Marlene's Piano

Jill Charles

ISBN 978-1-60145-867-4

Printed in the United States of America.

BookLocker.com, Inc.
2009

Dedication

This book is dedicated to my grandmother, Pearl Charles, my godfather, Joseph Makse, and my friend, Tobias Allen.

The story was inspired by Marge Stauffer, my great grandfather's sister, who played the piano brilliantly but did not find a stage.

With respect for her memory and hope to inspire my readers to unlock their talents, I wrote this novel.

CHAPTER ONE

"You are not going to music school, Marlene."

My mother's words fell like stones on the waxed kitchen floor. My face burned in anger and disbelief. I fixed my dark eyes on hers.

"Dad wanted me to go to music school. He always said so."

Her green eyes were sad but unyielding.

"Your father said many things, Marlene. He told Helen that she could be an opera singer and told Brendan that he could be an explorer."

I put my hand on the puffed sleeve of her black dress.

"Mother, he promised me since I was four years old that I would go to a conservatory. I've saved my allowance and I have seventy-two dollars."

She shook her head. Black strands of hair slipped from her bun like a veil around her pale face. It was four months since my father died, and she still wore black and prayed every day for the repose of his soul. Perhaps in her grief Mother had made an error, had not found the money set aside for my education. I wanted to believe that my father had some secret savings, but I knew full well he had never been able to save money nor keep any secret from Mother. She was always the practical parent, even now often holding the family's ledger in one hand and her handkerchief in the other.

"Marlene, your father believed his children could do anything and I loved him for that, but you and I both know that he never put by a penny. I kept all the books while he was alive and now that he's gone Joseph and I had to borrow money from your Uncle Luke to pay the mortgage on the house."

She put her arm around me and said "Sure you have as much talent as any girl at Julliard but we haven't the money to send you to a conservatory."

"Mother, what if I could make enough money? I made plenty playing the organ at the Varsity Theater last summer and I could give lessons and find a band."

Mother interrupted "Marlene, how many bands and orchestras do you know? Do any of them have a lady pianist? Or any ladies at all?"

I shook off her arm.

"I played in Laurel Catholic High's band for the last four years and in church concerts since I was twelve. I have more experience than most men my age and I'm learning new songs every week. I don't ever want to stop playing!"

Mother was calm but resolute.

"You needn't stop playing, but do not expect to make a life for yourself on the stage. Your family needs you now."

"What do you need from me?"

"Your uncle has asked me if one of my children would be able to live at the farm this summer. I thought you would be the best choice. Joseph's plumbing business is doing well and Amelia is a full-time nurse now at St. Luke's. Brendan makes enough money from his paper route to pay his high school fees. Helen has her job at the silk mill."

I felt tears welling up in my eyes.

"Mother, I want to help. I do, but please could I work at the Varsity Theater again and teach some music lessons?"

This got her Irish up; the color rose in her cheeks and her Ulster accent rang out in her voice.

"Jesus, Mary and Joseph, Marlene! What are you so afraid of? You're always going on about how you want to leave home."

"I wanted to leave Laurel, not home," I said, realizing how stupid that sounded.

"We have to repay your uncle," she went on. "You will earn as much as the farm hands but your work will be mostly indoors, canning with your aunt and boxing up the corn for market. You know that Aunt Josie could use help with the cooking and housework; Maud is always fainting or greensick."

"I don't know anything about harvesting or taking care of cows and hens." I said.

"Sure you'll learn it," Mother said. "Just like you learned to read and write and play the piano. Besides Aunt Josie will bring you home every Sunday when the Haydens come into town for church and on Saturdays while they're at market. Don't worry, Marlene. It's the hard times that teach us how strong we are and this too shall pass."

She hugged and kissed me and I clung to her, more tightly than I had since I was a little girl. Outside the kitchen window the blue hydrangeas nodded in the breeze, already waving goodbye to me.

I retreated upstairs to the room I shared with my older sister, Amelia. She was ironing her white nurse's cap and blue shirtwaist for her evening shift at St. Luke's Hospital.

"I heard that you've been drafted for the farm," said Amelia. "Mother mentioned Uncle Luke's offer to me, but I didn't think they would need you until the fall."

I lay back on the bed, my brown hair spread out on the pillow, trying to look as tragic as I felt. I took off my round silver glasses and rubbed my tired eyes.

"This will be the worst summer of my life," I said.

Amelia brushed her chin-length black bob, the short haircut that scandalized my mother and showed everyone that Amelia was a modern, independent woman.

"Will you miss Robert Schumann?" Amelia teased.

"Robert Schumann never looked at me anyway."

Like me, Robert had graduated from Laurel Catholic High in May, Class of 1922. He sang in the choir and performed in almost every school play. I would stare up at him from the piano in the orchestra pit when he was Romeo or Julius Caesar. He never glanced down at me. For all four years of high school, I had been obsessed with his handsome face, his golden tenor voice, his wry smile and social grace and obvious - though not always academic – genius. In my underwear drawer, I kept a picture of him in a top hat and suit that I had found outside his locker. I thought of Robert whenever I played *You Made Me Love You* or any other love song.

Amelia sat on the edge of my bed and patted my shoulder.

"Cheer up, Marlene. Maybe the farm will help you forget Robert. It'll be good to see Aunt Josie and Sven and Isaac will be fun to work with."

Sven and Isaac Madsen were Norwegian orphans taken in when they were eight and six by my aunt and uncle. Their father and mother had died of consumption in a steerage bunk on their way across the Atlantic. Sister Patricia, a Carmelite nun and oldest sister of my father and Aunt Josie, had worked in a New York orphanage and asked the Haydens to take the boys in so that they would not be separated. Aunt Josie treated them like sons and taught them to read and write, but Uncle Luke insisted that they were field hands, and must sleep in the bunkhouse and eat separately from the family. Sven and Isaac were much kinder than my cousins Maud and Boyd. They respected my uncle, but when he wasn't around they called Aunt Josie "Mama".

"It's Maud and Boyd I worry about," I replied, sinking my face into my pillow.

"I wouldn't worry," said Amelia. "Maud spends most of her time in bed imagining she has a headache and Boyd sneaks out of the field every chance he gets to steal Uncle Luke's whiskey and cigars."

When Amelia left for her evening shift, my younger sister Helen came in. She had been embroidering silk handkerchiefs in the living room while Mother and I argued, and had heard the whole thing, no doubt. Too sweet and shy to interrupt, Helen probably sympathized with both of us.

She sat beside me on the bed, hugged me, and laid her beautiful blonde head on my shoulder. At fourteen, Helen still wore her hair in ringlets, but already had a sweetheart, our neighbor Edward Malone. Dad used to call her "Helen of Troy" and I envied her for being the prettiest of the Piper children. Helen worked six days a week at Stolzfus Silk Mill, choosing a first job instead of attending high school as Joseph, Amelia, myself and Brendan had done before her. She told Mother she "was never much good at school" and enjoyed sewing clothes from extra silk and working with Edward and her friends Ruby and Rachel.

"I'm so sorry you can't go to Julliard, Marlene!" Helen said. "I know how you always wanted to go away to school."

"Thank you, Helen," I said, hugging her. "I really do want to make money and help Mother. I just want to play piano too."

"Maybe you can get a job at the silk mill after the harvest," Helen suggested. "They won't need you on the farm in winter. You could rent a room at a boardinghouse if you didn't want to live at home."

"I just know I can't make a living at music in Laurel," I said. "Not even if I play organ at the Varsity Theater and at church and teach piano lessons. I've got to get to New York or Philadelphia to some theaters or nightclubs."

Helen's hazel eyes widened with surprise as she asked "Would you play in a bar full of drunk people?"

Like Amelia and Mother, Helen was a strict teetotaler and believed in Prohibition, which I often questioned, though I never drank.

"I'd play in a bar, Helen. I feel like the music is alive inside me and I'll go crazy if I can't let it out. I'd play the piano for the Devil if he'd pay me."

She clapped her hand over my mouth and said "Shhh."

From downstairs, Mother called "Helen, some friends are here to see you."

Helen took my hand and squeezed it, like I did to comfort her when we were little kids.

"Ask God to help you, Marlene," said Helen. "And pray to St. Cecilia."

She rushed downstairs. Saint Cecilia, patroness of music, had sung for three days in a steam bath where the Romans tried to kill her with the heat, before cutting her throat with a sword. As a child, I prayed to her daily, but as an eighteen-year-old, I doubted the martyr would bless my ambition to play a piano in a nightclub.

I looked out the window and watched shy, red-headed Edward Malone take Helen's hand. Rachel and Ruby fluttered around her like chickens, giggling and gossiping on their way to the ice cream parlor. My little sister felt contentment I could no longer find in Laurel.

I leaned out the open window, slipped one foot out after the other, and carefully sat on the sloping roof. The shingles still held the heat of the May day and felt warm against my back. From the roof, I could hear everything in the yard and from the open windows of the house, while safely concealed behind the dense green leaves of the maple tree. No one could see me lying there in my nightgown, but I could catch glimpses of the yard and street below and watch the stars come out. The roof let me escape from home without leaving the yard. Mother always warned me that I'd fall and break my neck. I risked it anyway and taught my brother Brendan to climb out and sit there too.

A rustle in the maple tree below me caught my attention and I looked for a blue jay or squirrel. Instead, I spied Brendan's birds' nest of brown curls and his eyes blue as robins' eggs. He climbed up toward his window on the second floor.

"Hey, Brendan!" I whispered.

He looked startled, then climbed up to sit beside me.

"Where were you all evening? Mother was furious when you didn't come home for dinner."

"Don't squeal," he said. "But after my paper route, I rode my bike to Mill Creek to meet Isaac."

Our swimming spot, by the stone bridge at Mill Creek, was a mile from our house, but twelve miles from Uncle Luke's farm where Isaac lived and worked.

"Isaac told Boyd that there was peep show at the fairgrounds. When Boyd went into the tent to look, Isaac ran away. It was just a livestock tent and all Boyd saw were the rear ends of mules!"

We both leaned back on the roof and laughed at our cousin Boyd, who had bullied us since early childhood. Lately Boyd called Brendan "a queer" and tried to slap my behind every time I passed him.

"What are you doing on the roof?" Brendan asked.

"I'm trying not to throw myself off it," I said. "Mother just told me I can't go to music school and I have to work for Uncle Luke."

"I though Dad saved money for you to go to a conservatory," Brendan said.

I shook my head.

"Damn," he said. "I offered to work on the farm during the harvest, but when Aunt Josie asked Uncle Luke, he said 'I'll get more work out of Marlene than that pansy.' "

"I hate him," I said.

"At least you'll be with Isaac and Sven."

"I'll be canning and boxing corn, not catching frogs in the creek like you do," I said.

"We weren't catching frogs," he said softly.

"What were you doing?"

"We miss each other," Brendan said, although he saw Isaac weekly at church and Sunday dinner at our house.

A sputtering motor interrupted us and we looked down to see Joseph's Piper's Plumbing van pull up in front of our yard. Our older brother took great pride in Piper's Plumbing, the business he started, and his pale blue van.

Stubbornly independent and first-born, Joseph had enlisted in the Army during the Great War, over our Irish mother's objections that "no more men should die for the British Empire". When Joseph's right leg was amputated below the knee in a French field hospital, he never wrote to us about it. When he married Katrina, a Belgian nurse, in that same hospital tent, he didn't write to tell us. In 1918, they came home triumphant and the whole family loved Katrina for her cleverness, kindness and devotion to him. Mother had emigrated to marry Dad, so she understood Katrina's homesickness and helped her with her English. Amelia pressed her for details of the battlefield, which Katrina spoke freely about, but Joseph refused to mention. We all thought that Joseph's new stiff gait was a military step until Mother walked in on Katrina helping him bathe in her bathtub. When Mother saw the stump of his right leg and the artificial limb, she fainted.

Now Joseph strode confidently up the path to the house, and none of his customers or neighbors would guess that this plumber who crawled under houses and behind toilets had a wooden leg. He kept his brown hair short and his face clean-shaven. Katrina wore red lipstick and put her hair up in a neat French twist. She sang a French lullaby to three-month-old Harry, who lay half-asleep in her arms. They had named him Harold after my father, who got to see his grandson only twice before his last illness.

"Mother, where has Brendan gone?" Joseph called out like a drill sergeant.

With our father gone, Joseph tried to mold Brendan, like plaster, into "a real man" as the army had done for him. Brendan flamboyantly resisted.

"I'm not going in," said Brendan.

"Me neither," I said.

The stars all shone down on us now like diamond beads on deep blue velvet. Crickets chirped. At this hour, I would normally sit at the piano to play *Over There* and *Frere Jacques* for Joseph and Katrina, with Helen singing in her sweet soprano and the family joining in, one by one.

"Marlene, do you remember when Dad took us to see Eva Tanguay at the Franklin Theater?" Brendan asked.

"I do," I said. "That was when I knew I wanted to play piano onstage."

"That was when I knew I had to get out of Laurel," Brendan said.

We lay there quietly on the roof and remembered that night so many years ago.

It was 1914; I was ten years old and Brendan was eight. Usually our entire family went to plays or vaudeville shows, but on that night all the other Piper children were still sick with chicken pox.

Brendan and I had recovered, but Joseph and Amelia, (then aged fifteen and twelve) had more severe cases and were still spotted and itching. Six-year-old Helen had only a few spots on her face and hands, but wailed like a lost soul whenever she saw her reflection. Mother was at her wits' end, drawing oatmeal baths and smearing her children with calamine lotion. The whole house felt humid and feverish. She was scrubbing oatmeal out of the tub when Dad bent down to kiss her white neck and gently tell her we were leaving.

"Aileen, dear, I'm taking Brendan and Marlene to the Franklin. We'll get some sandwiches at Caprello's. Don't bother cooking anything tonight; you've worked hard enough today."

Mother kissed him goodbye and didn't even ask the name of the show.

We savored our provolone and meatball sandwiches at the Caprello Deli. The smells of aged cheese, salami and pickled peppers seemed much healthier than the calamine odor at home. The shop was busy before the show, but Guiseppe Caprello leaned over the counter to joke with my dad.

Mr. Caprello said "You're going to see Eva Tanguay? She's French Canadian, you know. Oo la la."

Then he gyrated his thick hips in the silliest feminine way, and the customers chuckled.

"I'm just giving my kids some culture," Dad protested, which amused everyone even more.

Dad led us through the golden doorway of the Franklin Theater, past the marble columns, up the red-carpeted steps and into the big balcony known as "peanut heaven". Usually Mother bought one bag of peanuts for all of us kids, but Dad bought us each a whole bag of our own. During the opening acts, Dad showed us how to throw shells at rich people – like Mr. Howard Bainworth in a box seat on the side of the theater. Dad bounced a shell right off the part of his pomaded gray hair. Mr. Bainworth turned around scowling under his waxed, curled mustache, but it was too dark to see who threw the shell. I saw Audrey Bainworth, his only daughter, kissing a young man in the third row. She wore a black hat with white egret plumes; Brendan and I hit several others before finally striking her, but she didn't even notice.

We sat in the very front row, with a terrific view of the jugglers, the dog trainer and the dancing girls with their twirling parasols and spinning crinolines. We were excited to see Eva Tanguay; Marco and Tony Caprello said she was the most beautiful girl in the world but their mother wouldn't let them have a picture of her because she danced the "hoochy-kooch". Eva was the headliner and danced and sang three different songs. She had bright brown eyes and curly brown hair, with a big smile and a sweet Quebec accent when she sang.

For the first number, she wore pink chiffon and sang sweetly about her mother. Next she appeared in blue velvet and sang a French love song, kicking her legs like a ballerina. Eva wore a white leotard with glittering pearls, tights and a tail of white ostrich plumes trailing behind her like some exotic bird-of-paradise. Her arms were bare and the tights made her legs look naked and showed off her hourglass figure. As she kicked her legs and swirled her hips, the men hooted and whistled and the women laughed and fluttered their fans. I really believed Eva could have flown off the stage if she wanted to, swooped over the crowd and out the theater door into the starry night sky. I had never seen anyone like her and the notes and words of her third song always stayed with me:

They say I'm crazy, got no sense
But I don't care.
They may or may not mean offense,
But I don't care;
You see I'm sort of independent,
Of a clever race descendant,
My star is on the ascendant,
That's why I don't care.
I don't care,
I don't care,
What they may think of me.
I'm happy go lucky,
Men say I am plucky,
So jolly and care free.
I don't care,
I don't care,
If I do get the mean and stony stare.
If I'm never successful,
It won't be distressful,
'Cos I don't care.

The next day Brendan and I made Joseph, Amelia and Helen laugh by imitating the dance Eva did. Joseph was very jealous that we got to see the "I Don't Care Girl", but paid Brendan ten cents for the program showing Eva kicking her long legs. Dad bought me the sheet music to play on the piano. Mother was annoyed that he took us to see a "cooch dancer" but Dad insisted "The children should hear fine music. Marlene will play at the Franklin Theater one day."

Mother said "Playing piano? Yes. Dancing like a burlesque girl – no."

Whenever anyone made fun of Brendan or me we would sing or hum *I Don't Care*. We taught it to our friends and siblings. The song became our private prayer, a rosary against a world that never understood us. Now, so many years later, without our dear Dad, the song still sustained us.

Mother and Joseph came upstairs, from room to room, calling out "Brendan? Marlene? Where are you?"

Up on the roof, Brendan and I joined hands and sang, too softly to be heard:

I don't care,
I don't care
What they may think of me…

CHAPTER TWO

On the farm, I felt like a failure at everything I did. No matter how hard I worked and how much Aunt Josie, my father's sister, tried to make me welcome, I knew I was a poor relation. I lived in a wooden room adjoining the barn, better than the bunkhouse for the field hands: Sven and Isaac Madsen and David Dunn, but plain and drafty compared to the two-story farmhouse where Uncle Luke lived with Aunt Josie and my spoiled cousins Maud and Boyd Hayden.

Every morning before five, Aunt Josie would wake me, opening my door and whispering "Good morning, Marlene" as sweetly as she could.

On my first morning there, I could not believe the hour and the fact that I would have to wake up before five every morning until November. As I washed my face and combed my hair into a neat braid, I tried to hurry, but moved like a sleepwalker. I resented the pink sun peeking over the horizon outside my window and the ugly whimpering cry of the rain doves in the barn.

Before we could eat, Aunt Josie, Maud and I would make breakfast for the men. I helped Aunt Josie brew the coffee, and cook the oatmeal and bacon. While I fried the eggs, my cousin Maud flounced into the kitchen in an immaculate white dress and apron. She wore neat blonde ringlets and a sour expression. She sat on a stool beside me, not working, but criticizing everything I did.

"Those eggs are going to stick, Marlene. Lift the edges. No! No! You've scrambled them. They're ruined now."

"Why can't you do this?" I asked.

"Marlene, you've got to learn. I can't believe you're eighteen years old, graduated from high school, and still can't fry eggs. What kind of wife will you be?"

"I'm not getting married," I said. "I'm going to play the piano."

"Don't worry," she whispered. "No one would have you anyway."

Neither Maud not Boyd had attended high school and they both thought that Joseph, Amelia, Brendan and I were spoiled because our father had taught history at Laurel Catholic High and we got free tuition. At twenty and nineteen, Maud and Boyd could not stand the fact that I might know more than they did, despite being younger.

I carried oatmeal, eggs and bacon into the dining room. Uncle Luke, Boyd, Sven and Isaac and David Dunn sat around the table, eating their fill before going out to the cornfield to pick until noon. Uncle Luke scowled into his *Old Farmers' Almanac,* his face and hair as dull and tan as its worn pages. Boyd leered at me like an evil blonde cherub, his blue eyes looking me up and down as no one should ever look at their first cousin. The new field hand, David Dunn, ate silently without glancing up from his plate. Only the Madsen brothers, Sven and Isaac, smiled up at me, recognizing a childhood friend and not just one more worker. If Uncle Luke weren't in the room, I would have hugged Sven and Isaac.

"Look at the new field hand," Sven joked. "She's a sight prettier than David Dunn."

"Smells better too, I bet," said Isaac.

"You boys pipe down," said Uncle Luke.

As children, Sven and Isaac always played with my siblings and me. No matter what my uncle said, I thought of them as kin, not hired help, and admired the way they looked out for each other. Sven never learned to read very well and he depended on Isaac for that, while skinny Isaac depended on his big strong brother for protection from Boyd. Isaac had gone to the optical shop with me when we were six and five, to get our first glasses. He told me that anyone who called us "four eyes" should be called "no brains". We used to hide Maud's dolls in the pumpkin patch and frighten her with toads. As we grew older, it became obvious that Sven loved Maud, even when she called him "common and dirty" or ignored him outright. I pitied him and wondered what he saw in her. The feeling seemed as unnatural as an ox falling in love with a housecat.

When Maud set down the coffee pot, Sven smiled and said "Thank you, Miss Hayden," but she rushed past him without a glance.

"Marlene, have you met David Dunn?" Isaac asked. "Your uncle hired him for the harvest."

I noticed the third field hand sitting across the kitchen table from Isaac and Sven. My uncle occasionally hired extra hands when the corn was ripe, but I never got to meet any of them because they kept busy in the fields and stayed in the bunkhouse. This man was a sharp contrast to the sunny looks of the Madsen brothers and my blond cousin and uncle. His curly black hair was like a storm cloud and he looked down as he ate breakfast, keeping his thoughts to himself. His hands were huge and sinewy, his arms wiry and his movements precise as he cut his food. He dressed like an ordinary farm hand in tan pants and a round-collared white shirt, but something in his manner made him look cleaner and more intelligent than the Madsens. He looked up at me suddenly with eyes like two masterful sapphires. His black eyebrows relaxed and his wide mouth spread in a strange smirk.

"I'm Marlene Piper," I said. "Pleased to meet you."

I reached out to shake hands with David, who shook my hand firmly and said "Good morning, Miss Piper."

When I touched his hand, a shiver ran through me and I felt cold all over. My initial feeling about David was fear, though I could not have said why. My second feeling about him was a prickling curiosity, which I knew well enough to conceal. His accent was unmistakably Irish and I wanted to ask him what part of that country he came from and to tell him that my mother was an immigrant too. His dark hair and pale skin reminded me of my mother; they were what my uncle called "black Irish".

"Marlene, you're not to fool with the field hands," my uncle said sharply. "Get back in the kitchen and eat breakfast with Josie and Maud."

"And bring me some bacon," Boyd added, slapping my backside as I passed him.

I whirled around, horrified, and he winked one devilish blue eye and licked his lips. Uncle Luke had seen this, but ignored it. Isaac and Sven averted their eyes and David glared at Boyd, but no one dared to challenge Boyd in front of Uncle Luke. Slamming the door, I rushed back to the kitchen. My face burned with shame, although I knew that nothing Boyd did to me was my fault.

Aunt Josie and Maud showed me where all the tools and dishes were kept and which fruits and vegetables were ripe. I weeded the garden and boxed up the corn. Sometimes I would feed corn to the chickens and slop to the hogs, hay to the horses and the cows. It would take me some time to learn to gather the eggs and milk the cows. My main work would be cooking and cleaning, but I soon learned that the kitchen could be as exhausting as the field. I would help Aunt Josie and Maud dust, sweep and mop every room in the house and wash all the laundry. My arms felt exhausted as I soaped and rinsed the clothes, pressed them through the ringer and hung them out to dry in the sun. How strange it was to handle the underwear of everyone in the house! I smelled the sweat on the men's cotton undershirts, and watched their undershorts flapping on the washline like seagulls.

After the men went into the cornfield, Aunt Josie, Maud and I delved into the work of canning. Peeling, chopping and slicing vegetables and fruit, stirring pectin into jam, I sometimes felt as if I were trapped in a giant mason jar. Steam collected on the windows, even when we opened them in futile hope of a cool breeze. Beads of sweat rolled down my back and my green cotton dress clung to me like wilted lettuce on a greasy plate. I wiped the steam off my glasses and tucked my brown hair into a bun.

When Aunt Josie sent me down into the cellar to shelve jars of preserves, the coolness relieved me. I leaned my face against the wall and wished I could live in that dark, quiet place between the wash ringer, the huge sink and the old wooden chairs. All I would need was a cot, a water closet and my piano.

"Marlene, come upstairs, please."

I sighed and followed Maud's shrill voice up the creaking wooden steps.

"I can't can tomatoes today," she said.

Why not?" I asked.

Aunt Josie and Maud exchanged knowing glances then looked back at me.

"Tomatoes will spoil if you can them during your monthlies," Maud said smugly.

She turned on her heel and began to skip upstairs, unburdened by any care or cramp. This time Aunt Josie saw through the clumsy lace of Maud's "symptoms".

"Just a moment, Maud," she said. "There is no reason on Earth that you can't start shucking vegetables for the chow chow."

Maud stopped in her tracks, sighed indignantly and rolled her blue eyes. On the kitchen table, she lined up string and lima beans, corn, celery, onion and red and green pepper. Her thin pale hand moved through the vegetables as neatly as a seamstress cuts through cloth.

Meanwhile, Aunt Josie showed me how to slip the skins off hot tomatoes by plunging them into cold water. We canned seven jars of tomatoes and a big pot of catsup, and then helped Maud boil vegetables for chow chow. The smells of tomatoes and vinegar made me hungry and I nibbled a few fresh peas and carrot slices.

"Don't eat between meals, Marlene. You're fat enough already," Maud scolded.

At one o' clock, we set both the tables for dinner: chicken corn soup with dumplings, cherries, snap peas, spinach salad and raspberry gelatin. The midday meal on the farm was always the largest. By one, the men had worked for eight hours in the field and the heat was unbearable. On the hottest days, they might take a nap after dinner, then go out to pick corn for a few more hours before supper at six.

Unlike Maud, I could never use my monthlies or a headache to dodge work. Unlike Boyd, I couldn't sneak off behind the barn with Uncle Luke's cigars or borrow the truck for a drive into town. My only escape from the farm was Sunday visits to Laurel for mass at St. Anne's Church and dinner at my mother's house.

Every evening after supper on the farm, I would go into the living room to play the piano.

Sometimes Uncle Luke would want to read his newspaper in silence and would bellow "Stop that darn racket!" Then I'd retire to my barnhouse and flutter my fingers over the tabletop as if it were a piano. I remembered the place of every piano key and heard the absent notes inside my head.

Luckily, Uncle Luke often retired upstairs to get ready for bed right after supper. Aunt Josie encouraged my piano playing. She and my father had played duets on her piano when they were children. She could still play by ear, though she had never been able to teach Maud and Boyd, who complained that piano lessons were dull and they would rather just buy records.

As I sat on the piano bench, I remembered Dad teaching me to play when I was four years old. He said "You have long fingers and slender hands. You're a natural piano player."

As I played, I remembered sitting on the bench with Dad before my legs were long enough to reach the pedals. He would pedal for me and my little fingers would follow his big strong hands over the ebony and ivory keys. On Sundays, after church, we would practice. He sat at the piano bench with me on his lap and guided my little fingers.

Plink, plink, plink. Plink, plink, plink.

Heart and soul, I gave you everything.

Hot and cold, you've taken everything…

Dad had a rich baritone voice and he could have joined the church choir if he had not been so opposed to joining things. My voice was like a screech owl, but when I was four I didn't know this and I sang with him as loudly as I could.

"You play beautifully," Dad said. "And some day, when you are grown up, we will send you to music school. You can play at the Franklin Theater downtown and hundreds of people will come to see you."

Had Dad really believed that I would succeed, or only said these things out of love?

"Music makes people forget their troubles," Dad always told me. "Always remember that when you play. You don't just make music for yourself. When you play the piano, your song is for everyone."

Now in my Uncle's living room, I slid the lid back from the keys and began to play *Keep On the Sunny Side.* Uncle Luke and Boyd had gone up to bed. Aunt Josie sang along and Sven and Isaac joined in, sitting on the floor next to the Hayden ladies on the sofa. Sven nudged Maud, hoping to hear her pretty soprano voice, but she just shook her head and silently embroidered pansies on a tablecloth.

Sven said "Play *Shenandoah*; it's my favorite."

I played and he sang:

"*Oh Shenandoah, he loves your daughter. Away, you rolling river. He'll take her 'cross the rolling water...*"

I thought of Sven's love for Maud and how angry Uncle Luke would be to discover it. It was Sven's one secret sorrow and, though I couldn't understand it, I began to admire his devotion. Would anybody ever sing about me like this?

"Can you play *The Foggy Dew?"* David Dunn requested.

He stood in the doorway, his face in shadow. I hadn't noticed him there, but I turned around on the piano bench to face him.

"I do know it," I said. "My mother is an Irish emigrant."

Although I disliked my weak alto voice, I sang all the words. David approached the piano and sang with me, his powerful baritone voice singing about how the Irish tried to rebel against Great Britain during the Great War, failing when the Germans never arrived with their promised weapons. It was a song my mother appreciated but forbade me to ever play in front of my proud veteran brother Joseph. Aunt Josie, Maud and the Madsens looked shocked as I played a song that made the Irish rebels martyrs.

"And I kneel and pray for you
For slavery fled,
O glorious dead
When you fell in the foggy dew."

I am playing for David Dunn and for myself, I thought, and at this moment no one else matters to me. David leaned on the piano and smiled at me for the first time.

CHAPTER THREE

As I tried to fall asleep at the farm, I prayed for my family and for my father. After my prayers I spoke to him. Sometimes I dreamed about Dad at night and woke up to remember, with a sharp pain, that he was dead.

"God, why did you have to take him?" I asked out loud.

Dad had been very sick in the flu epidemic after the war, and when he recovered Dr. Bauer told us that his heart was weakened. Dad pretended that nothing was wrong as he returned to teaching his history classes at Laurel Catholic High, taking his long, rambling walks and sitting on the porch swing reading Tacitus and Edward Gibbon and smoking a corncob pipe. It was in January of 1922 when he came home late from the library and gave his coat to a beggar woman.

"I wanted to be like Saint Martin," he joked.

When he caught a cold, Mother gave him chicken soup and allowed him to drink hot toddies, although she was a stern teetotaler. I think she knew, even early on, that it would be his last illness. Mother had always forbidden drinking in the house, after seeing too many men consumed by drink in Ireland, including her own widowed father. Dad was Pennsylvania Dutch and considered beer *das flussige brot,* "liquid bread" and nothing more. He got around her rule against drinking in the house by buying bottles of beer from the corner bar and drinking them on the front porch. When she let him drink whiskey for medical reasons, all of us children began to worry about him.

On February 11, two days after my eighteenth birthday, I passed Dad in the hallway. He wore his red striped pajamas and a royal blue bathrobe. His face, hands and feet were pale as alabaster and the damp smell of sickness clung to him, so unlike his usual smell of clover and sweet tobacco.

"Dad, can I get you anything?" I asked.

"No, thank you, Marlene," he said, and then he started to turn away. "But wait, maybe just one thing, dear. Would you go downstairs and play *Danny Boy* on the piano? I can hear it from up here. Go ahead now."

I tried my best to play loudly and not to sink into the sadness of the song. My mother sang it in Gaelic sometimes; it was the first song they ever danced to when he was a traveler in Ireland and he took her to a village dance in Dungannon. I tried to think of his funny story of how they met, when he broke a boot heel and she waited on him at her father's shoe shop, and crept out a window to go dancing with him that night. I pictured Dad as young Harold Piper the adventurer, eloping with his beautiful Aileen Dobhailen and bringing her to America. It hurt to hear him coughing weakly in the room above me. When I finished playing, Mother went upstairs to bring him his tea and could not wake him up.

Could Dad ever have imagined me living here in this wood shelter attached to my uncle's barn? Dad had worked his way through college to become a history teacher and scrimped and saved enough money to travel in Europe, his lifelong dream. His folks worried about him, and neighbors thought his wanderlust was crazy, but it led him to my mother. No matter how long it took, Dad would want me to find a way to play the piano on stage.

Sometimes, just after I said my prayers, I would speak to him, hoping his soul might listen.

"I won't disappoint you, Dad," I said. "I'll help Mother any way I can. I know you must be in Heaven now and not in Purgatory, no matter how ornery Mother said you were. I'll do whatever I have to do here and then I'll find a way to get out of Laurel and play piano. I love you, Dad, and I'll make you proud of me."

It was hard to feel proud of myself, as I sweated in the dusty barn, boxing up the corn for market. Boyd would bring wheelbarrows of corn in from the field and dump them on the barn floor, running away laughing while I picked up and dusted the pale green leafy ears. I neatly packed a dozen ears in each wooden box, and four boxes in each crate. I stacked the crates in a corner of the barn to prepare for market day.

Flies buzzed around the corn and the manure in the horse and cow stalls. The barn was shady, but just as hot and humid as the outdoors. I wanted to sit and rest, but Boyd would run to Uncle Luke and squeal on me. Uncle Luke would walk by, saying "Marlene, I don't pay you to lie around." If I fanned myself with my paper fan, he'd say "Too hot for the lady of leisure?" and spit on the ground.

During my first week on the farm, I asked "Uncle Luke, may I come into town with you on Saturday?"

"What would you do at market?" he asked.

"Mother said I could come into town with you on Saturday and see her."

"The hell you will!" he said, reddening. "What do you think this is - a union shop? You work for me six days a week. Now get your lazy ass back in that barn!"

I never got to go home on a Saturday. Uncle Luke took Boyd, Isaac and Sven to market, but never David or me. The Madsen boys were good merchants; Sven conversed with every customer and remembered their usual orders and favorite foods while Isaac added up all the prices in his head, made change and kept a list of Uncle Luke's profits. Boyd did nothing at market but lean against the side of the stall staring at ladies' legs or sneak off to buy ice cream sodas. More and more often, Uncle Luke took the Madsens to market instead of his son. He told Boyd "I expect you to stay here and keep an eye on the micks," but I suspected that he enjoyed leaving Boyd behind. By "the micks", my uncle meant David and me, although I was only half Irish.

One hot Saturday, I had gone to the pump to refill my big mason jar of water. Through the poplar trees, I could see the blue shining creek and almost feel its tempting coolness. Leaving my jar by the pump, I dashed toward the creek. As fast as I could, I unbuttoned my dress and kicked off my shoes and socks. Wearing only my brassiere and underpants, I raced into the cool, thrilling water. I ducked my head under and dived as deep as I could, feeling smooth rocks and tiny waterweeds against my kicking feet. Floating to the surface, I did a lazy backstroke for a few minutes. It would be easy enough to remove my wet underclothes, put on my clothes and go back to work refreshed. If anyone noticed my wet hair, which the boys probably wouldn't, I'd say I stuck my head under the pump and give them a good laugh.

When I turned to glance at the shore, I saw Boyd sitting on the log where I had left my dress. He narrowed his eyes at me and rubbed my dress against his lap. He buried his hands in the cloth, but focused on me. My breasts, white belly and thighs floated above the surface of the water and my underwear was sheer with wetness. I was so embarrassed to see Boyd that I dipped my legs underwater and struggled to a part of the stream where I could poke my head above water, but hide the rest of me.

"Boyd, what the hell are you doing? Give me back my clothes!"

"No! Come out and get them, you lazy bitch!"

I stood up, covering my bosom with one hand and my crotch with the other. I felt angry at Boyd, and ashamed of my cousin seeing me wet, lazy and mostly naked. The rough rocks hurt my feet. Boyd jerked my dress frantically in his lap.

"Give me my damn clothes!" I screamed, pulling on the dress.

Boyd covered his privates with one hand and squeezed my left breast with the other. I fell backward, horrified. Boyd laughed at me for an instant, but then cried out in pain. David Dunn had punched him in the face.

"Let her alone, Boyd!" yelled David

David came out of nowhere, like a summer storm, first punching Boyd from the side, then leaping in front of him and knocking him off the log onto his back. Boyd scrambled backwards on his hands and feet, like a terrified crab.

"You black Irish bastard! I'll tell my father!" he gasped. "You'll both get fired!"

David calmly said "I'll tell Marlene's brothers. You'll get killed."

David spat on the ground as Boyd dashed off through the trees. I awkwardly put on my dress, socks and shoes.

"Are you all right, Miss Piper?" David asked, holding out his hand.

I took it and held it.

"Please call me Marlene. I'll be all right, thank you. Boyd has always teased me, but never like that. Maybe now he'll learn his lesson."

David squeezed my hand and said "If Boyd ever interferes with you again, you let me know and I'll wring his neck."

"Will you help me box the corn?" I asked.

David actually smiled and said "I'd be delighted."

I went to my room to change my clothes, then took David to the barn with me to box up the corn for the rest of the afternoon. It was our first chance to have a real conversation. I had been curious about him and I trusted him now.

"Where are from, David?" I asked. "I mean, where were you born? Where is your family from? I can tell that you're Irish, but I wondered."

" I was born in Kildare," he said. "I have no family anymore."

"Are they deceased?" I asked.

"My father died when I was seven and my mother and stepfather had no use for me. I was the eighth of nine children and I was farmed out to my uncle in Longford when I was twelve. My stepfather hated me and my mother told me to my face that she never wanted me. When I was fourteen, my grandmother died and left me a little inheritance, enough to get to Dublin and onto a ship."

"My mother came from Dungannon," I said.

"Northern Irish," he said, unimpressed. "Is she a Protestant?"

"Hell no!" I said. "Her maiden name was Aileen Dobhailen and most of her family were Fenians."

My swearing embarrassed me, but made him chuckle.

"Don't pretend to me that you're Irish," he said. "Your father and your aunt are Pennsylvania Dutch and that's what you are, ain't?"

"That's not all I am," I said. "The Irish is part of me too even if I can't speak it. The music and the stories my mother told me..."

He stacked the last crate of corn and we sat side by side on milking stools. I sat on one next to him.

"How long have you been in America?" I asked.

"Six years," he said. "I'll be twenty on January 17. Before I came here I worked in the coal mines in Wilkes-Barre. The pay was better than with farm work but my lungs started burning inside, so I had to leave. I've been on farms for two years now."

I loved the sound of his brogue; he didn't try to hide his accent as my mother did. I wanted to keep him talking.

"Do you like America? Do you ever miss Ireland?"

"Do I like it here? You're the only person in six years to ask whether I like it here. I like the hot summers and the chance to travel where no one knows me and find work. I have no one to miss in Ireland, but I miss the places sometimes, the green fields and the Shannon, the peaceful silence. I don't feel that in America, even on a fine evening like this in a field of corn. I know it's all for sale, for profit and not for beauty."

"I know what you mean," I said. "I've never wanted to sell anything. What I want to do is play the piano."

"Are you working here until you find a husband?" he asked.

"I'm not holding my breath for that," I said.

He chuckled. I noticed the faded but beautiful leather of his black boots, with a sheathed knife in the left one. I had never seen him take it out or whittle sticks like Boyd did. David never fidgeted; he sat calmly observing everything like a bird of prey. Even now, he looked at me out of the corner of his eye, as if disinterested.

"Uncle Luke and Aunt Josie wanted me here for the harvest," I said. "But I think they really hired me because my father died this winter and my family needs the extra money. In winter, I'll look for another job. I don't want to stay in a place where I'm not needed."

"I know what you mean. Sure I do."

Slowly he turned toward me and took my hand. Lightning raced up my arms, but I smiled serenely. I wanted to clasp his big warm hands, but he turned my hand over in both of his, studying it instead of holding it.

"You have nice long fingers," he said.

"Thank you."

"You should be a spinner at the silk mill. I'm going to apply at Stolzfus Silk this winter. I could take you with me."

We heard Sven and Isaac walking back from the field, pushing each other and laughing. David dropped my hand, stood up, and went into the house without so much as a backward glance. I dashed off to the kitchen before Sven and Isaac could see me. If they saw me talking to David, or to any man, the teasing would be merciless.

Later that evening, I roasted corn in the brick oven behind the kitchen and made potato salad with egg and sliced celery. Blue crabs had been on sale at the market, and Aunt Josie had steamed ten small ones. Maud and I set the table on the front porch for supper, because it was too hot to eat indoors. Aunt Josie's face glowed with sweat and Maud fanned herself.

"I feel faint," she said. "Why can't Marlene bake the biscuits?"

"Because she'd burn them," Isaac teased.

"I would not!"

I kicked Isaac under the table when we sat down, but he just laughed. Sven defended his brother's long skinny feet and pressed his dirty boot on top of my shoe.

"Stop that now," said Uncle Luke. "You boys don't fool with Marlene."

"Excuse us, Miss Marlene," said Sven.

Isaac made a mock bow and his smile almost cracked open with laughter.

Boyd sat down next to me and snatched the butter plate just as I was about to dip my knife in it. Uncle Luke didn't seem to notice.

"Where's David?" asked Aunt Josie.

"He went for a walk," said Isaac.

"Why would he go for a walk at this hour?" my uncle complained.

Then, for reasons I have never fully understood, Isaac leaned toward me and whispered in my ear "David is down by the creek."

Perhaps Isaac had noticed my love for David. Isaac quietly absorbed everything and I always wore my emotions on my face like a rash. Even better, perhaps David asked Isaac to tell me where he was. I had my own plans now. All I had to do was say:

"I'll find David."

I stood up and rushed down from the porch before anyone could object.

Uncle Luke shouted "Hurry back!" as I scurried through the kitchen garden. The fresh delicious smells of tomato plants, basil, mint and peaches lingered in the air. The tall brown farmhouse shrank behind me as I rushed into the cornfield.

I caught a firefly in my hand. I looked into my fist and saw my handsome prisoner, his body striped black and red, his posterior glowing green with phosphorus. Dad had once said that fireflies had the only light without heat in nature. The firefly looked less mysterious up close, but just as interesting. He crawled around desperately in my dark, hot hand. I thought of all the fireflies that Boyd kept in Mason jars until their lights flickered out in death and the ones Joseph and Brendan released in the Varsity Theater. Suddenly I felt sympathy for the little insect. I opened my hand and let him find a mate.

I wove my way through the cornfield like a shuttle through a tapestry of green. My feet remembered the quickest way to the creek. Sure enough, David was wading in the creek, his tan pants rolled up above the knees. His calves were pale but strong and covered with soft black hair. I kicked off my shoes and socks, hitched my skirt up and waded in after him. He heard me splashing along behind him, stopped, and turned around.

"Marlene!" he said. "What brings you all the way out here?"

"I... it's ... it's supper time," I said. "Did you hear the bell?"

"Yes, but I wasn't hungry."

"Oh, you should eat anyway. Aunt Josie would be so hurt if you didn't eat with us."

"Oh, would she now?"

"Yes, and so would I," I said "Have you been swimming?"

"What if I have?"

"Do you swim fully dressed?"

"No, Marlene. I swim as God intended, in my skin. I don't wade around in my underclothes like you do."

"Were you spying on me like Boyd?"

"Sure I wasn't, but I was amazed that you could swim so well. You looked like a selkie."

"My mother told me about selkies. They slip off their sealskins and turn into women."

"If a man steals the sealskin from a selkie, then he can marry her," David said.

Without noticing it, we stepped closer to each other. He trailed one cool, wet hand up my arm and stroked the nape of my neck.

I tried to joke with him "Did I look like a fat brown seal?"

"You looked like a beautiful woman," he said. "I should have stolen your dress and kept you that way."

He smiled at me. He had beautiful clean white teeth. Uncle Luke and Boyd had called David a dirty foreigner, which only proved that they had never really looked at him. Dark whiskers made shadows on his face, but he was entirely clean.

He wrapped his arm around my waist and we kissed each other. We clung to each other's mouths like drowning people gasping for air. I had wanted to kiss David for so long. My knees quivered and I rubbed my wet ankles against his. What had I been so afraid of? I wrapped my arms around him and squeezed. The bell rang again but David only held me tighter. He pulled my hair out of its slovenly bun and ran his fingers through it. The water rippled around us and crickets chirped in the distance. It wasn't a dream and it didn't have to end when I opened my eyes.

When David finally ended the kiss, my lips felt swollen, almost bruised.

"Promise me something," he whispered.

"Yes," I said.

"Never, ever bob your beautiful brown hair."

"I promise I won't bob my hair. Now promise me something, David."

"Yes, Marlene?"

"Promise to take me swimming with you."

"Tonight," he said, and kissed me again.

We walked hand in hand through the cornfield, both of us looking left and right in case anyone saw us.

"We mustn't tell anybody, ever," I said. "Sven and Isaac wouldn't tell on us, but they'd say something by accident and Uncle Luke would find out. He'd fire you and maybe me too."

"Don't I know it. If he knew that a mick field hand was sparking his niece, he'd reach for the shotgun."

We let go of each other's hands as we neared the house. Aunt Josie glared at us as we walked up the porch steps.

"Where were you, David?" she said. "The crabs are getting cold."

"I like them cold," he said, settling down and cracking one.

Only Boyd paid any attention to me. He leaned over and whispered, too low for anyone else to hear him.

"Marlene, who let down your hair?"

CHAPTER FOUR

As I washed dinner dishes in the stinging hot water, I thought of David's kisses. The moments with him were my real life; the dirty dishwater and slop buckets were a bad dream from which I would soon awaken.

That night I sat up by candlelight and waited for him, not daring to light the lamp for fear someone in the house might see it. I kept hearing a clicking sound which I hoped was footsteps, but it was only crickets and katydids. The lights of the Hayden house went out one by one. The stars waved to me from the midnight blue: Ursa Major, Cassiopeia, Draco, Deneb, Altair and Vega, the Summer Triangle. I remembered summer nights when Dad sat on the porch with all his children and taught us the names of the stars.

"Deneb was a king. Vega was a princess. Altair was a cowherd, but he and Vega fell in love..."

My father held baby Helen in his arms and teaching her the word "moon".

"Moon. Moon," she said, stretching up her little white arms as if the moon were a white balloon that she could catch.

Now the moon was waxing gibbous, soon to be full. When I looked at it I thought of Robert's white face, David's shadowy face and my father's face. "Dad" was the first word I said, the first man I loved. I reached my hand up toward the moon in my window and let my tears fall. Dad was gone and Robert was only with me for a moment. David was not coming. It was too late. I was ugly and alone and orphaned.

My shoulders shook and my hot tears fell on the pillow. What if it went on like this every night of my life: my cold feet, my trembling hands, my adult longing and childish fears? How stupid and weak I was. I flipped the pillow over to the cool side and tried to settle into sleep. The cotton sheets were cool on my skin and I told myself I was comfortable and sleepy. I closed my eyes and lay on my side, pulling the covers up to my chin. Just as my consciousness began to fade, I heard a knock at the door.

"David!"

I leaped out of bed, put my glasses on and nearly tripped on my own nightgown. Before I opened the door, I peered through the lace curtain. He stood there in a white shirt and clean twill pants. I opened the door a crack. Lucky for me it was too dark for David to see that my eyes were red from crying.

"David?"

"Yes, Marlene?"

"Wait just a minute; I'm not dressed."

He pushed the door open and took me in his arms. I kissed him, then wiggled out of his arms to put on a cotton shirt and skirt. I turned my back to him but could feel his gaze on me. David sat on the edge of my bed, half-lit by moonlight.

"It's a nice little room you've got here."

"I hope it's warm enough for night swimming."

"The water will be warm," he said.

He led me by the hand through the cornfield and past the poplars. I slipped on the muddy bank and scratched myself on a raspberry bush. David took my hand to steady me.

"Are you all right?" he asked.

"Yes."

The moon smiled up at us from the creek.

"Get in the water as fast as you can," he said. "The mosquitoes will eat us alive."

He whipped off his shirt, revealing a pale wiry chest covered with lush black hair.

"The mosquitoes do not concern me," I said.

He chuckled, turned his back to me and kicked off his shoes and pants. Before I could get a clear look at him, he dashed into the water. He was naked; I had seen that.

I pulled off my skirt and shirt, set my glasses on a stump and followed David. The night air thrilled my naked skin. When I hit the water, it felt unexpectedly warm. It had absorbed the heat of the day like a jar of my aunt's sun tea. The creek had been waiting all day as I had. My feet skittered over rocks and squelched in the chilly mud. He swam out into the deep black center of the creek, then beckoned to me with one hand.

"Come here, Marlene."

I shook my head and shivered. As I treaded water, weedy tentacles twisted around my ankles. During the day I hardly noticed the waterweeds, but they spooked me now.

"Can't you swim? Come on out here, you wee shivering coward!"

I took a deep breath and swam toward David as fast as I could. Kicking and splashing, I tried to stay on the surface of the water. When I reached him, I clung to him with my arms and kept kicking my legs.

"Stop kickin', fool. I've got you."

He wrapped his strong arms around me. The little hairs on his arms and chest hung straight down like notes on a sheet of music. Submerged up to my throat in the water, I looked up into his face, but it was shadowed with the moon behind his head like a crown of light. I twisted one hand into his wet hair and pulled his lips down to mine. His kiss poured into me like hot tea into a cold china cup.

Suddenly, David loosened his embrace, pressed one hand on the crown of my head and shoved me underwater as hard as he could. With my mouth wide open, I choked and gasped. Floundering underwater, I looked up to see his feet swimming away. I tried to catch him, but he was too quick. The deep black water chilled my skin as I struggled upward. I had only been under for a few seconds, but it felt like a terrible stretch of time.

I burst through the surface of the creek, coughing and flailing. The water stung my nose and throat, tasting of mud and algae. I swam toward the shore and ran smack into David, who stood in the shallow water. He turned around and reached out his arms to hug me.

"Oh Marlene, you should have seen your face!"

"Don't you touch me!" I snarled, yanking his hair.

"Ouch! Are you angry at me?"

"Hell yes, I'm angry at you! You tried to drown me, you son of a bitch! Let me go!"

"Oh Marlene, I was only joking with you. That's how my da taught me to swim by throwing me in the water and letting me figure it out."

His eyes looked sorry but I was still furious.

"Did he jump in after you when you started to drown?"

"No! He wouldn't coddle me that way."

"When I was little I almost drowned here and my father jumped in after me. It made all the difference in the world."

I pushed my way out of David's arms and staggered back to the stump where my clothes were.

"You can't go back to bed now!"

"Watch me!"

I yanked my clothes on, shoved my feet in my shoes and ran back to the barnhouse as fast as I could. I locked the door behind me, pulled the curtains and flopped down on the bed, moist and miserable.

David was just using me. He must have hated me to tease me like that. He was like Elizabeth and Barbara in grade school, pretending to be friendly with me, then tripping me with the jump rope and laughing. David liked kissing me, but did not live on daydreams of kisses as I did.

When I woke up the next morning, my hair was tangled and my pillow was damp. But when I opened my door, I found a small blue bottle of white tuberose blossoms. As I placed the flowers on my windowsill, my heart softened again toward David Dunn.

All that summer and long into fall, David and I kept our secret from everyone. At night he would wait until Sven and Isaac snored and wheezed in the bunkhouse and then sneak out and knock on my door. In summer we swam naked in the creek together and in fall we curled up together under my quilt. Over and over he promised "I'll marry you," but I held his hands back and whispered "Wait."

You're killing me, Marlene," David said. "I need you."

"I need you too," I said. "But I don't need a baby."

"I'll marry you," he said, as a fact, not a proposal.

"I want to be a piano player," I said.

"You can always play," he said. "I'll get a job at the silk mill and take care of you. I'll help your mother out as much as I can too."

I laid my head on his chest and cried as I had once cried on my father's shoulder. The curly black hairs covering his white skin reminded me of half notes on sheet music. I told myself that I was safe, that the love of this good man and my own piano were all I needed for happiness. Where would I go, anyway, if I left Laurel? No one would pay to see me play. I could give lessons and perform at church sometimes. It would have to be enough.

One night in November, David and I were lying in my bed kissing. He twisted a lock of my long brown hair around his finger and I laid my hand on his heart. I had lit a few candles and the light was soft and golden. The room was drafty but we were warm under the covers. Soon we will be married, I told myself and I will never fall asleep cold again.

"I wish you could stay with me all night and creep back into the bunkhouse early tomorrow morning," I said.

"It's too dangerous," he said. "I know I would oversleep. I always hate to leave you."

I began to kiss him again, then stopped.

"David, did you hear something?'

"Yes. There's someone on the roof."

"What? One of the barn cats?"

"No. Listen."

Something heavy scraped against the tin roof, much larger than a cat or chicken and crawling on all fours. David rolled out of bed and reached for his boots, but he was too late. When I looked up at the skylight, I saw Boyd's devilish face looking down at me. Even in the dim light we could see his evil smile.

"I'll kill him!" David hissed.

"Quiet! Don't move."

We heard more scuffling and the heavy sound of Boyd crossing the roof and stepping down. He had a ladder; he had planned to catch us. Possibly his dirty mind had suspected this for a long time. I stood up and held David back as Boyd went into the house.

"Get back to the bunkhouse," I said. "Boyd might not say anything to his parents."

"Of course he will! He hates me and he still wants a piece of you. I've no doubt he's jealous."

"He won't wake his parents up and admit to spying on us. It would look too suspicious. Even if he does, you could say you were asleep in the bunkhouse. Go on!"

"All right, I'll go. But when I get kicked off this damn farm, I'm taking you with me."

"I love you, David," I said.

The next morning when I went to the house for breakfast, Boyd waited for me on the front porch, blocking the door. When I reached for the doorknob, he hissed in my ear.

"I always knew what kind of girl you were, Marlene, even when we were little kids. You ain't sweet and clean like Maud or Amelia or Helen. You'd love a roll with any man you could get and I think you could do a lot better than David Dunn."

"I'm not afraid of you." I said. "I know I'm a good person and I don't give a damn what you imagine about me."

"I saw you! When I tell the family, no one will respect you any more. Your own mother won't take you back."

"Go ahead," I said, trying to sound calm.

Uncle Luke, Aunt Josie, and Maud came downstairs. The others all began to eat, but my fear had killed my appetite. Boyd did not choose his moment with any care, he simply blurted out his slander.

"David Dunn did it with Marlene."

"Boyd, don't you ever speak that way in front of your family!" said Aunt Josie.

Everyone stared at Boyd, then at me. Maud looked outraged. My aunt covered her face with her hands. Anger reddened my uncle's face.

Aunt Josie sat down, white with worry, and avoided my eyes.

"Dunn, what do you have to say for yourself?" my uncle demanded.

"I've done nothing wrong," said David. "I love your niece, Mr. Hayden, which is more than you could ever do."

"You drunken smutty bastard!" my uncle shouted.

David stood up and shouted back. "We're getting married. We won't work another minute for you."

"You ought to be ashamed," Uncle Luke growled.

He stood up too. Aunt Josie held his hand and looked frightened of a fight.

David kept yelling "No, sir! You ought to be ashamed of working your own flesh and blood like a slave and making her sleep in the barn like an animal!"

"She sure acted like one," said Boyd.

"You Irish are all the same - trash," said my uncle. "Get off my land, both of you."

"No," said Aunt Josie. "Marlene should go back to her mother."

"I love David," I said. "I'll go with him. Thank you for your kindness, Aunt Josie."

David walked out and I stood up to follow him. As I passed my uncle, he said "You're a light skirt, just like your mother."

I spat in his face.

David and I held hands as we marched out to the bunkhouse. He packed his pipe and his few clothes in a carpetbag and wrapped himself in a long coat, muffler and cap. In my room, I packed my picture of my family, Helen's doily, Brendan's duck painting and my clothes and bedding in a laundry bag. I rolled up my quilt and used all my ribbons to tie the quilt and bag into an awkward bundle to wear on my back. The trunk I'd brought was too heavy to bring with us now. I had no idea where we would sleep that night, and imagined us huddled under the quilt in an alley.

David saw my shoulders shaking and pulled me into his arms. I began to cry.

"I'll take care of you," he said. "I have thirteen dollars saved and the silk mill is hiring now. Don't worry, Marlene."

"I'll miss Sven and Isaac and Aunt Josie," I said.

"She's a good woman," said David. "It's a shame she married that horse's arse."

David and I walked off the farm hand in hand. He never glanced back, but I did. Aunt Josie and Maud stood on the porch. My aunt cried while Maud comforted her. The men were walking out to the barn, preparing to slaughter one of the hogs. Sven saw me, and waved, even smiled. I waved back. No one else looked for a good-bye.

CHAPTER FIVE

David and I walked twelve miles into town. We found the cheapest boardinghouse in Laurel, Mrs. Green's, a three-story stone Colonial house near the stockyards and the railroad tracks. The parlor had peeling red and green poppy wallpaper and a strong smell of cigarettes, mold and mice. A middle-aged woman sat bent over an account book on the desk.

David said "My wife and I need a room."

I kept my gloves on to conceal my lack of a wedding ring, fearing that Mrs. Green would refuse to rent a room to an unmarried couple. Instead, she led us upstairs without a word. The room had a dresser with one missing drawer and a sagging double bed. There was an empty fireplace but no heater and one bare light bulb swinging overhead. David looked out the tall narrow window at the cows in the stockyard, then pulled down the blind.

"Don't worry," he said. "We're free now. Tomorrow we'll get jobs at the silk mill and then we'll get married. No matter what I've lost, I have you, Marlene. That's all I need."

I kissed him and said "I don't need a diamond ring, David. I love you and I always will."

He tried to lift my nightgown, but I said "No, please."

"Marlene, we're engaged. In our hearts we're already married and God knows that."

"You can wait another week for me," I said. "I don't want our first time to be in this shabby cold little room."

"What did you expect? A honeymoon in Europe? I'm not a rich man like your father."

"Dad wasn't rich, and that's not what I mean. I just want a wedding night."

"I've waited all my life for that bliss. I suppose I can wait a few days more," he said.

I fell asleep with David's arms around me and he didn't let go all night.

The next morning we walked three miles to the silk mill instead of taking the trolley. My feet still ached from our hike into town the day before. We'd spent twenty cents on breakfast, which was dry biscuits and burned bacon. At least I couldn't hear my stomach like yesterday.

A "Help Wanted" sign hung on the metal gate of Stolzfus Silk Mill. Men and women formed two separate lines in the courtyard. One by one, they were led inside, interviewed and sent out.

Mr. Schwichtenberg, the foreman who interviewed the women, was a short, bald toad-faced man. Helen had complained to me about his wandering eyes and hands since her hire.

I smiled at Mr. Schwichtenberg and shook his hand firmly.

"James Schwichtenberg, weaving foreman," he said.

"I'm Marlene Piper," I said.

"What work experience do you have, Marlene?" he asked, looking doubtful.

"I've baby-sat, taught piano lessons, played the organ at the Varsity Theater and worked on my uncle's farm."

"Have you worked with cloth before?"

"I can card, knit, crochet and weave wool. I can embroider silk handkerchiefs and I've sewn my own dresses and clothes before."

"Can you work a twelve-hour shift from seven in the morning until seven in the evening, six days a week?"

"Yes, sir. I'm used to long hours on the farm."

"Marlene, I will consider you. Come back here tomorrow morning at a quarter to seven. There will be a list of new hires posted on the gate."

His hands lay on the desk as if reaching for mine. Should I shake his hand again? Yes.

"It's been a pleasure meeting you," I said. "I hope to see you tomorrow."

He squeezed my hand with a wry smile and a wink. I already loathed Schwichtenberg, but I knew I had the job.

The next day David and I read our names on the list. At ten before seven, the whistle blew and we filed into the factory to begin our new jobs. Now I was a weaver and he was a packer. David stayed on the first floor, to begin boxing silks and loading them on trucks. I kissed him goodbye in the cloakroom, then put on my blue and white striped apron and went upstairs to join the weavers. I recognized most of the girls there, including Ruby, Jenny and Rachel who had gone to St. Anne's Church and school. Helen was shocked to see me.

"Aunt Josie drove into town by herself yesterday," said Helen. "She told Mother that you ran off with David Dunn."

"It's true."

"Marlene! Why? That dirty field hand."

Her hazel eyes widened as if she'd seen a spider.

"I love him," I said. "He's good to me. He's kind and smart and honest. David's the most *real* person I've ever known."

"What do you mean, 'real'?" she asked, tossing her honey-colored French braid.

I sighed. How could I tell my sister what I felt when David and I went night swimming? For the first time in my life, I didn't feel ashamed of my longing. The smoke of his pipe was worth more to me than diamonds. How could I say this to Helen, my innocent fifteen-year-old sister in her pressed white shirtwaist?

"He says what he really thinks about things and follows his heart and his own conscience. David isn't afraid of anyone."

"Well you should be," she said. "Mama's going to kill both of you."

"I love him," I said again, trying in vain to smooth my wrinkled clothes.

The repetitive motions of weaving, the simple act of lifting up my arms hour after hour, left them weak and aching. Sometimes my hands shook, but Rachel said that would go away with time. Sometimes I ran my fingers over the long table as if it had piano keys, playing the notes of the songs that filled my head. The slapping and swishing sounds of the thread machines became part of my daydreams. I would not always be in this factory; I would play again at the movie theater, in church, in a spotlight at a concert hall. The other girls stared at my mad fingers on the table, but I did not care.

I begged my parish priest, Father Hulings, to marry David and me as soon as possible. To my great surprise, he agreed. In the confessional he was not at all shocked by my spitting on my uncle or living with David at Mrs. Green's.

"You know your own mind, Marlene," said Father Hulings. "I'll marry you and Mr. Dunn on Saturday."

Mother and Joseph refused to attend our wedding, but Amelia, Helen and Brendan stood by me in St. Anne's Church. Isaac and Sven lied to Uncle Luke about needing to go to town to buy horseshoes so they could be David's groomsmen.

David smiled at me as we kneeled on the hard floor and Father Hulings prayed over us. We held hands as we took our vows and David pulled the golden ring from his pocket. We had no ring bearer, but I felt proud that David had been able to buy my ring himself, though it came from a pawnshop. I did not have or miss an engagement ring.

When he said "I do," David squeezed my hand so tight that I could barely feel my fingers. When I said "I do," he kissed my hand and slipped the ring onto my finger. Dad had once told me the ancient Romans believed that a vein in the ring finger of the left hand went directly to the heart. Amelia later told me this was a myth, but on my wedding day, I could feel my blood racing from my ringer finger to my drumming heart and through every blood vessel in my body.

I heard Father Hulings' gentle Irish voice say "You may kiss the bride."

David kissed me eagerly and we held each other tight, as if trying to force ourselves into one person. Many people whispered and Sven and Isaac clapped. Amelia had borrowed Arthur's car for us and Brendan and the Madsens had festooned it with tin cans, old shoes, and a "Just Married" sign.

We could not afford a honeymoon, but we had just rented our own house from Mr. Nussbaum, an old friend of my father's. We had no furniture, but looked forward to steam heat and hot and cold running water. Amelia drove us to the door and I kissed her goodbye, took David's hand and climbed the steps. We forgot all about the old tradition of carrying the bride over the threshold.

David fumbled with the lock, then opened the door. We rushed upstairs to the pile of quilts and pillows where we would sleep until we could buy a bed. Although I made every effort to be a modest bride, all day long I had shivered with anticipation of going to bed with my husband. I took off my blue cloche hat, black wool coat and the white silk dress Helen sewed in haste for me. David had already flung his Sunday clothes on the floor.

He was eager but not awkward, his skin hot despite being out in the cold evening air. David unhooked my garter belt and unlaced my corset, kissing the back of my neck and clutching my breasts.

"I love you, Marlene," he said.

"I love you, David."

I turned around and kissed him, running my hands all over him and rubbing my cold nose into the black hair of his chest.

"You're like a cat," he said. "Are you my kitty?"

He grabbed me between the legs with one big strong hand. The force of his fingers first startled, then delighted me. I stroked him too until he gasped for breath and pulled me into bed with him.

There was a moment of pain, but no blood and I didn't feel torn open, only filled. David was a virgin too, I knew, and he struggled to keep his rhythm and balance as he lay on top of me. I stroked his hair and kissed him but he clenched his teeth with lust, then shuddered and sighed. For a long time, I clasped him in my arms, not wanting him to leave me, one with him at last.

"I'm so happy," I said. "I love you so much, David."

"And I love you," he said. "I'll always do my best to make you happy, Mrs. Dunn."

He rolled off of me and I kissed him and went to the bathroom to wash up and brush my teeth before bed. David took his turn in the bathroom and I picked up and folded his rumpled clothes for the first time. As he entered the room, he smiled at me, but his blue eyes were sad and faraway as an ocean horizon.

"David, is anything wrong?" I asked.

"No, dear. You've done nothing wrong. I was just thinking that you are the only person in this world who truly loves me."

"What! David, that can't be. Write to your family. At least let them know that you have a job and a home and a wife now. Your mother will be happy for you. I'm sure that she loves you and misses you and has just never been able to say it."

"Marlene, please don't pretend you know anything about my mother because you do not. I have written letters and they have never been answered."

"What about your brothers and sisters then? Surely at least one of the eight would-"

David kissed me, not lovingly, but to stop me from speaking.

"No, Marlene. My family didn't cling to each other like grapevines the way your family does."

"You are in my family now," I said.

"Tell that to your mother and Joseph."

"They'll come around," I said. "I just wish that my father could have been there to see us married."

I told myself that Dad would have seen the good in David even though he did not have an education or a profession. Dad had been a field hand for four summers and taught evening piano lessons to work his way through teacher's college. He would not think less of David for being a laborer, as Aunt Josie, Uncle Luke and my mother had done. Dad would have made peace in the family somehow. I let David cling to me even after he fell asleep. I no longer thought of myself as an orphan; even in mourning I had never been as alone as David. I vowed that, while I lived, he would never be so alone again.

CHAPTER SIX

The house on West Lemon Street was a two-storey red brick structure with a green roof and one big white shingled gable in the front. Big square brick pillars lined the porch. There was no fence around the lawn and a weather-beaten old brown barn out back, which David quickly turned into his woodshed. Mr. Nussbaum offered to sell the house to us once we could save enough for a down payment. Until then we would pay rent.

The house had hot and cold water, and push button electric lights. The parlor had a fireplace and sliding doors leading to the dining room. There was also a narrow spare room on the first floor which I called my sewing room, although I had no sewing machine. Mother had taught me needlepoint and knitting and crocheting when I was little, but I seldom sewed except for simple mending. It was too early to declare that room a guest room; my mother had discouraged my siblings from visiting for more than a few hours.

The kitchen had a black and white checkerboard tile floor, a new gas stove, double sink, ice box and kitchen queen cabinet with compartments for sugar, flour, tea and coffee. A door in the kitchen led to the cellar where I stored the Madsens' jars of preserves on shelves between the coal furnace and the washing machine with its wringer and removable tub. After the spartan room and board at Mrs. Green's, I looked forward to washing clothes and cooking meals whenever I wished in these rooms.

The main staircase led up to the two bedrooms and bathroom on the second floor. David and I bought all of our furniture second-hand, buying one item each payday. For the first week we slept in a pile of quilts and blankets, but then we bought a curved metal bed frame and a new mattress. We ate seated on the floor until we bought a maple table and six chairs at an estate sale. Next we bought a long maroon couch, then a green armchair and footstool, then a tan wingback chair. I had brought my dresser and chest from home for our bedroom and bought a few second-hand rugs that could pass for Oriental. I made rag rugs for the kitchen and crocheted a blue oval rug for the bathroom in a rare burst of needlework.

On the weekends, David chopped wood in his shed and made stools, a bread box and small tables to stand beside beds and chairs. No matter how cold the weather, he enjoyed his work, wearing a sweater and scarf as he sawed and hammered. I brought him tea and kissed his red face, but David hardly glanced up from his carpentry table. His breath steamed out in the cold shed by the milky light of one naked bulb.

"David, honey, wouldn't you rather work on this inside? I wouldn't mind the sawdust and even the cellar would be warmer."

"Don't nag me, woman," he said. "I'm busy."

I went back inside and dumped the tea down the sink drain. I began to draw up plans for the garden, both vegetables and flowers. My fingers ached for a piano. I still ate Sunday dinner at Mother's but David hardly ever accompanied me. I played Mother's piano for my siblings and sometimes for my friends if they stopped by on Sunday afternoon. My own house felt silent and empty, even when David and I ate dinner together talking over factory and family gossip and the daily news. I began to sing as I washed the dishes and hung laundry in the cellar. One day David came inside, heard me singing and jokingly asked if I was mad. Then I remembered the sad sound of my mother's Irish songs in empty rooms, a voice her children just barely heard.

I told my mother that the quiet of the house disturbed me.

"You want the pitter-patter of little feet," she said, beaming like the full moon.

"No," I said. "I never think about babies. I want my piano."

"Marlene, you never had your own piano. What are you talking about?"

"I miss playing," I said. "I miss doing the thing I do best. Did you think I would just forget about it?"

Mother looked taken aback.

"Of course not," she said. "I always thought you would keep playing and maybe teach lessons or something, but you will have to save a lot of money to buy a piano of your own.

"And Marlene, I don't believe you never thought about having children. Don't be so afraid of it. Sure it's time you put someone else before yourself."

That Christmas, I was surprised with a gift. It arrived on Christmas evening, after David and I had eaten an uneasy ham and pumpkin pie supper at my mother's house. We had come home and he refused to shovel more coal into the furnace, even though I shivered in my sweater.

"We're about to go to bed anyway," said David.

"It's only eight o' clock."

Suddenly we heard a knock at the door. When I opened it, Helen and Amelia stood there. A truck sat parked in front of the house, with Joseph in the driver's seat and Sven, Isaac and Brendan hurrying to unload a large square item covered by an old blanket. As they wheeled it up my front walk, I recognized the shape.

"You shouldn't have!" I exclaimed.

"Don't be silly," said Amelia. "We pooled our money and we bought it second-hand from St. Nicholas Church."

My brothers and the Madsens struggled up the steps and through the front door with my present. Brendan whipped off the blanket with a flourish and bowed. The piano was an old brown upright, no doubt out of tune, but I knew now that my house would never really be empty again.

David laughed and I cried from happiness and hugged everyone, one by one.

"You should know that this was Mother's idea," said Helen. "Amelia told her how much you miss playing and I complained that no one we know can afford a piano. Then Mother said we should all pool our money and Sven and Isaac said they could help move the piano once we found it."

"I found it," said Brendan.

"This is a wonderful Christmas," I said. "Thank you. I'll thank Mother too."

The piano needed tuning and I resolved to call Mr. Zimmerman to help me with it as soon as possible, but I had to invite everyone in and play a few songs right then. My siblings crowded into our parlor, some sitting in my dining room chairs, all drinking tea and eating pfeffernuss cookies while I played one carol after another and everyone sang. I wished Mother had come with them, but I felt grateful to her all the same. Perhaps one day, most likely when David and I had a child, she would come to our house.

At last I said goodbye to everyone and stood waving to them from the window. David looked over my shoulder at the truck driving off in the falling snow, with everyone waving exuberantly and Joseph honking the horn.

"You never do cut the apron strings, do you?" he asked.

"What do you mean?"

"Your mother only put them up to this to show me up, to imply that I can't provide for you. She wants you to feel indebted to her and superior to me."

"No one thinks that! They all knew I was saving money for a piano and just wanted me to have one a little sooner. Helen sees me every day at work running my fingers over the weaving table like it was piano keys."

"And she took pity on her poor musician sister!"

"Why are you angry that I got a gift? I'm very happy tonight with my family and with you. They're your family too now. Why can't you accept that?"

"Your mother still won't set foot in our house. They are not my family, Marlene and never will be. I have no family, no one but you in this world."

I put my arms around David and kissed his whiskery cheek.

"Let's not fight," I said. "Come to bed with me."

David took my hand and we climbed the stairs together. After every argument, we would make up with kisses and caresses. David and I never went to bed angry, but although I sometimes apologized, he never, ever told me he was sorry.

CHAPTER SEVEN

In 1923, Amelia and Dr. Arthur got married and Maud surprised everyone by finally accepting Sven's proposal of marriage. Maud did not invite me to her wedding but Amelia asked me to be her matron of honor. David scarcely spoke to any of my relatives at Amelia's wedding, where Mother and Joseph were coldly polite to him. Every Sunday I went to Mother's house for dinner with the whole Piper family and David found some excuse to leave early, but I stayed late to play the piano and sing with my siblings.

"Why don't you cut the apron strings?" he scolded me. "You act like a child."

I worried about David spending so much time by himself. When we lived at the Hayden farm, I assumed that David was only solitary because we were isolated. He was more serious than Sven and Isaac so he could not become a close friend of theirs. I had always told myself that David's brooding was a sign of intelligence, not just melancholy, that I was the only one who understood him. When he began work at the factory, he made friends with two other packers, named Jim Dougherty and Sean Peterson.

David began to eat lunch with Jim and Sean rather than me and encouraged me to eat with Helen, Rachel, Ruby and the other girls. I didn't mind this at all as I loved to gossip and David and I had every breakfast and dinner to enjoy together.

"I'm glad you have some new friends," I said. "Maybe Jim and Sean could come over to our house for dinner one night."

I invited Jim and Sean to our house on many occasions, but they always declined. I thought this was very strange. Both of them were bachelors who lived with their mothers and I thought they might enjoy dinner at someone else's house. I didn't know either of them well, but Jim went to Saint Anne's Church and Sean was one of Arthur's patients. Why wouldn't they want to see where David lived and meet his wife? They scarcely said more than "Hello" to me when I happened to pass them at Stolzfus Silk Mill or at church.

Jim and Sean invited David to their houses to play poker with them every Friday evening. I was glad to be able to play my piano as late as I liked. David went to bed by eight every other night, and I had to stop playing then because he slept lightly. Even when I went to bed with him, I would get up later and read library books or draw or write in my diary in an armchair in the living room.

One Friday evening in early spring, I was making Easter decorations. I drew Easter nests with chocolates, colored eggs and bunny rabbits. David would think these pictures were childish, but I loved Easter decorations and he would not let me "waste eggs" by dyeing them. I couldn't convince him that a dyed egg is as edible as a plain one. After I had drawn my pictures in colored pencil, I looked for my scissors to cut them out and couldn't find them.

Frustrated, I went out to the wood shed. David had probably taken the scissors out and forgotten to bring them back in. The room was cold and the dirt floor was damp. There was a strange smell in the air, a smell between varnish and wood. I looked through the drawers of David's carpentry table and found the scissors. Still curious, I began to look through the bags and boxes underneath the table. I found screws and nails, sandpaper, tins of wood stain and varnish and an unlabeled green bottle. I pulled the cork and sniffed at it. It was liquor.

I had rarely smelled spirits before, but the odor of alcohol was unmistakable. I took a tiny sip to be sure and the smoky amber liquid burned my throat. It was whiskey. David must have spilled some of it somewhere for the room to smell so strongly. I wondered where he had gotten it, how much and for how long had he been drinking.

Should I put it back and act like I hadn't seen it? I really had no right to look through his things, but even if I hadn't searched the room the smell was obvious. If he came to work smelling like whiskey, David would be fired and most likely arrested. Many of Laurel's citizens drank privately, but the Stolzfus family were teetotalers and would fire anyone with a hint of alcohol about them. Why did David drink anyway, especially alone here in the wood shed? Was he so unhappy with me? A few drinks with Jim and Sean would be disappointing but not as disturbing as the lone hidden bottle.

David often came home from his poker games after I had gone to bed. He always washed thoroughly because Jim and Sean smoked cigarettes and he smoked his pipe when he was with them. David knew I couldn't stand the smell of smoke in the house. That night I waited up for him in the living room, ready to sniff like a bloodhound.

He looked red-eyed and surprised to see me.

"Marlene?" he said. "Why are you up so late, dear?"

I said nothing, but sprang up and kissed him. His mouth tasted like cigarettes and whiskey. Startled, he grabbed me by the shoulders and almost pushed me away.

"You kiss too hard. Are you trying to smother me?" he asked.

"You've been smoking cigarettes and drinking," I said.

"Yes, I have. Jim offered me a beer and it would have been rude not to take it. You told me once that you weren't a teetotaler like your mother. What do you care if I drink?"

"It's against the law, David. If I don't care, the foreman will."

"I'd never drink during the week."

"You went to Jim's house last Tuesday and Thursday."

"Don't you dare question me!"

He pushed me down into the armchair and when I stood up, he pushed me again.

"Stop it! Let me alone!" I yelled.

"You let me alone! I'll drink what I like when I like. I'm the man of the house and I'll be the boss here, not you, Marlene."

"Do you drink because you're unhappy?"

"No. I drink because I like it. I haven't been unhappy with you until this moment. I thought you had more trust in me."

"If you don't think anything's wrong, why didn't you just tell me about it? Is this why Jim and Sean never associate with me?"

"Not every man you meet finds you fascinating, you know," he said with a sneer. "I need something else in life to amuse me and you should thank God it's only a little beer and not another woman."

"No woman wants a drunk."

He slapped me across the face.

"David, how could you?"

"Don't start screaming, you'll wake the neighbors. I didn't even bruise you."

He hadn't hit me hard enough to knock me off balance, but I was furious.

"Why did you hit me? Why? I'm your wife and I love you. Why do you want to hurt me? If I've upset you, tell me so, but don't ever raise your hand to me again! Apologize."

"No. You've been coddled all your life; that's what's wrong with you. Don't you ever tell me what to do and call that love, Marlene."

"If you were walking across a railroad track and I saw a train coming, would you expect me to just stand there and let you be crushed or try to warn you and save your life?"

"You're all upset over nothing, Marlene. The drinking makes me happy. It doesn't make me sick. I'll never do it at work and I'll never be caught, so don't worry about that. If you love me, you've got to trust me."

"If you love me, you've got to apologize and swear you'll never raise a hand to me again."

"I don't have to apologize. You know I'll never hurt you."

"David, you *are* hurting me."

"I'm going to bed," he said.

I lay down on the sofa.

"Don't be dramatic," he said. "If you want to stay down here and sleep in the cold it doesn't make the least bit of difference to me."

I turned my back to him and heard his footsteps on the stairs. I took some old blankets out of the hall closet and curled up under them. The clock on the mantel sounded like a heartbeat and kept me awake. After two, I finally dozed off.

David made oatmeal and tea the next morning and kissed my face gently as I woke up.

"You'll ruin your back sleeping on this old sofa," he said. "You're so stubborn. Can't you see that I love you and I don't want to be angry with you?"

David sat beside me and put his arms around me. I laid my head on his shoulder.

"Tell me that you are sorry."

"Marlene, I won't grovel to you. I love you and that's enough."

He handed me a mug of tea and I drank it. We ate together quietly.

"I promise not to strike you again," he said. "But you must promise not to tell anyone about my drinking."

"I promise," I said.

He kissed me and encircled me in his arms. I breathed in the honest smell of David's skin and hoped that I would never smell whiskey or beer on him instead of this. If he had been able to keep his drinking from me, surely no one else would discover it.

CHAPTER EIGHT

Though I told no one about David's drinking, it began to visibly weaken him, like carpenter ants in the walls of a fine wooden house. As summer cooled and autumn descended, it became difficult to get him into our bed at night and out of it in the morning. He'd stagger home and bang on the door because he had forgotten his keys. Once he sat on the porch steps singing in Gaelic until I came down to drag him inside. I'd lead him upstairs, praying that the neighbors wouldn't hear. David would babble incoherently in Gaelic, which he never spoke when sober. He'd swat at my face and shoulders sometimes, but he was too drunk to have much strength or a good aim.

"Stop being such a brat," I'd grumble, as I yanked off his shoes and clothes.

As he drifted off to sleep, words dripped out of his mouth like mud, Gaelic and English, curses and prayers. Often he called for his mother, and then cursed her.

"Saint Jude...*pog ma thon*...God damn...Jesus, Mary and Joseph...Mam, I want to stay with you... He's a damn dirty man, Mam... Don't send me away!"

I'd have no peace on those nights. David was either too drunk to make love to me, or clumsy and rough in his attempts. Once he collapsed into sleep, he snored like a sawmill. Unable to roll him over, I'd creep down to the living room to sleep on our couch.

In the mornings, I'd make oatmeal or eggs and biscuits, with bacon or sausage if we had been paid recently. David would curse when I woke him, then cut himself shaving and curse some more.

"I'm not goin' in today, Marlene. I've got better things to do than haul silk all feckin' day."

"It's better than getting drunk all feckin' day," I'd mutter.

Then I'd try sweetness.

"Have one of these biscuits, David. They're so good with butter and honey."

"I can't eat, Marlene. I'm sick as a dog."

He had shadows under his eyes and cuts on his chin, but he combed his black hair neatly. I found his derby hat, and wrapped a biscuit in a napkin and tucked it into his pocket.

"You'll want it later," I said. "Let's go."

Then we'd grab our twin lunch pails and dash for the Number 17 trolley. It was so full we had to stand and David swayed badly. I always feared that he'd fall on someone or upchuck from the motion, but luckily neither ever happened. By the time we reached the factory he could pass for sober. Before I went upstairs he would kiss me.

One morning Schwichtenberg saw us kissing, pressed up against the wall. David's mouth tasted sour and I felt the uneasy weight of Schwichtenberg's gaze on me, even before I opened one eye and saw him on the steps. He swung his pocket watch with one hand and buried the other in the pocket of his checked trousers.

"You shouldn't be doing that in public, Dunn," Schwichtenberg scolded.

"She's my wife," David said. "I'll do whatever I like with her, and if any other man lays a finger on Marlene, I'll kill him."

He kissed me one more time, and then stalked off into the courtyard. Schwichtenberg pretended to be fascinated by his watch. I tried to rush past him, up the steps, but he caught my arm.

"You're twenty minutes late to work, Marlene. What do you think this is - a charity school?"

"No, sir. Our trolley was late."

"It was not late, Marlene. You missed it. Ruby rides the Number 17 too and she was on time. If you and your husband can't scrape yourselves out of bed in the morning, there are plenty of others that can. This is your only warning. If you're late again, I'll dismiss you. I've never approved of married women working here anyhow."

I told Helen "Old Shittenberg just scolded me for kissing my own husband."

"I hate him," she whispered. "He looks like the backside of a mule."

At work I tried to lose myself in the repetitive motions of weaving, imagining the notes of music I would buy from Zimmerman's music store. Sometimes one of the girls would catch me humming and warn me to be quiet. Ruby, Rachel, Helen and I all loved to gossip and always went to the water fountain or the ladies' room in pairs. Schwichtenberg liked to creep up behind a girl and pinch or slap her bottom, but he would never try it when anyone else was present. Sometimes I would walk by the window and look down at David loading boxes in the courtyard, with as much hopeless longing as before we were married.

One morning I passed Sean on the back stairs, grabbed him by the collar and pushed him against the wall. He looked startled and terrified of me, even though he was a head taller.

"Sean, I want to know why you and Jim keep buying my husband alcohol and sending him home drunk. Why?"

"I don't know what you're talking about," he said, offended. "David always brings the whiskey. I don't even know where he gets it from. And he only comes home drunk because he's afraid you'd beat him for staying out all night. I believe you would too, you fat bitch!"

He shoved me aside and hurried down the stairs.

That night after dinner, David came up behind me while I washed the dishes. Expecting a hug and kiss, I leaned back into my husband's arms. David grabbed my neck and right shoulder and squeezed hard so hard that I cried out in pain.

"Why did you scream at Sean on the stairs today?" he demanded.

I tried to pull his hand away from my neck, but he grabbed my right arm and twisted it behind my back.

"Ow! Let go of me, David! What's wrong with you?"

"You promised not to breathe a word about my drinking to anyone."

The pain in my arm didn't intimidate me; it doubled my anger. I wriggled out of David's grasp.

"Sean knows! He drinks with you!"

"Do you want the neighbors to hear you screamin'! Pipe down! You cluck like an old hen and I'm sick of hearin' you."

David stormed out to the shed. My hands shook with frustration, but I was too ashamed to tell anyone that I fought with my husband. If David tired of me so quickly and turned to drink, I must be failing him somehow. I said nothing to him and buttoned up my collar the next day to hide the bruise.

In our second winter together, I began to suspect that I was pregnant. My monthly period did not come in November; I scarcely noticed in December when it was absent again. I didn't feel weak or nauseated; I wasn't gaining weight yet or craving any strange foods. The first month, I told myself that it might be something else, but by Christmas I was certain.

David had given me nothing for our anniversary, saying that we had to save money for the down payment on the house. I gave him a book of Yeats' poems, which I am sure he never opened. I postponed telling him my suspicion until Christmas. My family sang carols and baked cookies as usual. Amelia and Arthur invited everyone to their house to drink hot cider and string popcorn garlands on the tree. I played *Silent Night, The First Nowell* and *Star Of The East* their piano. Maud boasted to everyone that she was already expecting and so sick that she could hardly stand to eat anything except fruit, gingerbread and her favorite homemade fudge. Sven doted on his wife and bought her oranges at the farmers' market. David sulked outside smoking his pipe for hours in the bitter cold. Helen gently asked him what Christmas was like in Ireland.

All he said was "Cold, wet and hungry, like any other day."

Helen shrank away from him and the rest of the family spoke to him as little as possible, directing all their questions to me. David gave me a cookbook instead of the sheet music that he knew I wanted. I gave him a new pair of boots, which he slipped on without a word. He left my mother's house early without telling me he was going. I was so angry that I put off telling him my news.

On New Year, my mother and I cooked pork chops and sauerkraut.

"Grandma Piper always made this for New Year's Eve," Mother said. "The Germans believed that killing a pig at New Year was good luck."

David turned up his nose at the sauerkraut and said "How can all that rotten cabbage be good luck?"

I kicked him under the table and he stormed out. I wished he could be sweet to me for one whole day so that I could finally tell him my good news. Lately all he talked about was how much money I wasted on coal, meat and my new winter coat. He rationed the coal and told me to put another sweater on when I got cold. I put my piano over a heat vent, and tucked an old blanket around it, fearing that the cold would weaken the strings. When David went out, I rushed to the piano like a secret lover and played for hours. If David came in and found me playing, he would yell at me to "Stop that noise and go to bed!" If he could not bear the noise of music and the expense of a new coat, how would he tolerate the constant hungry cries of a newborn?

I would love my baby; I knew that, but the birth would anchor me in Laurel. Now I would never be able to play in New York or Philadelphia. I had kept on dreaming of travel; even a few weeks off in the summer to play a few clubs would have been heaven. Now that would not be possible for years, and maybe not at all. I dreaded staying home all day with no company but the baby. Even at my dull factory job, I had the company of Helen and the other girls. Surely I would learn the good habits of motherhood from my own mother and from Katrina. I began to practice *Brahms' Lullaby* on the piano and *My Blue Heaven.*

Just Mollie and me
And baby makes three
We're happy in my blue heaven…

On the next payday at Stolzfus, and Mr. Schwichtenberg called me into his office. I wondered what in the world I had done wrong. He often chided me for trivial things like slouching and not smiling, but he had never called me into his office before. What if he had finally found out that I called him Shittenberg? I sank into the hard wooden chair across from his broad oak desk and leather office throne.

"Marlene, I want a word with you," he said. "It's about your husband."

"Yes, sir?"

"He's been late to work several times in the last few months. You have been late too, of course, but I am more concerned about David. When he does report to work, he appears to be under the influence of alcohol."

"No, sir."

Schwichtenberg leaned over his desk toward me in a most disturbing way.

"Don't fib to me, Marlene. You're smarter than that. Two of the foremen have made complaints. One of the truckers noticed it and spoke to me, and those truckers don't notice much. This morning I watched David Dunn drop a whole crate of silk handkerchiefs in a mud puddle and curse like a sailor."

"So would you if you dropped a whole crate of silk handkerchiefs."

"Don't be impertinent, Marlene. I won't tolerate impertinence in male workers and I detest it in females. You and David both know that Mrs. Stolzfus is a member of the Women's Christian Temperance Union. I don't know what you pot lickers drink at home and I don't care, but this sort of behavior will not be tolerated on the job."

"Why are you saying this to me instead of David? I've never been drunk in my life."

"David's foreman has spoken to him twice before. If he comes to work smelling like liquor or appearing to be intoxicated, we will be forced to dismiss him. I say this to you because it's a wife's job to keep her husband on the straight and narrow. Men need a guiding moral influence in life, especially Irishmen."

Now I hated Schwichtenberg more than ever. I wanted to gouge out his bulging, fishlike eyes with a dull knife. How could I sit here and take moral advice from a man who stood under the staircase to stare up girls' skirts?

"I'll do my best, sir."

"Here is your pay."

That night I cooked shepherd's pie, David's favorite dish. He had not met me at the silk mill gate after work and none of the men knew where he had gone. Usually he at least warned me in the morning that he might be going to Jim's or Sean's. I had watched both of them walk out the factory gate without David. If he's fired, we're ruined, I thought. We spent all my pay on the rent and his on all our other expenses: food, coal, water bills, everything. We never had more than five dollars in savings.

The day faded into a dark cloudy night and snow began to fall. Nine o' clock came, but I felt too restless to go to bed. Instead, I played the piano. The room was so cold that the ivory keys felt like teeth about to chatter. I played sad songs: *Danny Boy, Lass of Augrim, Downhearted Blues* and *What'll I Do?,* which I sang:

What'll I do when you are far away
And I am blue?
What'll I do with just a photograph
To tell my troubles to?

I pulled a sweater on to warm my cold shoulders, telling myself that David would shovel more coal into the furnace when he came home. I started a fire in the fireplace with wood and old newspapers. The grandmother clock ticked too loudly on the mantel and icicles cracked and fell from the roof. It was half past midnight when I heard heavy, uneven footsteps and the front door swung door swung open.

"David?"

I wanted to run into his arms, but I told myself that he did not deserve a warm welcome. Instead, I sat at the piano and waited for him to come into the parlor.

"David?"

"Who else were you expecting?"

His face was red and his eyes were bloodshot. His legs swayed and his hands shook as he drew near. It hurt me to see him as raw and red as an open wound.

"Where are your mittens?" I asked.

He mocked my voice, in a high nasal tone nothing like mine.

"*Where are your mittens?* You mean 'Where is my money?' don't you? I'll bet you'd like to know, wouldn't you?"

I tried to answer calmly "Yes. Yes, I would."

"It's all gone," he said.

"What? Didn't they pay you?"

"Oh, yes. They paid me. They begrudged me every cent, but they paid."

I stood up and faced him, trying to stare him down, but his unfocused eyes wandered around the room. I half expected him to say he had been fired and prepared my sympathies.

"What happened, David? Did you lose the money?"

He smiled stupidly, but his blue eyes were cunning, serpentine.

"No, I didn't lose it. I'm not a child. I drank it."

"Drank it? Where? How could you drink that much?"

"That's none of your affair," he said. "It's my money, Marlene. Not yours, not the mill's, not the landlord's, but mine. And I'll do what I like with it."

"Where will we get money for food?"

"*Where will we get money for food?*" he screeched. "How the hell should I know? You think I'm a real villain? You don't know anything!"

"Why did you do that?" I cried. "Why didn't you come home, David? I missed you. I was worried."

"You're not my bloody boss! Don't you ever question what your husband does in his own house. My mother never questioned her husbands, either of them, in her life. My stepfather wrenched my arm out of the socket once, for smoking his pipe. Mam just stood there silent and popped the bone back in when he was done. She knew her place. A woman should obey her husband and never fight him in anything, like the Bible says, like St. Augustine says."

His whispers stank of whiskey and choked out any sympathy I might have felt for him.

"The Bible says 'Avoid strong drink' and you've never read St. Augustine."

David struck my face, hitting my cheek and my left eye.

"Stop hitting me, you god damn bully!" I screamed.

"Somebody needs to beat some sense into you. You play the table at work like it's a piano. You still think you're going to play Carnegie Hall. You're a lunatic, Marlene, and I'm ashamed to have you in my house!"

"It's *not your house!"* I screamed.

"Oh! Is it your house, bitch? Did Mammy rent a little house for you? You're spoiled; that's what's wrong with you. Your daddy coddled you and told you that you had talent, made you believe that you were something special!"

He fixed his eyes on my sheet music: *Lass of Augrim, What'll I Do?,* and especially *Danny Boy.* I had been playing *Danny Boy* just before David walked in; it had been the last song I played for my father. David snorted at the picture on the cover, a grave surrounded by shamrocks and roses.

"What do you know about Ireland? What do you know about anything?"

He grabbed all the sheet music, crumpled it in his fists and flung it on the fire. I shrieked and sprang toward the fireplace, pulling the pages out just as they began to catch fire and trying to smother and flatten them with the rug. Black holes were seared into every page and the edges crumbled. Somewhere above me David was laughing.

I reached for the metal tongs and struck his knees with them as fast and hard as I could. He ripped the tongs out of my hands. Expecting him to strike me, I shielded my face with one arm.

Instead, David thrashed the piano keys with the tongs. The piano screamed out in A Minor and I sprang toward it, stretching my arms across the keyboard. David laughed demonically and slammed the tongs down on my left hand. The pain shot up my left arm and I screamed in agony. David shoved the piano away from me one final time and spat in my face.

"You're mad and you're useless!" he roared. "I rue the day I ever married you!"

I held out my injured hand and whimpered as he stormed upstairs and slammed the bedroom door. Had he ever loved me? He hated me now, hated everyone, even himself. David hated being alive. I knew then that I didn't want to be married to him any more. No matter what, I had to leave David before he destroyed me.

When I moved my fingers, I realized that only the left ring finger and pinkie were broken. I put the lid down over the keys and covered the piano with its quilt, wishing I could take it with me. My piano was the only object that I would really miss if David smashed, burned or pawned it. In my haste, all I took was the rest of my sheet music from the piano bench. I pulled the metal screen in front of the fire and left it to die alone. I put on my coat and boots. The last trolley had passed so I walked all the way to my mother's house, wet up to my calves from the snow. I pressed the doorbell for two full minutes before she came downstairs in her nightgown and slippers.

"Marlene? What are you doing here at this hour?"

Brendan and Helen stood behind her. They had been expecting only burglars at this hour, not an honest relative. I walked through the dark parlor into the dining room, and turned on a light.

When Mother saw my face, she screamed.

"Oh Marlene! I knew he would hit you! I always told you he was no good and now I see that I was right. What were you fighting about?"

"He came home drunk and said he spent his whole paycheck on drinks. I screamed at him and we fought, He broke two of my fingers."

Helen tried to take my hand, but I held the injured left hand with the right one.

"Oh, Marlene, what will you do?"

"I'm leaving him," I said.

"The hell you are," said Mother. "Divorce is a mortal sin and you have no grounds for an annulment. No matter what he's done, you are bound to him."

"I don't care if I'm married or not, but I won't stay in the house with him for one more day. If I can't stay here, I'll go elsewhere."

I turned toward the door.

"Oh stop being so melodramatic," said Mother. "You must stay here tonight. Helen, take your sister upstairs and clean her up."

"We won't let him hurt you, Marlene," Brendan whispered. "I promise."

Helen washed my face with soap and cold water; the skin was bruised but not cut, like a fallen apple. We jumped when we heard a knock on the bathroom door, but it was only Arthur and Amelia.

"Your mother called us," Arthur said discreetly. "She said you had two broken fingers."

All of us went into the bedroom Amelia and I used to share. Amelia gave me a stinging shot of painkiller in my hand and Arthur set the fingers and wrapped them in little wooden splints with clean gauze.

"Don't move them for a week," he said.

Brendan took Arthur to his room to ask him something in private. As soon as the door was shut, Amelia spoke her mind.

"I don't care what Mother said; I think you did the right thing by leaving David. No woman should tolerate that kind of cruelty. You leaving David is no different from Mother leaving her father. What if she had refused Dad and stayed there, being slapped and screamed at all her life, out of some false sense of obedience? God gave her a way out and she took it."

"I don't know if I have a way out," I said. "I'm pregnant, Amelia. I don't want a baby. I don't want someone as angry as David and as stubborn as me in this world."

"Don't talk like that, Marlene," Helen said. "You know that if David won't help you, all of us will. We won't abandon you."

"Mother told me to go back to him, but I can't bear to go. He may apologize. He may even be kind for a while, but it will always come back to this. I thought that if I only loved him enough..."

"Don't go back to him," said Amelia. "Get a divorce if you have to."

"But he has my house."

"We'll take care of that," said Amelia.

That night I slept in my childhood room and Helen slept in Amelia's old bed to keep me company. I cried quietly on the pillow. I missed my own house and hated to think of what else David might destroy while I was away, cutting my piano strings or burning my books. It *was* my house, which I had worked for and swept and scrubbed, with the flower bulbs I planted all around it. Now more than ever, I resolved to own that house and live in it until my death. I would not let David steal my home from me.

CHAPTER NINE

The next morning I insisted on going to work.

"Stay here," said Mother. "How can you weave silk with two broken fingers? You look disgraceful."

Helen had disguised the bruises as well as possible with make-up and thick powder, but I was still purple around the eyes.

"I have to go," I said. "If I skip work, they'll fire me."

I got on the trolley with Helen and felt the other passengers' stares. At the silk mill, a few people noticed my bruises, but no one spoke a word. I'm sure they knew what had happened; I had heard gossip about other wives in the same situation. I dreaded confronting David at work but he never came in.

All that morning, I felt sick in body and spirit. My head felt dizzy and empty as a tin top and my abdomen felt like knots of rope. Was this morning sickness or just the physical symptoms of my misery? I told myself that it would pass soon, that I was safer behind the thick red brick wall of Stolzfus Silk than anywhere else in town. Perhaps David was already in jail for being drunk and disorderly. I hoped so; it would keep him out of the snow and me out of danger.

Mr. Schwichtenberg came in late that day and didn't see me until eleven o' clock. He looked grave and beckoned to me.

"Mrs. Dunn, please step into my office."

I knew I was in trouble; he never called me "Mrs. Dunn". He shut the office door behind me and frowned.

"Your husband has been dismissed," he told me.

"Has he been here this morning?"

"No. He was dismissed yesterday when he received his last paycheck. Weren't you aware that your husband was fired for drinking?"

"I knew he was drunk but I didn't know he got canned." I said flatly.

Schwichtenberg sighed and shook his head as if my very presence gave him a headache.

"Mrs. Dunn," he said. "We cannot have workers coming into the factory in your condition."

"What condition?"

He lost his composure and his face turned red.

"I won't have you coming in here with bruises and two broken fingers. You look like a dog's breakfast. Go home at once."

"But I need the hours, sir. I feel fine."

"Mrs. Dunn, you misunderstand me. I want you to take your coat, your hat and your lunch pail, walk out the front gate of Stolzfus Silk Mill and never come back."

"But I've done nothing wrong! I've never been drunk! Why are you firing me for things my husband did?"

"Stop screaming, Mrs. Dunn. It's unladylike. If you don't walk out, I'll call the guard and have you removed."

"Go to hell, Shittenberg!"

I spat on his green leather account book and stomped out, slamming the door behind me. Later, I would hear that workers on all three floors heard the door slam. I stalked down the hall toward the stairs, not really looking where I was going. I got my coat, hat and lunch pail from the cloak room. In the dark rows of damp wool, I heard Helen's quick light steps behind me.

"Marlene, were you fired?" she asked.

"Yes. Shittenberg blames me for my busted fingers."

"That's so stupid!"

"I'm going home," I said. "Could you do me one favor and pick up my last check?"

Helen nodded and gave me a big hug.

"I know you'll find another job, Marlene. Something better."

I felt a cramp in my belly, like the worst menstrual cramp of my life. It hurt so much that I almost doubled over. Inside I felt like my internal organs were choking each other. It was not diarrhea or any normal pain from pregnancy.

"Excuse me," I said, handing Helen all my things and rushing down the hall to the women's lavatory.

I sank down on the toilet and leaned my face against the rough, unforgiving brick wall. My womb clenched like a fist and I looked down to see that I was passing blood. Tears welled up in my eyes.

"I'm sorry, baby," I said. "I don't deserve you."

Now I had lost everything. I tried to stand up but the pain in my belly held me down. I sat there in the cold bathroom stall, crying silently. The door opened and – thank God – it was Helen.

"Marlene, are you in here? Are you all right?"

"I'm dead," I said.

"Come on, be serious. Get up."

I pulled myself up and exited the stall.

"Come on, wash your hands. Were you throwing up? Is it morning sickness?"

"I'm not pregnant," I said. "Not anymore."

Helen's hazel eyes widened and admitted the truth.

"Oh Marlene, I'm so sorry. I love you."

Helen hugged me and we both cried.

"I'll be all right," I said. "It was not meant to be."

"Go straight home now," Helen said. "Tell Mother what happened."

Helen buttoned my coat, tied my scarf and handed me my lunch pail as if I was a child.

Mother was much more sympathetic than she had been the previous night. She made me chamomile tea, as she always had when I was sick. She asked me how I felt.

"Mother, I had a miscarriage today," I said.

"How far along were you?" she asked.

"Less than two months. I never told David. He wouldn't want it. I didn't want it, but I do miss the child, you know. What if this was my only chance to have a child and I lost it?"

"It happened to me three times," she said. "It was no fault of yours, I am sure. I'm sorry, Marlene, that you've had to endure so much. You know that I don't approve of divorce, but I do not expect you to live with David again. If you must live separately from him because of his mistakes, then that is no sin of yours."

"Thank you, Mother," I said.

"I love you, my girl," she said, giving me a hug. "You go on upstairs and say your prayers and get some rest. Pray to Jesus for strength and pray to the Blessed Mother, who knows how it feels to lose a child. Maybe one day when you're ready, the Good Lord will send you another child. Until then, don't blame God for this and don't blame yourself."

I prayed as best I could and asked God to help me get free of David and keep my home. I thanked God for my family and vowed not to become pregnant again until I could provide my child with two loving parents. As Mother advised, I prayed to Jesus Christ and Mary for strength and patience. Then I tucked myself in and fell into an exhausted slumber.

The next morning I had recovered my senses enough to look for work and the first person I thought of was my old friend Peggy Hobbes. I hadn't thought about Peggy Hobbes in months, but as the head housekeeper at the Ottoman, she could possibly hire or at least recommend me for any open position there. I put my mittens on to hide the splint on my hand.

Peggy and I had been inseparable from age seven to twelve, even when girls like Elizabeth Campbell and Barbara Jacobs called Peggy "nigger" and me "nigger lover". Boys, black and white, threw rocks at us, but we flung the rocks back at them and cussed. My parents both told me "In the sight of God, all races are equal," but they ominously warned me not to provoke white neighbors by bringing Peggy into their houses.

"Folks don't understand," Mother said. "And you don't want Peggy getting hurt, do you?"

Once, Peggy did get hurt because of me. Peggy's mother worked as a washerwoman and allowed Peggy and her brother Jerome a lot of freedom, but that abruptly changed when she remarried. Everson Pratt, Peggy's new stepfather, thought that Peggy was too uppity for a twelve-year-old girl and too old to run around with white kids. He resented Creoles and Catholics (Peggy's father had been both) and tried to make Peggy give up her gold earrings, which came from her maternal grandmother in Louisiana. In sixth grade, Peggy already had more schooling than both her parents.

One evening I walked her home from Mill Creek after her curfew. Mr. Pratt waited for Peggy on the front porch. She tried to run past him into the house, but he grabbed her by the arm.

"You come home on time for supper, you hear? And stay on this side of Lincoln Street!" he snapped. "I told you to stop runnin' with white kids. They got no respect for you."

"I respect Peggy," I said, loudly but calmly.

Peggy looked him right in the eye, defiant, and called "Goodbye, Marlene!"

Mr. Pratt flung open the screen door and shoved Peggy into the house. She was a big strong girl, not easily pushed around. I heard her stumble, but she didn't cry out. Her mother looked out through the screen door, but said nothing.

Mr. Pratt glared at me and yelled "Peggy don't need your damn charity! Get the hell off my property! And don't ever come back!"

Terrified of Mr. Pratt, I took off running. Peggy and I stopped playing together after that.

I saw her a few times in passing over the years, mostly at Central Market. She and her mother and Jerome started going to the Baptist church Mr. Pratt attended, although they had all been baptized Catholic. Peggy never took the last name Pratt. She always called herself Peggy Freeman. At age thirteen she got a job as a maid at the Ottoman and moved into a room at a boardinghouse. At sixteen, she married Jeremy Hobbes, a neighbor boy she'd always loved, who worked as a bellhop at the Ottoman. He was sweet and gentle, and they had two boys, Fred and Nathan. The last time I'd seen Peggy was at market in summer, pushing both boys in a stroller and balancing a bag of vegetables on top. She told me she had heard about my father dying and she was sorry. I'd told her I how I left my uncle's farm, got a job at Stolzfus and married David Dunn.

I approached the Ottoman Hotel from the servants' entrance in the alley. A black doorman and maid were smoking cigarettes and telling jokes. Peggy opened the door and called them back inside. When she opened the door, she saw me. Her stern expression softened; she transformed from head housekeeper to old friend in one glance. The doorman and maid went inside and Peggy and I were alone, two girls in the alley again.

"Peggy, you're looking well," I said.

She wore a long black dress and white apron and wore her white ruffled hat like a crown. Her hair was bobbed and curled and a gold and pearl brooch glittered on her breast. She stood tall and plump, more confident than ever. Peggy's brown eyes were bright but her broad smile folded up like a fan when she saw a bruise under my eye.

"Marlene, what happened to you? Who hit you, honey?"

"It was my husband, David Dunn," I said. "I can't stand his temper anymore."

"Are you still working at Stolzfus Silk?"

"No, I was fired because of this."

I took off my mitten to show her my two broken fingers.

"Oh, that's awful!"

"David left town and now I'm looking for another job. Peggy, I hate to come here and ask for anything because I haven't seen you in so long."

"I'm glad to see you at all, Marlene. Lord knows I'd hire you today if I could, but nothing's open."

Peggy thought for a moment.

"Marlene, do you still play the piano?"

"Yes. I've got my own piano now and I'll play for people every chance I get."

"I know a place that's looking for a piano player."

"Where is it?"

Peggy looked up and down the alley, stepping closer to me and whispering.

"Well, I haven't actually been there, but Jeremy knows the owner and he's a good man."

"Is it a dance hall?"

"It's a speakeasy," Peggy whispered in my ear.

"Oh."

"Now, whether you get hired or not, you must never tell a soul about this. And you never heard about it from me, understand?"

"Yes."

"I don't know a thing about the place," Peggy went on. "Not even where it is. Jeremy knows I don't drink and he only goes there to play clarinet. He makes more in one night there than in a whole week here totin' bags all day. Wait here while I bring him."

I waited in the alley, warmed by the steam from the cellar laundry rooms, listening to the splashing and clinking of hundreds of Ottoman china dishes being washed in the massive kitchen. At last the door opened and Jeremy followed Peggy out. He looked handsome in his red and white bellhop uniform and shook my hand politely.

"It's a pleasure to meet you, Miss Marlene. I know you're Peggy's old friend."

"It's nice to meet you too, Mr. Hobbes. I wanted to ask you about the place that needs a piano player."

Jeremy glanced at Peggy, who assured him "Go on, sugar. I'd trust Marlene with my life. She's no squealer."

"This place is in a cellar under Vintner's Hardware Store. It's open seven nights a week."

"Is it for whites or blacks?"

"Both," said Jeremy. "It's the only speakeasy in Laurel, as far as I know, so it has to be a black and tan club."

"I never knew that Laurel had a speakeasy."

"It opened a month after Prohibition started and it's never been raided. They pay a dollar a night for musicians, and they'll hire men or women, black or white. Can you play jazz?"

"Yes," I said. "I buy new songs at Zimmerman's every week and I can improvise."

"I heard you playing the organ at the Varsity Theater," said Jeremy. "I'll put in a good word for you."

"Thank you very much, both of you," I said.

Jeremy gave me one more piece of advice.

"If you go, wait until at least ten o' clock this Saturday night and knock on the back door three times, then twice. Tell the bouncers that Jeremy Hobbes sent you and they'll let you in."

He went back inside the hotel.

Peggy hugged me and said "I better get back to work now. Take good care of yourself, Marlene."

"I will, Peggy. I'm independent now. Tell me one thing, before I go. How is your family doing?"

Her face brightened, like a lampshade lit from inside. She felt shy telling me about her happiness.

"It's been good," she said. "It was hard at first, but my Ma helped us. She takes care of Fred and Nathan while I work and they're good boys. Jeremy's been wonderful."

"I'm so glad," I said. "Thank you, Peggy, for telling me about this."

We hugged and kissed each other on the cheek, then said goodbye.

"I'm sure we'll meet again, sooner or later," she said.

When we were kids, Peggy and I would always separate after we came home from Mill Creek, me walking toward Lime Street and her walking toward Lincoln Street. We used to always turn back to see if the other one was looking until we were too far apart to see each other anymore. Now I looked back at the Ottoman Hotel and watched Peggy still standing in the doorway until I rounded the corner.

CHAPTER TEN

No one had seen David since he was fired. To my surprise, I found no trace of him when I returned to my house. David hadn't smashed or burned anything and had only taken a carpetbag and a few clothes.

"Maybe he hopped a train and skipped town," said Brendan. "No one would hire him in Laurel now."

"Stay with me tonight," I said. "He's not gone, Brendan. I know it."

I had no food but potatoes and the water bill hadn't been paid, so Brendan and I melted snow to boil the taters and make tea. We stayed up late playing hearts. Last thing before we went to bed, we bundled up to dash to the outhouse. Being a gentleman, Brendan let me go first. When he took his turn, I started walking back to the house.

The sky was purplish-black like a bruise, with no hint of dawn. All of my neighbors' windows were dark and West Lemon Street sat silent, without even a dog barking or a crow cawing in one of the bare trees.

My footsteps sounded loud: crunch, crunch, crunch. *Crunch.* When I stopped suddenly, I heard one extra footstep and broke into a run. I didn't stop or even glance backward, but I screamed like a scorched cat and dashed toward the shed.

I scrambled up the ladder, clumsily knocking it to the floor as I jumped into the hayloft. Only then, did I turn around and see David below me.

He looked like he'd crawled out of his grave. His black hair stood up in tufts and his face and hands were red with cold. His eyes and teeth looked sickly yellow and long black whiskers darkened his face. David's coat hung open and he reeked of beer and blood. Bruises encircled his right eye and blood stained his lips. His hands clutched the ladder like claws.

I screamed so loud that my throat felt raw, but somehow I could still hear his raspy breathing. Could Brendan hear me in the outhouse? Would the neighbors come running?

"You bitch, I'll kill you!" he growled.

The ladder slapped against the hayloft and he began to climb. I tried to shove the ladder backward but he was too heavy to push over. One hand reached out for me but I kicked it. His bloodshot eyes glared over the hay. I stood up, held onto a rafter and kicked David as hard as I could. My boots struck him in the forehead, in the eye, in the nose, the mouth, the throat. I kept kicking and stomping on my husband, like a black spider.

"Die," I said through clenched teeth. I gave him one last kick, to the chin. He reeled backward and hit the frozen ground. The shed seemed to shake. David let out a groan and a sickly choking sound. I peered over the edge of the hayloft, gripping the beam with white knuckles.

"David?" I whispered. "David."

His eyes were open but his chest stopped rising and falling. He could be lying still on purpose, waiting to grab me when I climbed down. But the ladder had fallen on top of his legs, so I couldn't come down. I felt too scared to jump, like cat in a tree who couldn't remember how or why she climbed so high.

I heard feet rushing through the snow and saw Brendan in the doorway of the barn. Now I hoped that none of the neighbors had heard my screams, but, if so they had disregarded them. The worst struggle of my life had only taken a few minutes.

Brendan set up the ladder and helped me down. He held his hand above David's mouth, careful not to touch him.

"He's dead," he said flatly.

"I know," I replied. "I killed him."

"We should call the coroner," said Brendan. "It will look suspicious if we wait."

"Look at his face," I said. "They'll know I killed him. They'll know."

David's eyes were bruised and blood trickled from his nose and lip. His head looked like a sickly plum that had fallen to earth and split open.

"You did not kill him. You found him," Brendan dictated to me. "You saw the barn door open and came out to find out why. When you saw him, you screamed and became hysterical. I heard you and came outside. We suspect that David had been drinking, got in a fight and come home to recuperate."

"He did have blood on his lips before," I said.

"Yes," Brendan went on. "When David came home and found the door locked, he went into the barn. He tried to climb up into the hayloft, fell off the ladder and hit his head. This is the story that we will give to the coroner."

We positioned the ladder back over David's legs where it had been. Both of us wore gloves; there would be no fingerprints. I peered outside to confirm that no one watched us.

"I'll speak to the coroner," said Brendan. "That might be best. One of his daughters was in my algebra class at St. Anne's. You wait upstairs. You're too upset to see anyone and if he insists on seeing you, just tell him that you found David and started screaming."

My vision blurred. Tears watered the world down. I began to realize that I was a murderer, worse now than David had ever been. He would wait for me in Hell.

I remembered how much I had loved David Dunn, our wedding night in this cold house, swimming in the creek. He had led me off the Hayden farm; if not for David Dunn I would still be crying myself to sleep in that little shed by the barn. He had been the only one to protect me from Boyd. After all our hard work, didn't we deserve some happiness? For months now, I had already been mourning the loss of my husband. What I wanted was to have my David back, the young man who smiled at me in the cornfields, not this stinking, drunken beast.

He had been robbed all his life, by his mother, by his stepfather, by the coal mines, by my uncle and now, robbed of his life by me, his own wife. Here is your American fortune. I cried so hard that Brendan had to help me into the kitchen.

"You had to kill him," said Brendan. "David wanted to kill you. That's why he came back here instead of skipping town. It's not a sin to defend your life, you know. Not all of us are born to be martyrs."

"I'm not pure enough to be a martyr. I enjoyed killing him. I kicked him in the face a dozen times. I must have broken his skull."

"Impossible. That would be like kicking through the Kaiser's helmet. The fall killed him. That's why he groaned when he hit the ground."

"But I wanted him dead," I said. "That's a mortal sin, even if never go to court, or even if I'm legally not guilty. Brendan, I've been angry since I was a little girl. I only played the piano because it calmed me down. I used to bully Helen and fight in the schoolyard. I hated Mother. I hated the nuns."

"Everyone hated the nuns, Marlene. Children hate their parents because they want to be free. I've felt like a freak show in Laurel all my life. I don't want to work in the silk mill and get married like everyone else. I'm hopping a train to New York City first chance I get. Then I'll bring Isaac with me."

"Isaac would leave Sven?"

Brendan stared out the window at the pink sliver of sunrise in the eastern sky.

"Sven has Maud," Brendan said. "And Isaac needs me and I need him."

I remembered all the times Isaac and Brendan sneaked away together to fish or skinny-dip, long after they were boys. I remembered Sven punching Boyd for calling them queers. When he was about twelve, Brendan found the myth of Apollo and Hyacinth in Dad's mythology book. He asked Dad if a man could fall in love with another man. Dad said "Yes."

"I love him," said Brendan. "No one else knows. Now we understand each other. Even if we never tell another living soul, I have your secret and you have mine."

"Be sure to save me a seat in Hell," I said.

"This life is hell," said Brendan. "A man who beat you, men who would lynch Isaac and me. This shitty little town is our hell, Marlene, but we will get out of it - both of us. You broke out of your hell tonight and I will break out of mine."

I held his hand and started crying again.

"I'm as cruel as David, Brendan. I think that's why I married him. I was afraid of him at first, but I still had to have him. He was like the part of myself that I was afraid of. It was all wrong. I'm a killer now; I'm not natural."

I laid my head on the table and sobbed. Brendan patted my back and actually smiled.

"Marlene, you are supremely natural. Your temper saved your life today. If you were meek and mild, it would be you lying out there dead. I don't want to hear any more about it."

"Brendan, I'm not the same."

"You *are* the same, Marlene. We will never tell anyone. No one will ever suspect you."

"Mother will know," I said. "She always knows anything I've done wrong. I wish Dad were alive. I could tell him, tell him I'm sorry."

Brendan pulled his chair close to mine and hugged me.

"Take it to confession," he said.

"No. To my grave."

I buried my face in his bony shoulder.

"Go upstairs now, Marlene. I need to call the coroner before the neighbors wake up. You lie down. I'll get you when this is all over."

In the bathroom, I found my sharp scissors and began to snip my hair. I cut clumsily, angrily at first, then straightened the haircut out. When I finished, I had a passable bob.

I looked into the bathroom mirror and gasped at my short dark hair and pale face. For a split second, my reflection looked like David, with bloodshot eyes and short dark hair. I put my glasses on and smiled at my own face.

I looked down into the snowy backyard to see Brendan talking to two men in long black coats. The coroner was short and stout with a long white moustache. The other man was younger and drove the hearse. I saw the dirty brown boots in the back of the hearse as Brendan shook the coroner's hand and smiled.

The engines rattled and the hearse drove away. I stopped crying. For the first time in months I felt completely safe.

CHAPTER ELEVEN

Brendan spoke to Mother on the telephone, as he had spoken to the coroner, knowing that Mother would dispense the information to our siblings and neighbors by the time I went to her house for supper.

"Marlene's very distraught," said Brendan. "She's not able to speak of it yet."

My family had avoided speaking to me about David in his lifetime, and I doubted that his name would be spoken much after his death. Part of me wanted to tell everyone I loved the whole truth, but I feared gossip. Even if the coroner said the death was an accident, the Laurel community would believe otherwise.

I missed my family and needed to be near them, even though I could never tell them the whole story. That afternoon I took the streetcar to my mother's house, dressed in my black sweater and skirt. Joseph and Katrina and Amelia and Arthur were there too and everyone rushed to hug and kiss me.

"Marlene, we are all so sorry for your loss," said Helen.

You have no idea, I thought to myself. I thought about how Jack the Ripper was never found out, how everyone who saw him supposed he was a nice English gentleman. No one knew he carried butcher knives in his fine leather bag.

Joseph hugged me hard, the way men hug each other. He had seen soldiers die and never spoken of the lives he took except when raging at David. My knocking my husband off a ladder paled in comparison to the deaths he and Katrina must have seen in Belgium and France. I feared that Joseph might notice the change in me and recognize the graveness of one who has survived a life and death struggle.

"You'll be all right, Marlene," he said. "We'll all take care of you."

"I can take care of myself," I said gently.

Mother stared at me like a stranger and I wondered, for an instant, if she knew. No. She had always despised David and now felt relief and shame for feeling that relief, nothing more.

No one asked me what had happened; they believed Brendan when he told Mother we found David in the shed with a cracked skull. My siblings all hugged and kissed me and murmured sympathies in my numb ears.

"You should stay here tonight," said Mother. "You can wear my black dress for the funeral tomorrow."

"What will you do for a living now?" Amelia asked. "There may be an opening in the hospital kitchen for you."

"Thank you," I said. "I'll apply everywhere I can."

"Don't worry too much about that now," said Katrina.

I slept, or pretended to sleep, in my old bedroom that night. All I could focus on was the clock ticking in the parlor downstairs.

At mass the next day, I felt sick and unworthy to stand before God or take communion. I had killed my husband and I could not forgive myself. No one prayed a rosary for him that day, but I would pray many, asking that his soul could rest in peace, although mine never would. It was not a funeral mass; David's name was only a footnote.

"Let us also pray for the repose of the soul of David Dunn," said Father Hulings.

David, I hope you're only in Purgatory, I thought. *I hope that's where I end up too when my life is over. We can bear any agony, David, if only we know that it will end someday. Nietzsche was right that suffering makes us stronger.*

At the burial that afternoon, my family stood silently around the grave. Father Hulings recited *Patrick's Breastplate* because he knew that the deceased was an Irishman like himself:

I bind unto myself this day
The power of God to hold and lead
God's eye to watch, God's might to stay
God's ear to hearken to my need
Christ be with me, Christ within me,
Christ behind me, Christ before me
Christ beside me, Christ to win me
Christ to comfort and restore me.

But who had ever shielded David from pain, I asked myself? Joseph and my mother looked angry, as if the pine coffin still held something infectious. Each one of them comforted me, but only I cried. No friends attended the funeral. Jim and Sean were either at home with their families or out drinking and playing poker without a thought about their old friend. Mother had arranged the burial in haste and not even put an obituary in the *Laurel Intelligencer-Journal.* Aunt Josie,

Sven and Isaac were there, but the other Haydens stayed at home. The tombstone read:

David Dunn
Born County Kildare, Ireland
January 17, 1902
Died Laurel Pennsylvania
November 13, 1923

He had only been twenty-one years old, such a young man, but so jaded and hopeless. I wept for the husband I had lost and the happy home and children we'd never had.

Sven hugged me and whispered "He knew you loved him, Marlene. You loved him more than anyone else ever had. But you can't save another person; he has to save himself."

I shook my head and said "I wish he'd never met me."

Helen took my arm and led me away from the grave.

"Marlene," she said. "I know it sounds silly, but I really do like your hair short. It looks so light and free."

I squeezed her hand and managed to smile.

True to his word, Brendan skipped town the day after the funeral, taking Isaac Madsen with him. The note left on Brendan's pillow read:

Trying our luck in New York City.
Will write when we get work.
Love,
Brendan Piper and Isaac Madsen

The note was in Isaac's handwriting.

Mother cried harder than she had since Dad's funeral. Aunt Josie worried aloud about Isaac and Brendan "getting swindled, or worse." Joseph refused to speak about it and Sven was silent for a whole week. Naturally Maud blamed Brendan.

"Those high-hat Pipers think they can do anything! My Sven just wanders around the house like a flat tire and won't even speak to me!"

The days after David's death were an anxious time for me. I played the piano for hours to fill the silence and practice for the job at the speakeasy. After three days, I slept peacefully alone in my house. I could cook a big pot of beans, ham and potatoes and live on it for days. Each morning I marched downtown to apply for every position I could find.

I wondered how many people in Laurel had heard about David's drinking, his firing and his sudden death. Everyone at St. Anne's Parish would read it in the bulletin and the news would spread like measles through Central Market, the downtown shops, the Varsity Theater, up the 50 trolley lines, in the six high school and 27 churches of Laurel, into many of its 50,000 homes. My reputation as the widow of hard-drinking Irishman would precede me.

I applied at St. Luke's Hospital kitchen, but they wanted someone with culinary experience. I applied at Xavier's Hat Shop, but they wanted someone more fashionable. Buying sheet music at Zimmerman's, I asked about their "Help Wanted" sign.

Without even looking at me, Mr. Zimmerman said "I only hire men, Mrs. Dunn."

"Maybe you could use someone to play the Steinway in the window and draw the customers in."

Mr. Zimmerman scowled at me over the narrow rectangles of his glasses.

"This is not the midway, madam. My shop is a serious music store for professionals, not some place for bums to play for tips."

"I've been shopping here all my life, Mr. Zimmerman. My money's good enough for you; why aren't I? Half your clerks can't even play the piano."

He blushed with annoyance, all the way up to his receded hairline, but spoke to me like a baby.

"Marlene, dear, why don't you teach lessons? That's what ladies do when they're short of money."

"I'm not a teacher, Mr. Zimmerman," I said. "I'm a serious musician."

As I left the shop, I kept my face down and prayed that no one I knew would see my misery. My reputation was shot; I had failed on the farm, at the mill and in my marriage. Laurel had always found me odd with my glasses, my Irish immigrant mother and my inexplicable father, a teacher who loved to walk barefoot and steal black walnuts out of other people's yards. Dad had taught me, and all his children, to be proud that we were unique. Now, in the worst time of my life, I thought of Dad as I passed the golden marquee of the Franklin Opera House and the smiling statue of Ben Franklin.

I remembered the night when Dad took Brendan and me to see Eva Tanguay. Now I had lost Dad, lost Brendan, lost my job, lost my husband, lost everything but the music. In spite of everything, I remembered the song, and I walked through the back alleys singing:

They say I'm crazy, got no sense
But I don't care.
They may or may not mean offense,
But I don't care;
You see I'm sort of independent,
Of a clever race descendant,
My star is on the ascendant,
That's why I don't care.

I don't care,
I don't care,
What they may think of me.
I'm happy go lucky,
Men say I am plucky,
So jolly and care free.
I don't care,
I don't care,
If I do get the mean and stony stare.
If I'm never successful,
It won't be distressful,
'Cos I don't care.

At ten o' clock that night, the streets of downtown Laurel were empty except for a few beggars and young couples walking arm in arm out of the Varsity. No one noticed me, but my heart fluttered like a butterfly in a net. I found the address of Vintner's Hardware Store, 611 Grant Street. No lights were on inside and as I peered through the front window, I saw neat rows of paint cans, coils of rope and wire and metal bins of nails, screws, nuts and bolts. This place was no Carnegie Hall.

The alley behind Grant Street stank of urine and rats scurried in the shadows. The back door that Peggy had mentioned was just a greasy slab of metal. After walking three miles to downtown, I had to try. I knocked three times, then twice, as Jeremy had instructed.

A metal slit in the door opened and a black man stared out at me. I could only see his thick eyebrows, bloodshot eyes, and the bridge of his nose, but he looked rather disgusted with me.

"What do you want, lady?"

"I'm here to try out for the piano playing job."

"We lookin' to hire a man."

"I play twice as well as any man and you won't have to pay me as much."

Another man's laugh came from behind the door.

"Them's fightin' words," said the laughing man as he pushed the first one aside. This was an older black man with gentle eyes.

"Who sent you, gal?" he asked.

"Jeremy Hobbes," I said.

"Well, shoot, if you're a friend of the Hobbes family, you must be able to keep a secret."

"I never tell secrets," I said.

"You better not," said the first man. "Because the last man who tried to call the cops on us accidentally fell down four flights of stairs."

The door opened with a squeak and the two men hurried me into the dim hallway. The older one was thin and wiry with a gray beard in a purple suit and black leather hat, looking like a court jester. The middle-aged one was clean-shaven and wore a tan suit and fedora. Both carried themselves like gentlemen and I envied their fine clothes.

We descended a curving flight of stairs lit by one yellow bulb. The cellar smelled of coal and metal and the strange burned odor I'd smelled in the alley. It looked like an ordinary cellar with a coal furnace in one corner, boxes of tools and stacks of lumber. The older man slipped behind a stack of lumber, then opened a trap door and climbed down a metal ladder. It was dark in the room below him and I could barely see the ladder.

"Ladies next," the middle-aged man said sourly.

I gripped the ladder and crept slowly down the hole. To my surprise, I stepped onto a blue tile dance floor, painted with yellow starfish and tropical fish of every color. The room was surprisingly large and warm, with dark hardwood walls with yellow and green lights shaped like starfish. A gas stove and metal sink gleamed behind the bar. Twenty stools sat at the long walnut bar and all kinds of chairs and armchairs surrounded the tables. There were four long sofas against the walls: red and green plush and black and brown leather. Green and gold Japanese lanterns painted with fish dangled from the ceiling. On each table sat a candle in a red glass jar. Three steps led up to the stage, which held a drum set and a piano. A purple curtain edged with gold hung behind the stage.

"It's beautiful," I said.

"Thank you, ma'am," said the older gentleman. "I laid these floor tiles myself and Chauncey put up the wood paneling."

"Don't be tellin' her our names!" snapped Chauncey.

"Why not?" said the older man. "She's gonna be hired tonight; I can feel it."

"My name is Marlene...Piper," I said. It was the first time I had used my maiden name since my wedding, but I knew as soon as I spoke it that I would never be Marlene Dunn anymore.

"I'm Emmett Davis," the old gentleman said, shaking my hand. "Good luck to you, Miss Piper."

The purple curtains parted and a tall, dark man emerged, handsome as a Greek god. He smiled with a broad generous mouth. He had a long nose, strong jaw and high forehead and his large eyes shone like onyxes. He had pomaded black hair and a navy suit; his shoes shone and his tie was green silk. I couldn't believe I had ever seen this man before, wearing a green apron and weighing nails at Vintner's Hardware Store.

Emmett said "Sir, this lady wants to play piano for you."

"Can you play jazz?" asked the man in blue.

"Yes, sir. I can play Charleston, black bottom and any new music you'll give me."

"How about rag?"

"I know *Maple Leaf Rag, Tiger Rag* and lot of Joplin songs."

"How about blues?"

"I couldn't sing 'em, but I can play *Downhearted Blues* and *St. Louis Blues."*

"Well, stop braggin' and play us a song," said Chauncey.

"Like Mark Twain said 'It ain't braggin' if you can do it!'" I snapped back.

I sat down at the piano and tore into *The Entertainer*, then *Black Bottom Blues*, then *My Blue Heaven* and *Yes, We Have No Bananas*. I ended my set with *I Don't Care*, although I cared more about impressing these men than I'd ever cared about an audience. Emmett smiled and tapped his feet. Chauncey looked disgusted to hear a white woman play jazz. The man in blue showed no emotion, but listened carefully to the notes; I could tell he knew a lot about music.

"Why don't you sing?" asked Chauncey.

"My voice isn't the greatest," I said. "But I can sing back-up alto if you need it. I can play anything by ear and play new music the first time I read it. I used to play the pipe organ at St. Anne's Church."

"Well, that ain't no organ," said Chauncey. "And this ain't no church."

The man in blue handed me some sheet music.

"Play that," he said.

I tapped out sharps and flats, my feet bobbing on the petals. The tempo was frantic 4/4 time with rumbling low notes and jingling high ones. I had to spread my fingers wide to strike two chords at a time. I missed two or three notes entirely, but didn't pause, hoping the three men wouldn't notice. Sweat moistened my brow as I stopped playing and turned to my audience. Only Emmett clapped.

"What's your name, miss?" asked the man in blue.

"My name is Marlene Piper."

"My name is Alphonse Vintner, but all my friends call me Al. I own The Starfish and of course, the hardware store. I'm pleased to make your acquaintance."

Al shook my hand firmly and smiled.

"Can you work from ten o' clock at night until five in the morning?"

"Yes, I can," I said. "I'm a night owl."

"You will have most Sundays off and some Saturdays if we have a band in. If we have a band or other musicians in, could you play with them without arguing?"

"Yes. I've played with others all my life, in church, school and at home. I don't care if someone else has the spotlight as long as I get to play."

"Most important, can you keep The Starfish a secret from everyone, including your own family and your best friends? The mere fact that you've been in here could get you a year in jail."

"Or worse," Chauncey murmured.

"I won't tell anyone." I said.

"Good enough," said Al. "You're hired."

He shook my hand and I struggled not to kiss him or faint. Chauncey and Emmett heard a barely audible secret knock and climbed up the ladder to let the first patrons in. Al motioned for me to take a seat at the bar.

"You must have a drink to celebrate," Al said. "What would you like?"

I had never drunk anything but wine, communion wine at mass, (usually greenish Benedictine or watery red) and a few glasses of chianti or Riesling at weddings and parties. I'd never had a cocktail or even considered beer.

"What do you have?" I asked.

Al chuckled and unlocked a huge carved wooden cabinet behind him. "We've got it all, sister. Bourbon, Scotch, Irish whiskey, gin, brandy, cognac, light and dark rum and ten liqueurs. There are red and white wines, champagne, port and beers: pilsner, ale, porter and stout."

The bottles gleamed like jewels: amber, garnet, peridot, emerald, diamond and citrine. There were men I had known who would kill for Al's tiny silver key to the liquor cabinet. The smell of David's whiskey breath still haunted me. Still, not to drink would be an insult to The Starfish and make me look cowardly.

"Watch this," said Al.

He stepped over to the sink, which had three faucets instead of two.

"Here we have state of the art plumbing technology."

He turned the faucets as he spoke, the left, then right, then center.

"Hot water, cold water and Laurel Lager."

The middle faucet ran with a golden stream of beer! Al filled a pint glass with it, not wasting a drop, switched off the faucet and took a sip.

"Where does Laurel Lager come from?" I asked.

"From Laurel, and that's all anyone ever need know. I protect the identities of all my suppliers. I'm the only one who knows where the booze comes from, in case we ever get busted."

"I'd like something that tastes like lime," I said.

At that moment, limes were the most exotic fruit I could think of and the green color had to be lucky. I thought of the limeade and Key lime pie Mother made in the summer, a taste gentler than lemons and full of sunshine.

"Gin and tonic," said Al. "The classic. I'll have one with you."

Al reached under the bar for ice from a small icebox and dropped it into two tall glasses. He poured gin in till they were half-full, then added bubbly tonic water. He cut a lime into thin slices, perfect as playing cards and its fresh scent filled my nostrils. Later I would observe that Al always had a clean smell of bay rum and limes. The lime slice floated on the bubbly drink.

"The British invented gin and tonics, and although I'm Portuguese I have to admire their practicality. Gin and tonic is a remedy first used in India. The tonic water has quinine, which cures malaria. The lime slice has Vitamin C, which cures scurvy. The gin itself cures anything else that ails you."

I giggled and we clinked our glasses.

"To the Starfish," I said.

"To the Starfish," he agreed.

The gin and tonic tasted as bright and sweet as laughter, like evergreen and lime. Its clear bubbles made it look innocent and I tried not to enjoy it too much. I sipped it slowly as the first customers came in, three middle-aged white men and one young black lady.

"We won't need you tonight," said Al. "There's a band coming in. But be here on Monday at ten and I'll introduce you to the bartenders and the other regular musicians. The band has been called The Starfish Six, but now it'll be The Starfish Seven."

CHAPTER TWELVE

When I arrived at The Starfish at 9:51pm, Chauncey scolded me.

"No one shows up here before ten o'clock – ever," he told me witheringly.

"I'm sorry," I said. "I'm used to showing up early before I play. No one saw me; I'm always careful."

Before the other musicians arrived, I had time to practice a bit on the piano and try another cocktail, an old-fashioned. The sugar cloaked the whiskey deliciously and I savored the maraschino cherry. Only one cocktail a night, I told myself, but try as many different kinds as possible.

Al introduced me to the other musicians one by one. Although we were called The Starfish Seven, we would not all perform together every night. Most of the others had day jobs and only came in three or four nights a week. There were other occasional performers from Laurel and sometimes visiting bands, but the Seven were the inner circle, relied on by Al and the customers

The first two were the saxophone player, Howard Davis and his sister, Iris, who played the drums.

"Howard and Iris are my sister Shirley's kids," said Emmett.

Both Howard and Iris were well into their twenties and neither looked much like Emmett. Howard was tall and lean and silent, usually dressed in black. Iris was plump and pretty with bright eyes and pin curls. She favored frilly dresses, cloche hats with cloth flowers and round hats with demi veils. Her lipstick and fingernails were royal purple, but she pounded the drums and cymbals with more vigor than any man.

"It's so nice to have another girl in the band," said Iris. "The other five are all boys."

"I'm very pleased to meet you," I said.

Iris showed me the doors of the two washrooms (ladies' and gents') and three dressing rooms, one for the men in the band, one for her and me and a third for visiting performers. Each room had closets of hats and clothes as well as sheet music, reeds, mutes and spare strings.

The bass player was tall shy fellow with raven hair and large graceful hands. He wore a loose green sweater and round black glasses that made his eyes look dark and severe. I thought I recognized him from somewhere but could not think of his name until Al said it.

"This is Aaron Bauer, our bass player," said Al. "Aaron, this is Marlene Piper, our new pianist."

"You're Dr. Bauer's son," I said. "It's nice to meet you."

I held out my hand but Aaron looked at it like an unwanted present and complained to Al.

"I can't believe you hired a white woman to play jazz piano. Every week you bring in another stupid skirt who thinks she can sing. I'm sick of it!"

"If you're sick of it you can scram," Al snapped back. "I hire performers because they can play and I don't give a damn what color they are."

"Stop your belly achin', Bauer," said Howard. "I wasn't keen on having a Jew bass player, but I got over it."

Aaron muttered "Al always favors the broads," and slunk off to tune his fat bass fiddle.

I sat down at the keyboard, played a few scales and chords and pounded out a jelly roll on the high and low keys. The loud notes bothered Aaron, but he didn't ask me to stop, just went to the bar for a pint of Laurel lager. Iris came up behind me and patted me on the shoulder.

"Don't let him rile you," she said. "Aaron's a great musician. His family gives him grief, though. They wanted him to be a great Jewish doctor like his old man and he ended up a payroll clerk at Stolzfus Silk Mill."

"I never liked Stolzfus much either," I said, hoping that Aaron and I might have some things in common.

The trombone player was an even more familiar face, Frank Caprello, the third of the eleven children. He had the black curls and fine olive complexion of all the Caprellos and wore a full mustache over his constant smile.

"Frank!" I gasped. "Does your father know you work here?"

"Oh yes," said Frank. "The whole family knows, but they keep it quiet of course. Papa and Mama were mad about me having a night job, and not coming into the deli until after two, but they don't complain about the wine I bring home. The Caprellos have never been temperance people."

"My family is," I said. "I haven't said anything about working here and I know Mother won't take it well."

"I'll blackmail you as necessary," Frank teased.

The guitarist was Oliver Untermeyer, Joseph's friend and sometime plumbing partner. He was tall and lanky with thinning maple-colored hair and long dextrous hands. Oliver was a joker, like most of Joseph's friends, and it didn't surprise me to see him playing at a speakeasy.

"I've been trying to get your brother in here for ages," said Oliver. "But he won't dance and he won't leave Katrina and Harry alone for even one night."

"He's a great dad," I said.

I wondered if Joseph had ever told Oliver the real reason he didn't dance. After the war my brother hid his prosthetic leg, fearing that he would be considered an invalid and unable to work. He kept the leg concealed and never danced or swam or risked revealing it, even after securing a good reputation as a plumber. Perhaps the loss reminded Joseph of the war and he could not bear to let others see that it had changed him.

Jeremy came in with his clarinet and I shook his hand gratefully.

"I told them you sent me, Jeremy," I said. "Thank you so much for helping me find this job."

"It's no cake walk," he said. "Some days I steal a nap on one of the hotel beds. The money is good, though, and Peggy doesn't mind. She tells Fred and Nathan that I work nights at the hotel. One day they'll ask where their college fund came from and by then they'll be old enough to understand."

"I understand," I said. "I know that Peggy has a good life with you."

"She spoke highly of you too, Miss Marlene."

Iris introduced me to the crowd "Tonight the Starfish Six become the Starfish Seven again, with a new piano player – Marlene Piper."

"I can't believe they got a white girl playin' piano," an old black lady complained.

"What's she gonna play? Mozart?" said a white college boy.

The first song we played together was *When the Saints Go Marching In*. Iris sang and Howard played a dazzling saxophone solo. Jeremy followed him with a clarinet solo and then nodded his head at me. I played the melody and added a few high chords, playing high Cs when Iris sang "Oh when the bells begin to chime."

The crowd danced and cheered. Men and women, black and white, stood up and applauded us. I felt happier then than I had in years. The music had been inside me like an underground spring and now it was a release for all my feelings and a pleasure for the audience. No one heckled me onstage after that; I had earned a place in the Starfish Seven. We played for hours and took many requests.

I liked everyone in the band, even sulky Aaron, whose respect I wanted to win. His pessimism disappeared when he played the bass and he plucked the strings with perfect rhythm. Jeremy, Howard, Frank and Oliver joked and chatted and never tired of playing. Iris was sweet to me and flirtatious with the crowd of black men who came to adore her, much to her brother's dismay.

Jeremy and Howard usually played leads, and sometimes I did. All of us had frequent solos and could play songs of our choice alone while the other players took breaks. Oliver could play solo or rhythm guitar and sing. Iris sang too sometimes, which looked odd while she drummed, but sounded beautiful. She had a soprano voice and could sing old-fashioned ballads or improvise whole jazz songs by herself. Jeremy had a fine bass voice, but preferred clarinet to vocals.

We took breaks and I met the Starfish's two bartenders: Dennis Arinopolous and Zach Bloomquist, both of whom worked at Vintner's Hardware during the day. Dennis was old and bald with a gray beard and glasses. Zach was young and blond with a cute boyish face. They served drinks tirelessly and usually only worked one at a time, but that night they had both come to meet the new pianist. Al and Emmett would tend bar too when the place got busy. I met the other bouncer too, Pete Romanovich, a big silent Russian with a black beard, who guarded the entrance with Chauncey.

At five o' clock that morning Chauncey and Pete helped the last customers up the ladder. Dennis and Zach washed the last glasses. After Al left, Oliver asked me if I wanted to know a secret.

"The pianist before you was a great singer named Shane Marshall," Oliver said. "Al quarreled with him and threw him out of The Starfish."

"What did they fight about?" I asked.

"What do you think, sister? It was about a woman of course – Blue Maria. Lots of men fall in love with her and Al ignores it, but he couldn't ignore Shane. Maria adored him and Al walked in on them right there in the dressing room. He fired Shane and told him to get out of town. Shane threatened to go to the cops and rat us all out.

"He fell down four flights of stairs in an apartment building in Pittsburgh. His neck was broken when he hit the bottom. They say Shane owed people money there, but...

"Hey, Marlene, you look white as a ghost. What's wrong?"

"Joseph must have told you how my husband died."

"Oh, I'm sorry, Marlene," Oliver said. "I didn't even think...I shouldn't be telling you any of this gossip. It wouldn't interest you and I hate to remind you of your loss."

"You didn't mean any harm," I said. "And I must confess that all gossip interests me."

"It's a shame about your husband," said Jeremy. "But I'm sure he'd be proud of the way you're supporting yourself."

"David might be proud that I work in a speakeasy, but he never liked my piano much," I said.

"What was your husband's last name?" asked Emmett.

"Dunn," I said. "David Dunn."

"Why do you go by Piper, then?" asked Chauncey. "No point in using the maiden name if you ain't a maiden."

"Piper means musician and that's what I am," I said. "I belong to myself and not my dead husband. Are you married, Chauncey?"

"Humph! Ain't no woman in Laurel fine enough for me."

He stalked off to mop the floor behind the bar.

Emmett chuckled and whispered "No woman would have him, the bitter ol' pill. I lost my Bethany three years ago and not a day goes by that I don't miss her."

Emmett stood by the piano as Jeremy got up to pack his clarinet. He leaned over to confide in me.

"Miss Marlene, David Dunn used to come in here sometimes."

"Did he come in with Jim Dougherty and Sean Peterson?"

Emmett nodded. "At first he came with them, but after a while he kept borrowing money from them and stopped paying it back. Dunn couldn't pay his bar tab and Al told him to get lost until he had the money. One night he showed up here with a fistful of dollars and bought beer for everyone in the bar."

I remembered the night David had come home drunk and broken my fingers. It enraged me to know that he bought beer for strangers who probably laughed behind his swaying drunken back while his wife sat home cold and hungry.

"I guess he thought he was being generous," Emmett went on. "But he got ornery and knocked over a chair. He tried to pull Blue Maria out on the dance floor and when she wouldn't go with him, he threw a beer in her face. She kicked him so hard he fell over and Chauncey and Pete jumped on him to drag him upstairs. Al banned him from The Starfish for life."

"He never told me he went to a speakeasy," I said. "But he drank and fought too much."

"Shameful thing, picking fights with women," Emmett said. "We don't allow that kind of thing at The Starfish. No ma'am."

I felt comfortable at The Starfish, even though some of the patrons were foolish, no one was permitted to be loud or aggressive. Chauncey disliked me but would stay out of my way and The Starfish Seven, Al and Emmett were wonderful. Some of the men and women recognized me from school and church and waved or winked, but never asked for details of how I came to work here. Iris gave me a cobalt glass bowl to leave on the piano for tips and those who requested songs always put in a few coins. I hoped that no one in my family would hear about what I was doing, but Laurel was a small town and gossip moved through it like bubbles through beer.

On Sunday, I scraped myself out of bed after four hours' sleep to go to mass and then to Mother's house for Sunday dinner. I had been paid, enough to cover all my bills and give my mother twenty dollars. With tips, the money was much more than I anticipated. Mother counted out the bills in the thick envelope and stared up at me with suspicion. She pushed some of the bills back toward me.

"Marlene, I can't take all this. You need to save some."

"All my bills are paid, Mother, and I put some in savings. Don't worry."

"You didn't mention your new occupation," she said.

"I've been playing some private parties," I said, keeping the lie as parallel to the truth as possible.

"You've been up too late," said Mother. "You have circles around your eyes like a raccoon."

"I work late, but that's why I'm paid extra," I said. "And I sleep in the day."

"You seemed to be nodding off at mass," said Mother. "Are these drinking parties that you go to?"

She smelled the truth like a dog smells pheasants in tall grass.

"Some people drink there," I said. "But I don't."

Mother put her hand on mine and pressed it against the table.

"Obey your conscience, Marlene, no matter how much money anyone offers you. Don't dance with men who drink and don't take a ride in an automobile with anyone who's been drinking. Alcohol destroyed my father and could destroy anyone in my family, especially the women."

"I won't get drunk," I said. "You know I won't do anything dangerous."

"I couldn't bear another disappointment," she said.

"Be proud that I found a place to play. I can work and be independent and help to support you. Thank God for that; I do."

She regarded me gravely. We both knew that I was a criminal, and that I could get hauled off to jail anytime for playing in a place that broke Prohibition. But where else could I make a living as a musician and keep a roof over my head and hers? Mother held my hand but couldn't quite smile.

"I love you, Marlene," she said. "But don't ask me not to worry. I wish life could have turned out differently for you."

"Mother, my life ain't over yet."

CHAPTER THIRTEEN

I recognized Blue Maria the first time I saw her, perched on a bar stool at the Starfish. First I noticed her hat, a circle of royal blue felt with one peacock feather. Her pin-curled auburn hair made me wonder why no one called her "Red Maria" until I saw her heaven-blue eyes. She wore a sleeveless scoop-necked flapper dress with beaded fringe whispering above her slender calves and bare arms. Blue Maria had a large white bosom like a swan; she was not one of those flappers who bound their breasts in a corset to look boyish. She wore silver sandals and red polish on her fingernails and toenails. Her earrings, bracelets and necklace were silver. A large round sapphire in a braided silver ring glittered on her left hand. Later I would learn that Al had given her this ring, but though she always wore it, it was not an engagement ring. Blue Maria smiled knowingly, prepared to seduce the whole world.

As I played, I glanced up at her again and again as she sipped a mimosa and smoked a cigarette in a gold holder. She tapped her feet to the music and smiled up at me.

The song I played was *Don't Bring Lulu.* The whole band was there and Oliver sang:

We all went to a party, a real high-toned affair
And then along came Lulu, as wild as any Zulu.
She started in to "Charleston,"
And how the boys did stare...

When I took a break to get a glass of water, Al introduced us.

"Maria, darling, this is our piano prodigy, Marlene Piper. Marlene, this divine chanteuse is Blue Maria."

I took her hand and said "I'm very pleased to meet you."

"I love your music," said Blue Maria. "Would you accompany me?"

"I'd love to."

I had feared that Blue Maria might be vain or competitive with other women. Growing up, I had often been snubbed and insulted by pretty girls. Although Blue Maria knew her own beauty, she was not soured by vanity. She loved to talk to everyone, from other musicians, like Iris and me, to Chauncey and Emmett, to old widows who called her "Honey" and weathered railroad men who told her their whole life stories. I could have envied Blue Maria, but I liked her too much from the very beginning.

"I have to ask," I said "Why are you called 'Blue Maria'?"

"Blue is my favorite color," she said. "It's always been lucky for me and I always wear something blue, at least a ribbon or a blue stone."

"I love blue too," I said. "I used to hate wearing pink dresses when I was little."

"I have something for you," she said, reaching into a handbag decorated with beaded bluebells.

She pulled out a white silk scarf printed with blue butterflies and gently tied it around my neck. It stood out against my plain navy dress.

"Thank you. It's so beautiful."

"Keep it," she said. "It looks better on you."

The first song we performed together was *My Blue Heaven*. Blue Maria told me that her mother was an unwed vaudeville singer and she herself had been on the stage since she began singing and tap-dancing at four. She never knew her father; her mother either would not tell or honestly did not know who he was. Blue Maria and her mother had traveled all over the country, from Atlanta to Los Angeles to Seattle to Boston. Now Blue Maria sung with Helen Morgan and at Texas Guinan's club in New York City. As she described her life on trains and stages, I pictured myself at her side.

Like so many others, I went to the bar to lose myself. Music was my real life, the thing I loved best, but it felt good to crawl down into darkness and shut out the ordinary daily life of Laurel. The Starfish was its own world, with its own rules and its own time. The nights I spent there melted into each other. Sometimes it all felt new, even after years of work there and sometimes the dark hours seemed so long, as if I had always played the piano at The Starfish and my former life had only been a dress rehearsal.

The Starfish was smoky. Thick clouds of smoke hung in the air around the piano as I played. Young ladies held gold cigarette holders in satin-gloved hands. Businessmen smoked cigars. Farmers smoked corncob pipes and college professors smoked clay ones. Black and white men and women shared matches and Lucky Strikes, the small courtesies that all smokers in the world show one another. I never had any desire to smoke, but ignored the smell until I went home to wash my hair and collapse into bed. Smoke was part of The Starfish, almost as much as the drinks.

Everyone talked while I played, sometimes so much that the music was hardly audible. There were always a few happy couples dancing and I told myself that they needed me for this. I played with all or any of The Starfish Seven and dozens of guest performers.

I bought new music every week at Zimmerman's Music Store and could also play new pieces that other performers brought in. I wished I could tell Mr. Zimmerman that I now made more money than any of his stuffy clerks, but instead I just smiled smugly. All I needed was sheet music, or to hear a song played once and it was mine, filed away like a card in a card catalog. Sometimes I made mistakes but if the songs were jazz, no one minded or really noticed. A flat or sharp would weave its way into the clinking of glasses and tapping of dancers' feet, the occasional crash when a drunk fell to the floor.

When Chauncey had to remove a drunk from The Starfish, he would spin him (it was almost always a him) around until he was confused, then sling him over his shoulder and drag him up the ladder to throw him out in the street. Pete Romanovich would fill in for Chauncey and sometimes both of them had to break up fights. As drunks were carried up the ladder, squirming like angry babies, Emmett would call up after them:

"Don't come back till you can hold your liquor!"

Occasionally I would get to dance, when someone else took my place at the piano. I liked the Charleston and the black bottom, much better than waltzes where I could smell the noxious fumes of my partners' breath. No one should really dance the black bottom unless they are drunk; slapping your own backside is too ridiculous and painful for a sober person. The Charleston is much more graceful, but I liked to see drunks reach for their knees and grab someone else's or trip over each other's feet. I admit I slipped once or twice when I'd had too many gin and tonics, but I jumped right back up and kept on dancing. The only thing I hated was when old drunk men tried to grab me. I'd slap their hands and shove them away, but they'd just laugh. Chauncey would shake his fists at a man who was too persistent with me; he protected every woman in The Starfish, even those he disliked.

Sometimes when I played, other people would sit beside me or ask me to give them a turn, but I never did unless Mr. Vintner had hired them. I loved The Starfish's piano so much that my piano at home probably got jealous. Maybe I was rude, but I hated to let some boozer pound on the keys. Sometimes Al would push people away from me and say:

"Stop that, now. Let Marlene play."

If they persisted, he would shout "Sir, take your hands off my pianist!"

The bar would then erupt in laughter.

If Al saw a few great dancers, he would call them into the center of the floor to compete individually. The crowd would scream "Get hot! Get hot!" Whoever got the most applause won a free drink.

At the end of the night I would help the bartenders clear away the glasses and wipe down the tables. Iris and I might wash and dry the dishes. Al would massage my tired shoulders and tell me not to wear myself out. Chauncey would glare at us with disgust and Emmett would just whistle as he swept the floor. Al would kiss my hand and bid me goodnight.

I told myself that he was just being friendly because Al flirted with all ladies, young and old, black and white. Al was too polite to make eyes at someone else's wife or girlfriend, but he would compliment women in a way that flattered them and their men. He'd always smile and his black eyes would flash.

"There are so many pretty girls in here tonight. Who wants to dance?"

He'd find some young shy wallflower or an old lady who hadn't danced in years and spin her around the floor. Some men envied him but no one ever insulted him to his face because he owned the only speakeasy in Laurel. Many women fell in love with his Latin good looks? but the only one he fell for was Blue Maria. From the rumors I heard, she had other men in New York City and Philadelphia and he had other women in Laurel, but whenever Blue Maria was in town, they were inseparable.

One time I went backstage to get my coat and hat and found the two of them entangled. She sat on a table with her arms around him and her knees under his elbows. Blue Maria had nothing blue on except her sapphire ring and earrings and Al only wore an unbuttoned white shirt. They both stared at me, but I said "Don't mind me, I'm just passing through."

I was drunk that night and very lonesome. The sight of Al's legs like marble columns in the half light did nothing to console me. Al Vintner was a beautiful man. I would never have anyone that beautiful

– I knew – just as surely as I would never be able to afford diamonds. He was not a rich man, just another immigrant's son, a Portuguese Catholic with a tool shop and a plain-looking two story house. The Starfish was like Aladdin's lamp to Al Vintner, granting him wishes and greatness. Playing there almost every night, I sometimes forgot that it was illegal and, like Aladdin's lamp, it could be stolen from Al, me and all of us at any moment.

CHAPTER FOURTEEN

I tried to leave all the intrigues behind at The Starfish but one of them, too large to conceal, overflowed into my daytime life. The secret concerned two people I loved and envied: Al Vintner and Blue Maria. Though I wanted to support them, their excesses weighed me down, like morning glory and clematis climbing up a trellis, intertwining with each other and spreading their wild blooms over everything in their path.

Al approached me at the bar and asked me for a favor. Before I saw him, he laid his hand on my shoulder and my heart hit a sharp note. He must have felt my pulse quicken, though I tried to look calmly into his black eyes.

"Marlene, I wouldn't normally impose upon you, but I need to ask your help with something."

"Yes, Al?"

"Blue Maria was staying at the Ottoman, but they need her room for a visiting congressman. I have a deal with one of the managers there, but all the rooms other happen to be full. I'd take her to my house, but I'm going out of town on business for the next three days. She needs a place to stay, just for the weekend, until she can get her room back. If you could put her up, I'd give you twenty dollars for your trouble."

The offer of money made me suspicious. Blue Maria was an independent woman and, despite her total lack of interest in cooking and cleaning, she could easily secure room and board somewhere in Laurel for a few days.

"Twenty simoleons is too much," I said.

Al chuckled and pulled out a bar stool for me. We sat side by side and he motioned to Zach to give me a second complimentary gin and tonic.

"You never know with Blue Maria. She likes to dine out on the strangest dishes at the strangest hours and go to the pictures and shopping. I wouldn't ask you to pay for any of that and I'd just as soon give the spending cash to you. She's liable to drop it all on a new blue hat."

"I see. Have you spoken to Blue Maria about this?"

"Yes. She would rather stay at my house, but I insisted that she have a chaperone. She said you're her only female friend."

"That surprises me."

"That she considers you her friend?"

"No, that she doesn't have more women friends. Most of the women in the bar like her just fine."

"Most of their men like her too much, if you know what I mean. That's why I'd rather not leave her alone for a few days."

"Al, Blue Maria loves you. Can't you trust her?"

He looked down and rested his head on one hand.

"We love one another very much," he said. "But, as you know, our lives are complicated. Many men have already proposed marriage - among other things - to Blue Maria. She could live very comfortably on her beauty alone and she knows it."

"That's only half a life," I said.

"There's a man from New York who's been pursuing her, a big butter and egg man named Bertram Chambers."

Al looked around to make sure no one overheard us and drew a newspaper clipping out of his pocket. It showed Mr. Chambers, a short stout man in a three-piece suit and top hat, cutting the ribbon on a new cannery. He had white hair and sideburns and was at least sixty, affable but self-satisfied. Blue Maria stood to his left, clapping her silk-gloved hands as the rest of the audience applauded the ribbon cutting.

"I've heard of him," I said. "He owns Chambers Canned Goods."

"He bought her a diamond ring," said Al. "I found out that she hocked it, but she went up to New York last week to see him. If you see him anywhere near her, tell him to get lost. Don't let Blue Maria know that you know any of this."

"Al, Blue Maria is my friend and I can't spy on her or tell her what to do. No one can control her."

He clasped my hand, not to charm me, but because he really felt afraid.

"Marlene, if Blue Maria takes up with that man she will leave Laurel and never look back. Do you want that to happen?"

"No, of course not."

"Then promise to help me, just for these two days."

"I promise."

I looked forward to Blue Maria's company. When Zach drove me home that morning, I told him what Al had told me and swore him to secrecy.

"It'll backfire, Marlene," he said. "I bet you it'll cost you more than fifty dollars too."

"I thought you liked Blue Maria."

"Everyone likes her, that's why she attracts trouble like a light bulb attracts moths."

The next day I picked up Blue Maria at the Ottoman. She packed up most of her things and stored them in a basement room there; I helped her carry the boxes down. A long black Ottoman Hotel cab waited to take us back to my house on West Lemon Street. I saw Peggy and we waved to each other, but she was too busy to say much to me.

"Blue Maria will be staying with me for the weekend," I said.

"Good luck," said Peggy. "She's a sweet girl, but she's up all night and has the strangest callers."

"Does she have a caller named Bertram Chambers?" I asked.

"I don't ask the gents their names, Marlene."

"I want to thank you and Jeremy again for recommending me for my piano job. It means the world to me."

"You always had the talent," she said with a smile. "Jeremy says you're the best pianist he's ever seen there."

"You should come down some night, Peggy."

"No. I don't approve of alcohol. I don't judge you at all, but I know I wouldn't be happy there."

The cab driver honked his horn impatiently. I said goodbye to Peggy and rushed downstairs. The back of the Ottoman Hotel cab held Blue Maria's trunk and two suitcases and her hatbox rested in her lap.

"It's sweet of you to spend the weekend with me," she said. "Not that I need a babysitter, as Al seems to think."

"I'm glad to have you," I said. "My house is no Ottoman Hotel, but I think you'll like it."

Blue Maria had never visited my house. I had prepared the back bedroom for her, with a new blue chenille spread on the bed, clean blue and white towels, a china bowl and pitcher and vases of blue hydrangeas. That was the room I had shared with David, now renamed the guest room, but never used since all my visitors lived in Laurel and had no occasion to sleep over. Blue Maria admired the house, the bluebells and scarlet runner beans in the backyard and my old upright piano.

She happily ate sugar snap peas and corn on the cob and helped me make sun tea. While I played the piano, Blue Maria sang every silly song she knew from *Yes, We Have No Bananas* to *Makin' Whoopee*. She insisted that I sing along in my mediocre alto:

But don't forget folks, that's what you get folks, for makin' whoopee.

Her voice sounded clear and bright, without the haze of cigarettes and liquor and other people's conversations. I loved to hear her sing in the shower and watch her drift down the hall in a negligee as light as blue smoke.

She had her bad habits, of course. Blue Maria mixed whiskey with her coffee and gin with her lemonade. One of her suitcases was full of bottles and she wore a hip flask in her garter, having no qualms about reaching up into her skirt for the comforts of liquor.

"I need some hooch," she said, offering me a helping.

I gently declined. Drinking outside of The Starfish seemed dull and drinking out of Blue Maria's hip flask seemed dirty.

Blue Maria also smoked, even though I begged her not to light cigarettes in the house. On Friday night, I smelled smoke coming from her room. She was leaning out the window and smoking, even though I had insisted that she only smoke on the porch. If I knocked on her door, she would throw the cigarette away and deny everything. Like a child, she had to be caught in the act of mischief. Stealthy as a cat, I climbed out my bedroom window and crawled over the sloping roof to the open window where Blue Maria sat. She wore an almost transparent negligee over her long pale limbs and hourglass chassis, looking like a beautiful moth in the twilight. I was barefoot, wearing my white nightgown. She looked surprised to see me, but she kept on smoking.

"I was just keeping the mosquitoes away," she said, daring me to stop her.

"Please don't smoke, Blue Maria. I can't bear the smell of it in my house and I smell it all night at The Starfish."

"It's going out the window, don't worry. Stay there, I'll come out."

She emerged from the window with a large jar of orange juice.

"Where did you get that?"

"I brought my own oranges and a juicer. I squeeze my own juice every morning. The Ottoman has oranges year round, not just for Christmas. Here, it has gin, your favorite."

"To you and Al," I said, before lifting the jar to my lips.

Blue Maria averted her eyes.

"What's wrong?" I asked.

"Al doesn't want to get married," she said. "He loves me, but he says he won't ever settle down with any woman."

"Do you want to settle down?" I asked.

"Yes. I love my music and I love traveling, but I want to have children too. I'm thirty-two, Marlene. I'm not a young flapper anymore."

It surprised me to hear Blue Maria say that she wanted children. I couldn't imagine her changing a diaper or wiping up spilled milk. I thought that she was like Al, content to flit from one place to another, from one lover to another, like a butterfly. It hurt me to see that she was an ordinary unsatisfied woman, not a goddess smiling down from the stage.

"Al could be a good father if he wanted to," I said. "He takes care of so many people and he's smart and patient."

"He would love his children," she said. "But he'd still be going to Canada to buy whiskey and having flings with flappers. He wouldn't be there when I needed him to be. He's thirty-seven. If he was going to settle down, he would have done it by now."

"I always thought he wanted to marry you," I said.

"No. He can't be faithful to me and I won't accept anything less."

She took a long drink from the jar.

"Are you faithful to him?" I asked.

"Did your husband really fall off that ladder?" she asked, narrowing her eyes like a snake.

"Yes!"

Neither of us spoke for a long moment. I knew that there had been gossip about me. No one would ever openly accuse me, but there would always be suspicion about David's fall, even among people who had never met him.

"I'm sorry, Marlene," said Blue Maria. She put her arm around my shoulder, tipsy and affectionate, and kissed my cheek.

"You're a sweet girl," she said. "I wish you nothing but the best, but you know that everyone has their secrets and their sins. We all do what we have to do to get by, and women are encouraged, if not compelled, to deceive in order to survive."

"Do you deceive me?" I asked.

"Rarely," she said. "I trust you. I trust very few women and no men."

I hugged her and kissed her cheek.

"Please don't leave The Starfish," I said. "You're the biggest star in Laurel. You know that, don't you?"

She snickered.

"That's like being the biggest parrot in a cage. You know I'm going to leave Laurel, Marlene. I've been here on and off for two years and that's a record for me. Mama raised me like a gypsy. If I do settle, it can't be in a little backwater town. It will have to be in New York City."

I hugged my knees to my chest. There was nothing I could offer her, no jewels, no fame, no true love, no family. The stars began to come out above the rooftops and the crickets chirped like little beggars. I remembered the sorrow in Al's dark eyes and felt it in my heart like an open wound, an empty space. Blue Maria would leave me.

"Don't look so sad," she said. "I want to take you with me."

"What? But I live here. I just got a mortgage."

"I don't mean that you should move, silly. But I'm going up in two weeks to record an album and I get to bring an accompanist. You could take the train up there with me. Al would give you the days off; I already asked him. Once you're recorded, thousands of people will hear our songs and you'll have many more chances to play on your own. I'll take you to Texas Guinan's club; she's a friend of mine. We can go to Daly's Theater and see Mae West. You can play in Greenwich Village and maybe even on Broadway one day."

I had never been to New York City and I longed for it now as much as any immigrant ever wanted to read those words at the base of the Statue of Liberty: "I lift my lamp beside the golden door." Every great musician went to New York, from torch singers to jazz men to concert pianists. Blue Maria offered me my sweetest dream.

"I'd love to go with you," I said.

"Then it's all settled."

We shook hands, businesslike and she offered me the last of the gin and juice. I accepted and drank. Then we hugged each other goodnight and crawled back inside, replacing the screens on the windows to keep out the mosquitoes.

The next morning at breakfast, Maria told me all about the things we could see in New York: the subway, Central Park, Broadway, the Metropolitan Museum of Art, Carnegie Hall, and the ballrooms and nightclubs where we could play. It was a siren's song and I did not resist.

I had told Blue Maria how Brendan and Isaac took off to New York and never let us know where they went. We picked through Brendan's postcards and noted all the places he mentioned, especially theaters and restaurants.

"There are a couple night spots where we might find Brendan, if he wants to be found," said Blue Maria. "Don't get your hopes up too much, but we'll try."

That afternoon, I took Maria downtown. She wore a ruffled green dress and a sun hat and I wore a blue polka dot dress that she said she liked. I bought her a Chinese fan with peacocks on it and she insisted that I buy myself one with a picture of a nightingale. We ate dinner at the Black Orchid Café; I had Crab Louis and she had Chicken Veronique. I even took her to the Varsity to see John Barrymore as *Don Juan*; it felt like a date. We walked arm in arm, despite the summer heat. Every time a man whistled at her, I scowled at him until he looked away, ashamed.

On Saturday night, Blue Maria went to bed early. I felt restless and lay awake in bed for a long time. When I heard her quick light footsteps descending the stairs, a feeling of dread swept over me. I tiptoed after her and listened from the hall as she opened the front door.

"You shouldn't have come here," she whispered.

"I had to see you, Maria."

I peeked at him, a snowy-haired man dressed all in white, a Panama hat on his head and a black tie around his thick neck. He was shorter than Blue Maria; he might have been her father or even her grandfather. How dare he come to Laurel to steal her away from Al!

"I'll be up there in two weeks," she whispered. "You have no reason to worry about me."

"I love you, Maria. I think of you every day. I know that Al Vintner is out of town, so I thought I'd drop by. Peggy at the Ottoman told me where you were."

"This is Marlene's house and she works for Al. You shouldn't be here."

"Can't we go for a drive somewhere?"

I crept up the steps and called to her from upstairs, trying to sound as if I'd just woken up.

"Maria? Are you all right?"

"I'll be right up," she said.

I heard whispering and kissing, then the door shutting.

Maria ascended the stairs like a guilty teenage girl facing her mother, even though she was eight years older than me. We avoided each other's eyes.

"I suppose you heard Bert and me talking," she said.

"Some of it."

"It's none of Al's business or yours," she said.

"Please don't leave," I said.

She glided past me and shut her door firmly behind her. I went downstairs, but Bertram Chambers was nowhere to be seen.

On Sunday, Blue Maria went to mass with us. As a Protestant, she had to stay in the pew during Communion, but she loved the Latin and the hymns and prayed silently with closed eyes. She wore a modest blue and white striped summer dress and a hat with daisies.

After church, we ate dinner at Mother's house with the Haydens, Madsens and Ritters. My mother was delighted to meet Blue Maria. Amelia, Katrina and Helen asked her all about the places she had traveled in her singing career. She mentioned again that I would be accompanying her to New York.

Maud narrowed her eyes and said "Marlene, can you even afford a trip to New York? Hotels and food are so expensive up there. And how do you know your album will make any money?"

"I have some money saved," I said.

I looked down, annoyed, but not wanting to fight with Maud in front of all my relatives.

"Have you any idea how talented your cousin is?" Blue Maria asked Maud.

"I beg your pardon?" Maud said indignantly.

"No, beg her pardon," said Blue Maria, pointing at me. "She's a piano prodigy, in case you never noticed. Marlene can play jazz by ear and improvise better than any pianist I've met, and I've met hundreds. In less than a month, our album will be on sale from here to California and on the radio. She'll get a hundred dollars to start and ten percent of all our sales."

"We're all very proud of you, Marlene," said Aunt Josie.

Blue Maria winked at me across the table and I winked back. My family always enjoyed my music, but my work at The Starfish was not discussed. I had provided some of our Sunday dinner with my earnings, which commanded as much respect as anything Maud did or refused to do. Now my songs would play in homes across the country and people I would never meet would tap their feet and dance to the notes that sustained me.

CHAPTER FIFTEEN

The day we left for New York City was a hot one. Before we boarded the eight o' clock train that morning, Blue Maria and I were already fanning ourselves and rustling the necklines of our cotton dresses to simulate a cool breeze.

Blue Maria had been to New York many times, as a little girl and as an adult, but I had never been there. She told me all about Coney Island: about riding the ferris wheels and the carousels, watching the monkeys and magicians and swimming in the Atlantic Ocean. I looked forward to going swimming and braving a few roller coasters, but I was more interested in her descriptions of Carnegie Hall and the Metropolitan Museum of Art and Central Park.

"We'll see all the cultural sites tomorrow; don't worry," she told me. "That's why we took two days off."

I had read about New York and seen many pictures of its landmarks, but nothing could have prepared me for the size and activity of the city. It buzzed like a beehive, even on that sweltering day. I was dazzled by the high vaulted ceilings and marble floors of the train station, but Blue Maria took my hand and pulled me through the crowd. In the street, thousands of automobiles honked their horns as drivers and pedestrians cursed each other in a dozen languages. Barefoot children unscrewed a fire hydrant and leaped over and through the pounding stream of water. The height of the buildings made me dizzy; the tallest building in Laurel was Bainworth's Department Store, with only eleven stories.

As soon as we stepped off the train, I began to look for Brendan. My mind knew that New York was too big a city for me to find anyone, especially someone who went there to hide, but my heart kept looking. Every young white man with curly brown hair distracted me for a moment, with the hope that I might see my wayward brother again.

"Stop ogling the men, you fool!" Blue Maria joshed me. "It's supposed to be the other way 'round."

We caught a trolley car to Central Park and walked across the Great Lawn, under the spreading green trees. The shade felt delicious and I longed to kick off my high-heeled shoes and press my toes into the cool grass. Luckily our hotel was near the park, a new brownstone building with Oriental carpets and bouquets of red and yellow daylilies.

Our room was shady and much cooler than outside, with a big white double bed. Blue Maria tossed her clothes on it and I sat down.

I almost wished I could catch the subway to Coney Island that day to eat hot dogs and ice cream on the boardwalk and not have a care in the world. I felt so nervous that I couldn't eat. I hadn't had anything, not even cereal or toast for breakfast, yet I felt full of energy and devoid of hunger.

Blue Maria and I both bathed and powdered ourselves in the little bathroom down the hall, then slipped into our blue and white floral print dresses and straw sun hats. I had wanted to wear suits, but she said that we would be much too hot and would look better if we dressed alike, "like a sister act", she said.

On our way to the recording studio, we passed Carnegie Hall. I stared at it like a pilgrim might stare at Our Lady of Lourdes. The round Roman arches in the red brick seemed eternal and I laid my hand against one of the walls and prayed. If I were a real pianist, I thought, I would belong in here.

"Marlene, come here," Blue Maria said, beckoning me in through a side entrance.

"Have you been here before?" I whispered.

"Bertram took me here for the symphony. Come on."

We slipped through the marble lobby and up into a balcony, to stare down at the orchestra on stage. The woodwinds and violins sang like birds, the drums thumped and the piano pulsed like the heart of the orchestra. The conductor stopped to correct one of the cellists and ask the bassoons to play softer. Only then did I notice that this was only a rehearsal; there were less than a dozen people sitting casually in the audience. The gray-haired man at the piano cracked his knuckles.

"I always wanted to be a real concert pianist," I said.

Blue Maria put her hand on my shoulder.

"You are a real pianist," she said. "You don't need music school to know how to play, Marlene. Your music is in here."

She took my right hand and laid it above my heart. It felt like a sacrament.

"Come on, let's not be late," she said, leading me out of my sanctuary.

The recording studio was on the eighth floor of a white brick building that also housed two radio stations. Our songs would play on both of them. We arrived a half an hour early and sat in the waiting room. I tried to read *The New York Times*, but felt too nervous to focus on anything. Blue Maria talked to Cora and Della Deveraux, two black Creole sisters from New Orleans, who sang jazz.

"New York is a tough town," said Della. "We tried playing on the street for extra money, like we do back home, but people just walk on by."

They recorded before we did. When our names were called, Blue Maria squeezed my hand once and smiled. As soon as I began to play, I calmed down some. My energy flowed through me into the piano and even when we had to do a song over, I didn't get flustered. We recorded ten songs, all of which would be on the record. Only two of them would play on the radio, our rendition of *My Blue Heaven* and an original song that we had written called *Starfish Blues*:

You thought that my life was over
The day you said goodbye
And now you see me wild and free
And dare to ask me why.
You break my heart, I'm torn apart
Yet always I survive.
My heart, she is a starfish
And keeps herself alive.
You lied to me
You cried to me
You tried to keep me bound
My heart, she is a starfish
And you can't hold her down.

Then I had a pounding piano solo with a jelly roll around high C and eight notes played like light raindrops with my left hand. Then we repeated the second verse:

You break my heart, I'm torn apart
Yet always I survive
My heart, she is a starfish
And keeps herself alive.

We had written those words together, late one night at The Starfish. I had scribbled the words and then the notes on a blank Vintner's Hardware invoice that Zach left on the bar. Blue Maria felt so proud of the rough beauty of the notes and the woman's refusal to despair. We had practiced it after the rest of the Starfish Seven left. Howard and Jeremy would have added solos to it and Aaron would have carped about my "side project" and "hogging the spotlight" with Blue Maria.

Chauncey had objected "That noise ain't sad or sweet enough to be a blues song!" but the name stuck and *Starfish Blues* was our baby. The producer agreed with us that our album would be called *Starfish Blues.* Now we signed our names to a contract and received our checks, the largest sum of money I had ever received for my music.

As we strolled out into the sunshine, Blue Maria asked me "How does it feel to record your first album?"

"I feel terrific," I said. "And very hungry!"

We dined on bagels and lox and full-sour pickles in the nearest deli and split an egg cream from the soda fountain. The food was new to me, but I'd always loved fish and pickles and liked the soda as soon as I realized it had a lot of chocolate and no egg. Cold food was all I could stand on that sickeningly hot day.

It was a relief to go underground to the subway. We rode to Coney Island and held hands so as not to lose each other in the crowds. The sound of a John Phillips Sousa march rang out and the hot air smelled of popcorn, hot dogs and ice cream. We made a beeline for the Wonder Wheel, which was two ferris wheels, one inside the other. When we rode on it, our car moved from the inside to the outside track. Blue Maria rocked the car and I laughed, fearless. We rode the Racing Derby Carousel, the Whip, a swing ride and three roller coasters. I screamed and screamed as the cars rattled over the wooden frame of the Mile Sky Chaser in Luna Park, plunging down six huge hills. Blue Maria laughed at me so much that she stopped feeling any fear of her own. Our last ride was a nice slow carousel. I had ridden some carnival rides in Laurel, but nothing like a double ferris wheel or a gigantic roller coaster.

We wanted to go swimming and instinctively avoided the crowded swimming pools and made our way to the beach. It was no less crowded but the saltwater swept over us in cool waves. I wore a black and red striped wool bathing suit and Maria wore a green one with a pale blue flowered swimming cap. After our swim, we walked on the boardwalk and into fun houses and penny arcades.

We hopped back on the subway, which only cost a nickel. Blue Maria and I ate spaghetti and meatballs in a cellar-level Italian restaurant.

"This is delicious. Marco would like this," I said.

"It's great, but it makes me crave red wine so badly," she whispered.

After we finished our spumoni, Blue Maria took me to a club run by Texas Guinan. Texas was not there, but Blue Maria introduced me to everyone from the manager to the chorus, who danced like a flock of golden pheasants in yellow feathered flapper dresses. Blue Maria kissed the bartender hard on the mouth and handed him her hip flask, saying "Rum, please." I told him about our album and he gave us free champagne cocktails, which was lucky because they cost a dollar each. We danced a few dances, but my feet hurt and my partner was a sailor who squeezed me too tight. Before we left, the manager booked us for a show in late August.

Back at the hotel, Blue Maria opened her hip flask and a jar of maraschino cherries and combined them with two cold bottles of cola. She tried in vain to teach me poker, and we played at least ten games before I finally beat her once.

As she slept that night, Blue Maria rolled over and put her arm around me. Deep in sleep, she murmured "I love you, Al."

"I love you too," I said.

She rolled over again, oblivious. Moonlight crept through the blinds. The formerly spotless white room now smelled of rum and sweat. I turned my pillow over, searching for the cool side and finally sinking into sleep.

The next day we felt slightly hung-over and skipped breakfast. We wound our way through Central Park, toward the Metropolitan Museum of Art. Again and again, I searched for Brendan on the street, but he was nowhere, not in a café window sipping coffee, not selling sketches on the sidewalk or peeking out from an office window.

"I keep hoping I'll see Brendan," I finally admitted. "I can understand his wanting to leave Laurel. All day yesterday I kept looking at every house and every apartment and imagining what my life would be like if I lived here and played at a different club every night. No one would know me and I could start my whole life over."

"Brendan had to start his life over," Blue Maria said. "I'm sure he's happy here, Marlene. I've asked all my friends to keep an eye out for a

Brendan Piper or an Isaac Madsen. Texas and Mae West know a lot of theater boys, a lot of Brendan's type."

"Thank you, Blue Maria," I said. "Maybe there is some chance I'll see my brother again. You're lucky to have so many famous friends."

"You're my best friend, Marlene" said Blue Maria. "No matter what happens, I will always think so."

"You're my best friend too," I said.

We spent four hours in the Metropolitan Museum of Art, until Blue Maria got bored and dragged me out. I marveled at the golden jackals of Egypt and marble heads of Greek muses, the Dutch *veritas* paintings of cut flowers and dead fish, Renoir and Matisse's Impressionist paintings. Dad had showed all of his children these paintings and sculptures in his art books, wanting us to love art and the hands that formed it, in other lands and other centuries.

I remembered the discovery of Tutankhamen's tomb in the fall of 1922. Brendan and I had pored over news articles about it when I was home from the Hayden farm, thinking how much Dad would have loved it. Of course, David could not understand all the fuss about a boy king who had been dead for three thousand years.

"Dad went to this museum," I said. "He wanted me to see it sometime. Brendan has been here too; he sent Mother a postcard of a gold sarcophagus. I feel close to Dad here. Even though we never went here together, museums and libraries always make me think of him."

"He'd be proud of *Starfish Blues*," said Blue Maria. "And of Brendan's art."

"Mother doesn't always think so," I said, only half-joking.

"Whatever we've done wrong – and none of us is perfect – we have at least brought some more beauty into the world," Blue Maria said.

Those words would sustain me, even more than the memory and hope of New York City. My piano playing was on records now, in music stores and on the radio. How many people would hear those songs and be touched by them? If I never achieved fame and fortune, which I never honestly expected, at least I would have a few achievements and adventures. At home, I put my photographs and postcards of New York City in a scrapbook, promising myself to return there and travel on to other cities until those beige pages were full.

CHAPTER SIXTEEN

I did return to New York again in August. Blue Maria and I received lots of applause and drank Tom Collinses with Texas Guinan after our show.

"You can go anywhere you want if you just keep playing," Texas told me.

Texas and Blue Maria talked about men, the ones who bankrolled them and the ones they truly enjoyed. Blue Maria compared her sapphire ring from Al to a gaudy spiral of diamonds from Bertram Chambers. I thought of the wedding band I had pawned, but I said nothing.

"Are you married, Marlene?" asked Texas.

"No, ma'am. I'm widowed."

"I'm sorry."

"I'm not."

We laughed and clinked our glasses, downing cheap gin like the waters of Lethe, as if we could leave all our troubles behind.

I found trouble waiting for me when I returned home. Mother was playing her *Starfish Blues* record and ironing when I dropped by her house. The parlor smelled of steam and hot metal and I could almost smell trouble. At her home, I still felt like a naughty little girl, as if she were about to lecture me for hitting Helen and hiding up in the maple tree.

"How are you, Mother?" I asked.

"I'm very well, thank you. The baptism was beautiful. You should have been there."

Maud and Sven had baptized their son Eugene Gustaphus Madsen, who had been born on August 9. He was a small, crimson and angry, like a red ant, with fuzzy blond hair and an unbelievably loud cry. Maud told everyone that Gene had colic and sensitive skin and rarely let anyone else pick him up, even his doting father. Helen later told me that when Father Hulings baptized Eugene, his cry could be heard across the street.

"Mother, I'm sorry. I just forgot. I bought a wooden boat for him, from Coney Island."

I reached into my bag and showed her the carved wooden tugboat. Mother sighed and set the iron upright. She didn't meet my eyes or examine the toy, and she always liked to pick out children's toys.

"I don't believe you forgot, Marlene, and neither do Maud and Sven. You didn't care enough to be present. If you cared about Gene, you would have remembered."

"Of course I care about Gene! I love Sven and Maud too! But Maud doesn't exactly treasure my company. She only wanted me to be there so she could show off the fact that she has a husband and son and I don't."

"That's ridiculous!"

"That's the truth. She told Harry that 'Aunt Marlene plays music for bad people'. Joseph had to shut her up and tell his son the truth. I didn't pitch a fit when Maud didn't come to my wedding and she has no business pitching a fit now!"

"Stop your yelling!" Mother yelled.

"I'm sorry if I embarrass you, Mother," I said. "But I don't give a damn what Maud thinks of me and I never will."

I still played at The Starfish at least five nights a week, but Blue Maria was absent more and more, often going to New York by herself. Al brought in new bands and singers, but he didn't dance as often. He smiled at everyone and sometimes gave out a round of free drinks on holidays, but when he turned away from the crowd his eyes were sad. All the pretty girls in the world couldn't fill up the empty space Blue Maria left behind.

"You and Blue Maria are getting' too big for your britches," Howard teased.

Aaron carped "Men only come to your shows to stare at your boobs. Nobody cares if a frail can play or not."

"Shut up, Aaron!" said Iris. "You never wanted any gals in this band, but Marlene and I play better than you and you know it. Do you think people go to see Ma Rainey and Bessie Smith and Helen Morgan just to stare down their gowns? In music it's how you sound not how you look!"

Emmett clapped for his niece and Aaron looked down and tuned his bass fiddle. Everyone in The Starfish had congratulated me on my album, but only Iris and Jeremy wanted records for themselves. It hurt to know that our band would never record or tour because we were so mixed: three blacks, two whites, an Italian, and a Jew.

The Starfish Seven attracted all types of folks and the most unexpected customers I ever saw at The Starfish were locals – Amish. One evening I spotted two round black hats and one white bonnet hovering over the bar. If unicorns had pranced in and ordered a pitcher of Laurel Lager it could not have surprised me more.

Many Amish and Mennonites lived around Laurel, growing corn and raising dairy cattle on their verdant green farms. Like other farmers, they came to town on market days to sell produce, meat, butter, milk and cheese, and to buy the tools and dry goods they needed. Since Colonial times, the Amish had kept mostly to themselves, speaking a Low German dialect that sounded like a cocktail of English and German. Mennonites spoke English and mingled more with their less religious neighbors, but were still set apart by their plain clothing and temperance.

I wondered where these four had left their horse and buggy. If their families knew they had been drinking, they would be shunned completely. The plain people had always practiced temperance, long before other denominations dreamed of Prohibition.

I went behind the bar and tugged on Dennis' sleeve. He squinted at me through his glasses; I must have looked as startled and indignant as I felt.

"Marlene, what's the matter?"

"Dennis, what are you doing serving beer to Amish people? Don't you know they'll be shunned for drinking?"

Dennis chortled so hard he almost bent over, pressing a hand on his belly to stifle his laughter.

"Oh Marlene, you're such an innocent girl. Haven't you ever heard of the *Rumspringe*?"

"The what?"

"*Rumspringe.* It means 'running around'. In their teenage years, young Amish people are allowed to try a few worldly things before they decide if they want to be baptized or leave their church."

"Their parents let them drink?"

"And smoke and dance and party all night without chaperones. Yes, their parents did it themselves when they were young. I've yet to see an Amishman who didn't choke on his first drink and run home to his farm."

"I guess they have to know what they're missing or it would be ignorance and not sacrifice."

The concept of parents trusting their children that much made my head swim. Mother and Dad would never have allowed any of their children to try drinking, smoking or wild parties, let alone decide not to be baptized or confirmed. The decision of my baptism had been made when I was a week-old baby, asleep until dipped into the baptismal font.

"Something like that," said Al, who had overhead us talking. "Anyway, make them feel welcome. I want them to know that not all English are wicked."

I looked at the two boys and the girl, all about sixteen with rosy skin and clear eyes like cherubs. The girl's blond hair was twisted so tightly beneath her bonnet that I wondered if it hurt her. One brown-haired boy had his arm around her waist and the other looked enough like her to be her brother or cousin. I smiled at them and they smiled back. They talked and laughed loudly, speaking a few English words to Dennis. The drinks had gone right to their heads.

I wanted them to try dancing and whispered a few words about it to Blue Maria, Iris, Oliver, Aaron, Jeremy and Al. Instead of taking my usual place at the piano, Blue Maria I approached the three Amish kids.

"Come here," I said. "We have a surprise for you."

They looked puzzled; I wondered how many words of English they understood.

Blue Maria said "We have a gift for you. Please come with us."

She pantomimed the act of giving a gift and pointed to where her dressing room was behind the stage's purple curtain. We helped all three of them off their bar stools and took them by the hands. I led the brown-haired boy and the girl.

Under the golden light of Blue Maria's Japanese lanterns, we introduced ourselves, pointing to ourselves and saying our names. The girl was Rebecca and her beau was Daniel. Eli was her *alter bruder,* he proudly explained.

Maria rummaged through her steamer trunks and behind the peony curtain of her closet. She brought out two fedoras, suit jackets and ties. Daniel and Eli took off their black hats and put on the fine clothes, tilting the hat brims at rakish and ridiculous angles, crowding around the full-length mirror while Iris knotted their bright silk ties. Blue Maria dressed Rebecca in her beaded lavender shawl, with a pattern of blue dragonflies, and draped a pearl necklace around her pale throat. Then she offered her a silver comb and hair brush, and a wide silver ribbon to tie back her hair. Rebecca timidly removed her bonnet and sat at the vanity table to brush out her hair. Her hair was soft and yellow as butter, hanging down to her waist. Daniel stared at her hair with wonder. Maria put red lipstick and rouge on Rebecca's face and blue powder on her pale eyelids. She sprayed Rebecca with violet water from one of her many perfume bottles and gave the boys some lime musk cologne that must have belonged to Al. They smelled like delicate plants in a greenhouse.

We led them out onto the dance floor as Jeremy, Oliver and Aaron played *Paper Moon* while Iris sang. I had asked them to do slow songs, no Charleston or foxtrot, nothing with steps that the Amish wouldn't know and couldn't guess. Al saw Rebecca hesitating by the stage, bowed to her and took her hands. They danced gracefully, instinctively gliding across the floor. Blue Maria and I danced with the boys. Eli rested his head on Maria's shoulder, intoxicated by the jasmine scent of her auburn hair. I danced with Daniel, who stared longingly at Rebecca over my shoulder. Rebecca stared at him too, until we took pity on them and gently pushed them together. Daniel stroked Rebecca's beautiful hair and she laid her head on his shoulder and closed her eyes.

Al took me in his arms and we waltzed.

"Have we led them astray?" he asked, smiling wryly.

"No, I think not."

Daniel and Rebecca were kissing. Blue Maria kissed Eli, their lips brushing like feathers, then covering each other. Al kissed me, a soul kiss, and I kissed him back. He breathed into me like God into Adam and I trembled, but no one seemed to notice or care. Al smiled at me, friendly, as if we had just played a good joke together.

"They'll go home," I said. "None of them will take up drinking, but they'll always remember this. When Daniel and Rebecca are an old white-haired couple, they'll laugh together about this night, when he wore your hat and she wore make-up."

I surveyed The Starfish and glanced up at Al with moist eyes.

"That's the real reason I made The Starfish," he said. "To make people happy. It's not for the money, because I could lose all that any day. It's nights like these that I think it's all worth it, that I am a good man, that I've done something worthwhile."

"I'll always remember this night," I said.

Al did not kiss me again and we didn't speak of it afterward. If Blue Maria noticed, she did not care. There were other times when I kissed men on the dance floor, but I never let it lead to anything. The Starfish was a dream world, like living in a motion picture and when I emerged into the cold light of morning, I left the grand illusion safely behind me.

During the twelve days of Christmas, Dennis and Zach served up rum punch and egg nog at The Starfish. We played *Joy to The World* and *O Come All Ye Faithful* and all the drunks sang along. Even Aaron, who complained about the "Christmas madness", cracked a smile listening to a toothless old chicken farmer and his wife warbling the "Glo-o-o-o-o-o-o-o-o-ria" from *Angels We Have Heard On High*.

Mrs. Vintner made a rare visit to The Starfish, bringing sugar cookies and fruitcake. She was a petite and pretty, with a thick Portuguese accent and silver hair under her black lace mantilla. Even the roughest barflies loved her immediately; she reminded us of our own dear mothers and grandmothers.

"Alphonse was such a good boy," Mrs. Vintner said. "He won so many holy cards at school, but at home he would never stay in his room and study. His papa would tell him 'You stay home, read your books' but Alphonse would climb out the window and run down the alley to play with the other boys."

Al looked sheepish, but everyone else laughed, even Blue Maria. Al had obviously inherited his charm from Leonora Vintner. Many of the older drinkers spoke fondly of her late husband – Oscar Vintner – who had started Vintner's Hardware Store.

"Our name was Vindonho," she told her adoring masses. "My Oscar and I – we worked in the vineyards. His family had always picked grapes. I was so angry at Ellis Island when they changed our name, but Oscar said 'Vintner' means the same in English."

She told us about Al's five younger siblings, two brothers and three sisters, all of whom were married and had children. Three of Leonora's children had left Laurel but she lived with the youngest – Bianca – and her husband and son in the old Vintner house.

"It's so good to see Al's other business," she said. "His father would love this place. I think Prohibition is unnatural, so cruel not to be able to drink and be happy. Even Jesus and the Blessed Mother had wine at the wedding at Cana."

Blue Maria seemed slightly shy in the presence of Al's mother, maybe expecting her to act like a short-tempered mother-in-law. Mrs.

Vintner loved Blue Maria's singing though and told her how beautiful and sweet she was. Most likely she harbored some matrimonial hopes for her wayward son, so that he would finally marry and have children as all his siblings had done, but she tactfully refrained from expressing them.

"Al is lucky to meet you," she said, kissing Blue Maria goodbye.

"I'm lucky I met him, and you, Mrs. Vintner," said Blue Maria.

Al escorted his mother and Blue Maria up the ladder at the end of the evening. It would be the last time he escorted Blue Maria anywhere.

Two days before Christmas, The Starfish suffered its first break, but unlike its namesake it could not repair itself. During a break that evening, I helped Blue Maria dress, standing behind her at her dressing table to fasten the buttons on her silver satin gown. I counted thirty of them, tiny and shaped like foreign coins. When I looked down at her hands, I noticed that Blue Maria was not wearing her sapphire ring. I hoped that she had just taken it off because it clashed with her dress. Mr. Chambers' heavy diamond spiral was still on her left ring finger. She fastened a silver and opal necklace around her pale throat.

"Blue Maria, where's your sapphire ring?" I wondered.

"It's in the safe in the storeroom."

"Why did you take it off? Did you and Al have a fight?"

She had tried to return the ring once before when Al was spending too much time with a torch singer named Louise Blake. They fought often, I told myself, but it was always resolved. Blue Maria shook her head, and her diamonds glittered like ice crystals. A foreboding chill crept up my spine.

"I'm going to New York, Marlene," she said.

"Can I come with you?"

"No."

I resented this. "Are you going to see Bertram again? You ought to break it off with him; he's too old for you."

"No. I'm going to New York to stay."

"What? Why?"

"Marlene, I don't have a future in Laurel or with Al. I want a permanent home of my own. I can't live in hotels and have love affairs all my life. Bertram wants to marry me and I said yes."

I dropped to my knees next to her and grabbed her arm. I must have looked hysterical because she looked frightened of me.

"Please don't do this! You'll never be happy with an old man. You need music and drinks and dancing and stages, even small stages like The Starfish. I need you to sing with me."

"I'll still sing with you on the second album. I won't give up performing. Bertram loves my music and takes me out to clubs all the time. It isn't as if I'm going to prison. You can visit me whenever you like."

"What about Al? You've been with him for four years. Are you just going to throw him over for a richer man? Be Blue Maria, not a damn gold digger."

Her eyes burned and she wrenched her arm out of my grasp.

"I thought you were my friend, Marlene. Did Al pay you to be kind to me? Women are never kind to me."

"I love you," I said. "I am your friend and I won't let you throw your life away. You love Al and he loves you. I've seen you together."

She smirked and turned away, saying "You've seen too much, you Peeping Tom. Fifteen minutes of jazzing on a tabletop is not love."

"Al still made you happier than Bertram ever will."

"Hey, Marlene! Maria! Stop flappin' yer gums and get up here on the stage!" called Aaron.

"Can it!" I fired back.

Blue Maria laid her hand on mine.

"Don't say anything," she said. "I don't know what Al would do if he knew I was leaving. You know what happened to Shane, don't you? Al looked the other way when I had flings with strangers, but when I fell in love, he went mad with jealousy."

"Al would never hurt you," I said.

"Marlene, Al has hurt me more than you can possibly imagine."

She rushed out onto the stage and I had no choice but to follow her. I kept my eyes on the keys and the sheet music, trying hard not to cry. An old farmer put a bottle of homemade hard cider in my tip bowl and said "What's the matter, doll face?"

I said, "I lost my best friend."

"He'll be back," the farmer said, patting my shoulder.

I tried to corner Blue Maria, but she avoided me all evening. When I tapped her shoulder, she turned on her heel and stalked off. I felt like I was on a sinking ship and couldn't shake the awful feeling that I would never see her again. We had planned a second album; I had written new songs for it. We had planned a train trip to Chicago in the summer to record the album and play some shows there. Would anyone want to hear me play without my glorious singer?

If only I could say the right thing and talk Blue Maria out of it, say something more intelligent than "I love you" and "Please don't leave me". I couldn't bear to talk to anyone, not Aaron who kept scolding me for my mistakes or even Iris when she asked me what was wrong. Al had gone out of town to buy provisions and wasn't expected back until the next afternoon. By then Blue Maria would be in New York. She had planned her escape, a clean break for herself and a landslide for the rest of us.

At the end of the night, she started toward the ladder, carrying a round blue suitcase. Before she could go up, Al came down the ladder. He was home early! My prayers were answered. I didn't even have to spill her secret because he understood the suitcase at once. Dennis, Iris, Howard, Aaron, Oliver and I all froze and stared at Al and Blue Maria. Chauncey and Emmett followed Al down the ladder and stood by silently.

"Blue Maria, where are you going?"

His eyes looked dark, haunted.

"I'm going to New York, Al."

He walked toward her and I hoped that they might kiss, but he put his hand on the handle of her bag and scowled.

"Leave your clothes here. Don't you trust us?"

"I've never been able to trust you, Al."

He wrapped his arm around her waist, possessively and without tenderness.

"You're impossible. If you go to see Chambers one more time, I'll..."

She laughed bitterly and wormed her way out of his grasp.

"What? You can't get rid of him as easily as you got rid of Shane Marshall."

Al fell silent.

"Marshall tried to get our whole place shut down," Chauncey murmured. "He had it comin'."

She didn't even glance in our direction. Blue Maria and Al glared at each other like deer in a deadlock.

"I love you," said Al.

"Not enough," she replied.

"I'll marry you."

She hesitated and almost dropped the suitcase.

"Blue Maria, listen to the man who loves you," said Iris.

"It's too late. You never gave yourself completely to me, Al. There were always others and I won't share you. I don't want half a man."

"I'm more man than that old bastard. He'll be dead in five years and you'll come crawling back."

"I'll never come back," she said. "I'm having a baby."

"Whose?" Frank blurted out.

"Mine," said Al.

"No. You always took precautions. It's Bertram's. I wanted a child and we agreed on it. I'm four months along already. So you see Al, I can't come back to you."

He looked down, not dejected, but holding in his rage.

"What do you think you're going to do? Become a society matron? Society will never accept you. Your past will be smeared all over the papers and when they catch you with a butler or a gardener the whole damn country will hear about it. You will have no friends, no music, **no life whatsoever with that man**!"

"I already have a life with him! Bert loves me! He loves our baby! I'm the only woman for him! You think I did it for the money? I did it for love! I love Bertram and he loves me. He keeps his promises."

She stepped onto the ladder. Al made no move to stop her.

"You'll regret this!" he shouted.

"Send your thugs after me! I'd rather be shot dead than stay in this hole with you!"

No one spoke. For a minute, no one even moved. Iris began to cry and Aaron handed her a clean handkerchief. Frank whispered to Howard "She can't be serious."

"Go home, all of you," said Al. "Don't come back until after Christmas. Take three days off. I know I will."

"Al, she'll change her mind," I said.

He shook his head.

"Marlene, sweetheart, you don't know her."

His shoulders drooped and he crept away like an old man, slow and lonely.

CHAPTER SEVENTEEN

As I sipped my third glass of champagne, I promised myself that 1927 would be different. This time next year I would have recorded a second album with Blue Maria and I would have someone to kiss at midnight. Joseph and Katrina stood next to me, kissing passionately. He wore his Sunday suit and she wore a red fringed flapper dress I had never seen before. Katrina had sipped Brandy Alexanders and shimmied on the dance floor for hours, so different than the usual clean quiet nurse I saw every Sunday. Joseph had been to The Starfish before with Sven, but this was Katrina's first visit. Harry and her new daughter Clarice kept her busy at home. Over the years the family had quietly accepted my night job, and Joseph and Sven began visiting The Starfish "just to keep Marlene safe, Mother", as Joseph said.

"Your mother was so good to watch Harry and Clarice!" Katrina said. "We haven't been out dancing since before he was born."

"Mom is an angel," Joseph said, savoring his Laurel Lager.

At Mother's house we had woven wreaths of stolen holly and ivy from neighbors' yards and hung popcorn garlands and paper ornaments on a fir tree that Joseph chopped down. Mother still hung stockings for us, filled them with oranges and chocolates, and put our presents under her tall tree with its bright glass ornaments and satin angel. My life had not unraveled when Blue Maria left. We had played together in New York, Philadelphia and Boston but never gone west to Chicago. She hated to leave Bertram and their daughter, Violet, who was four years old now.

"I feel empty," I said to Joseph.

"You're certainly full of champagne," he said. "I see you're anxious. Let's go."

Katrina insisted on one more dance, but then we could leave. Louise Blake was singing and Al had given me the night off. We had to push through the crowd to get to the exit. Chauncey was carrying passed out drunks up the ladder, including many women.

"Won't they get arrested?" Katrina wondered aloud.

"The cold'll sober 'em," said Chauncey. "I'll never leave a soul down here, no matter how drunk they are. If anybody pukes on my floor, I swear I'll rub their nose in it."

He wasn't joking.

Joseph, Katrina and I climbed up into the bracing cold night to find a light snow falling from the purple sky. He had parked the car six blocks away because the crowds for New Year at The Starfish were huge. We each slipped a little on icy patches, holding each other's arms so we wouldn't fall.

"Mother sure loves that radio you got her for Christmas," Joseph said.

"That's so funny," I said. "She called it a new-fangled contraption, but now she has it on whenever she and Helen do the dishes. She'll even sing along with it."

As we crossed the trolley tracks on Liberty Street, we heard the guttural sound of a man vomiting. Joseph pulled his scarf up over his mouth and nose. Katrina took a step forward, ready to offer help and unafraid of the stench.

"Don't look, Marlene," said my brother, assuming that I was more sensitive than he.

I could not help staring at the figure in a black wool coat, crouched on all fours behind a parked trolley car. I was about to pass him by when he lifted his pale face out of the shadows.

"Robert!"

He glanced all around like a frightened mouse, trying to tell where my voice came from.

"Robert Schumann? It's you, isn't it?"

I stepped down onto the trolley tracks. Joseph and Katrina stopped and looked back at me. I kneeled down beside Robert and gently lifted him to his knees, my hands under his arms. He looked red-eyed and smelled like misery. I was overjoyed to see him, even in that putrid state.

I had loved Robert Schumann through all four years of high school. I had heard nothing of him for years, except that he had left Laurel for New York City to pursue the stage. I still kept a photograph of him in a top hat and tuxedo that I had found in the school hall. Sometimes on the Hayden farm or even now, at home alone, I would take it out of my underwear drawer to gaze at Robert's perfect smile and bright brown eyes.

"Do you remember me?" I asked.

"I'm terrible with names. Please excuse me, ma'am. I know your face though, from Laurel Catholic High."

"I'm Marlene Piper. This is my brother, Joseph and his wife, Katrina."

Robert sat back on his knees and waved weakly to them. Katrina also climbed down to help him, but Joseph looked disgusted. We each took one of Robert's hands and helped him to his feet.

"Where do you live, Mr. Schumann?" Katrina asked.

"I was staying at a boardinghouse, but I can't go back. It's past curfew there and...Oh, my head!"

"I'll bet you live at Mrs. Green's," said Joseph.

"That's not much living," I said. "Let's take him home with us until he dries out."

"I don't want puke in my car!"

"I won't do it again," said Robert. "I'll lean my head out the window just in case."

Katrina and I helped him stagger along with his arms over each of our shoulders. I grinned at Joseph and he rolled his eyes. Robert didn't notice as he spent all of his remaining energy putting one wobbly foot in front of the other.

"I have a spare bedroom," I said. "And I can make you some coffee and give you a nice bath."

"A *cold shower*, you mean," Joseph said severely.

"No, I'm freezing. Just somewhere warm..."

"Don't let him pass out," Katrina said. "Lay him on his side in case he vomits again."

His breath reeked and I averted my face, praying that he wouldn't retch again. I had never been drunk enough to vomit and never wanted to be. Even David had held his liquor, in my presence at least. Anyone who upchucked in The Starfish was 86'ed immediately. I'd only heard the heinous splattering on the floor a few times in my four years there.

Katrina and Joseph dropped us off at my house and walked us up to the porch.

"He'll be all right," I said. "Just let me get him inside."

"Marlene, don't make an ass of yourself," said Joseph.

Robert crept upstairs to the bathroom, sank down on the toilet and struggled to undo his belt. I unbuckled it and stepped out of the room until I heard a flush. Robert stood at the sink trying to wash his hands and dropping the soap on the floor.

"Here, let me help you," I said. "I'll give you a bath."

I pulled off his shoes, his stinking holey socks, his sweaty shirt and jacket. I had always imagined undressing Robert Schumann, but never under these god-awful circumstances. His boxer shorts were silk and his sleeveless undershirt was soft and snow-white. He was beautiful, even in this delirious state, his chest smooth, his forearms and legs muscular with fine brown hair.

Once Robert was naked, I pulled him into the bathtub and ran the water in. He wasn't embarrassed, just cold until the warm water covered him up to his neck. I washed him with lavender soap and a washcloth. As I shampooed his hair, he leaned his head back and closed his eyes. He asked for water and I gave him my china mug. I helped Robert dry off and put one of my flannel nightgowns on him.

"I'm sorry I don't have any pajamas for you," I said.

"I don't mind. This is nice and warm," he said.

He brushed his teeth thoroughly and combed and dried his wet hair. Then I led him to the upstairs guest bedroom. Robert crawled under the quilts and held his arms up to me like a child. I bent down and kissed his lips lightly. It thrilled me but maybe it was just a creature comfort to him, something he wouldn't remember in the morning.

In four years at The Starfish, I had kissed many drunks: traveling salesmen, college boys, soldiers and sailors on leave. I had even slipped into the dressing room with a few of them, but I always took precautions not to get into trouble and never brought any man out of the twilight world of the speakeasy and into my house.

I went down to the cellar and washed all of his clothes in the washing machine. I shoveled more coal in the furnace and hung his clothes up next to it. The heat would dry them by morning. The socks were past saving; one of them fell apart in the wringer. I put a pair of my wool socks with his clothes, hoping that they would fit him.

As I went up to bed, I peeked in at Robert. He dozed peacefully without snoring and lay on his side. The rhythm of his breathing soothed me and I wanted to crawl in bed beside him. What if he woke up in the morning and didn't know where he was? What if he felt embarrassed and left before I could wake up? He would probably be very ill in the morning, so I put an old chamber pot on a chair next to his bed. I decided to lie down beside him, between the top sheet and the blanket. Even under two blankets and the quilt that room, the room David and I had shared, still felt cold. Being near Robert made me shiver with excitement and I couldn't wait until morning.

CHAPTER EIGHTEEN

I woke up before Robert did, but I kept my eyes closed for a long time, savoring the warmth of his body under the blankets and the sunlight through the white curtains, unusually bright for a January morning. He breathed steadily and did not throw up again. I tried not to roll over too much to avoid disturbing him. The last man who had shared my bed – David - had yelled at me and kicked when I rolled over and shattered his brittle sleep.

At last, Robert opened his eyes and looked at me. He looked comfortable but confused.

"Marlene…Marlene Piper…where am I?"

"You're at my house. I found you by the trolley tracks downtown." He reached around under the blanket, realizing that was wearing my nightgown.

"Where are my clothes?" he asked.

"I hung them by the coal furnace," I said. "I'll go get them."

"Are you married, Marlene?" he asked.

I almost laughed. No doubt he couldn't remember any of the previous night and wondered how he had gotten into bed with me.

"If I were married, you'd be in heap of trouble. I'm widowed. I live here alone."

I got up to get Robert's clothes.

"I saw you at The Starfish," he said.

I was astonished that he could enter the same room as me without my sensing it immediately. I had watched Robert on stage so many times that it seemed strange to think as one silent face in an audience, but the place must have been crowded and maybe he didn't stay long.

"Were you there on New Year's Eve?"

"Yes. It was my first time. I'd been in New York…"

He hesitated and shivered, so I rushed to get his clothes. I brought him some water too. Katrina had told me that a hangover is dehydration and water - sipped slowly - cures it better than black coffee or an agonizing cold shower. Robert drank thirstily and stood up to dress, turning his back to me but not overly modest.

"Is this a spare room?" he asked.

"Yes. My room is down the hall."

"I thought so. It's so cold and bare in here."

I looked around at the prints of lilies and hyacinths on the wall, the closet, the dresser and the trunk at the foot of the bed. It was hardly an empty room, but he was right about its constant coldness. No guest ever stayed there more than one night, and Robert probably wouldn't linger either, I thought sadly.

"How long have you been back in Laurel?" I asked.

"I came home for Christmas and was here most of December. I didn't know how long I'd be here so I got a room at Mrs. Green's."

"Why didn't you stay with your folks?" I asked.

"I did for the first three weeks, but they got tired of me. My sister Elaine and her two kids live with them, so they couldn't spare the room."

"I see."

Mother had told me that Elaine Schumann left town when she got married, then divorced and returned home last year with her son and daughter.

"Where do you work now?" I asked Robert.

"I'm giving guitar lessons," he said. "Here, see my card."

It was a powder blue card printed with navy curlicues and Victorian script, which read:

Robert J. Schumann
Actor, Singer, Guitarist, Avant Garde Personality

"That's great," I said.

"I have three pupils now and anticipate seven more," he said. "I'm doing all right, but unfortunately I won't get paid until the end of next week. Mrs. Green expects me to pay her by the fifth."

"I could loan you some money," I blurted out without thinking.

"No, I couldn't take your money. That wouldn't be right. It was very kind of you to take me home and look after me, especially after not seeing me since high school."

"I was going to ask you about that," I said, settling on the bed beside him. "I heard that you went to New York City after graduation, but that's all I heard."

I wouldn't tell him that I kept a copy of his portrait tucked between silk slips and stockings in my underwear drawer. The photographer had kept it on his wall as a sample and I had bought a copy. On difficult days I would unfold the black frame and stare at his in his three-piece suit with his cocked hat and pocket watch. I had imagined that he was a successful actor by now and would never return to Laurel. Was it wrong that I was glad to see him back here, even if he was drunk and broke?

Robert looked down, almost dejected, but then gave me a wry smile.

"In the last five years, I've sung with three different bands and acted in a dozen plays."

"Wow!" I said.

He waved his hand dismissively.

"I never made it to Broadway or Carnegie Hall, nothing that big, but I had a wonderful time. I rented a room no bigger than a closet from this sweet old Jewish widow named Ida Leibowitz. I stayed out until well after midnight most nights and slept most of the day. Mrs. Leibowitz would leave a plate of dinner in the icebox for me; she treated all her boarders like her children. When I told her I had to leave, she actually cried."

"I believe it," I said. "I bet it was expensive to live there."

"Yes. I want to go back, but I had hoped to stay here and save my money for a couple months first, just do some lessons and live as cheaply as I can. The thing I really need is a good accompanist."

"Do you now?" I said. "I accompany almost everyone who plays at The Starfish, you know. I'm in the band, The Starfish Seven, but you mustn't tell anyone."

He crossed his heart and pinched his lips shut with one hand.

"Maybe I could get you a show there," I offered. "The Starfish Seven are probably all hung over today and Al told them attendance was optional."

Robert laughed and gulped some more water.

"You just can't top that," he said. "You work at a speakeasy and you get paid holidays. That's better than a union."

"It's a darn sight better than Stolzfus Silk Mill," I said.

My stomach growled audibly.

"You must be hungry," said Robert. "If you're not busy this morning, maybe I could return your kindness and take you out to breakfast?"

"Are you sure you feel like eating?"

"No, but that's no reason you shouldn't. I'm not ill now; I think I could manage a few slices of toast. There's a cook at Neptune's Diner who owes me a meal."

Suddenly I felt embarrassed to be sitting there in my flannel nightgown and slippers with uncombed hair and spotty glasses. I liked being alone here with him and was excited but not nervous to have him in my house. When I thought of going out with Robert in public, though, my heart twitched like a cornered mouse. Someone we knew was bound to see us together and what would they think? I told myself that I didn't care what kind of impression I made on anyone. Even if Robert left for New York next week it would be fun to spend a few hours with him.

"All right," I said. "Just let me get dressed."

I washed up and brushed my hair, putting on some of the jasmine perfume that Al had given me for Christmas and some lipstick. I never wore make-up in the daytime, only in the evenings when I performed and then just some brown eye shadow and red lipstick, no rouge or kohl around my eyes. I wore a wine-colored sweater and a long navy skirt with a deep purple cloche cap and my long black wool coat.

As Robert and I boarded the trolley, he took my hand to help me aboard. He kept holding my hand as we sat together, leaned toward me to look out the window and point out places that he had missed while he was away from Laurel. I couldn't imagine missing Laurel, but found his happiness vaguely reassuring. He told me how he and Pietro and Marco Caprello had lit firecrackers behind St. Anne's school, leaving scorch marks on the blacktop, but never getting caught.

We rode through downtown, across the railroad tracks, and out onto East Peach Street. We passed through a stockyard where pigs squealed and stank in their stalls, then a lumberyard and Dutzer's Junkyard. The few houses in this neighborhood were rickety and far apart with faded fences and barking dogs. I had a rough idea of where Neptune's Diner was, but hadn't been there before. This was a part of Laurel that I never visited.

At last we got out and took a shortcut down an alley to a street of dusty shops selling antiques, pine furniture and guns. Icicles dripped loudly from tin roofs, making puddles in the trodden snow. At the end of the street sat a long green railroad car trimmed with gold. A painted sign read "Neptune's Diner" and showed Neptune and Amphitrite in a chariot pulled by dolphins.

"Who's the lady with Neptune?" Robert asked.

"That's Amphitrite, the Queen of the Ocean," I said. "Dad read us all the Greek myths when we were kids."

"He was a great teacher," said Robert. "The whole town misses him, you know."

"Yes. I know."

Inside the diner, two families and some old men ate their breakfast in the padded leather booths and an Al Jolson record played from the kitchen:

You made me love you
I didn't want to do it
I didn't want to do it…

I froze and Robert whispered "Don't you like the place?"

"I love it," I said. "I just remember that song from our senior year."

The song always reminded me of Robert, though I never dared to tell anyone.

The only employee in Neptune's Diner on New Year's Day was a cook with black whiskers and a filthy spotted white apron over his massive belly. He grinned at Robert from the kitchen and rushed over to us with a coffee pot and two mugs.

"How are you doin', Robert? Happy New Year, ma'am."

"Happy New Year," I said.

"Larry, this is my friend Marlene Piper. Marlene, this is Larry Huntzacker."

"Pleased to make your acquaintance," he said. "Cup o' joe?"

"Yes, please, and some water if you don't mind."

"My pleasure. You pick out anything on the menu and it's on the house."

Larry laid down two menus and hustled back to the kitchen.

"He's a nice man," I said. "How come he owes you a meal?"

"I met Larry the first night I came into town and I beat him badly at a poker game. He paid me as much as he could then and offered me some free meals."

"Are you a card shark?"

"Yes, I am. Poker has saved me from going hungry on several occasions and it's a quick way to make friends."

Robert ordered some sourdough toast and I had an omelet with ham, cheese, mushrooms, peppers, onions and black olives. It was a meal in itself but it came with a slice of orange and a sweet corn muffin with butter and honey.

"This is delicious," I told Larry.

"You kids drop by any time."

"I haven't gone out to eat in ages," I told Robert.

"You deserve a treat for helping me out," he said. "I must have looked like a lost soul last night."

"I'm glad I found you."

He laid his hand on the table and covered it gently with mine. He lifted my hand to his lips and kissed the palm. No one had ever kissed my hand like that before and shivers ran up my arm and all through me. We ate and talked, lingering in Neptune's Diner for over two hours. When Larry asked us if we wanted lunch, we thanked him and left.

Thick feathery snowflakes fell like a merciful blanket laid on the weary tin roofs and faded walls of East Peach Street. We caught the trolley back into downtown and I hated the thought of saying goodbye to Robert. I needed to go home and take a nap before getting up to play that night and he needed to go back to Mrs. Green's.

"Could you meet me at The Starfish tonight?" I asked.

"Marlene, I'd love to, but I'm broke right now."

"I could buy you some drinks," I said. "And if you sing you'll get at least one for free, more if Zach is tending bar."

"Would they let me sing there?"

"Of course. We have guest musicians from New York and other cities all the time. I need a new singer since Blue Maria's gone to New York and gotten married."

I felt comfortable telling him everything about The Starfish. Chauncey would have snapped me in half like a toothpick if he could have heard me gossiping about the place.

"I saw Blue Maria sing with Texas Guinan," he said. "She's a goddess."

"We all miss her," I said.

Robert and I parted ways downtown, right in front of the Caprello Deli. He hugged me and gently pressed his lips to mine. I could have dropped on the street and made a snow angel for joy.

"I'll see you tonight," he said.

The door of Caprello's Deli swung open with a warm rush of cheese-scented air. Mrs. Caprello stood behind me with Marco. Marco winked at me, but his Mama looked offended.

"I see that Robert Schumann is back in town. He probably thinks he's a big shot now," Marco said.

Mrs. Caprello laid her hand on my shoulder and said "Be careful, Marlene. All actors are liars, no matter how gifted."

CHAPTER NINETEEN

That night I arrived at The Starfish before the other Six, so eager to see Robert, but determined not to tell anyone. I feared that he might not show up. Iris and Howard Davis came in, moving slowly. Jeremy Hobbes was sober, as always, but too polite to tease any of us. Aaron Bauer, who never got drunk and had only sipped one whiskey and one beer on New Year's Eve, looked at the Davises and then me with a smug grin.

"Marlene, you look positively fried," Aaron said.

"I feel fine."

I was wearing a purple silk dress that Helen had made me for Christmas and a necklace and earrings of amethyst. Iris looked me up and down and then winked at me.

"Who you waitin' for, Marlene?"

"Nobody."

Robert came in at half past ten when we were tuning up. It was all I could do not to run toward him and throw my arms around him. Shyly, I turned around on the piano bench and beckoned to him.

Iris said to Howard "Look out, here comes Marlene's 'Mr. Nobody'!"

Robert wore a long black coat and scarf and a gray wool hat and carried a guitar case and suitcase. The luggage worried me; he could be taking the morning train to New York. His brown hair was slicked with pomade and he smelled of musk. He wore a black three-piece suit, a red tie and two white gardenias on his lapel. Robert sauntered over to me, smiling, and pinned one of the gardenias on my bosom.

Emmett and Chauncey exchanged knowing looks.

"He must be an old friend of Marlene's," said Emmett.

"Friend, humph! A young widow should watch herself," said Chauncey.

I introduced Robert to everyone, one by one, saying.

"This is my friend Robert Schumann, a singer from New York."

Everyone greeted him politely, but only Iris looked genuinely pleased to see him. I asked the band if Robert could sing with us and he sang:

Boys and girls together
Me and Mamie Rourke
Tripped the light fantastic

On the sidewalks of New York.

The band clapped and Howard said "He sounds okay to me, but ask Al."

Zach made me a gin and tonic and gave Robert the brandy he asked for, looking slightly confused when Robert asked him to warm it up. Robert swirled the brandy in his glass, sniffed it and sipped, pronouncing it "Excellent."

"It should be," Al said icily. "It's from Ireland."

"The Irish have excellent taste," said Robert, beaming at me.

I gathered up his clothes and suitcase and carried them to the dressing room. As I passed Al, I casually said "I thought Robert might like to sing with us tonight, if you don't mind."

"That's the band's decision."

"They're all for it," I said honestly. "But Howard said I should ask what you thought of him."

Al shook his head.

"You don't need my permission for whatever you want to do, Marlene. I'm not your dad."

"Of course not, but let me know what you think of his singing."

Robert was already singing *Yes, Sir, That's My Baby* with Iris and Howard and Aaron backing him up on the drums, saxophone and bass. He had just finished the first verse when Al leaned over to me and whispered.

"He's a cake boy."

"What?"

Robert wasn't rich or effeminate or obsequious, the only "cake boy" characteristics I knew.

"He's a cake boy, Marlene. He'll drink here as long as someone else pays and he'll sing as long as the audience keeps clappin'. He won't last a year in this business."

"That's ridiculous! Robert's been a singer for five years now and an actor too."

"I believe he acts and sings and possibly juggles. If the Starfish Seven want him, that's no problem for me. But he's no prince. There's nothing special about being a failure in New York."

Al brushed past me and stood behind the bar all night sulking. Now I feared that he would ask Robert to leave. Had I made a mistake by bringing him here and thinking everyone else would worship his talent the way I did? Apparently I wasn't the only one who loved his baritone voice. Everyone in the audience danced when he sang:

It's three o' clock in the morning,
I've danced the whole night through.

Halfway through the evening, I looked down and noticed that the eight tables closest to the stage were full of ladies, old and young, black and white. Robert's audience loved him, whereas mine only loved my music. I didn't envy him for that; it had been the same way with Blue Maria. I never expected to be on center stage. Some players feel overshadowed by a lead singer, but I never felt that way. If Jeremy or Howard got more solos than I did or if Iris and Oliver took the spotlight to sing, I never felt slighted. We were like a bouquet of flowers, each distinct and beautiful, not runners racing against each other.

When we took a break, Iris took me aside. We shared a pitcher of water in the dressing room after playing for five hours straight and dancing after Oliver came in with new guitar songs that didn't call for a piano or drums. He and Robert had sung some duets.

"Your Robert is a fine singer," Iris said. "I hope he'll stay with us awhile."

"He's not really mine," I said, embarrassed.

"They never really are, honey," she said. "Just like my cats. I love 'em and they love me, but they can't be owned."

"Howard and Aaron seem to like Robert. I wonder what Al has against him."

"Don't let that bother you, Marlene. Al wants to be the only sheik in this oasis."

I wanted to ask Robert about the suitcase, but I couldn't work up my courage to do it until after four o' clock. I sat next to him at the bar.

"Are you going somewhere right after this?" I asked.

"Oh, you noticed my suitcase? Mrs. Green needed a room for her son who just came back from the Navy and she turned me out this morning with no notice."

"That's terrible! Did you at least get your money back?"

"I hadn't been able to pay her yet for this month. I told her I'd have the money by tomorrow, which is true now. It's too late, though, and she didn't like me coming and going at night either. It made her suspicious. Really, it's just as well she sent me away. My room had mice and she refused to fix the radiator. I fully intended to pay her -"

"No, you shouldn't! Sending you away without even three days' notice is completely unfair."

I leaned close to him and laid my hand on his.

"You could stay at my house again," I offered.

"Do you sometimes get lonely in that big old house?" Robert teased, stroking my hand.

"I like being alone," I said.

"You're very generous to let me stay with you again. I'll be much better company this time, I promise."

He kissed me full on the lips. Zach made a sound halfway between a cough and choking and Al loudly announced "Break's over. One more set!"

At the end of the night, Oliver gave Robert and me a ride home. We talked affably about people we knew, who had left Laurel and who had stayed, who drank and who didn't.

"I wish Joseph would come into The Starfish more often," said Oliver. "I offer him a free drink every time I see him, but we were lucky to get him and Katrina in there for New Years."

"They were lucky to get Mother to baby-sit. They left her house after the pork and sauerkraut supper saying they had a party with the fire marshal. Mother believed it because Joseph had worked on those hydrants, so she took care of Harry and Clarice."

"I know that your mother and Amelia don't approve of drinking," Oliver said to me. "Thank God Katrina is a European and sees Prohibition for the sham it is."

"Joseph doesn't like to get drunk because he's seen veterans who drink too much," I said bluntly.

"I hope you're not referring to me, Marlene!" said Oliver, feigning indignation.

We all laughed together and Oliver shook Robert's hand.

"It's great to have you back in town, Robert."

"Thanks, Oliver."

As Robert and I climbed up the steps into the cold dark house, I was already sinning. I made bargains with God. *Dear Lord,* I pleaded, *if you will let me sleep with this man just this once, I will get him a musical career and a place to live and I will never sin again after this one occasion. I know it is wrong, but through my love and my sacrifices I will make it all right.*

We could see our breath inside the house and Robert said "I'll shovel some coal in the furnace."

I lit his way down to the cellar and began to follow him downstairs, but he called out:

"You don't have to come down, Marlene. Go ahead and get ready for bed. You said you like to wash the smoke out of your hair. I'll be up in a minute."

"All right, thank you."

I bathed every inch of me with rose-scented soap and shampoo, shaved my armpits and legs and anointed my skin with cocoa butter lotion and a tiny amount of jasmine perfume. I brushed and flossed my teeth, combed my hair and dried it with a towel. My flannel nightgown looked nubby and shabby to me all of a sudden and the purple silk dress smelled too much like smoke now. I wore my lacy black slip under my blue robe that looked like velvet, but wasn't. My slippers were blue Chinese silk.

Robert kissed me quickly on the lips and went into the bathroom. I could hear him washing up, but I wouldn't let myself spy on him, so I went to the guest room and turned down the bed. As soon as I went upstairs, I had turned on the radiators in both bedrooms. Mine was as warm as toast, but the guest room still felt frigid. The floors creaked and the sheets and pillows felt cold.

Robert entered wearing crimson silk pajamas and leather slippers. His brown hair was clean and soft without the pomade and his skin looked new, pink and clean. He smiled but then shivered. Instinctively, I drew close to him.

"It's like a tomb in here," he said.

I laid one hand on his shoulder and said "You don't have to stay in the guest room."

Our arms fastened around each other as quickly as the clasp of a necklace. Robert kissed me hard and my knees trembled. He stroked my neck along the jugular veins and hot blood surged through me. I pressed my mouth into his and opened my eyes for an instant to convince myself that he really was here kissing me. Robert opened his eyes too, without embarrassment. He kissed my neck and reached his long graceful hands into my robe, pressing my back through the slip.

"I'll do anything you want me to," he said.

I took his hand and steered him down the hall to my bedroom.

"Oh, this is much better," he said.

I rubbed his strong arms and broad back through the red silk. My robe fell to the floor and I staggered backward toward the bed, still kissing Robert. He closed his eyes and lay back luxuriously, like a cat.

He lifted my left hand and kissed the palm.

"Such gorgeous hands. Piano playing hands."

Then he gently rolled me onto my back to massage me, from my neck to my feet. His kisses landed lightly and teased my skin, like butterflies.

"Do you want me to finish?" he asked.

I nodded.

"I'll pull out."

Robert moved with deliberate slowness, breathing hard. He caressed me with one hand and supported himself with the other arm. I rocked my hips against his and stroked him all over, eager but wanting to prolong this. He smelled delicious, like musk or clove, a smell that I now realized was his own sweat. I kissed and nibbled his neck and moaned. Lust sang from my mouth, loud, off-key, rhythmic and beautiful as jazz.

"Go on and scream if you want to," he said. "No one can hear us."

He pulled away from me at the crucial moment and we lay kissing for a long time.

"I always loved you," I confessed.

"Shh."

He kissed me again.

"You've given me more than I deserve," he said.

"You deserve every happiness in the world," I said.

Robert pulled on his pajamas and brought me a washcloth to clean myself. We settled into my bed, side by side. He curled one arm around me and I felt complete joy and safety. I did not ask or care what would happen next. I told myself that if I died the next day this would be enough.

CHAPTER TWENTY

Robert was renting the back bedroom from me; that was the story we agreed to give to both our families and all our friends. Folks at the Starfish might wink and nod at my behavior, but my family would be horrified. My union with David had been such a disaster that I hesitated to tell them I had a new man. Certainly I would not let anyone find out that I had slept with him.

"For the moment, let's just let them think that we're good friends," Robert said.

The next Sunday I was surprised that he wanted to accompany me to church.

"You told me you were an agnostic now," I said. "Have you changed your mind about that?"

"No, but mass won't hurt me any. I miss the people in my old parish," said Robert. "I never went to church in New York and now my parents and Elaine only attend on the Holy Days of Obligation. A lot of the church women were very cruel to Elaine. She can't take communion now that she's divorced. Lance and Gwen can't understand why she has to stay in the pew with them."

"The church is wrong about a lot of things, including divorce," I said. "But faith has been the rock I cling to in hard times."

"I know it's important to you," said Robert. "So it will be important to me too."

He hugged and kissed me and we hurried to get dressed in our best clothes. I felt slightly hypocritical and wore my plainest black wool skirt and sweater over a high-necked white blouse. Robert looked as handsome as ever in a blue suit and his gray hat. No matter how cold it was he wore a felt hat with a brim, never a stocking cap or a furry hat. His ears turned as red as two crawfish as we walked down the snowy block to St. Anne's.

We took the streetcar and then walked about eight blocks through the old neighborhood. Our feet crunched in the snow and frost sparkled on the trees. Robert and I talked about our childhood classes and masses.

"Remember old Sister Boniface, who we used to call Sister Bismarck? She rapped my knuckles once for shouting out a correct answer in arithmetic."

"I do remember and I felt sorry for you," I said. "We were all scared of her, and when she got really angry she would speak German without meaning to. *Ach du lieber!*"

"Her robes were so long I used to think she had no feet," Robert said.

As we neared St. Anne's, other churchgoers joined us on the sidewalk. Mothers held their bundled-up babies and fathers took their little ones' hands to lead them across the street. Old men and women tottered across the snow, leaning on their canes and supporting one another. A few wealthy families parked their automobiles on the street. Some people I knew waved to me and Robert.

When Robert entered the church, he instinctively stepped toward the front, where his family used to sit. I plucked at his sleeve and pulled him to the pews on the right side of the altar with the Pipers. Mother sat in the center of the pew, with Helen on one side and Amelia, Arthur and their baby girl Florence on the other. Joseph, Katrina, Harry and Clarice sat behind them. Robert and I slipped in beside Joseph. He looked surprised but not displeased to see Robert. Helen noticed Robert and jerked her head to point him out to Amelia. Amelia turned around, startled, then smiled knowingly at me.

My gaze switched back and forth like a metronome from Robert to my mother. She could smell smoke or gin on me from across a room. She would know that I had slept with Robert, even though neither of us would ever speak of it. I didn't hear one word Father Hulings said or one note of the hymns, which I usually loved. Jesus might have some mercy on my sins but I expected none from Mother.

Robert was oblivious to my nervousness as he sang *Gloria* with moist eyes. I wished that I could lose myself in the mass as I had in childhood. Now the only place I felt prayerful was behind the organ and I only played a few holiday masses each year. Mrs. Binewski was pounding on the pipe organ now and it cried out like a nauseated cat. I knew I could do better, even if I arrived sleepy from a long night at The Starfish.

At the kiss of peace, Mother turned around to shake hands with us and saw Robert. Her mouth smiled tightly but her eyes did not brighten. He shook hands with her and said "Peace be with you, Mrs. Piper."

"And with you, Robert."

I felt so nervous that during communion, I dropped the host. Father Hulings frowned at me, but the altar boy caught the host on a brass paten and held it up again for me to take. The altar boy smiled, feeling helpful and amused by my mistake.

After mass, Robert lingered in the entryway talking to half a dozen of his old friends and their wives. He hadn't seen any of them since high school and was now meeting their children for the first time. It bored me because I saw them every week and they never bothered to speak to me.

Harry and Florence rushed up to me and launched themselves into my arms.

"Aunt Marlene, Grandma wants to talk to you."

"Thank you, sweethearts."

I hugged and kissed them both and followed them down the steps, beckoning to Robert to follow us. Mother stood there with her children and grandchildren, imperious as a czarina in her red wool coat and white rabbit muff.

"I presume that you are coming to Sunday dinner as usual."

"Yes, if that's all right with you."

"It would be polite to bring your friend to join us."

Robert was close enough to overhear that and agree.

"I've always had great respect for the Piper clan," he said. "Especially Mr. Piper. He was the most intelligent historian I've ever known."

"Yes, he had great insight," Mother said, unmoved by the compliment.

At Mother's house we drank mint tea and creamy coffee and ate egg pudding with sausage, home fries and applesauce. Joseph told knock-knock jokes to Harry and Florence and Clarice and pulled pennies from behind their ears, like my dad used to do with us. The rest of the family politely yet thoroughly questioned Robert.

"What brought you back to Laurel, Robert?" asked Joseph.

"I came to visit my parents for Christmas and I hope to make a little extra money here before I go back to New York."

"What was your employment there?" asked Amelia.

"I've been in three bands and acted in a dozen plays. The last one was *Playboy of the Western World* by Casey."

"That caused a great stir in Ireland years ago," said Mother. "My sister Sheila wrote me about it. There was a line about girls in their shifts that started a riot. The playboy is some storyteller who comes to town and all the women are mad after him."

"Yes, that was my role," said Robert, blushing.

"What are you doing for work now?" asked Helen.

"I teach guitar lessons," he said.

He told them about the three boys he was teaching, from nine to twelve, and their guitars and their families. Robert taught in the afternoons after the boys got home from school. He had told me he expected seven more pupils but they never appeared.

"Are you staying with your parents now?" Katrina asked.

This was the crucial question and I felt glad that I didn't have to answer it.

"I had been boarding at Mrs. Green's, but Marlene is renting a room to me."

Everyone fell so silent that I could hear the clock ticking in the next room.

Mother glared at me and said "Is that so?"

"Yes, Mother," I said. "I lived at Mrs. Green's and I wouldn't want a friend of mine staying there."

"I have other musical engagements too, thanks to your daughter's recommendation," Robert added.

I nudged him in the ribs. Hadn't I told him that Mother didn't approve of The Starfish? She put her elbow on the table and rested her face on one hand, always a terrible sign. Arthur blurted out what he, Mother and Amelia were all thinking.

"Why don't you apply for a job at Stolzfus Silk Mill? They always need more spinners and weavers and they'll train you."

Robert looked indignant.

"Come on now, Art. Spooling is fine for some folks, but I was born for the stage. Marlene here is just the same."

He held up my hand in his, palm outward, displaying it like a found treasure.

"Look at these hands. Do they look like the hands of field worker or a silk weaver? These are pianist's hands. We are musicians by our very nature."

"All the Dobhailen women have elegant hands," Amelia said. "Those hands could do just as well stitching up wounds or sewing silk blouses or holding a baby."

As she spoke, she gestured toward herself, then Helen, then Mother.

After the meal, Amelia, Arthur and Katrina and Joseph kissed Mother goodbye and left with their children. Amelia invited me to come and see her soon. Mother steered me toward the kitchen to help her with the dishes and Helen followed.

"Where did you find Robert?" Mother asked

"I've known him since grade school, Mother."

"You know what I mean. Where did you meet him again in the last month?"

"At the New Year's Eve Party at The Starfish."

"Was he drinking?" Helen asked.

"Everyone there was drinking."

I wanted to list myself, Joseph and Katrina as examples, but I knew better. Helen's naiveté annoyed me.

"I don't like that man's airs," said Mother. "Any man who claims he's above working turns out to be far beneath it. You were a fool with David. Don't be a fool again, Marlene"

"I won't be. I have no plans to remarry. Robert is a boarder at my house and a singer for the band. I need someone to sing with me if I'm ever going to play in New York again or have a chance to record an album or travel anywhere else. You must know that. No one will pay to see me playing on stage all alone or buy a plain instrumental record."

"Make music with him if you must," said Mother. "But don't live with him."

CHAPTER TWENTY-ONE

I went to see Amelia two days later at her house. She told me to come between eleven and one, when Florence was taking her nap. The Ritters' white row house was three stories tall, with green trim and a green awning over the red brick porch. It was on Plum Street, six blocks from Mother's house. Snow frosted the big maple tree and carpeted the big backyard. Frost sparkled on the forsythia bushes but Arthur had shoveled the front walk.

Not wanting to ring the doorbell and risk waking Florence, I peered into the front room, found it dark, then looked in the kitchen. Amelia was washing dishes, wearing one of her white hospital aprons. When I tapped on the window of the side door, she opened it.

"Come on in. It feels cold out there."

"It is," I said. "Here, I can dry the dishes and put them away if you tell me where they go."

"Thank you."

Amelia kept her whole house in apple-pie order, cleaning vigorously while Florence napped. Many young mothers complained of tiredness, but Amelia actually seemed restless at home after years of working twelve-hour shifts at the hospital. She made raspberry tea and brought out some ham and bean soup and biscuits for our lunch.

We sat in green armchairs in her yellow living room with a coffee table between us. Photographs of Amelia and Arthur at their wedding and in Boston on their honeymoon hung on the mantel, with a picture of them and Florence. The cherry tables were polished and the lamp with stained-glass grapes shone, but wooden blocks and a metal top littered the floor. It relieved me to see that her house wasn't perfect.

"When Florence is potty-trained, I'll be ready to have another child," said Amelia.

"We want two of them and Arthur and I think it would be good if they're close in age so they can play together. I still miss the hospital. Sometimes I walk down there with Florence to visit with the doctors and nurses. They'll have me back anytime, Dr. Lowry said."

"That's wonderful. It's too bad you can't work a few days a week now."

"I could work a night shift or two each week, although Arthur doesn't like me to be away at night. He would be here with the children though. I'll definitely go back to work when they're both in school, at least part-time."

"Yes, you should," I said. "You're a great nurse. I see patients of yours at The Starfish who ask how you're doing."

She shook her head, but she still smiled.

"I hope you don't mind, Amelia, but I came to you for medical help today."

"Really?" she looked interested. "What's the trouble?"

"There's no trouble. You once offered to get me birth control if I ever needed it. I wanted to take you up on that offer."

"I see."

She paused and sipped her tea.

"I can pay whatever it costs."

"That's not a problem, but I will have to ask Arthur. He'll get you what you need and I'll bring it to you. There... Is there anything else you want to tell me?"

"Robert Schumann lives me now, as you know, and we're in love. I don't want to remarry yet or to have any children, not for a few more years anyway."

"Yes, I can understand that. I won't say anything to the rest of the family, of course, but they can probably guess what's going on. Tell me something, Marlene. Does Robert like to drink?"

"No. He's not like David, Amelia. He'd never hurt me."

"He'll never strike you, but that's only one kind of hurt."

"He has one or two cocktails a night at most, which is no more than I have. I drink in moderation for my own enjoyment, just like Dad used to, and no more. You don't have to worry so much about me."

Amelia took off her glasses and wiped them with a corner of her skirt, as she always did when something frustrated her. Perhaps, subconsciously, she hoped she could see everything clearly if only the lenses were clean enough.

"You know I don't approve of your drinking, Marlene, but I never worry about you becoming a drunk. I worry about Robert, though. He's intelligent and very charming, but I can tell he's not as responsible as you are. He seems to believe that the world owes him a living."

"He will earn a living with me. Robert has a perfect tenor voice and all the stage presence that I lack."

"You're a better musician than he is and you've never been conceited about your talents. I hope you both succeed, I really do, but you can also succeed on your own."

We talked until two o'clock, when we hugged each other goodbye and Amelia went to wake Florence up from her nap. The next day Amelia came to my house with a diaphragm and instructed me about how to use it. She also gave me a book by Margaret Sanger, which I promised to read.

Robert and I lived and worked comfortably together, our lives intertwined like dance steps. We slept during the day and went to The Starfish at least five nights a week. Robert did not always sing but he always walked me to work and had a few drinks. He almost never got to play his guitar unless Oliver wanted a back-up guitarist or took the night off. Then Robert might go home to sleep, but he'd return at dawn to walk me home. He came with me to Central Market to buy groceries. I had been carrying my own heavy bags since my first marriage and when Robert helped me, the lightness was amazing. I went to church and Mother's house on Sunday, but Robert rarely accompanied me. He maintained his agnosticism. We each visited our friends and had dinner guests at the house sometimes.

"I'd like to have your parents and Elaine over here sometime," I said. "Do you think they would disapprove of your living here as much as my mother does?"

Robert shook his head and said "They don't approve of anything I do. We'll see them at Easter. That's soon enough."

"Are they angry at you for something?"

"It's not just one thing. They don't drink and they hate modern music. My father works at Stolzfus, like most everyone in town and wonders what the hell is wrong with me that I can't settle down in Laurel. Mama always asks why I'm not married and Elaine resents my freedom because she's stuck here in Laurel with two kids."

"You should spend more time with them and get to know Lance and Gwen better. They'd love their uncle. I do."

He hugged me and laid his head on my shoulder.

"The Schumanns aren't a perfect family like the Pipers are. I don't feel deprived or anything, that's just how it's always been."

"My family used to be perfect," I said.

CHAPTER TWENTY-TWO

"My family isn't as sociable as yours," he warned me.

We were riding the streetcar to his parents' house for Easter dinner. I was nervous, but excited to meet them. I had only seen his parents from a distance at church and had not spoken much to his sister Elaine because she was three grades ahead of us in school. They were all intelligent with an aristocratic bearing, but somewhat reserved.

The Schumanns had emigrated from Prussia and during the Great War there was some gossip about their sympathies for the old country. This didn't make me think less of them at all; my own mother considered the war a pointless sacrifice for the British Empire and had objected when Joseph joined the army. After the war, I too believed it had been a waste and wondered how anyone could blame Germans in America for the Kaiser's mistakes.

"My parents speak a lot of German, especially Mama," he said.

"That's all right. I studied German in high school, remember?"

The Schumanns lived in a green row house with neat boxwood hedges and lilies-of-the-valley blooming around the porch. Mrs. Schumann let us in, cordial but not happy.

"It is good to meet you, Marlene," she said.

"Thank you, Mrs. Schumann."

I gave her a jar of strawberry jam that I had made, which she whisked off to the kitchen. Mr. Schumann sat in a rocking chair reading the newspaper. He said "Good afternoon," to each of us, but did not stand up to greet us or even shake hands. Elaine hugged and kissed Robert and me. She looked pale and pensively beautiful with large dark eyes like her brother. Elaine wore her brown hair long, almost to her waist and wore a white cotton dress trimmed with Venice lace. She moved slowly, directed by her mother, but dwelling in her own thoughts. Elaine reminded me of a princess in The Red Fairy Book.

Lance and Gwen rushed down the stairs to meet us and hugged Robert and me around the knees. Lance was four, Gwen was two and both were excited to see us. Elaine had dressed Lance in a white shirt, tie and knickers and Gwen in a yellow daisy dress with two neat brown braids, but both of them had dirty shoes and sticky fingers.

"Uncle Robert, is this your wife?" asked Lance.

"No, this is my friend Marlene Piper."

"Are you like the Pied Piper?" Lance asked.

"No. I'm good and I don't steal children. I play the piano."

"Me too!" both children cried.

They sat at the piano and pounded on the keys. I played some songs they could sing with, *Ba, Ba Black Sheep* and *Row, Row, Row, Your Boat* and tried to guide their little fingers to the right keys. Robert and Elaine smiled and conversed behind us.

"Your children have great talent," said Robert. "I don't know how you keep up with them. Having kids would wear me out."

"I'll bet Marlene wouldn't mind having a child," said Elaine.

"No, I wouldn't."

Mrs. Schumann requested a song about the Lorelei and sang in German while I played:

Ich weiss nicht was es bedeutet

Das ich so traurig bin...

Grandma Piper had told me the story of the Lorelei, singing mermaids who lived in the Rhine River enticed boatmen to sail toward them and die when their ships crashed on the rocks. Mrs. Schumann looked happy only when she sang, one elegant white hand on her breast, her silver hair and starry black eyes shining. She trilled like an opera singer; I had never heard such a dazzling soprano except on stage. Mr. Schumann twitched his thick mustache and scarcely looked up from his newspaper. Lance and Gwen tried to reach for his hand or climb in his lap, but Elaine shooed them away.

"You sing divinely," I said to Mrs. Schumann.

She nodded and smiled, absorbing the praise without feigning modesty. Mrs. Schumann knew the beauty of her face and voice even if no audience applauded her.

Dinner was leg of lamb with rosemary, German potato salad, hard rolls and green peas. Dessert was glazed pears in vanilla sauce. I wished for a nice glass of Riesling or a mug of hefeweizen, as my father would have had with this meal, but the Schumanns were strict teetotalers.

"Robert, how is your employment?" asked Mr. Schumann.

"Very good, sir. I'm giving many lessons and Marlene and I have been playing private parties."

I had never expected him to tell his family the whole truth, but it upset me to hear him lie so blatantly. At least my own family now knew what I did for a living, even if we collectively refused to speak about it.

"We plan to go to Chicago to record an album called *Twilight Melodies*," I said.

Robert explained "My friend Lou Cunningham, who moved to Chicago, wants to record us. We'll record there and then tour all the way to Los Angeles. MGM and Warner Brothers are always having casting calls and I plan to audition."

"All this travel won't be cheap," Mr. Schumann said with a snort.

"No, but we'll be played on the radio and we can sell records in every town we stop in on the way home to pay for our trip," Robert explained.

"I hope they pay you very much," Mrs. Schumann told me. "You play beautifully."

"Thank you, ma'am. I have been lucky to accompany Robert."

Robert repeated that to her in German and she looked pleased. He told them that he was renting a room from me and his parents asked when he would have enough money for a house. Elaine talked about her work, taking in washing and doing housekeeping for wealthy families. She hoped to find another secretarial job once her children were in school. I spoke to her privately after the meal.

"I don't get a dime from Wayne," she said. "He lives with his mother in Wilkes-Barre and she supports him completely, living on a railroad pension. What a spineless man!"

"Does he ever visit the children?" I asked.

"Only once in two years," she said. "He spent all his money on gambling and other women, so I packed up and left him just after Gwen was born. If he wants to see us he knows where to find us."

"It must have taken a lot of courage to get the divorce," I said.

"Any idiot can get a divorce," she said, flicking away the compliment. "I would like to find another husband. Several men are interested in me..."

She talked on and on about her gentlemen callers, none of whom I knew, though they all worked at Stolzfus.

"I understand that you're widowed," she said. "Do you think you will ever remarry?"

"I hope so," I said.

"I've never known Robert to stick with any girl longer than a month," she said. "You're quite lucky."

Before I left, I invited all of the Schumanns to come and visit us any time, suspecting that they would never take me up on the offer. I gave Lance and Gwen two Jacob's ladders that Isaac had made out of ribbon and smooth wood. Robert and I waved goodbye and walked toward the streetcar. Lance and Gwen waved with both hands and leaned over the fence to watch us walk away.

"They're little monkeys," said Robert, only half joking.

"I love them," I said. "I like your whole family. I wish they went out more often."

"Mama is self-conscious about how little money they have. Her father was a count and my father was the gardener's son. They eloped to America, you know."

"Like my parents, except my father was American."

"And your mother didn't leave a fortune behind. Mama will always think of herself as impoverished nobility."

"Do you think of yourself that way?" I asked.

"Yes. Ancestry has a lot to do with a person's character, whether we like to admit it or not."

"I hope you don't buy into that eugenics nonsense. I don't. I've seen too many smart and talented people of every race and class. It makes me sick that some people believe Irish are born drunks and Italians are born criminals. The Irish monasteries were great seats of learning even in the Dark Ages and Italy gave the world Rome and the Renaissance. How can some pasty-faced faced Englishman think he's superior to that?"

Robert whistled, amused by my anger. "I guess that got your Irish up," he teased. "I certainly don't think the English are the brightest people on Earth. There are some clever people from every country; America is proof of that. But don't you think that certain character traits run in families? Like melancholy or drinking or the music in your own family?"

"I suppose so, but even in families there are exceptions. All of my siblings are different."

The last family celebration before we left town was Helen's June wedding to Edward Malone. It took place outdoors in the Malone family's orchard with pink and white apple blossoms all around. Helen had sewn her white silk dress, her lace veil and the yellow and pink floral dresses for her bridesmaids Jenny, Rachel and Ruby. Edward's brother Jack was the best man and had also brought a guitar to play. Edward dressed all in white too, which suited his pale freckled face and red hair. They blushed, pink as the roses Helen carried, as they kneeled in the grass while Father Hulings blessed them. Even as I prayed for their happiness, I knew that Edward and Helen's honest, innocent love would sustain them both.

Helen and Edward had saved their money for a year to afford the wedding and a brief honeymoon in Washington, D.C. Edward had nailed together the long tables and benches and Helen had arranged vases of orange blossoms on the tablecloths. Edward's father barbecued pork and roasted corn for the wedding supper.

"It's so tactless serving barbecue at a wedding," Maud complained.

Sven and I looked up her, surprised, our mouths stained reddish-brown with sauce.

"I think it's delicious," he said.

"I admire Helen and Edward for saving their money for so long. They did this all themselves," I said.

"Is it true that they're moving into your house?" Maud asked.

"Yes. Robert and I will be gone to Los Angeles until at least next January. I'm not charging them any rent though. They need to save money for their own house."

Maud scowled and said "Anyway, it's rude to discuss money in public. I would have preferred an indoor wedding myself. There are too many flies out here and Eugene will get a sunburn."

Robert had looked bored during the ceremony and hadn't touched the food. He complained that Helen hadn't asked him to play guitar. When everyone began to dance to Jack Malone's guitar music, Robert led me away from the wedding party.

We wandered through the pink and white orchard where a soft wind scattered petals from the trees. The evening air was warm and heavy with the smell of blossoms. Robert held my hand and helped me over a fence into a meadow with a duck pond and a willow tree. He sat down at the base of the tree and beckoned to me.

Robert looked so handsome there with his pale blue shirt and navy tie, his tan jacket spread on the ground for me to sit on. His brown eyes shown like amber and his smile promised me every happiness in the world. I sat down and kissed him eagerly, but when I reached for him, he pressed something into my hand.

It was a white gardenia with a ring on its stem, a plain golden wedding ring. I was utterly surprised and dropped the gardenia. The ring slid from its stem and he picked it up and offered it to me, on one knee.

"Marlene, you are the only person who has ever understood me and loved me completely. My music was never complete without you and my life never will be. I don't ever want to have to hide our love from anyone or check into a hotel under false names or pretend that I am just your accompanist. I want to be with you every day and every night of my life, even when I'm old and gray and my voice is cracking."

"I'll still love you," I said. "I always loved you, Robert, but I'm afraid."

"You can't be afraid of me?"

"No, I ... you know how it was when I married David. We began with such optimism, but when he began to fail and feel trapped, he blamed me for it."

"Marlene, you know I would never hurt you. I could kill that man for what he did to you. Don't look away."

He turned my face toward his.

"Robert, what will you do if we don't succeed in Hollywood?"

"I'll play music wherever we go, here, there or anywhere in between."

"If I had children, I would want to bring them up here."

"I understand that. You have a wonderful family and I know Lance and Gwen would love to have cousins. We can always take a train to Chicago or New York from here. I would hope we could have a few years to ourselves before we have children, to establish ourselves."

"Yes," I said. "I have no intention of giving up my piano. You must never ask me to stop playing in public even after we have kids."

Robert took my hand and spoke soothingly.

"Don't worry, Marlene. I'd never ask you to stop playing and when we record our next album, we should have enough money to hire babysitters when we need them. I'd never expect you to be a housewife any more than you'd expect me to spin silk at the mill."

"I love you, Robert John Schumann, and I accept your ring."

I pulled off my white gloves and slipped the ring onto my finger. Robert and I kissed again and again. We lay down together in the cool grass, unbuttoning but not removing our clothes, joining together but springing apart at the crucial moment. I was determined not to get pregnant yet and still felt some guilt about my lust for him, which was no purer with the gold ring on my finger than it had been on New Year's Day when I undressed him in his drunken stupor.

We would be happy together, I knew, but there would be long weary travels and disinterested audiences and tight times. My family would not approve of my second marriage and I knew that Robert and I would not be married in the church. I put my glove on over the ring, so that no one saw it as I kissed Helen goodbye. That night, Robert and I plotted our wedding together.

CHAPTER TWENTY-THREE

Robert pinned a gardenia on the lapel of my lavender dress. It was an ordinary cotton dress printed with bluebells.

"I couldn't wear white," I said. "Not after my marriage to David. Not after all we've done."

"I'm glad you're not a virgin," Robert said. "And you know I'm not; I told you about Eve and Janet and Pauline. The important thing isn't being each other's first lover; it's being each other's true love."

"You were the first man I ever loved," I said. "Sometimes I wished I could have run off to New York with you after high school."

"But I had to leave Laurel for a few years and to find myself. I'm glad I didn't get married any earlier than this. At twenty-four, I feel like I'm just old enough now."

We admired ourselves in my bathroom mirror. I wore a white hat with a floppy brim, trimmed with sky blue ribbon and live bluebells, forget-me-nots and daisies. I wore a braided silver bracelet that had belonged to Grandma Piper and pearl earrings on extended loan from Blue Maria. I dropped a penny into my open-toed white shoe.

Robert wore a cream-colored suit with a powder blue shirt and jade green bow tie, a Panama hat and a gardenia on his lapel. We might have been going to a summer picnic or an afternoon tea dance. No one noticed us on the streetcar or downtown.

Our two witnesses and only wedding guests were Elaine and Larry Huntzacker from the Neptune Diner. Elaine brought us a bouquet of yellow daylilies, purple irises, blue hydrangeas and orange blossoms. She wore a peach-colored Sunday dress and Larry wore a navy jacket with gold buttons and held the golden ring on a silk pillow. The official who married us was a mousy-looking little man with thick glasses, but he couldn't help smiling at us as we took our vows.

"You may kiss the bride."

Robert swept me back in his arms and poured a kiss into my mouth. Larry clapped and chuckled.

"Aren't you going to throw the bouquet?" Elaine asked.

I flung it over my shoulder and into her arms. She hugged me.

"Mother and Father will be furious that you didn't invite them," she told Robert. "I told them I was going out to buy milk! I won't say anything, of course, but I do think that once they get over the shock, they'll be pleased. We all love you, Marlene. I wish you both every happiness in the world."

"Thank you, Elaine, " I said.

"Mother and Father are furious no matter what I do," said Robert. "I didn't ask them because I knew they would want a church wedding with a big reception and punch and orange blossoms and dozens of their friends who I don't even know. I'll be gone for a year and give them a chance to miss me."

"We'll be back in my old house by this time next year."

"Unless we get lucky," Robert said.

We sat on benches on the lawn behind the court house to eat our modest wedding feast. Elaine took our photographs by the hedges with my camera. Larry brought a platter of cold cooked shrimp, crab cakes, figs, cherries, Roquefort and gouda cheese. He even baked a white cake with blue icing roses.

"Where are you kids staying for your wedding night?" asked Larry.

"An old friend is putting us up," I said.

That afternoon we heard the Laurel Symphony Orchestra play Mozart and Bach in the park. We crept into an afternoon tea dance at the Ladies' Auxiliary Hall, doing the fox trot and stealing lemonade and powdered tea cakes. That evening we knocked on the servants' entrance of the Ottoman Hotel and Peggy opened the door.

She wore her white summer uniform and carried a huge ring of keys.

"Congratulations," she said, hugging me and kissing me on the cheek.

"Peggy, I remember you from first communion class," said Robert. "You're looking very well."

"I am well, thank you, Mr. Schumann. I remember that Marlene always liked you, although she wouldn't admit it in third grade. I always knew that one day she would end up with you, just like I ended up with Jeremy Hobbes."

"We owe you a great deal for this," said Robert.

Peggy refused to take any money from us, saying "You deserve a wedding present and this doesn't cost me anything."

"If it weren't for you, Peggy, I would never have found work at The Starfish and very likely never have met Robert again. I owe everything to you."

"You would have found the place, I'm sure, and been hired there eventually, but I was happy to help you."

"I wish I could pay you back somehow," I told Peggy.

"I have everything I need in life," she said. "But if there is ever any favor I need from you, I will let you know."

We rode the elevator to the top floor, a penthouse suite often used by honeymooners. It was amazing that no other couples had reserved the room in the middle of July. Peggy assured us that no one would object to our occupying the room.

"I've helped Mr. Sims out dozens of times and he knows he owes me favors. When my mother had surgery, he let me put her up in a room here for a whole month. If I put you on the register, no one will question it. Besides, it's only one night."

"You really do run the Ottoman Hotel, don't you, Peggy?" said Robert.

Peggy beamed and unlocked the door to the suite. An electric fan whirred softly above the white chenille spread of the huge brass bed. I rushed into the bathroom, dazzled by the white marble and full-length mirrors.

On the balcony were potted topiaries shaped like lollipops, two wicker lounge chairs and a bucket of ice with a chilled champagne bottle. I knew that Peggy did not approve of drinking and never drank herself. Had Peggy procured this for us or did the Ottoman always discreetly supply champagne to wealthy newlyweds? I asked Peggy about this, but she just winked at me and said "That's complimentary. You kids enjoy yourselves now."

We sat on the balcony sipping champagne and looking down over Laurel. Those lights had dazzled me when I was eighteen, but now, five years later they looked insignificant. After Philadelphia and New York, the low white lights were like a patch of alyssum compared to a rose garden. Still, I felt powerful because I could see the whole town, but no one could look up and see us.

"Tonight we're on top of Laurel," said Robert. "But soon we'll be on top of the world."

He spread a lush comforter over one of the lounge chairs and sprinkled rose petals over it. He undressed, lay down, and beckoned to me, as pink and white and perfect as Venus on the Half-Shell. I could not believe I was lucky enough to have married this man. I lay down beside him and kissed him." I've always loved you," I said. "You're the most beautiful person I've ever known."

"You're the greatest musician I've ever known," he said, kissing my hands.

A light breeze blew over our naked skins as we joined together, high above Laurel and already far beyond it. We took a bath together in the claw foot tub and slept on the brass bed. The next morning at ten o'clock, the telephone rang with our wake-up call from Peggy. Robert and I had one last romp on the horsehair sofa, packed our bags and checked out. I felt that I had stolen something and gotten away with it, and blushed and tingled all over with the secret delight of my wedding night. I was Mrs. Marlene Schumann and nobody around me knew.

When we got to my house, my mother was upstairs in my room. I took off my ring and hid it in my pocket. I had forgotten that Mother had offered to come over that day and help me pack.

"It must have been a late night at The Starfish," said Mother. "I called you at eight o' clock this morning, and at ten I came on over to help you pack your things."

"Thank you, Mrs. Piper, but that's hardly necessary."

Robert laid his hand on her arm but she swatted it off like a mosquito.

"Sure it is! Marlene stuffed every piece of clothing she has into six cloth bags. Do you honestly call that packing? And do you really think you'll be wearing a wool coat and galoshes in California?"

"I'm sorry," I said, feeling real guilt about lying to my mother.

"I think I'll go and see my family," said Robert. "I want to say a proper goodbye to Elaine and the kids and I know they won't want to go to the station tomorrow. I'll have supper there."

Robert kissed me on the lips before rushing downstairs.

"Why are you angry with me, Mother?" I asked.

"I'm not angry about you leaving; I'm pleased that you're able to see the country the way you've always wanted to. I do know what it's like to be young and want to escape, but you know that I don't trust Robert. He loves bright lights and big cities, and while you may want to come back to Laurel and settle down, he never will."

She snapped the latch of a suitcase and sat down on my bed.

My stomach boiled; I almost blurted out the truth which I had wanted to hide until I left town.

"That's not true. He wants to marry me, to come back here and have kids."

"That's what he says now, when he needs your music to have any kind of chance at a career as a singer. If he could do it alone, he wouldn't be here now."

"I love him and he loves me!" I protested. "He's the only person who has ever understood me, except possibly Dad."

"Robert Schumann is nothing like your father!"

"I don't need your help, Mother. I had everything packed the way I wanted it before you came in."

"I'm not leaving until the dishes are packed. And don't think of going out there without an electric fan!"

She stayed most of the afternoon, our arguments giving way to calm preparations as I packed every household item I might need into two big wooden crates, two trunks and two suitcases.

"It is good of you to let Helen and Edward stay here while you're away," she said. "Why don't you come to my house for supper? I can invite Joseph, Amelia and Helen and let them see you one more time before you go away."

"All right."

I left Robert a note and took the trolley home with Mother. We ate with Joseph, Amelia and Helen. The table seemed larger with just my immediate family, no spouses, children or Haydens as there had been last Sunday. Helen joked about movie stars she'd like to meet and Joseph asked about which trains we would be riding on. Amelia gave me a little first aid kit with medicines and bandages and insect repellent. We sat out on the porch after supper, eating watermelon and spitting the seeds.

"I'll miss you all so much," I said.

"You won't be gone forever," said Amelia.

Helen said "Besides, you might get famous in Los Angeles and bring us all out there to live with you."

We hugged and kissed each other goodbye. As Amelia drove me home from Mother's house, I felt peaceful. I knew that nothing here would change in my absence, that everyone would welcome me back no matter how long I had been gone.

The next morning, Joseph woke me and Robert before five, pounding on the front door. We stuffed all our luggage into the Piper Plumbing van and rushed to Buchanan Station, picking up Mother, who insisted on seeing me off. She told me she loved me, wished me luck and gave me a package of blue wisteria stationary and orders to write. Only as the train pulled away did I see her crying and holding onto Joseph as he waved his white boater hat and smiled.

CHAPTER TWENTY-FOUR

Robert and I recorded *Twilight Melodies* in Chicago, spending a week there before embarking on our western tour. We played at a club in Tower Town, close to the Chicago Water Tower. I loved riding the elevated trains, and hoped that someday every city in America would have them whizzing above the honking cars on busy streets.

We played at a dance at Green Mill Gardens and bought new hats at Marshall Field and Company, the world's largest department store. Robert looked through all thirteen stories, admiring ties and shoes and cute salesgirls before finally settling on a gray felt Stetson with a braided band. I bought a broad-brimmed straw hat with a black and white ribbon, a simple summer hat that would match anything I wore. Robert loved new clothes more than I ever did because he knew he was attractive and everything looked good on him. He preened like a peacock before the mirror, practicing his expressions.

I joshed him "Do all men practice being handsome in the mirror?"

"Yes," he said seriously. "And some of us succeed at it."

We left from Union Station, bound for St. Louis. On our way out of town, our train passed the Union Stock Yards. The smell of manure was sickening in the heat and flies buzzed everywhere. Cows and sheep plodded passively in their pens, but the pigs squealed loudly, as if they knew that death awaited them. I looked over thousands of brown and white backs of cows and sheep and the desperate pink pigs. Robert grabbed me by the arm and rushed me away.

"Don't stand there staring, Marlene. This place reeks."

"I want to see everything, not just the pretty things," I said.

On every train, we had our own sleeping car, folding down our seats at night to make a comfortable bed by the window. We made love with the rhythm of the rails clicking underneath us and moonlit fields of wheat and corn whipping by outside our windows. In the dining car, we ate from china plates, enjoying orange juice and Lobster Newburg, which we could not have afforded back home. Mr. Cunningham had paid for our train tickets and every meal on the trains.

We took a thousand copies of our record on tour with us and by the end of the three weeks we had sold them all. The money from ticket sales was ours to spend on cheap hotels, meals in a diner or cafeteria, cab and trolley fare. I insisted on saving as much as we could for Los Angeles, so we lodged and ate very modestly except on the train. Robert wanted more new clothes, but I talked him out of it.

In St. Louis we played at two nightclubs in one night and a bankers' company party the next day. Everyone had heard *Starfish Blues* as sung by Blue Maria and the crowd did not want to hear a man singing it. When Robert began to sing, both men and women booed him. No one had ever booed us before, so we continued to sing and play louder.

"Pipe down, cake boy!"

"Let the piano gal sing it!"

"I can't sing!" I screamed back.

One man flung a beer bottle on the stage and it rolled at my feet, unbroken. Enraged I threw it back at him and he caught it. He actually looked amused. He was a strapping Polish man with his shirt unbuttoned, and sleeves rolled up. He had downy blond hair on his chest and forearms and strength I would never admit I admired.

Robert whispered "What the devil is wrong with these Missouri people?"

I yelled "You asked for it, jackass!"

I began the song again, pounding the piano and singing my heart out. Robert just stood back, admiring me and beaming. I ended the song by rolling my fingers up and down the keys. The whole crowd was cheering, and they kept cheering when Robert sang, and shouting out requests. The big man introduced himself as Karlo Doperialski and bought us a pitcher of beer.

"You have a good woman here," he said to Robert.

In Kansas City we were the opening act for a fifteen-piece band at a club on Vine Street. We tried to dance but could hardly keep up with the stomping and kicking of the other dancers. We went into three different clubs, drinking gin and whiskey. Every place had a band and there were many brilliant black musicians. The next morning I sent Iris a postcard saying that she must come out here some day. I sent every one of my family members and friends at least one picture postcard, knowing that I would crave their letters once we settled in Los Angeles.

As we rode through Colorado, I was overjoyed to see the blue peaks of the Rocky Mountains after the long flat monotony of the Great Plains. We played at a wedding reception for a city councilman's daughter, and the next night at an Italian nightclub. Robert mentioned that we were newlyweds and the owners gave us a bottle of pink champagne. There were over two hundred people singing and dancing and more flooded in every minute, parking their cars all over the front lawn.

"Aren't they at all afraid of the police?" I asked.

Robert pointed to an off-duty policeman in the corner, chatting amiably with the owner's wife, with a gin rickey shining as brightly as his badge.

"I feel safer knowing he's here, don't you?" said Robert.

It shouldn't have astonished me that every city we visited had its gin mills and cops and politicians who either turned a blind eye or profited from the night spots themselves. Robert and I had expected every kind of corruption in Chicago and St. Louis and Kansas City, but as our train wound its way west, through the rolling hills of Utah, we began to feel uneasy. We had bought bottles of gin and whiskey at the Denver nightclub, fearing that we might finally be entering a truly dry state.

The sugar-white Mormon Temple, the dome of the Utah's gray marble Capitol Building and the stone lions and beehives on Brigham Young's houses were stately and mysterious. The Temple was unlike any Catholic bell tower or Baptist steeple I had ever seen; it looked ancient and Biblical. The shady porches, quiet Zion mercantile shops and the blond children walking Salt Lake City's spotless streets all seemed too clean to be real in the middle of the desert. The brownstone buildings looked whitewashed and we wondered what lay underneath.

"The state motto is 'Industry'," I observed. "You have to admire the Mormons' hard work, building all of this in such an arid place."

"I don't have to admire anything about blind faith and hypocrisy!" Robert snapped.

"Thank God you're not so hard on Catholicism," I said.

"The Catholic Church committed atrocities in the Crusades and the Inquisition, but they never attempted anything so stupid as Prohibition. I cannot love any church that would condemn dancing in the street like King David or drinking wine among friends like Jesus."

"Some people don't need to drink to be happy, and they do love music or else we wouldn't be here."

We played at a private garden party; I loved the sweet peas, hollyhocks and the native sunflowers that waved and smiled even in sandy soil. At the party, a young man who had been expecting us invited us to a speakeasy in the basement of a house far out in the desert.

We rode in his truck over miles of crackling gravel and dirt roads. He pointed out that the trees among the sagebrush were junipers, fragrant evergreens that thrived in the hot dry weather. The moon hung low in the sky, golden as a ripe peach. A whitewashed farmhouse with a weather-beaten gray barn loomed in the distance. I counted twenty cars and trucks parked all around it. This was the place.

Our driver introduced us to his mother, Mrs. Tate, who operated the speakeasy. Her husband was in jail for brewing his own beer and gin, but now bootlegging was the only way for his wife and eight children to support themselves until his release. Her two oldest sons were bouncers at the door, three of her daughters were barmaids and her school-age children wiped tables and washed glasses.

"We've paid the ten percent tithe all our lives," Mrs. Tate says. "But the Mormon church won't give me a dime now and my own family shuns me."

"I know what you mean," said Robert, proceeding to tell her all about his parents misunderstanding his musical vocation.

Nothing Robert had ever felt could compare to living in the desert with eight children aged twenty to six, brewing beer in the cellar and gin in the attic. Robert and I depended on the goodwill of our audiences, but that was nothing like opening your own home to dozens of desperate drunken men and a few jaded women every single night. Mrs. Tate made the best of it, kissing her children and sending the little ones up to bed. She gave us a free pitcher of amber beer and we toasted her with gin fizzes. She shooed everyone else out of her home at two in the morning, but invited us to stay in her guest bedroom. The next morning, we weren't too hungry for breakfast, but she gave us a bag of cherries and some peach turnovers to eat later. Mrs. Tate drove us to the train station herself.

We were glad to leave the gray sagebrush of Utah for the golden hills and cypress trees of California. I shrieked when I saw my first palm tree outside the train window. Before that I had only seen them in books.

In San Jose we played in a nightclub with a Spanish tile roof to an audience of fruit farmers and railroad men. The bartender gave us a bottle of Napa Valley zinfandel and a cabernet from Sonoma. I went to mass which was crowded with Mexican ladies in mantillas and white women with broad-brimmed hats. The church was sweltering hot and the ladies' bright fans moved like hundreds of butterflies. Robert bought bread and cheese and grapes at a farmers' market and we wandered the quiet streets of Mission-style buildings.

Of all the cities we visited, I loved San Francisco the best. I loved the Victorian gingerbread houses and the fog rolling off the Bay in the morning. Robert and I walked along the Embarcadero watching sailboats and ate sweet and sour prawns in Chinatown. The afternoons were sunny but mild as we rode a trolley up the impossibly steep hills and checked into a seedy hotel in the Tenderloin.

We played at a college party in Berkeley and students lined up for autographs. Girls begged to dance with Robert while I played. I nodded to him and smiled, feeling proud of him and amused to see the girls blush and giggle. I had Robert now; there was no need to be jealous. An hour later I would pounce on him in our shabby hotel room and make the bedsprings beg for mercy.

I was sorry to leave San Francisco but excited to go to Los Angeles. The sizzling asphalt of the studio lot seemed like a mirage. I remembered Dad reading me the Greek myth of the ivory and horn gates of Hades where true and false dreams departed into the world of the living. When our train entered Los Angeles, I told Robert that we were entering the gate of dreams. He laughed and clutched my hand nervously.

Mr. Cunningham had found me a job playing music for a silent movie called *Twilight;* our *Twilight Melodies* was named after it. I would play piano and organ on the sound stage in the morning and have all afternoon to watch the actors and actresses. On my first day in the studio, I watched the cast and crew for three hours. There were dozens of takes before the director even let the film roll and he barked directions at the actors constantly. During a break, I held out my hand to introduce myself and he walked right past me. It was strange to hear actors and actresses speaking their lines aloud, after watching silent pictures all my life. The sound men gossiped about the next innovation in film; next year there would be movies with actors speaking their lines aloud.

"It will change everything."

"No audience will watch Clara Bow when they hear her Brooklyn accent."

Robert had been out all day looking for our next home, and when he came to get me at seven o' clock that evening, he had found one. He hailed a cab and held his hands over my eyes as we neared our destination. When he let me take a look, I saw a beautiful white bungalow with green trim and a red brick porch. There was no upstairs or cellar, just a kitchen, bathroom, living room and bedroom, with large closets in the bedroom and hall. We lay down between two cotton sheets with an electric fan on to keep us cool.

"An apartment would have been cheaper," I said.

"Yes, and hotter and full of cockroaches. I know we'll be happy here."

CHAPTER TWENTY-FIVE

It felt bizarre to wake up in the morning smelling the ocean, to hear the wind rustling the palm trees, to step out behind our bungalow and pick avocados, oranges and grapefruit for breakfast. The "back yard" was a narrow patch of scratchy yellow grass where I grew my potted geraniums and marigolds. The bluebells and bleeding heart I planted withered in the hot dry ground, no matter how carefully I watered them.

The heat was a shock to me too. I dried my hair in front of the electric fan and pointed it toward me while I cooked and washed our dishes. Robert and I took lukewarm showers and lukewarm baths, sometimes together, washing each other with lemon-scented soap and rosewater. I powdered myself with talcum powder until I looked like a sugar doughnut, but during a long day at the studio, I sweat so much that I had to bathe again when I got home.

Robert said it was a waste to bathe twice a day, but I refused to take criticism from a man who spent half an hour shaving his face with a badger brush, bay rum and a steamed towel. Despite the heat, Robert slicked his hair with copious amounts of pomade. A mosquito once flew into Robert's hair and perished.

We bought our furniture second-hand, one piece at a time, first a mattress, then two basket chairs, then a table, then bookshelves. I did not want to spend much on furnishing the house; I knew from the beginning that I did not want to settle in Los Angeles. We could not afford a piano; it was the first time in my life when I had not had a piano at home. When I came home, my hands and wrists were exhausted from playing piano and organ all day long, but I still missed playing my favorite songs at home. I tried to listen to more records, write more letters home, cook and bake and keep our little house spotless.

Robert had purchased a second-hand coupe with most of my first paycheck. He refused to ride streetcars with Mexican laborers and barefoot boys on the running board. When I took the streetcar to run errands, he teased me.

"Only the poor take the streetcar in Los Angeles. That might be good enough in Laurel, but I'd be ashamed if Douglas Fairbanks or Clara Bow saw me riding a streetcar."

Robert took me driving out in the desert and was very patient with me when I made mistakes. I usually preferred to let him drive, but if he ever felt tired or drank too much, it was nice to be able to take the wheel.

We did see Clara Bow and Douglas Fairbanks, Myrna Loy and Rudolf Valentino. Star-struck Robert got every one of them to sign the autograph book he always carried. One afternoon, he lit Joan Crawford's cigarette and gloated about it until bedtime. I always felt too embarrassed to ask any actor or actress for their autograph. I might blush and name a film of theirs that I'd loved while Robert insisted that I take out my camera and get a snapshot of him with any star he could put his arm around. He never asked me if I wanted to be in the picture.

Motion pictures seemed a lot less glamorous to me after my sweaty days on the sets. The director shouted at everyone and the actors wore pancake makeup with black eyeliner to emphasize their eyes and brows. They looked like a mockery of King Tut. I played the same songs over and over again until the notes stung my ears and fingers. I wished I could be at home in my shady bedroom where Robert lay sleeping until one every afternoon. He picked me up from the studio with a bottle of ice water in the car, knowing that this work exhausted me more than any night at The Starfish.

I made twice as much money as I had in Laurel, but there were new expenses, higher rent and gas for the car. Robert wanted to buy better furnishings for the house and better clothes, but I preferred to pay all our bills first and split the remaining money between a check to my mother and a savings account. I did indulge Robert sometimes, going out drinking and dancing on my nights off.

He had planned to teach guitar lessons as he had in Laurel, but there were hundreds of musicians already offering lessons and Robert could not attract any pupils. It took him two months to get booked in a club and he went out looking for bookings every afternoon while I worked. I tried to attend all of Robert's performances.

I say "tried" because sometimes I had to work evenings and nights. We filmed five night scenes and I had to be there for all of them, pounding away at the organ while the camera rolled.

I was on camera in one ballroom scene, playing the piano. I wore a black satin gown and the director insisted that I take off my glasses; luckily it was not hard to play *You Forgot to Remember* without my sight. Robert visited the set to watch the scene being filmed and brought me six red roses. The following year, Joseph and Amelia would take all the family to see *Twilight*. Clarice and Harry would shout "Aunt Marlene!" wildly when they caught a split-second glimpse of me.

In addition to playing clubs, Robert did screen tests at MGM and Warner Brothers, but none of them panned out. He found work as a movie extra, cheering in the crowd at a horse race. Robert insisted that I buy him a red and white striped summer jacket so he could be more visible.

"I need to draw as much attention to myself as possible," he explained. "Anything that gets me noticed will help my career. You see this silver cigarette lighter with my monogram on it? R. J. S. I want people to remember that. I don't smoke myself but I'll light a cigarette for an actress or a casting director. Oh yes."

"I don't want you to take up smoking," I said.

"What are you, my doctor?" he asked. "Smoking is harmless and it keeps you thin. You could probably drop a few pounds if you took up smoking."

"No thank you. I'd rather be plump and smell sweet."

I smelled plenty of smoke on the sets and in the studio and at nightclubs when I watched Robert sing. In the heat, I began to favor champagne cocktails and melon and lemon liqueurs as well as my beloved gin and tonics with lime. Robert drank whatever his fellows were having and always managed to get at least one free drink for singing at a club.

After his third solo performance, I asked him "Don't you tell club owners that we did *Twilight Melodies* together and that I can perform with you?"

"I always say that, Marlene. Most of them have never heard of it and the few who have say 'So what?' I have a better chance of playing a club if I meet their house band or the club's own pianist and they recommend me to the owner."

Although Robert and I delighted in each other's company and encouraged each other in everything, I missed performing with him. I was also much more homesick than he was and rushed to the mailbox every day to collect letters from my family and friends.

The first letter I received came from my mother. I sat on the mattress to read it, because we had not yet bought our furniture. My heart pounded as I opened the envelope. As soon as Robert and I had boarded the train out of Laurel, I had written letters to her and all my siblings telling them of my marriage. Hers was the first and most dreaded response.

Dear Marlene,

I was very disappointed to read of your decision to marry Robert Schumann. I feared that you might do something like this in California, but to find out that you married in Laurel and concealed it from your entire family hurts me terribly. If you love Robert and feel proud of him, as you claim, why not have a proper wedding and invite everyone in your family and his? Why couldn't you have waited six months until you both came back from California and then married in the church? You say that Robert is an "agnostic" but that is no excuse.

I know that you have loved Robert since you were a little girl (yes, I always knew) but he is completely unreliable. I am never in favor of divorce, but in your case I wonder if an annulment would be possible, now before you have any children.

You always claimed to want a musical career more than a husband and children. Why this hasty second marriage? If you have a child, you will not be able to play in smoky gin mills every night, much less go on tour.

Robert will go out singing and acting (barely earning enough to sustain a family) and dancing in dark clubs with flappers. Marriage is no guarantee that you will not lose his love to other women, drink and drugs. I know that marihuana and cocaine are common there in California. To drink spirits is dangerous enough; stay the hell away from any other intoxicant and insist that Robert do likewise.

You tell me that Robert is a musical and theatrical genius, like a Mozart or a Shakespeare. Don't you know that three of Mozart's children died from hunger while he drank and took laudanum? Don't you know that Shakespeare left Ann Hathaway and their three children in Stratford when he went to London to make plays? Your father also admired the works of the great artists, but he knew better than to imitate the mistakes of their private lives.

I know that your playing for the motion picture will be a success. I have always been proud of your musical talent and am glad you were able to travel. But I must ask you to come home when your contract expires. Please come home to Laurel without Robert. You don't need him on stage or in your life. You love him painfully now but that pain will diminish when you return to your real home and continue your career without him.

You can be happy without a husband. I have been a widow for five years and I am grateful to God for every day of my life. If you do join your life to someone else, it must be someone completely trustworthy and humble, as well as intelligent and loving. If you must have a man, choose one who will be an anchor and not a snare.

I love you, Marlene, and I say these things out of love and worry, not to condemn you. Please consider what I have said.

All my love and care,

Mother

Joseph and Katrina were also disappointed but less so and their letters were short and infrequent. Helen wrote to me regularly and it comforted me to think of her and Edward living in my house. I packed her first letter in my lunchbox between the tuna salad sandwich and the orange and celery. I read it in the shadow of a storefront set, on lunch break, ignoring the director's demands for soda water and the smoking and cursing of the camera men.

Dear Marlene,

I sit here in the living room with a sweater on even though it's August. Your house is always cool. At first I thought this was because the neighbors' chestnut trees shade it, but now I wonder if there is water underneath the cellar or some other source of the chill. The back bedroom upstairs is so cold that I do my ironing up there to stay cool. I'm not comfortable sleeping there, though, and neither is Edward. We have put our new bed in your room upstairs and moved your bed and things to the back bed room. Of course we can change all that when you return, if you want.

Edward and I both want to thank you again for letting us stay here. I love the gas stove and big icebox. On Sunday of course we go to Mother's house or the Hayden farm. Edward teases me about my "bride's cooking" and yes my last peach pie was a little damp, but I can make better mulligan stew and roast chicken than anyone, and Edward always devours all the leftovers from my meals.

You asked what I do in my spare time. I still sew a lot and have made a yellow daisy print dress for Florence and sailor suits for Harry and Eugene. I still make silk handkerchiefs and gloves and have begun to sew silk flowers to attach to handbags, hats, and clothes.

I admire Florence and Harry more and more (not so much Eugene) and feel that I am ready to be a mother too. I look forward to leaving Stolzfus, to a time when my arms don't ache at the end of the day. I imagine what I will say to Schwichtenberg before I leave. "I'm going home to my husband, you old toad, and I won't be back again. Take one last look at my gams while I'm walking away!"

I hope that you're enjoying your work at the studio and your avocados and oranges. That's great that Robert got Rudolph Valentino's autograph. Ruby made me watch "The Sheik" six times in the theater when it came out and we still think he's the most handsome actor ever.

I understand how you feel about Robert. I was sorry that you didn't ask me to attend your wedding because I would have, no matter what anyone in the family says. You must follow your heart and I will never think less of you for doing so. I miss you very much.

Your Loving Sister,

Helen

I got only one letter from Al Vintner while I was in California, but it told me all I needed to know about the goings-on in The Starfish. I missed The Starfish Seven badly. Everyone on the film crew was nice and the piano and organ were the finest instruments I ever touched, but I missed the friendship of playing with my band. Al's letter smelled of him, like lime and bay rum and I kept it in my underwear drawer to preserve the scent. He had enclosed a small snapshot of his head and shoulders with a glowing starfish in the background. On lonely nights when Robert played at clubs and I stayed home, I would stare at Al's picture and re-read his words, remembering his wise guy voice.

Dear Marlene,

Emmett took this picture of me on a slow night here. I want you to ponder it until you feel good and homesick.

Marco mentioned to me that you married Robert Schumann. He's a lucky man. I hope that you will tour for at least a few more years before settling down to raise a family. Los Angeles is a hard town and I'm glad you don't have to face directors, critics, and club owners alone.

Three of The Starfish Seven have also tied the knot this year. Frank Caprello married Sophia Zuchetto, a sultry beauty who had been sneaking out of her parents' house every night to hear him play trombone. Mrs. Zuchetto caught Frank walking Sophia home at five o'clock in the morning. She ambushed the two of them in the alley behind her house and told Frank if he didn't marry her daughter she'd tell Mr. Zuchetto and he'd bust Frank's head like a melon. Frank fell to his knees right then and asked Sophia to marry him Their wedding was in September and they both are very happy.

Howard Davis married Emily Jackson, a childhood friend of his. Emily is a teetotaler and a good Baptist. The only drink at their wedding reception was lemonade and I just about upchucked. Luckily, Emily has no objection to Howard playing in The Starfish Seven because the pay is excellent. Her parents only approve of gospel music but apparently they believe that Emily will "save" Howard.

Iris was not asked to be a bridesmaid and was very put out. I told her to quit moping and choose one of her many suitors. She seems to lose interest in any man in her life after three months or less. Lately she's looking as gloomy as Aaron Bauer, but they play as well as ever, so I can't complain.

Oliver Untermeyer surprised everyone by marrying Elaine Schumann (nee' Hartsell) in October. She'd never been to The Starfish until he brought her in one evening and introduced her as his bride. Oliver had known her when they were kids but hadn't spoken to her in years. He went to fix a clogged U-pipe under the sink at her parents' house and took Elaine dancing at Rocky Springs that night. You have probably already heard all about that from Robert.

Charlotte, Ralph and Henry all take turns playing with the band, but the audience agrees that no one could ever replace you. You are welcome to come back to The Starfish any time if you get fed up with L.A.

The hardware business is going swimmingly and I have opened a second Vintner's Hardware out on East Peach Street, next to Neptune's Diner. Dennis and Zach will be manager and assistant manager respectively. Should you ever desire a day job, I could certainly use a secretary to get my affairs in order.

Don't take any wooden nickels,

Al Vintner

Amelia wrote to me only once. She did not answer the letters I wrote to her and I thought she must be angry about my marrying Robert. I called my family on the telephone on Sunday mornings, when I knew they would all be at Mother's and Amelia sounded happy enough to speak to me, but she never did bare her soul over the telephone.

"I meant to write, but I've been so busy," she reassured me. "Of course I'm not angry at you."

Amelia's letter came on a rainy day in November. The palm trees whipped in the wind outside and thunder and lightning slashed the skies. It was the kind of storm Amelia, Joseph and I used to watch from the porch, thrilled but never frightened like Brendan and Helen.

Dear Marlene,

I have not shared this news with anyone but Arthur, but I want to tell you now. I am pregnant again. Arthur and I had been taking precautions, but as I warned you, both prophylactics and diaphragms can slip and fail. I hate to think of this as a failure or an accident, but it is a surprise to me.

I had hoped to go back to work three nights a week now that Florence is toilet-trained and sleeping through the night. I want to be excited about this child, who I know I will love dearly but I also miss my work at the hospital.

Mother cannot understand how I can miss being up all night, giving shots and emptying bed pans, listening to old people's aches and pains and helping screaming women with breech births, but I never ever tired of it. I felt so smart and strong and capable, and I don't feel that way while taking care of my own child. My work for patients was a respected profession; my motherhood is a duty and is taken for granted. I love Florence but I miss the company of the other nurses and doctors. I miss working beside Arthur which may never be possible again if I always have to be at home with the children.

Arthur says that I should enjoy my time away from work as much as I can, that I can always return to it when our children are in school. Katrina says she misses the company but not the work. I think that nursing always reminded her of the Great War, even in happy times like delivering a baby or taking a cast off a broken leg. She approaches her work with devotion but not with enthusiasm. Old nurses used to tell me that I would "get sick of sick people" but it never happened, not in my four years as a hospital volunteer and student or my four years as a nurse.

Enough of my rambling! How is Los Angeles? What are the studio and sound stage like? Can you get copies of the soundtrack from the movie? Are you and Robert playing in any good clubs?

I miss you very much but I know that you always wanted to leave Laurel and chase your dreams.

Your big sister,

Amelia

P.S. I like the name Brigid for a girl or Brian for a boy.

Thanksgiving left me empty, though I tried to be thankful for my husband, my career and my house. I filled a small turkey with cranberry walnut stuffing, candied the sweet potatoes and sliced almonds into the green beans. My pumpkin pie had a crack down the middle, not a smooth orange surface like my mother's pies. Robert sympathized; he took me out dancing, then drove us up into the dry hills to look at the Hollywoodland sign. Robert covered us with a blanket in the backseat and pressed his heat against my cool skin. He gave me ecstasy but not peace.

"I don't know if I can be happy here," I said. "Even if you do get more roles and I do get to play more movie soundtracks. I love you so much, but I miss home."

"How can you call Laurel home?" he asked. "When you were there all you ever wanted to do was get out and now you want to go back? Women are never satisfied."

CHAPTER TWENTY-SIX

Robert and I performed together only once in Los Angeles. It was a New Year's Eve party at a nightclub called The Flamingo. I'd invited the sound crew and everyone I knew on the set. Many of them were single and had come to Los Angeles from far away, so they had no family with them to celebrate the holiday. Unlike the cast and the directors and managers, none of us had invitations to glittering parties. Robert and I had spent Christmas alone with a wreath I made of holly and ivy. I gave him a new hat and shoes and he gave me some new sheet music.

Robert and I signed autographs and sold some albums. We played all our *Twilight Melodies* and many Christmas carols. The audience had guzzled a lot of egg nog and rum punch, so they sang along.

Robert whispered "There's something tragic about a room full of drunks singing *O Come All Ye Faithful.*"

I had to agree.

The club manager, Mr. Conroy, was a seedy-looking man of about sixty with a cheap maroon suit and sparse gray hair. He sat between us as we took a break and put his arm around Robert. He squeezed my knee under the table where Robert couldn't see it. Like a reflex, I kicked Conroy in the shin. He removed his hand and continued to grin like a baboon.

"You Schumanns make great music but you need to work on your image. Doll, you'd look a lot better onstage if you took off those granny specs. No one wants to see a woman with glasses."

Mr. Conroy reached up and took my glasses off, but I snatched them back. He smelled like musty cologne, rum and halitosis. He continued to wave his hand as if he had delusions of philosophy.

"Yeah, that's much better. No glasses, maybe a permanent wave in your hair."

"I can't read the music without my glasses."

"You might do something with your hair," Robert said.

"If you kids want to make it in L.A., you shouldn't neglect your appearance. First impressions are everything here. I know all the directors, De Mille, Griffith..."

"We've already made an album and toured seven cities," I argued. "People buy my album to hear me play, not to gape at my face."

"Well, your face ain't your biggest attraction anyway, but if you don't think men stare at your boobs while you're onstage, you're an idiot. When people pay money to see a broad, they expect her to be gorgeous and any fool can play the piano. You two want to be in pictures, don't you?"

I couldn't believe that Robert didn't leap to my defense, but he stared at Mr. Conroy, as passive as a child.

"We're already in pictures, Conroy," I said through clenched teeth. "How many have you been in? Why don't get up onstage and play us a song, since any fool can play the piano?"

"Marlene, don't scold the man," said Robert. "You embarrass me."

Mr. Conroy stood up and Robert followed him.

"I want you to sing a few songs with my Loretta," said Conroy. "She's the blonde at the bar with terrific legs. She's my niece."

He put his arm around Robert and steered him toward the bar. Robert shook hands with Loretta, a slim little flapper of about sixteen. She wore a gold beaded dress that kept sliding off her shoulders and a red poinsettia in her hair. Loretta nodded and smiled like a wind-up toy at everything Mr. Conroy said as he ran his thick red hand up her delicate arm. I hoped she wasn't really his niece.

"What the hell are you doing?" I asked Robert.

He scowled. "I'm trying to make us some money, Marlene. If you can't help, then stay out of my way."

I watched, disgusted, as Robert played three songs with Loretta. She hit wrong notes and played too fast. She smiled at the audience and they cheered and whistled.

I didn't want to argue with Robert in public or to waste any more of my New Year's Eve. I'd be happier at home listening to records or reading a book. On my way out, a few people complimented me on my playing and shook my hand, but my heart felt heavy. I hailed a taxi and watched fireworks bloom like gold chrysanthemums in the sky as I rode home.

I took a hot bath with lavender bath salts, but still could not sleep. I drank chamomile tea with warm milk and even prayed the rosary. Was this really the first hour of 1928? It had been New Year 1927 when Joseph, Katrina and I stumbled out of The Starfish and found Robert puking in the snow. The last twelve months had been triumphant. I had married the man I loved, recorded, toured and left Laurel behind. A year ago I could not have dreamed all that, but now who did I have to share this hour with?

If anything Robert was more dissatisfied in Los Angeles than he had been in Laurel. Here stardom and wealth were all around him, tantalizing, but no easier to grasp than in Pennsylvania. I wanted to believe that this was just one awful night, and that Robert loved and respected me too much to consider finding another accompanist. Why had he paid more attention to a vile-smelling old man we just met than to his own wife? Was Robert jealous of my success? If he did get into movies like he wanted would I be sitting here alone every night or worse, in some smoky club watching him flirt with other women and court the audience as he had once courted me? If we had a baby, would I be trapped at home alone in this strange city? I had expected exciting parties and crowds of musical friends, but none of that had materialized.

At four in the morning, Robert finally came home. I was lying in bed in the dark, wide awake. I lay on my side and did not roll over when he undressed and lay down beside me.

"I missed you," I whispered. "I wanted to kiss you at midnight."

"Why did you leave?" he said. "You shouldn't have run off like that without telling me you were going. Why are you so damn jealous? I don't care anything about Loretta, but she's a looker and I need to make a good impression."

"My music makes a good impression. Our album made a good impression. Why would you kick me off the stage just because some fetid old man wants you to play with his girlfriend? Why?"

Robert was silent for a minute. We lay on our sides with him facing away from me.

Finally he said "I need some success of my own, Marlene. You've recorded two albums, toured across the country and played a soundtrack for a movie. You're in a picture. If you died tomorrow, people would still remember your music and love you for it. Whatever happens next, you are a success."

I clutched his shoulder until he rolled onto his back. I turned on the bedside lamp and put my glasses on, so we could see each other as we spoke.

"You're a success too, Robert. You've done everything I've done except the first album and you've been in plays and a movie."

"No one remembers the plays, Marlene. I didn't make it in New York and in Hollywood I'm just a face in the crowd. I'm an extra in a movie; that means nothing. Any musical success I've had has been because of you and my acting has gone nowhere."

I wrapped my arms around him and he nestled his head between my breasts. I slid off my nightgown to comfort him with my soft skin.

"Men like Conroy have no talent," I said. "They envy and exploit people like you and me. That's why he told me I was too ugly to be onstage and that's why he wanted to push you around. We have youth and beauty and talent and he has none of that. Don't sink to his level, Robert."

I felt Robert's hot tears on my breast.

"Marlene, I'm so sorry I disappointed you. You mean more to me than anyone in the world. You believed in me when no one else did."

"I want to leave Los Angeles," I said.

"Me too."

Two days later we received a letter thanking me for my work on the picture and telling me that the studio would not renew my contract. My last paycheck was enclosed.

Robert and I sold or pawned everything we owned except for a few clothes, books, music and his guitar, the items we could carry with us on the train. I gave my potted plants to our neighbors. When we left the house I walked through every room to say goodbye to it. I stroked the trunks of the avocado, grapefruit and orange trees, the only live and lasting things from our home there. Robert had sold our car, so we went to the train station the way we came, on a streetcar. I took a last look at the Hollywoodland sign, but Robert refused to look back.

CHAPTER TWENTY-SEVEN

The trip home from Los Angeles was sweaty, humid and squalid. There was no glamour, no garden parties or champagne. This time we had no tour plan and searched desperately for places to play in every town we stopped in. On the train, we could not even afford bunks to sleep in. Robert slept on my bosom and I laid my head against the rattling window. No matter how much I shifted my arms and legs and neck, cramps chewed on my muscles and I woke up aching every morning.

We rode south and west, stopping only a few times to find places to play and raise enough money for food and the cheapest hotel rooms we could find.

"What a pity I can't play my piano on the street," I said.

"We're not beggars," said Robert. "I won't put my hat on the sidewalk no matter what happens."

We played in a smoky speakeasy in San Diego, another in Santa Fe and a third in Austin. Mexicans, tan-faced farmers, Navajo Indians and cowboys came to see us in Santa Fe. The Mexicans made me play all our songs a second time while Pilar, the house chanteuse, sang the lyrics in Spanish. I saw old mission churches and bought tamales at Mexican farmers' markets. Robert drank beer to cool himself, but I only craved water. The cacti of New Mexico and Arizona lifted up their arms like martyrs crowned with blood-colored fruits.

My mind waved in the heat like the broad flat deserts of Texas. Cowboys, college boys, Mexican farm hands and big-bellied ranchers screamed out requests for songs I didn't know. A banjo player with a gray handlebar moustache accompanied us and sang any song we didn't know, old cowboy songs and some from Kentucky and Tennessee.

In these towns at least Robert and I could stretch out on cheap hotel beds under whirring ceiling fans. No matter how desperate we were, Robert's body comforted me and I wanted to be alone with him as often as possible. In Austin, Robert told me it was too hot to make love, but I got a key to the hotel bathroom and pulled him into a cool shower.

"Imagine it's a waterfall," I said. "Imagine that you were lost in the desert and wandered for days and nights, near dying from thirst and hunger until you came to a narrow valley where the water pours down.

There are cactus fruits all over, with white and yellow and pink flowers. And you find me standing here in this waterfall."

We licked the water off each others' skins and shampooed each other's hair, frolicking until the manager began to pound on the door. We raced out, wrapped in towels and carrying our clothes.

"I run a respectable place here!" shouted the manager.

"We're married," said Robert. "We have a license for this sort of thing!"

The only pure joy of our trip east was Mardi Gras in New Orleans. I had planned our itinerary with the intention of going there and staying there for three days. We played at two different restaurants and wandered the streets, eating beignets and café au lait for breakfast and oyster po'boys and ham and olive muffaletta for lunch. We got free meals from restaurants we played in, crawfish remoulade, jambalaya and Oysters Rockefeller. I loved sucking the crawfish but Robert was squeamish about them.

We went to St. Louis Church, the old Ursuline Convent, and Napoleon House, which the Creoles had built in a vain attempt to attract Napoleon Bonaparte. I walked in the old cemeteries and watched families lay flowers before their ancestral crypts, knowing they would have a place there. Robert found the graveyards morbid, with the bodies above the soggy ground, and so many victims of yellow fever epidemics. I found a strange comfort in the closeness of the living and the dead.

"I feel scared of my own death, mostly because I fear hell," I said. "But I don't fear dead people in general and I couldn't fear my own departed relatives. Love is stronger than death and it's good that people here visit their family tombs."

"When you visit my grave, bring me a white rose and a bottle of whiskey," said Robert solemnly.

I could have argued with him and said (honestly) that I didn't know for sure that he would die before me and that I didn't want to imagine losing him. Instead I only said "I promise."

Parades passed by day and night, throwing hard candy and strings of beads. I gathered up beads of every color of the rainbow as souvenirs. With their white horses and red velvet masks the krewe men resembled the Knights Templar. Music poured out of every doorway: jazz organ, trombone, Cajun guitar and fiddle. Bands marched down the streets with brass and drums. At night the marchers carried torches. People of all ages, black and white, wore costumes; pirates, fairies, devils and saints surrounded us on all sides. The black people outnumbered the whites here.

New Orleans had dozens of speakeasies but the black jazz musicians here far surpassed us, so we played in white restaurants by day and drank in clubs at night. One bartender gave us Ramos gin fizzes, frothy orange water drinks which were "a sure-fire hangover cure". Robert and I danced until well after midnight, with each other and with other partners.

In the wee hours of the morning, we pounded on the door of a cheap hotel (a yellow brick house that must have been at least 100 years old) until the night clerk opened the door. He led us up three flights of stairs to a narrow room with a double bed and long screen window with open shutters.

We were footsore and sweaty, but full of oysters and rum. We peeled off each other's clothes like orange rinds and writhed on the sagging mattress. Robert held my hands down and kissed me so hard that our lips were bruised. I rolled on top of him and the mattress squeaked. Someone pounded on the floor below us, but we ignored it. At last we collapsed, satisfied, and slept in each other's arms. As I drifted out of consciousness, I dimly remembered that I had not put in my diaphragm.

That night I dreamed a strange dream. My father sat under a black walnut tree, alive and healthy. His eyes were bright behind his glasses and he smoked his corncob pipe. I approached him slowly, but he didn't notice me. He kept calling out to someone on his right "Bring them to me, Eva! Bring me the nuts!"

A beautiful little girl, about four years old, ran toward him. She had curly dark brown hair, bare feet and a pale blue summer dress. Her skirt was full of black walnuts and she gathered more ripe green pods that had fallen on the ground. Dad was teaching her to steal black walnuts off the neighbors' lawn, like he taught me and all his children. When he finally looked up at me, he said what he always said about it.

"We're just sampling the nuts, Marlene. Don't tell your mother; she might not understand."

"I miss you, Dad," I said. "Mother misses you."

"I miss my Aileen," he said, patting the grass beside him, inviting me to sit, which I did.

Eva dumped the walnuts from her skirt into his lap. My eyes met hers, which were dark brown, bright and sweet. She reached her little hands toward mine, but we did not touch. I recognized her oval face, pointed chin and high cheekbones. Eva was a Piper child, my father's granddaughter.

"You're my girl," I said.

She smiled and sat on the other side of Dad. I wanted to hold her, but I knew I wasn't supposed to touch her yet.

"I love you, Dad," I said. "Are you in Heaven?"

"Where do you think we are right now?" he said.

I noticed then that we were in a field with many trees and flowers and no fences, not in Laurel as it had first appeared to me. The sky was blue, gold and yellow like a sunset, but the sun, moon and stars were all visible at once.

"I don't belong here," I said sadly.

Dad took my hand and held it.

"I love you Marlene," he said. "When you wake up, I won't be with you, but Eva will."

I woke up before Robert and folded and packed our clothes. I had to jostle him awake and we rushed to the train station. My dream did not evaporate like normal dreams; it was tattooed into my memory. I wanted to tell Robert what I saw and heard and what I believed it meant, but I hesitated. He might not share my hopes.

He ran from the streetcar into the station, yelling back over his shoulder:

"Shake a leg, Marlene! You can run faster than that!"

We played in an Atlanta club to an audience of college kids, bankers and cotton farmers. The men smoked Cuban cigars and offered Robert whiskey and corn liquor. I didn't drink anything but water; the smell of whiskey made me almost sick.

In Charleston, South Carolina, I insisted on staying for three days. I was surprised by the antique beauty of its narrow cobblestone streets and the yellow and pink houses and palms near Battery Park. We bought fruit and vegetables at the City Market and felt a ghostly chill as we passed the Old Slave Market, though the day was sunny. We played twice at a club with a Confederate flag on the wall.

"Don't these folks know we won the war?" I whispered to Robert.

"Do NOT mention the war, Marlene!" he hissed. "You sure are crabby when you're sober. Why don't you try some of this good bourbon? It tastes like smoke and oak and heaven."

"No, thank you. I'm not much for whiskey."

"I'll get you your usual gin if you insist on it."

"No, thank you. I'd like some orange juice or pineapple if they have it."

"Pineapple? Are you insane?"

"I see one there by the bar. They're a symbol of Southern hospitality."

"We cannot afford pineapple, Marlene. You always eat the most bizarre food you can find. It's embarrassing."

"I'll ask if you want."

The bartender, a sweet old man with a gray handlebar moustache, sliced the pineapple and passed it out to all the patrons, serving me a tall glass of its juice.

"How much?" I asked.

"Not a penny!" he said. "Sweets to the sweet, darlin'. I bet you never drank anything so sweet up in Pennsylvania."

"No, sir," I said, licking my lips.

In Baltimore I laid a white rose on Edgar Allan Poe's grave and ate blue crabs. We could not find a place to play, so we had to take the next train to Washington, D.C. We saw all the monuments and little else, again finding no place to play and sleeping on our departing train.

Exhausted, we reached Laurel early in the morning. No one was expecting us; we had not known for certain which day we would arrive. We caught a cab home and dragged our suitcases up the front steps. Helen and Edward were asleep upstairs and I didn't want to wake them.

"I don't want to sleep up in that cold back room," I said.

We collapsed on the sofa and lay spooned on our sides, not stirring for hours. Soon I would be back at The Starfish. I had seen the palm trees of California, caught the beads from Mardi Gras and tasted pineapple in Charleston. For now, being home was enough.

CHAPTER TWENTY-EIGHT

From Ash Wednesday on, I felt certain I was pregnant, but put off telling anyone. Because my first pregnancy ended in miscarriage, I was afraid of losing this baby. Because Robert had left Los Angeles feeling defeated, I did not know if he would welcome a child or worry that he could not support a baby.

His parents barely acknowledged his efforts to make a career for himself in California. Robert told them all the high and low points of our months there over dinner at the Schumann house. While we were away, he had written only three letters to his mother. Her frequent letters, addressed to him and me, detailed the Schumanns' daily life and Elaine's marriage, but did not comment on anything Robert did. At dinner, Mr. Schumann said nothing about *Twilight Melodies* or Robert's movie scenes.

"I don't care for motion pictures," said Mrs. Schumann. "They make me seasick."

Robert left their house with his teeth clenched in rage, pulling me along by the hand.

It was different at the Untermeyer house on Cherry Street, where Lance and Gwen rushed out to wrap themselves around our legs and hug us like pythons. Elaine and Oliver asked us about every place we'd been and all about the movies. Elaine complained that Gwen demanded that they play our record every day, and Lance bragged that his aunt and uncle were movie stars.

"I wonder what it would take for Mother and Father to see my picture," Robert said, with his chin in his hand. "Maybe if I paid them a hundred dollars and bought the tickets."

"Mama loves your music," Elaine said. "She just wishes you had a steady job. Papa just isn't artistic; you can't blame him for it."

"It kills me," said Robert. "Even if I was a movie star, nothing I did would impress my own parents."

Helen and Edward were happy to see Robert and me. They gave me my old room upstairs and moved into the chilly back bedroom without any complaints. They were still saving money for a down payment on their house and I saw no reason to ask them to move out yet.

I visited Amelia and Arthur, Joseph and Katrina without Robert. Joseph still disapproved of my marriage and changed the subject when I mentioned Robert's acting and singing. Katrina had bought *Twilight Melodies,* but Joseph would not listen to Robert's singing; he asked Katrina to only play the album while he was at work. Amelia welcomed Robert, but she and Arthur bored and disgusted him (without meaning to) by discussing infected sores and German measles at the dinner table.

Robert was able to give lessons to six pupils, but still earned only half as much as I did. We never spoke about this, but I knew it upset him to ask me for money for new clothes and shoes, to give all his earnings to me as soon as he got paid. He went to New York to audition for plays, staying with actor friends of his.

On Sundays I went to mass with Helen and Edward, leaving Robert in bed alone. I would ask him, each time, to meet us at Mother's house for dinner, but he rarely came. Mother would send me home with a Dutch oven full of leftovers "for your heathen husband". Everyone else laughed at that, but she didn't sound like she was joking. Robert would claim that he had overslept or had a stomachache, that no one wanted to see him there anyway.

"You have to win their trust by being there on Sunday. You don't have to go to church, but be there for dinner with the family. Offer to help clean Mother's gutters or play ball with Harry in the yard. They won't say anything mean to you. It looks awful when I show up alone."

The first time Robert came with me for Sunday dinner at Mother's house was St. Patrick's Day. We ate corned beef, cabbage and potatoes, barm brack and bread pudding with raisins and caramel sauce.

In high spirits, everyone gathered around the piano after supper to sing every Irish song we knew. I played *Cockles and Mussels*, *The Foggy Dew*, and *The Wild Rover*. Helen sang *Danny Boy* in English and Mother sang it in Gaelic. Joseph played his trombone and Amelia played her flute; Harry played his harmonica. It was rare for them to perform with their instruments and even rarer for Mother to sing for an audience, but it was our tradition. She sang *Love Is Pleasing* so sadly and sweetly; each note struck me in the heart:

I wish, I wish, I wish in vain.
I wish I were a maid again,
But a maid again I can never be
Till the apples grow on an ivy tree.

I left me father, I left me mother
I left all me sisters and brothers too,
I left all me friends and me own relations,
I left them all for to follow you.

But the sweetest apple is the soonest rotten
And the hottest love is the soonest cold
And what can't be cured love has to be endured love
And now I am bound for Americay.
Oh love is pleasing and love is teasing
And love is a pleasure when first love is new
But as it grows older, sure love grows colder
And it fades away like the morning dew.

And love and porter makes a young man older,
And love and whiskey makes him old and gray,
And what can't be cured love has to be endured love,
And now I am bound for Americay.

I had always felt very sentimental about that song, and happy when Mother sang it. After all, she fell in love with my father, and came to America to marry him and have us children. Her life had some secret sorrow, but surely she got her happy ending. This year I understood the words as if hearing them for the first time. Now I knew what it was to miss my family and what it was to love a man who drank and raged and a man who despaired and turned cold. How many times had my mother longed for her dead mother, for her sister Sheila and her brothers Daniel and Gabriel? Her father had been harsh with her and drank heavily after her mother died; she had only hinted to us at how much she had suffered. I wanted Mother to tell me everything about her life and she never would. Tears cascaded down my face. Robert looked embarrassed and whipped out a clean handkerchief for my eyes.

Mother was cordial to Robert and wished him luck with his auditions.

"Don't feel too downcast about leaving Hollywood," she said. "You can act on Broadway and make music anywhere. I don't care where you tour as long as you always bring Marlene home to us."

"Yes, ma'am, I promise I will," he said, shaking her hand.

I thought about giving everyone my happy news then, but I held off.

That night at The Starfish Al gave The Starfish Seven a bottle of Irish whiskey and ordered us to drink a shot whether we were Irish or not. Robert asked for a shot and Howard scowled at him. I gave Robert my shot glass.

"What are you doing, Marlene?" he asked. "You're the only Irish one in the band."

"No, thank you. I told you I gave up drinking for Lent."

"But it's bad luck not to drink on St. Patrick's Day," he said.

"Come here."

I drew him into the restroom and locked the door. He looked worried.

"Are you sick?"

"Robert, I'm pregnant."

"Are you sure?"

"Yes. I felt sure at Mardi Gras, but I waited. I'm two weeks late."

He put his hands on my shoulders softly as if I had transformed into china and might easily shatter. His face was full of love and concern.

"Don't worry about a thing, Marlene. When I get my next role I'll make so much money that you'll never have to work after the baby comes."

"But Robert, I like playing here."

He didn't miss a beat.

"Then I'll hire a nursemaid and you can keep playing here a couple nights a week. I promised you I'd never ask you to give up your career if we had children and I meant it. I am absolutely proud of you as a pianist and as my wife and my child's mother."

I kissed him long and hard until an impatient drunk began to pound on the door.

Robert bought me orange juice, the most expensive drink at the bar. My other new favorite drink was soda water with lemon slices. It looked to all my friends like I was still drinking. I craved the lemons and ate the slices, which was bizarre even for my wide-ranging appetite. I did not want Al to know my condition, for fear that he might ask me to stop working, so I told no one at The Starfish. In less than a month, the bartenders would begin to talk about my teetotaling and the truth would leak out.

After Robert, the next person I told was Amelia. I had gone to visit her alone and she had put Florence down for a nap. We were drinking raspberry tea, which relieved the strains of her own pregnancy.

"My feet are swollen," Amelia complained. "I run to the bathroom every ten minutes. I've gained thirty pounds which is twice what I gained when I had Florence. I'm afraid I may be having twins."

We settled on the sofa and I felt the movements in her belly, a restless kicking and stretching.

"Yes, it could be twins," I said.

Amelia looked at me knowingly and laid her hand on my belly.

"I don't believe you gave up alcohol for Lent, Marlene."

"How do you know that?"

Her eyes sparkled behind her glasses, like when we were schoolgirls and she explained a law of science that I had not yet learned. Amelia still loved to tease me.

"Elaine Schumann told me that Oliver heard from Dennis that you drink soda water with lemon now. Al told Oliver that you look unusually radiant lately. I'm glad you finally listened to me and quit drinking."

"I didn't quit forever."

"I know that too." Amelia was serious now.

"How long have you known I was pregnant?"

"I knew when you came to Mother's house the first Sunday after you came back. I'm not even sure how I knew. You haven't gained weight yet and you ate the same amount and type of food you always eat. But I knew as soon as I saw you that you were pregnant. Are you happy about it?"

"Yes, I am. I want a baby. Robert's been wonderful."

"Does he have a role yet?"

"Not yet," I said. "But he has six pupils and we're still getting royalties from *Twilight Melodies.* I have royalties for *Starfish Blues* too."

"You'd better tell Mother you're pregnant," said Amelia. "And don't let her know that you told me first or she'll be jealous. It will save you the trouble of making any public announcement. She'll tell everyone in the family and at church, and your band will hear about it if they haven't guessed it already."

Amelia sent me home with a bottle of vitamins and Epsom salts for soaking my feet.

I didn't have to say anything to Mother. The next Sunday at her house I was helping her clear the table and wash the dinner dishes before I went home. If I was alone with her, I could work up the courage to tell her the truth. Everyone else had gone home already, with some prodding from Amelia.

Mother went upstairs to the bathroom. When she came back downstairs, she found me bent over with my head in the icebox, as furtive as a raccoon in the garbage bin.

"Marlene, what in the world are you doing?"

"Eating pickled watermelon," I said.

The jar of pickled watermelon was far in the back of the top shelf. The watermelon was pale pink and spiced with cinnamon, cold and zingy. My mouth was full of the last slice and my fingers were sticky. The flavor thrilled me all the way down to my toes. Aunt Josie had given the jar to Mother, who was too polite to reject any gift. No one in my family ate watermelon pickles, not even me.

Mother sighed and said "I haven't eaten pickled watermelon since I was pregnant with you. How many months along are you?"

"Just one," I said, facing her. "Only Robert knows."

She hugged me tight before I even set down the jar.

"You'll do all right, Marlene," Mother said.

She rushed out of the room and returned with a silver Miraculous Medal, hanging the image of the Blessed Mother over my nervous heart.

"You'll do all right," she murmured. "You'll do all right."

Mother repeated it low and soft like a prayer, willing it into being.

I worked all summer and fall, right up until the birth, trying to save money. I could feel the baby kicking, stronger when I played the piano and when Robert sang.

Amelia and Katrina both planned to attend my delivery. One evening when I got up from the supper table, my water broke. I began to cry because the contractions hurt, and I was terrified of the approaching pain. Robert was in New York playing Macbeth in a little theater. I wanted him to be the first to see his child, but I didn't want him to see me crying and screaming.

Edward carried me upstairs and Helen called Amelia. She drove over, dropping off her children at Mother's house and bringing Katrina with her. Amelia carried a black medical bag with a stethoscope, ointments, rubber gloves, scissors, forceps and gauze. She wore her nurse's hat and apron. Katrina wore an apron and carried towels, soap and washcloths. She knew how to clean before and after surgery, but had not assisted with births like Amelia had. I rubbed the Miraculous Medal necklace that Mother had given me.

"Don't be afraid," said Katrina. "We'll call Dr. Bauer if anything goes awry."

Amelia felt my belly with her warm callused palms and long medical fingers. Her touch made me feel calmer; I could not feel embarrassed in front of my sister and sister-in-law. Robert would have told me not to cry. Mother would have told me not to curse. Dr. Bauer would have been helpful, but bored with a birth that was sacred to me.

"The baby's head is facing down," she said. "It won't be a breech birth, fortunately."

A contraction clenched my whole body like a fist.

"How long will it take?" I asked.

"Too long," Amelia said knowingly.

They both laughed, but I whimpered.

My water had broken shortly after six in the evening and I was in labor until eight the next morning. Helen stayed up all night, making coffee and ham sandwiches for Amelia and Katrina and tying up my hair in a kerchief to keep it off my sweaty forehead. All three of them helped me go to the bathroom and brought me water when I was thirsty. Katrina wiped my brow with a cold washcloth and I clenched another between my teeth in pain and frustration.

Helen held my hand and spoke softly to me between the waves of labor pains.

"You're so brave, Marlene. Don't give up now. Robert will be so proud."

I swore vociferously in English then in German, curse words I had written in my high school notebooks to yell at confused enemies. I even used the few Polish profanities Ben Kowalski had once told me and Italian curses the Caprellos knew. Amelia and Helen always laughed at my swearing, but I hoped Katrina wasn't shocked.

"I'm sorry," I said. "I hope I don't offend you."

"Nothing offends me,' Katrina said. "In the war I heard every curse word in Europe – English, French, Dutch, German, Russian, Latin..."

"Latin?" I asked.

"Yes, I had to stitch up a priest once. The doctor had to take shrapnel out of his leg and we were low on morphine, so he said 'Don't give me any. Save it for the soldiers.' He tried to take it like a martyr but I never heard Latin like that in church!"

We all had to laugh.

As the sun rose, my womb felt like an open wound and I was drenched in blood and sweat.

"Good God!" I screamed. "Robert, where the hell are you?"

Edward got up to go to work and called through the door to wish me well.

"Hang in there, Marlene!" he said. "I'll meet the new Schumann when I come home."

At last Amelia looked between my legs and said "It's the crowning! I can see the head. You're getting close now, Marlene."

"Robert will be home in two hours," said Katrina.

I shifted between sitting up and lying down to ease the sharp pains in my back. Helen piled pillows behind me.

"Push now," said Amelia. "Go on. Go on."

"Be brave. Be a soldier now," said Katrina.

All three of them kissed my forehead. I felt too weak and agonized to hold their hands now but they rubbed my shoulders and back. I sat at the edge of the bed, hoping that gravity would help me. Amelia sat below me with a pile of clean white towels ready to catch the newborn.

"Yes! Yes! Come on!"

I bore down hard, closed my eyes and prayed. I heard a splattering sound and felt the hot blood and afterbirth coursing between my legs.

Amelia held up my child, a bloody bluish-white baby who cried loudly and flailed her little arms.

"It's a girl," said Amelia.

"My Eva," I said.

I collapsed back into the pillows, as Amelia cut the umbilical cord. Katrina wanted to wash Eva off at once, but I held her for a minute first. I wanted to be the first person she saw when she opened her eyes.

Eva's eyes were gray, the irises shifting like clouds. With one red hand she reached up and clasped my finger. She held the finger in her little rosebud fist and looked at me. She stopped crying and looked thoughtful.

"I love you, Eva Cecile Schumann," I said, kissing her sticky black hair. "And your daddy loves you too."

Then I let Katrina wash and dress Eva. Helen telephoned my mother and Mrs. Schumann with the happy news. I insisted that Amelia and Katrina go home to their families. I was utterly exhausted and fell asleep in my bed with Eva next to me. I was half-awake when Mother and Mrs. Schumann came in bearing baby clothes and took turns holding Eva. She woke me several times with her crying, but I could not get her to nurse yet.

I watched Eva in her sleep. Her bassinet and crib sat empty; I couldn't bear to move her away from me yet. She kept curling up her little pink fingers and closing her eyes like a blossom exposed to the cold. I found a wet spot on the sheet and changed her diaper for the first time. Eva wailed, hating the feeling of being cold and exposed. The folding and pinning came easily to me; I had diapered many babies for practice, including Helen. I had named my daughter after the fearless Eva Tanguay, and the first song I sang to my daughter was *I Don't Care.*

Later that afternoon I put on my sweater and wool skirt. I dressed Eva in a soft pink dress and hat and wrapped her in a green daisy blanket that Helen had knitted. When she fussed, I rocked her in my arms. We toured the house and yard and I pointed out everything to my little stranger. I wondered how many sounds she had heard in the womb and how strange it must be now to have the senses of sight, smell and taste, to have things to reach for and touch.

"See the maple trees? See the little squirrel? Listen to the leaves crackling under my feet. I smell a bonfire. Can you smell it, Eva?"

I heard footsteps coming down the street and before I even turned around, I knew who it was. Robert approached, carrying his suitcase and a big shopping bag. He smiled and ran, his brown coat flaring out behind his quick lean legs.

My first impulse was to run toward him, but Eva cried at the sudden motion when I took my first steps. I waited for Robert to wrap us both in his arms and kiss her, then me.

"My little Eva Schumann," he said. "My little angel child. Marlene, I should have been here. I'll never forgive myself for not being here."

"I forgive you," I said. "I'm glad you didn't hear me screaming. I would have blamed you for my labor pains, so it's better that you weren't in the house."

Eva opened her eyes and gazed at her father. She stretched out her little hands to him and he held her gently in his arms. His eyes were moist with tears.

"I've been paid, thank God," he said. "*Macbeth* will run for another month."

I told Robert all about the birth and how good Amelia, Katrina and Helen had been to me. He presented Eva with picture books, a winter coat with a rabbit collar, a jack-in-box and a stuffed teddy bear. Eva would name this bear "Bob" and sleep with him every night.

At dinner with Helen and Edward, Robert told us all about the play. I was very hungry but Eva cried constantly, so it was hard to eat. My breasts ached with milk, but I still could not get her to nurse. I sat, frustrated, on the living room couch while the others conversed at the table and Eva cried instead of suckling.

We all went to bed early that night.

"You should put her in her crib," said Robert. "We don't want to risk rolling over on her."

"No. I'll have to get up to feed her every few hours anyway. Eva hasn't nursed yet; she must be starving. I'll put her in the bassinet by my side of the bed. Then I can reach over and get her without having to get up."

"All right, Marlene. You may as well keep her close for now."

That night Eva nursed successfully for the first time. I lit the bedside lamp and watched her in the golden light. I was so proud and relieved that I woke Robert up to show him.

"That's lovely, Marlene," he mumbled, drifting off into sleep.

Eva's strong little mouth, her appetite and steady heartbeat reassured me that she was healthy and growing. I had worried so much about her, from the night of her conception and the dream of the walnut tree. Years later, I would tell Eva, and only Eva, about that dream. How happy my father would be to see us now!

Robert performed in three plays in New York that year and two at the Stuart Theater in Laurel. Everyone I knew saw him perform at the Stuart, but it paid very little. When he was away in New York, I no longer sat up and waited for him as I had in Los Angeles. With Helen and Edward in the next room and Grace and Eva in their cribs across the hall, I could never feel truly alone.

I did ask Robert to kiss me when he came home late and wake me if he wanted to. I didn't want him to feel that I neglected him for Eva. I loved him more now than ever, as a loving father, not only a handsome and talented man. The Starfish Seven did not complain when he came in to sing with them. Al still called Robert "Cake Boy" and gave our pay to me. I told Robert he should ignore it because Al always got along better with women and it wasn't anything personal. I lied.

In June, I took Eva out of Laurel for the first time, going by train to New York to visit Blue Maria. It was agony changing Eva's diaper in the narrow train washroom and washing out the wet one as best I could. Luckily the motion of the train rocked her to sleep for most of the journey.

Blue Maria's Violet loved Eva and we took them both swimming in the pool. We went to Central Park and the zoo and had dinner with Bertram. The French nanny fed the girls mashed potatoes and cream of chicken soup while we feasted on Cornish game hens and she took them up to bed before we had our desert of Bananas Foster, complete with flaming rum.

Bertram took Maria and me to Texas Guinan's club and bought us champagne flips and grasshoppers. I felt quite tipsy, but I suddenly remembered that Robert would be singing at a hotel that evening.

"Let's go and see him," I said. "It would be a nice surprise for him. Bertram, you've never seen my husband sing."

"I quite agree," said Bertram. "That would be lovely."

We leaned tipsily on each other in the Dusenberg, crowded into the backseat with Bertram sitting in the middle, "between these two divine ladies". He was good-humored and fun to be with, telling me all about the history of the buildings we passed and the hotel we were going to. Bertram would never be as exciting as Blue Maria, but I began to understand his appeal. Blue Maria had been a wanderer all her life and Bertram made her feel at home anywhere.

I rushed inside and asked the desk clerk where Robert Schumann was playing. Charles was parking the car and Bertram and Blue Maria stayed in it.

"He was in the grand ballroom for two hours," the clerk said. "But then he went up to Audrey Bainworth's suite."

"Where is that?" I asked.

The young man looked flustered.

"It's a private party, ma'am. I'm not allowed to give out guests' room numbers."

"But I'm Marlene Schumann."

"I'm sorry, ma'am. I can't give the room number to anyone."

Bertram came up behind me with Blue Maria on his arm. The clerk did not realize that we three were together. Blue Maria wore a sapphire and diamond necklace and a jade green silk gown and Bertram wore a double-breasted navy blue suit with silver buttons. I wore a plain black wool coat over my purple silk dress with some pearls Blue Maria had loaned me. I stepped away from the counter and waited by the elevators to see if Bertram and Blue Maria (who had overheard everything) could elicit a different response.

"Hello, William," said Bertram. "I see you've moved up the ladder to night clerk. Getting any studying done?"

"Yes, sir," said William, his face brightening. "I have my law book here to read when business gets slow."

Bertram turned to Blue Maria. "You see, darling, I have to become his friend now before he's a high-priced lawyer. Say, Maria, do you have the invitation?"

Bertram pretended to look in his pockets and Blue Maria reached into her sequined peacock purse.

"Dam- I mean darn it, Bert! I simply can't find it anywhere. For Pete's sake!"

"Audrey will be so annoyed; we're late already," said Bertram.

"It's Room 1113," William piped up.

"Oh, thank you," said Blue Maria. "You're too kind."

She walked over to the elevators where I was standing and linked arms with me. Bertram bowed and let us go into the elevator first. I saw the surprised look on William's face as the door closed, and I stuck out my tongue at him.

"What a jackass!" I said. "Why wouldn't he tell me the room number? Do I look dangerous?"

"No," said Blue Maria. "He was probably ordered to keep everyone out because the guests are up there drinking and there's a tiny chance you might be a liquor agent."

"Do I look like a lady cop?" I snapped.

A butler answered the door of Room 1113. He let us in without asking who we were. The room was smoky with French cigarettes and Cuban cigars. Bottles of gin, brandy, whiskey and liqueurs glittered like jewels on a bar against the wall. A girl in a black dress shook the cocktails with ice from a silver ice bucket and a maid collected the empty glasses. I heard murmurs of French, German, English and Spanish. The suite was as big as the ground floor of my house and at least a hundred people, American and European, mingled and danced to Robert's divine tenor voice singing *Lover, Come Back To Me*.

I followed the sound into the next room and found him next to the piano where a solemn man in a tailcoat tapped the keys. I waved at Robert and he saw me and raised one eyebrow. He sang three more songs while I waited to speak to him.

Blue Maria and Bertram had made a beeline for the bar and she brought me a pale purple cocktail that tasted of cassis and violets. I watched Audrey Bainworth sitting in a gold-leafed French chair like a princess, her attention shifting between Robert and her black Pomeranian dog, Caesar, who sat in her lap. She wore a black satin evening gown with golden Egyptian sandals and silver and diamond rings. Her hair was dyed black and bobbed short with bangs. Audrey had tiny blue eyes and thin lips with too much rouge and kohl. She was thin, with a long slender neck, elegant arms and legs and a completely flat chest, the perfect flapper shape that I had seen in only a handful of live women. I had heard a rumor that she had her breasts removed because flat chests were fashionable; this was so disgusting that I hoped it was false.

Audrey Bainworth had visited Stolzfus Silk on several occasions while I worked there, buying yards of silk: Chinese red, jade green, black or cherry blossom pink. Some of these silks were for upholstery and cushions as well as gowns, gloves, shawls and the bizarre turban hats she favored. Audrey carried Caesar with her everywhere in her large handbags or in her arms like a baby. Caesar refused to walk on a leash and snapped viciously at anyone but his mistress.

She would talk to him and ask him "Do you like the black silk, Caesar, or the lovely red?" as if she actually expected an answer from the little black beast.

Helen had whispered to me "If that stupid heifer buys silk for her dog's bed, I'm going to spit on it!"

Audrey had never been to The Starfish. Like most of Laurel's upper crust, she drank at house parties or at the Ottoman Hotel. Peggy told me that Audrey once got so pickled on champagne punch that she fell into the marble fountain in the hotel lobby.

"She had to pay off the editor of the *Laurel Intelligencer-Journal* to keep it out of the papers," Peggy had said.

"Didn't she get arrested for public intoxication?"

"Oh no," said Peggy. "Rich folks don't get arrested. Chief Carmichael was the one who pulled her out of the fountain."

When Robert told his audience he would take a short break, I approached him with a glass of water. Audrey Bainworth also approached him and handed him a five dollar bill. Caesar circled around her feet yipping.

"You have such a melodious voice, Bobbie," she cooed. "I swear you're the only talent that ever came out of Laurel, Pennsylvania."

Up close, I could see Audrey better; her movements were girlish but she had fine wrinkles around her eyes and mouth. Her rings glittered and the silver one on her ring finger was a coiled serpent with emerald eyes. Audrey held out her hand and Robert clasped it, bent down and kissed the serpent. *What the hell is he doing?* I thought. *She's not the damn Pope.*

"Miss Bainworth," said Robert. "I don't believe you've met my accompanist, Marlene Schumann."

"I'm Robert's wife, another talent out of Laurel," I said, reaching out to shake her hand.

She ignored it and picked up Caesar, who growled at me.

"Now, now, baby. Don't be mad when other boys kiss Mommy."

She kissed her dog on the lips and said "Bobbie, I do hope you'll sing *Beautiful Dreamer* before you retire to your room. It's my *favorite*. I simply adore it."

She flounced off to mingle with her guests. I hugged and kissed Robert, who felt immobile in my arms.

"How did you get in here?" he asked.

"The butler let me in," I said. "Blue Maria and Bertram are here too; I brought them by to see you. We were hoping you'd come back to the old manse with us."

"Not possible," Robert said sadly. "I get a free room here as part of my payment for this. I was playing downstairs and Audrey Bainworth recognized me and offered me one hundred dollars to play at her party."

"That's wonderful," I said. "She has great taste in music. But tell me, why does she call you 'Bobbie'? You've never been called Rob or Bob in your entire life, let alone Bobbie. It's awful."

"It's just a pet name," he said. "There's nothing wrong with it."

"Whatever you say 'Bobbie'," I said, kissing him.

"Marlene, I need to go and wash up," he said.

"Robert, can I stay here with you tonight?"

"No, dear, you need to be with Eva. She's back at the mansion, I presume."

"Yes, with Violet and the governess."

"Did she have a good day?"

"Oh yes. We swam in the pool and went to Central Park and the zoo and had Cornish hens for supper."

"Kiss her for me," he said. "I'll see her back in Laurel at noon tomorrow."

Robert turned on his heel and melted into the perfumed crowd. I saw Audrey Bainworth feeding an angel on horseback to Caesar and felt miserable. Bertram and Blue Maria were waltzing and smiling. I had no partner and no wish to dance so I made my way to the buffet table to pilfer as many oysters, sausage rolls, Brie cheese crackers, melon balls and oranges as I could stomach. I drank too much and had only a hazy memory of Blue Maria and Bertram holding me by the arms and leading me to a cab and then upstairs to bed.

I felt ill the next morning, but luckily Blue Maria had left a pitcher of water beside my bed. I woke up every few hours to drink another glass before finally rising at eleven to dress Eva.

At breakfast I asked Blue Maria "Do you think Robert stayed behind to see her?'

"I doubt it, Marlene," she said. "Audrey Bainworth is 47 years old. She's had flirtations with dozens of men, but they're all high rollers like her. A poor singer like Robert would be like a music box to her, no more."

"He's not a poor singer," I said.

"I meant poor in his pockets, not in his voice," she said.

When I got home, Robert was in the living room playing his guitar. As I opened the door, Eva squealed with delight at seeing her daddy. He was startled and broke a string.

"Where the hell have you been?" Robert demanded. "Do you know what time it is?"

I glanced at my watch and said "It's three fifty-one."

"I damn well wonder what's for dinner. I'm starving and Helen took off with Grace, not even leaving a note. Edward's working late or some damn thing."

"Daddy, shh!" said Eva.

She wrapped herself around Robert's legs and he patted her shoulder without looking down.

"Don't say 'damn' in front of Eva," I said. "I need to change her diaper and give her a bath right now. You can come upstairs with me if you like."

"Couldn't you fix me some food first?" asked Robert.

He avoided coming upstairs until I had thrown the dirty diaper in the covered pail of bleach water. Eva was big enough to sit up in the bathtub and play with a toy duck and wooden boat. I carefully shampooed and rinsed her hair and soaped her skin with a soft cloth. She laughed and cooed when I poured warm water over her. Robert came into the bathroom and smiled at his daughter.

"So how many albums did you sell at Audrey Bainworth's party?"

"Twenty eight," he said. "I have a list and your half of the profits right here."

He reached into his pants pocket.

"Leave it on the dresser," I said. "I don't need every penny right this minute. I trust you."

His eyes glistened but he did not smile.

"I missed you at Blue Maria's," I said. "I woke up three times last night and each time I was disappointed that you weren't there."

"You shouldn't travel with Eva," he said. "She sleeps through the night at home but you insist on taking her to a strange city with strange people and of course it upsets her."

I dried her off and put her nightgown on her. Eva fussed and stretched, not yet giving in to sleep.

"What do you mean 'strange people'? Eva had a wonderful time with Violet and Blue Maria. These are my dear friends, and they're not half as strange as Audrey Bainworth who feeds canapés to her damn dog."

"Not in front of the baby!" he scolded. "I made money in New York, Marlene, and you went up there just for pleasure. Don't criticize me."

"I just think it's a shame you couldn't come back on the train with us. You weren't busy today."

Robert rolled his eyes.

"Marlene, I was tired and hung-over and I just wanted to go home. I bet you weren't even up by ten."

"No. I deserve to drink and sleep in too, sometimes."

I put Eva into her crib in her room, though she wasn't sleepy. I wanted to connect with Robert again for both of us to feel glad to be home and alone together. He was leaning in the doorway of our room and I took him by the hand and led him to our bed.

CHAPTER TWENTY-NINE

The October day was ripe and golden like an apple. Yellow maple leaves covered my front yard and I went out to rake them, taking Eva and Grace with me. Edward wanted to rake leaves every day, but he came home exhausted from spinning at the silk mill and he deserved a rest.

Eva pointed to the four carved jack-o-lanterns on our porch, carved by Helen, Edward, Robert and me.

"Pumkin, Mama! Pumkin!"

I could not quite get her to say "pumpkin" or "jack-o-lantern".

Helen and I took our daughters over to Amelia's house. Grace rode in the baby carriage and Eva hurried along beside me, crying sometimes to be carried. I insisted that she walk, but held her hand to help her up Amelia's steps.

Amelia had made caramel apples and gave caramels to Florence, Eva, Brian and Gregory. Eva let Grace lick her apple; both of them were gleefully sticky and hated it when Helen and I wiped their faces. All the cousins ran around in the backyard, pushing each other in the wheelbarrow and flinging leaves everywhere. Helen, Amelia and I munched our apples and watched our kids from the dining room window.

Amelia told us that she was nursing two of her elderly neighbors, Mr. Zook, who had throat cancer and Mrs. Ross, who had severe arthritis.

"I visit Mr. Zook every morning at six, before Arthur and the kids are up," she said. "He still gets up at four to watch the blue jays and cardinals at his bird feeder. I don't know if he gets up so early because he was raised on a farm or if it's insomnia. It's some of both I guess. He has three kids in and around Laurel, but none of them come to see him.

"Mrs. Ross's daughter, Amy Miller, cooks and cleans for her, but I go over there at eight after the kids are in bed to give her a bath and make sure she takes her pills and vitamins. She forgets sometimes."

"Do they pay you anything?" asked Helen. "If you don't mind my asking?"

"Mr. Zook's son Walter pays me, but the Rosses don't. I don't care about that, though. Arthur and I are comfortable and I just want to keep nursing. Even when I'm tired, it's very satisfying. Mrs. Ross loves to play pinochle with me and Arthur's not much for games."

"It's great that you can still help sick people," I said. "I saw Amy Miller at the market on Saturday and she said 'Your sister Amelia is a saint'."

We all laughed.

"Edward and I will be able to get a house soon," said Helen. "Thanks to Marlene, we've been able to save enough for a down payment. We looked at a house on Prince Street yesterday. It had a big kitchen and three bedrooms, but Edward swore he could smell dry rot in it."

Helen and I went home to prepare dinner before Robert came home from his guitar lessons and Edward came home from the silk mill. I was peeling potatoes and she was making biscuits. Grace and Eva played with wooden spools, stacking them and rolling them across the kitchen floor. We heard the soft thud of the newspaper against our front door and – for no apparent reason - Eva and Grace both began crying.

"Eva, what's wrong? You're a big girl; you can wait for dinner. Can you get Bob Bear and Sally?"

Eva brought Bob, her teddy bear, and Sally, Grace's rag doll with blond yarn hair and a red dress. My mother had sewn Sally before Grace was born, expecting a girl. Grace always clung to Sally for comfort and Eva clutched Bob.

"Something's wrong," said Helen.

"With the girls?"

"No, it's something worse. I feel like a storm's coming but it's not that either."

Our mother was able to foretell many kinds of trouble, including when a clear day would turn cloudy and when someone would get sick. Eight times out of ten she knew which of her children was on the phone before she picked up the receiver. She knew which one of us was coming down with something before we even felt sick. When I told Mother she might be psychic, she laughed and said "It's only woman's intuition."

So far Helen was the only one of her children who was intuitive and her unexplained insights were rare. If she sensed a crisis it must be close and severe. I brought the newspaper inside and sat down on the sofa. I unfolded the news like a ticking bomb. It was.

"Helen! Helen come in here!"

The headline read:

STOCK MARKET CRASHES, BANKS CLOSED

Helen called every bank she could think of and got no reply, though it was before five. Then Helen called her friend Louise Risser, the secretary of the president of Laurel Bank. Louise was at home and she confirmed for Helen everything the paper had said.

Helen sank down on the sofa and burst into tears.

"I don't believe it!" she said. "It's all gone! All the money's gone, all our savings for Grace, our down payment for the house, everything!"

"I didn't think this could happen in the twentieth century," I said. "We don't have bank fraud like they had in the 1890's."

I was still reading the paper and trying to remember my one economics course in high school (where I had doodled Robert's face in my notes instead of learning about stockbrokers.) I read about how speculation had driven the stock market higher than ever and then sunk it. Dad and I had talked about Adam Smith's theories of capitalism, but greed and fraud of this magnitude baffled me. Where had all the money gone? Why had no one predicted this last week or last month?

Grace and Eva heard Helen crying. Eva led Grace into the living room, holding her hand. Grace toddled over to her mother and held up Sally, feeling sure that having a doll to hold would solve any problem. Helen was touched, and said "Thank you, Grace," then buried her face in her hands.

Grace began to cry too and I took her upstairs and laid her down for a nap. Eva followed me tentatively.

"Aunt Helen crying."

"Aunt Helen needs to cry for a while, sweetheart. Come on and help me make dinner."

I carried Eva downstairs, wanting to hold her to alleviate my own fears.

Robert came home first and I told him what had happened. The blood drained from his face.

"I passed Laurel Bank today and they were closed. Old National was closed too, but I thought nothing of it. My God, this cannot happen in America. The government will step in with treasury bonds and give the banks money to cover their losses."

"Don't bet on it," I said. "It's bad enough to lose five hundred dollars for Eva's college fund. We have seventeen years to get it back and we still have royalties from *Starfish Blues* and *Twilight Melodies*. Helen and Edward had two thousand dollars in the bank. They were about to buy a house."

"Did you try to console her?"

Robert was concerned now and laid his hand on my shoulder.

"Helen wanted to be left alone. She just waved me away and lay down on the sofa, pulling the blanket over her. I haven't seen her cry like that since Dad died. I remember she hid under the blanket on her bed and wouldn't come out. I went to get her out and she hit me."

My vision began to blur with tears and I sank into Robert's arms.

"I put Grace to bed," I said. "I didn't want her to see her mother like this."

When Edward came home, Helen sat up and spoke to him, her legs still wrapped in the blanket. She tried to explain it to him, but he just said:

"I know what happened, honey. I heard it on the streetcar coming home. We'll get through this. I'll tell you one thing, though, from now on I'm keeping all our dough locked in a steel safe in our bedroom."

Edward hugged Helen until she stopped crying. We ate dinner in silence and listened to the news on the radio, in disbelief and disgust. President Hoover said the Depression would end in a few months, but we already knew better than that.

The next day parents of every one of Robert's guitar students called to cancel the lessons. Robert stopped picking up the phone after the third call, so I had to bear the bad news to him. Edward came home from work early, holding a pink slip and his last paycheck. Stolzfus Silk had suffered, like every business and factory in town, and its board of directors had decided to lay off every worker who had been there less than five years. This was a third of their workforce, including over 200 men like Edward Malone, with young families. Aaron Bauer, who was also let go, told me these numbers.

Downtown stores closed and some stayed empty. The Caprello Deli stayed open and Mr. Caprello couldn't lay off any of his workers because they were all his children. He kept insisting that he'd been much poorer than this in Italy, living on polenta, but for the first time no one believed him.

Sven ran Hayden farm now, but it would always be called Hayden farm, never Madsen farm. During my year in Los Angeles, Uncle Luke and Aunt Josie had told Boyd to quit drinking or get out and he'd chosen the latter. Though I'd never seen him at the Starfish, Emmet said he'd been 86'ed from it years ago.

Brendan and Isaac would continue to work the ski lodge in Vermont each winter and every fall, and scrape by on Brendan's illustrating work and Isaac's work in greenhouses the rest of the year. Brendan sent Mother sketches of the woods and mountains.

"At least the two of them are together," Aunt Josie would say, reading postcards of the snowy mountains.

Joseph still had his plumbing business with Oliver, but customers now tried everything to avoid paying them. Now and then he came to The Starfish to drink a beer and collect himself.

"Today Mrs. Starr told me all her children would die of cholera if I didn't fix her toilet – for free! I told her she was a piss-poor example for those kids!" Joseph said.

"Literally!" Oliver added.

"Thank God The Starfish didn't lay anyone off," I said. "People keep on drinking no matter how lousy the economy is."

Al had called all of The Starfish Seven and his bartenders and bouncers on October 30. He had reassured us all that we still had our jobs and if necessary he would sell his house and live in Vintner's Hardware before letting anyone go. Dennis and Zach managed to keep the Vintner's on East Peach Street open and the original Grant Street store was as busy as ever. The Starfish's business declined slightly until Christmas, but then picked up again. Anyone who did not pay for their drinks was 86'ed and musicians only got one free drink per night now, which disappointed all of us (except Jeremy who never drank.) I kept asking if Robert could come in and sing but Al said no because it would take money away from all the other players. I got the band to let Robert come in for holiday parties, but that was all. They preferred the various female singers that Al continued to bring in.

My work at The Starfish and the royalty checks from *Starfish Blues* and *Twilight Melodies* were the main sources of income at my house. Edward applied for jobs every day, chopping wood and shoveling snow sometimes, often coming home exhausted after walking around all day chasing "Help Wanted" signs. Robert had no employment and detested helping around the house.

Once when Helen was kneading bread, which she made at home now, she asked Robert to change Eva's diaper. Robert was lying on the couch and Edward was coming up from the cellar with a basket of clean laundry.

"How can you ask me that?" Robert cried. "Isn't it enough that I can't find work in the movies or on the stage? Just because I'm between jobs doesn't mean I should slap on an apron and be completely emasculated!"

"Shut your piehole!" said Edward. "Sitting on your ass all day doing nothing is what makes you feel emasculated! I'll help you out, Evie baby. I ain't scared of a little shit!"

"Eddie! Not in front of Eva and Grace!" Helen scolded, but she told me about it later and we had a good laugh.

Ironically, the one friend I assumed was rich enough to escape the Depression unscathed was the one who lost the most. Blue Maria called me on Halloween to invite me to her husband's funeral. Her voice was calm, stoic and utterly miserable.

"Bertram found out what happened on Black Monday, in the afternoon. He jumped out of his office window on the twenty-third floor. His office boy called me. He said Bertram had seemed quiet, but nothing unusual, no tears or screams or even any last words. Maybe he couldn't face me, or more likely, couldn't face his family."

"You and Violet are his family."

"Marlene, you know what I mean. The Chambers clan have always had money and now that their canneries are bankrupt none of them want to live anymore. Bert's mother and sisters told me not to attend the funeral. The will left the house and all the bank accounts to me and set up a trust fund for Violet when she's twenty-one. Now Bertram's mother is trying to contest it. No matter what, the house will have to be sold for debts."

"Where will you go?"

She paused. "I'm going to play in clubs here until spring and then I'll go on the road again. I rented an apartment for Violet and me. I can't bear to live in this big empty home anyway."

The funeral took place the next day and I took the train up to New York to be with Blue Maria. Mother graciously loaned me her black mourning dress with the puffed sleeves, satin gloves and a black straw hat with a demi-veil that had been Grandma Piper's.

"I want you to look respectable," said Mother. "Your friend Maria shouldn't have to face those harpies alone. I'll be glad to have Eva here with me for the day."

"You're not afraid of the Depression are you, Mother?" I said.

"No. I'm sad that Edward was laid off and Joseph is short of work, and I worry about all my kids, but I also know that you'll take care of yourselves and each other no matter what happens. Think of all the medicine and care Arthur and Amelia have given us for free and how Sven and Maud are always bringing us milk and eggs and vegetables. We're very lucky. I have my health, thank God, and I'll go back to selling shoes if I have to."

I had worried a bit about Mother, because I could not afford to give her money as I used to, but Amelia told me she and Arthur would support her until Joseph's business improved and until I wasn't the only employed adult in my house. Mother more than repaid us by taking care of our children whenever any of us girls "needed a day off."

Blue Maria met me at Grand Central Station. By habit, I looked her over for a trace of her signature color. She wore a black mink coat over a black lace dress, black leather gloves and boots and a black wool hat with a veil over her face. Her only blue ornaments were a pair of opal earrings Bertram had given her. Violet wore a black hat and coat over a black velvet dress and patent leather shoes. She held her mother's hand and spoke little, except to blurt out what she knew about her father's death.

"My daddy is dead. He jumped out a window because all the money is gone."

Her voice was flat and dull, but she understood everything.

I was taken aback, but I managed to say "It's good that you and your mother have each other."

Blue Maria drove her own car now and I whispered to her on our way to the church.

"Did you tell Violet how it happened?" I asked.

"No," said Blue Maria. "I told her he died but not how. She overheard it from the maids. I had to let all the servants go and they cursed me and blamed me for putting their families in the poorhouse. His mother told me to my face that I drove her son to his death, that he had always been a good Christian before he met me."

"But think if he'd never met you and never had Violet, how empty his life would have been. He would never have married anyone else."

"That's true."

We stopped at a florist's shop and bought three pale blue irises.

The funeral took place in a huge Episcopalian church stuffed with white chrysanthemums, lilies and gladiolas. The shiny black coffin was closed and covered with white roses. Blue Maria and I laid our irises on it, and held Violet up to put her flower in the center. Mrs. Chambers and Bertram's sisters and brothers-in-law scowled at us, but no one dared remove the flowers. Blue Maria had also had the undertaker lay her peacock shawl and Violet's baby bonnet over Bertram's heart.

"I was the one who identified him," Blue Maria said. "No one in his family would come to the morgue; they were so ashamed and so busy trying to keep it out of the papers. The undertakers did everything to clean him up, but half of his face was crushed. It was the worst thing I've ever seen and I'll never forget it."

I held Blue Maria's black-gloved hand in mine. Many of the mourners cried and sniffled softly the entire time, but none of Bertram Chambers' family shed tears, except Blue Maria and Violet. Fortunately the newspapers had been paid off and no reporters or photographers invaded the scene.

"If only he'd called me," said Blue Maria. "I could have talked him out of it. I know how to get by on nothing. They all still think I'm a gold digger, but I never needed a fortune. I just need my baby's dad."

She began to weep then, into a handkerchief embroidered with forget-me-nots. Violet hugged her mother's legs and cried too.

There were many suicides in New York City, prominent men like Bertram Chambers who could not bear life once their wealth and power vanished. The wealthy in Laurel lost some money, but only a few went bankrupt and there were no suicides. Elizabeth Campbell Sloan and Barbara Thompson continued to dine at the Black Orchid Café and wear fox furs when they doled out soup to the needy with the Salvation Army. Audrey Bainworth was notably absent from *Laurel Intelligencer-Journal* photos of charitable rich ladies; Bainworth's Department Store had just laid off over one hundred employees, many of whom were in the bread lines now.

One afternoon in November it was beginning to snow and I was taking Eva to meet Robert at Buchanan Station. He had gone to New York to audition for a play. Eva sat on our front steps and whined. I had to pull her along by the hand.

"I don't want to go! I'm cold, Mama!"

"Come on, Eva, your daddy will want to see you. You won't be cold when we start walking."

Robert had not gotten the part but he was glad to see Eva. He'd brought her an illustrated book of Grimm's fairy tales, but I made him keep it hidden in his suitcase.

"For December 25," I whispered.

All the Schumanns loved fairy tales and Eva would be no exception. She and I believed her father was Prince Charming, elusive and mysterious, but able to infuse any time and place with happiness just by showing up.

We walked home together in the snow, Robert and I each holding one of Eva's arms and swinging her between us. Thick snowflakes drifted down like white doves and covered the naked trees and damp sidewalks. No matter how broke we were, Robert, Eva and I had each other and Christmas would soon come.

We were hungry in 1930 and as winter melted into spring, I began to forage for food. Everyone did it and I did not consider it stealing to pick a few cherries or raspberries on a branch that stuck out into the alley. I picked black walnuts up off the ground as Dad had done. My main find was dandelions. Dad had told me that their greens were just as nourishing as collards or spinach, and you could eat the root too if you boiled it. I told myself that no one would miss a few dandelions, although I saw other women and children digging them up too.

I would walk to Holy Cross Cemetery with my old brown leather purse and a sharp knife and spade to dig dandelion greens. I would slip the plants into a burlap bag inside my purse. I was keeping the cemetery neat and getting the plants that dogs were least likely to pee on. I would visit my father's grave and pour whiskey over it. He had asked me once not to put flowers on his grave, but sometimes I left black walnuts there. Dad wouldn't mind if it attracted squirrels; squirrels always made him laugh. The stone read:

HAROLD JOSEPH PIPER
Born August 28, 1867
Died February 11, 1922
Loving father, husband and history teacher

I wondered if Dad had ever been as hungry as I was now. He had told me about his father going on strikes at Stolzfus Silk Mill and his mother taking in washing to make ends meet. He had scrubbed floors and washed dishes in the cafeteria to earn his way through college, getting a merit scholarship too. Dad had seen depression and bank failure in the 1890's but not on such a huge scale.

Mother taught us children never to steal but Dad's rule was "never squeal" when he picked a peach off Mr. Hess' tree or gathered black walnuts off the ground. He believed that anything in the alley or on the ground was fair game. He always looked surprised when the owners of the trees rushed outside yelling.

"Harold Piper, you damn dirty thief!"

Dad would stroll away calmly, saying "Well, that guy's off his nut."

Even as a child, I knew that my father was not a thief, any more than the birds and squirrels were. He only took what he needed, nuts that would have rotted, fruit the owner would not miss.

Dad would not think less of me – I was sure – for pulling dandelions from graves or accepting boxes of fruits and vegetables from Sven. Maud said that the money I made at The Starfish was "dirty money" and Mother still forbade me to mention its name, even when we were alone. Dad wouldn't have objected; he would have enjoyed sitting on a bar stool sharing a pitcher of Laurel Lager with Joseph. Maybe he would have felt sorry that I played underground instead of in an orchestra, but he would have known that the chance to perform mattered most, even more than the records or songs on the radio. Dad always mocked Prohibition and said "What next? A ban on dancing?"

I missed my father terribly because he would have found a way to laugh at the things that made me cry.

CHAPTER THIRTY

Robert went up to New York four days a week all through January and February to play Duke Orsino in a small Shakespeare company. After *Twelfth Night* ended, he continued to go to New York every weekend, playing guitar and singing at a hotel in exchange for his room and meals. I missed him badly and begged to come up and see him just for the day, but he insisted that I spend his earnings on bills and not waste a penny, even though he kept wasting money on cigarettes and new ties and hats.

We argued about it on Easter Sunday. Robert had promised to come home on Saturday night but he wasn't there when I came back from The Starfish. I carefully filled Grace and Eva's Easter nests with chocolate rabbits, jellybeans and saltwater taffy. I'd saved my tip money to get them some Easter candy. Edward and Helen had dyed eggs and hidden them around the house for the girls to find.

Eva and Grace dashed around the house finding eggs on windowsills and under the sofa, delighted that the Easter Bunny had come. Helen, Edward and I looked forward to a week of egg salad sandwiches, instead of tuna fish or peanut butter. We dressed the girls in their white Easter bonnets and gloves, their matching yellow dresses that Helen had sewed.

At mass, Eva asked "When will we see Daddy?"

"At Grandma Aileen's," I said.

She started crying and I had to take her outside.

"Why doesn't Daddy go to church?" she asked for the first time.

"Daddy's in New York playing music. He'll be home soon."

But Robert did not appear at my mother's house. Eva and her cousins found hollow wooden eggs filled with chocolates in Mother's yard and enjoyed the ham with pineapple and cookies with pink icing. I could not enjoy Easter, though, without knowing where Robert was. Mother asked, and I had to admit I didn't know.

He finally showed up at our house late that afternoon. Eva saw him coming up the walk and ran to him.

"Daddy! Daddy!"

Robert picked her up, spun her around and kissed her. I stepped out onto the front porch. Robert took one look at the scowl on my face and picked Eva up and walked away. He left his suitcase behind him as if I were a bellhop who would carry it in and a maid to unpack it all for him.

"I'm taking Eva to the park to feed the ducks," he called over his shoulder.

Eva waved goodbye. I was furious, but as Robert knew, I refused to fight with him in front of her. That evening after supper I confronted him in our room.

"Why didn't you come home last night?"

"I played at a house party in Queens until three in the morning."

He looked me straight in the eye and lied to me. I could tell that he had rehearsed that line.

"Eva cried all through Easter mass. I told her you'd be at Grandma's but of course you weren't. Mother wondered where you were and I had no idea."

"Just tell her I'm in New York making money. I brought you twenty-three fifty."

"I'd rather have you home for Easter," I said.

Robert flared up.

"Well, I'd rather have you home taking care of our child than at The Starfish every night with Al Vintner, but I suppose we all have to make sacrifices."

"What? Why do you care about Al?"

"The man hates me, that's why. I'm just like Jesus Christ; I get no respect in my hometown."

"You're nothing like Jesus. He got crucified and He still showed up for Easter!"

"Marlene, what do you want from me?"

"I want you to keep your promises to Eva and me. You promised that you'd be home for Easter. Who in New York is as important to you as your wife and kid?"

"No one," he said softly. "Do I look like I can afford a girlfriend? I can hardly afford you."

"Stay home for the next two weeks."

"But I can make more money!"

"We don't need any more money this month. Spend more time with Eva and me, please."

Robert agreed, but he sulked around the house for the next two weeks playing his guitar and calling New York every day to try to book gigs.

In March, Blue Maria sent me a letter inviting Robert and me to play at the establishment where she now performed, a restaurant dance hall and secret bar called The Queen of Clubs. Now was my chance for a nice visit to New York with my husband.

"She's doing this to spite me, you know," Al grumbled. "She has a lot of nerve, hiring my pianist right out from under me."

"Al, it's only for one night," I said. "You have other pianists who can fill in and I could use the extra dough."

"You do what you want, Marlene. I don't own you. But be back on time the next night, no hangovers and no funny business."

Robert and I took the afternoon train up to New York and the subway to The Queen of Clubs. Exhausted and famished, we dragged our meager luggage a few steps down into the restaurant. It was a daylight basement with oak paneling, large comfortable booths and a broad hardwood floor.

Blue Maria rushed out to greet us, wearing an apron dotted with forget-me-nots over a cobalt velvet gown. Red-haired, blue-eyed Violet toddled along beside her. She remembered me and smiled and waved.

"I help in the kitchen during the day and sing here at night," Blue Maria explained. "We've got a little supper for you, included in your compensation."

An old Jewish couple emerged from the kitchen, carrying a big tray of food. The woman had silver hair in a chignon and moved like a queen; the man was shorter than her, with glasses, a big belly and a double-breasted suit. They shook everyone's hands and introduced themselves.

"I'm Kate Weinblum and this is my husband Jacob Weinblum," the lady said.

"Everyone calls us Kate and Big Jake," said her short husband. "We're so glad to meet you all. Blue Maria told us all about you and I know our crowd will love you."

"How was your trip?" Kate asked. "Have you eaten?"

I felt at ease at once. The Queen of Clubs felt more like a well-furnished living room than a smoky speakeasy. Kate and Big Jake brought a huge platter of pot roast with vegetables, cloverleaf rolls, tomato soup and a bottle of garnet-colored liquid.

"That's grape cordial, good for the heart," said Big Jake, with a wink.

We all poured ourselves a glass and sipped. It was a delightfully sweet wine, potent but with virtually no scent. Blue Maria had told us that the real drinks did not come out until evening and a bouncer always watched out for cops.

"This may not be legal, but I do believe it's kosher," Blue Maria whispered.

Before the show, Blue Maria showed us her apartment, a large two room flat with peonies and nightingales on the wallpaper. The curtains and the slip covers on the sofa and chairs were pale blue. A small table folded down from the wall in the kitchen, which had a little icebox, double sink and gas stove. African violets and blue hyacinths bloomed in pots on the fire escape outside the window. The bedroom had a trundle bed, and Violet slept on the pull-out mattress. Blue Maria's old traveling trunk sat at the foot of her bed, with labels from every American city she and her mother had traveled through on their vaudeville circuit.

"That trunk is the one possession I've had all my life," she whispered.

On the living room wall were pictures of Blue Maria and her mother and Blue Maria and Bertram with Violet.

"Blue Maria, how old were you when your mother passed on?" I asked.

"I was twenty-five," said Blue Maria. "Mom played vaudeville and traveled right up until the end of her life. I went with her until I was eighteen, then took off with a guitar player. We always wrote to each other care of Uncle Pete, her brother in Cincinnati. She wrote to me every week, and I never wrote her often enough. The last time we were together we met here in New York for Christmas, just a few months before she died. She was sixty, but her health had always been so good. I thought she'd live forever."

"She married late in life, like you did," I said.

"She was thirty-five when she had me, but she never did marry. She always had a lot of admirers, but she didn't know or wouldn't tell who my father was."

I sat silently for a moment, imagining how hard that must have been for Blue Maria.

"You have a nice place here," I said. "Kate and Big Jake are great."

"They are," said Blue Maria. "I had nobody to turn to after Bertram died. I couldn't believe how many people turned out to be fair-weather friends. I had only played here a couple times, but the Weinblums took me in and then told me their daughter Tamara had just gotten married, leaving an extra position in the kitchen and this vacant apartment upstairs."

"Do you mind working in the kitchen?" I asked. "Working in the silk mill used to drive me nuts."

"You told me," said Blue Maria. "It's not like a factory where a foreman is looking over you every minute. The customers can be difficult, but Big Jake, Kate and Esther are easy to get along with and the cooks and dishwashers and waitresses are all nice. I don't mind cooking and washing dishes and taking orders. My feet get tired, but my voice never does."

"Do you think we'll ever tour again?" I asked her.

"One day," she said. "It's hard now that we have children."

"I hate Robert for running all over New York and leaving me home." I said. "I told you how he came home late at Easter."

"Is he still mad about leaving Los Angeles?" Blue Maria asked.

"He's mad about not being a star," I said. "For me, the most important thing is being able to play the piano every day, to experiment and practice new songs and pour whatever I think and feel out onto the keys. Whether anyone hears my music or buys it is secondary. I love travel and I love royalties; don't get me wrong. But I never expected to get rich or famous. I won't feel my life was wasted if I don't get to play Carnegie Hall."

She held my hand said "Marlene, a life with you could never be a waste."

That night Blue Maria opened for us and introduced us as "the best piano player in the U.S. of A and her handsome husband". There were couples from age 16 to 80, white, black, Jewish, Italian, Polish, Russian and Irish. The two Weinblum daughters, Esther and Tamara, danced with their husbands. The Queen of Clubs was more cosmopolitan than The Starfish but I felt at home there. Robert and I made five dollars a piece and sold some of our *Twilight* albums.

"I think I could get you a regular gig here," Blue Maria said.

"Al wouldn't want me leaving too often," I said. "But I've had a wonderful time."

"I'd take the gig," said Robert.

Because of his audition the next day, Robert went to bed early, sleeping on Blue Maria's couch, but Blue Maria and I stayed up late, playing *Starfish Blues, What'll I Do?,* and *Makin' Whoopee.* Then we started taking requests.

From the back of the audience, a voice I recognized called out "Play *I Don't Care,* Marlene!"

Stunned, I searched for his face in the crowd, his curly hair, his bright brown eyes - any trace of him. I tried to step off the stage, to push my way through the dancing crowd and find him.

"Where are you going?" asked Blue Maria.

"Get back on stage!" said the first row of drunks.

"Play *I Don't Care*!" said a second voice from my past.

They were both in the room and I couldn't reach them. By the time I could leave the stage, they would dissolve into the New York night. Perhaps they planned it that way, but why come to hear me play and not speak to me? Defeated, I sank down on the piano bench and pounded my disappointment into the keys. Because the song always consoled me, and because Blue Maria didn't know all the words, I began to sing;

I don't care
I don't care
What they may think of me

As I sang, I heard the two voices drawing nearer to the stage and singing with Blue Maria and me.

I'm happy-go-lucky,
Men say I am plucky
So jolly and carefree
I don't care,
I don't care,
If I do get the mean and stony stare.
If I'm never successful,
It won't be distressful,
'Cos I don't care

They wove their way through the crowd and by the end of the song, I could see them at the foot of the stage, holding pints of beer, wearing new suits and caps, and smiling bigger than they ever had in Laurel. I struck the last note, jumped off the stage and caught them both in my arms.

"Brendan! Isaac!"

"Another pitcher, please, Jake!" Isaac called to the bartender.

Brendan and I hugged each other tight and I began to cry on his camel-colored jacket. He was taller, but still wiry and smelled of clover and sweet tobacco, like Dad once did.

"I have your record and I hear you on the radio, but it ain't the same," Brendan whispered. "I had to see you."

"I looked for you every time I came to New York," I said. "It made me almost crazy. I miss you so much. Mother and Aunt Josie miss you both so badly."

Isaac handed me the beer, which I gulped, and maneuvered us to some bar stools.

"Sven doesn't miss me," Isaac said. "And Mama - Aunt Josie - she never writes. They believe that we are lost souls."

"I know better," I said.

"We've been so happy here," Brendan told me.

He told me about his illustrating work and Isaac talked about his job at the greenhouse. They shared a house with actors and artists and went to plays, and movies and drag balls.

"Last Halloween I dressed up like Eva Tanguay," Brendan said. "Understand that I don't wish I was a woman but I always wanted to dance like her."

"I remember," I said. "You always could. I named my daughter after Eva Tanguay."

"And now you sing like her," said Isaac. "We all made it out of Laurel, Marlene. You have your piano act and Brendan and I have each other."

Under the bar, where no one could see, the two of them joined hands over my lap. I kissed them each on the cheek and we all told each other "I love you."

I gave them all the news I had of home, of Mother and Amelia, Joseph and Helen's families, and told them all about The Starfish Seven and Robert and Eva. Blue Maria introduced herself and said "I'm glad to finally meet Marlene's long-lost brother and long-lost friend. Isaac, where have you been keeping Brendan all these years?"

"Oh, I couldn't afford to keep him," Isaac said. "He pays his own way."

At the end of the evening, I asked Brendan one more time "Couldn't you please come to see Mother and meet my Eva?"

"Marlene, it's not possible."

"I'll buy you a ticket."

"That's not what I mean."

"Couldn't you just come home for a day?"

"Marlene, New York is our home."

Brendan kissed me goodbye and pressed an envelope into my hand. He and Isaac hugged me and then rushed to catch a cab to a party. When I opened the envelope, I saw a card with Brendan's sketch of himself and Isaac in suits with sunflowers on their lapels. I remembered Brendan's old picture of Oscar Wilde holding a sunflower, his favorite blossom. When I turned the card over, I read a neatly typed card with "Brendan Piper" and his office address. Now I could find Brendan in New York. He and Isaac were no longer lost to me. I hid the card in my wallet, deciding not to mention it to Robert or to my family.

The next morning Kate and Big Jake invited us downstairs for French toast and potato cakes. Robert had already left for his audition that morning; we'd agreed to meet later at a public library.

I waited for two hours and read fifty pages of The Count of Monte Cristo but Robert never showed up. I called the theater where he had auditioned but no one there remembered him. At last, more disappointed than worried, I made my way toward the train station. I ate a big cheese knish and full sour pickle to dull my pain. How could my husband forget me and ignore me as if we were still in high school? Didn't he love me at all?

By the time I got home to Laurel, I was angry. At the train station I looked around for him, though he wouldn't have known which train I was taking coming home and wouldn't sit around the station waiting for me anyway. When I got home, Helen and Edward were at Mother's house with Eva and Grace. They'd left a note for me and Robert. I found Robert's dirty clothes dumped in a pile on our floor. He had been home today, dropped off his soiled underwear for me as if I was his maid, then rushed out again to something or someone more important. Furious, I grabbed his dirty clothes and shoved them into his bureau drawer.

An envelope had fallen out of one of Robert's pockets and lay on the floor like a white gardenia petal faded to beige. I picked it up and smelled the musky scent of his skin on it. I hated how much I missed him, even in my anger. I sat down on our bed and pulled the letter out of the envelope, which Robert had already opened.

The envelope had arrived General Delivery at the post office, not at our house. The handwriting was unfamiliar with dark, angular letters marching across the page like army ants. Still, the handwriting had a feminine grace about it. The letter read:

Darling Bobbie,

Please come to my place as soon as you get into town. I've cried into my pillow every night that you've been away. Even little Caesar can't cheer me up and I haven't been out at all except to walk him. Oh my poor nerves!

My psychoanalyst says I am rootless because I have no husband and children to share my life. At times I do regret the flightiness of my youth – the baby I might have had – all the love I long to give weighs me down. The burden of my feelings is unendurable without you. I have never loved so deeply and earnestly.

My sweet Bobbie, I want to give you everything you've always wanted. I'll take you to Venice and the French Riviera. You can have all the silk ties and pinstripe suits you like. I will put you on stage in every opera house in Europe and on every radio station across America. I want to share your songs generously with the world and never try to clip your wings as your wife has done.

I know you have sacrificed two years of your life for a mistake and are sacrificing each day now because of your child. But Bobbie, you must put your past behind you. I know that you married that widow out of pity and not love. You deserve freedom and your child deserves a father she can be proud of, a famous man, not a henpecked husband trapped in a backwater town. Marlene can never truly love anything but her music; like most so-called artistic females she is more than a little mad. You must break free from the shackle of your marriage.

Think of your music, your acting, and our future, Bobbie. Do you want to die broke in Laurel, Pennsylvania? I know that you are a brilliant star and I will let the whole world see you shine.

I live only for you,

Audrey

I crumpled the letter and shoved it into my pocket. It would be easy to rip it to shreds and flush it down the toilet, to fling it into the coal furnace and watch it burn. Maybe I could even pretend that I had not seen it. I could pound out Beethoven's *Fifth* on my piano downstairs until my hands stopped shaking and my eyes no longer burned.

No, it was too late now to deceive myself, Robert or anyone else. I loved Robert so much and needed to believe he loved me and Eva. Whenever he had paid me a compliment, part of me had doubted it, wondering if it was all an act. I had seen him transform himself into Hamlet and Macbeth. It would be no great feat to disguise himself as a loving husband and father. I hated Robert. I felt like a murder victim, who realizes only at the end that the coffee was always sweetened with arsenic instead of sugar.

At that very moment, I heard the front door open and shut. I wanted to hide or sneak out the back door. The footsteps crossed the living room. I wished it was Helen who I could confide in, or Edward who I could avoid speaking to until I was calm or Eva (Oh my little Eva!) whose eyes would light up when she saw mine. I would have to lie to Eva, to pretend that I was all right, but already I felt my anger glowing through my skin like radium under glass. I recognized those brisk masculine steps, the sound of Robert's new Oxford shoes, not Edward's work boots, ascending the steps.

Robert appeared in the bedroom doorway like a comic character who just walked into an Ibsen play by mistake. He entered the room and smiled at me without seeing the darkness of my eyes, the way my shoulders slumped forward as if I were collapsing in upon myself. Robert settled on the bed beside me, wrapped one arm around me and lightly kissed my mouth.

I heard metal clinking in his pockets and looked down to see him draw out a silver pocket watch. As Judas approached Jesus Christ in the Garden, did Christ hear that same click of silver on silver, the sound of such a small amount of money extinguishing a great love? My eyes were downcast and Robert assumed I was looking at the watch.

"Isn't it elegant?" he asked. "A gift from an anonymous lady admirer."

He flipped the watch over to show me the monogram on the back: R.L.S.

"If she's anonymous, how do you know she's a lady?"

My voice sounded far away. I felt desiccated, like a seashell with a tiny crab suffocating inside.

"What did you say, Marlene?"

"I said 'HOW DO YOU KNOW SHE'S A LADY?'!"

I spoke so loudly that my voice warped. Robert shrank back when he saw the rage in my eyes. I pulled out the crumpled letter.

Robert lifted in from my hand and tucked it in his breast pocket.

"Audrey Bainworth admires me," he said. "Many women do. You must have known when you married me that I would attract many women. That's inevitable for a performer."

He tried to sound more calm than defensive.

"You're not a prostitute," I said.

"I'm an actor and a singer, Marlene. I am a star. And I won't be anchored to this shitty little town and that hole in the ground you call a nightclub. It's disgusting! I find some success and happiness and – yes, a beautiful woman for a change - and you accuse me of selling myself!?"

Robert stood up, irate now, and laid one hand on his chest as if giving a monologue.

"I worked damn hard for this. I want a place in New York; I won't stay in Laurel anymore! It's choking me, this provincial town, my narrow-minded parents. If you loved me you could understand."

I stood up too, torn between wanting to hold Robert and wanting to shatter his beautiful cheekbones like china.

"I couldn't bear Los Angeles, but I could live in New York," I said. "It's close enough to home and big enough for you."

He talked right over my words.

"I don't want you to come with me, Marlene. I didn't want to be with you today. You've gotten fat and you dress so plain. When we go out together I'm ashamed of you."

"What? I don't look any different than I ever did, Robert."

"You're different since you had the baby."

"Don't call Eva 'the baby' like she's some damn object!" I said. "I've always loved you. I wanted you even more after she was born and even while I was pregnant. I cried into my pillow at night when you pushed me away. I never denied you anything: love, money, trips to New York. You're wearing a silver watch and new shoes and I'm digging dandelions in the graveyard for food. Now you tell me it's my fault you're unhappy and I'm not good enough for you. Don't you *ever* tell me I didn't love you enough!"

I was roaring now and Robert's words were as thin and biting as a paper cuts.

"You do love me," he said. "And you did your best, Marlene, but I want more."

"I'll give you anything you want."

"I want Audrey," he said.

"Why?"

"She understands me and I understand her. We have all the same interests, the same tastes. We smoke the same cigarettes and laugh at the same fools we see on the street. Audrey will do anything for fun and never worry what her family thinks."

"She can afford that. She has no family."

"Neither have I," said Robert. "Not mine or yours. I need to get the hell out of Laurel; I always did. In Hollywood I had a chance but you, you had to come back here even before we had the baby."

"Eva! Say her name."

I tried to grab him, but he flicked my hands away.

"You can't hold me with guilt, Marlene. I'm a free man and I'll go where I want, when I want with whoever I want. I'll tell you right now that I never wanted a child. I tried to make the best of it, but there it is. Children are boring; children are stupid; children are greedy and daughters are the worst of all."

"Children are people. Why do you talk about Eva like she's a stranger? She's your own flesh and blood."

"I wonder," he said.

I tried to slap him then, but he grabbed my wrist and shoved me aside. He pushed past me through the hallway to the top of the stairs.

"Robert, where are you going?" I asked.

"This is not my home," Robert said. "I've wanted to tell you about Audrey since June. That's when it all began, at her party at the hotel. I knew then that I loved Audrey, not you, and that I want a divorce."

He walked to the top of the stairs, never turning his back to me. I followed.

"I'll never let you abandon me and our daughter. You have no grounds for a divorce from me. My whole family and yours will tell everyone I took wonderful care of Eva and you. You would have frozen to death in the gutter if it weren't for me."

"Don't try to follow me," said Robert. "I will divorce you. Audrey and I are going abroad, I won't say where, but it is a country with a bright climate and very lenient divorce laws."

I stood silently at the top of the stairs and watched Robert go out the front door. I staggered back to my room and collapsed on our bed, which still smelled of him. I cried until my sides and stomach ached.

Helen and Edward came home with Eva and Grace. The little girls were frightened by my sobbing and started to cry too, so Edward took them outside to play in the snow. Eva didn't want to leave my side, but I managed to kiss her and send her outside. Helen called Amelia and told her I was hysterical and needed a nurse and both my sisters. Slowly and painfully I told them what Robert had said.

CHAPTER THIRTY-ONE

Amelia and Helen insisted that I box Robert's things up and put them in the attic. For the first few weeks I thought he would come back for them. I imagined hundreds of cruel taunts and declarations of love that I wished I could tell him. No one had heard from Robert before he left town or knew where he was going. Helen told me Robert would come to his senses and return soon. Joseph told me I was better off without him, and to stop moping and looking out the window. Amelia felt sure he would return to see Eva no matter what happened but my mother told me not to hold any false hopes.

"I knew Robert was selfish," Mother said. "I tried to be kind to him, but I never trusted him."

His parents would not speak of him. Elaine was sympathetic and closer to me than ever, often coming to visit so Eva could see Gwen, Lance and Will. She told me how miserable she had been when Wayne left her and Lance and Gwen, and how much she hated the stigma of divorce.

"I can't believe my brother be can so cruel," she said.

Two months later I read in *The Laurel Intelligencer-Journal* that Audrey Bainworth had married Robert Schumann in Havana. Cuban law permitted anyone to get a divorce after living there for thirty days. I imagined a place full of palm trees and gardenias, the taste of rum and sound of Spanish guitars, everything Robert craved and I couldn't afford. My husband was honeymooning in the tropics with his new bride as Eva and I walked hand-in-hand through the cold gray slush in Laurel.

It hurt like hell when Eva asked me "Where is Daddy?"

Over and over again she would toddle into a room or rush around a corner and call out "Daddy!" At first her voice was expectant, then questioning, then tearful.

"Mama, where's Daddy?"

"Daddy's gone away, Evie."

"When will he come back?"

"He won't come back, Evie."

She would wait a few minutes and then ask again.

"But, Mama when will Daddy come back?"

She clung to my legs.

I shook my head.

"He went away. He won't come back, ever."

I didn't want to tell her until she was much older that Robert stopped loving me. I didn't want my child to know that love could end for no good reason. I could scarcely believe that myself. By the time I'd be ready to tell Eva the truth, and by the time she'd be ready to ask me for the whole story, she would already have overheard many fragments from relatives and neighbors. I didn't want to lie to my daughter, but I didn't want to beat her with the truth either.

"You should tell her Robert is dead," Mother said. "It would be easier for Eva to bear. She'd stop looking for him and couldn't blame anyone for his absence."

"Mother, you always wanted me to tell the truth."

"No one tells the whole truth," my mother said coldly.

"What if I told her he was dead and he came back to see her one day? Eva would hate me, and rightly so."

"Don't hold your breath for him to come back, Marlene," said Mother.

Eva had kept one of her father's handkerchiefs with his initials on it. I found it under her pillow, washed it with her sheets and put it back, not saying anything about it. Sometimes Eva would cry at night because she missed Robert. Grace would say "Shhh" and Eva would stop crying when I came into the room.

Once when I tried to comfort her, she slapped me. It made me angry but I didn't strike her. I looked her in the eye and said "Don't hit me. Don't you ever hit your mother no matter how mad you are. If you want me to leave you alone, I will."

Eva rolled over and sulked. Grace stared at me wide-eyed, then pinched her eyes shut and pretended to be asleep. At least they have each other, I told myself.

I went downstairs and played Pachelbel's *Canon in D Major* on the piano. It was the most peaceful song I could think of. I kept playing until the whole house was silent.

I went upstairs to check on Eva. She was asleep, clutching Bob Bear, with the handkerchief lying across her pillow and one foot sticking out of the covers. I pulled the sheet and blanket over her foot. Grace was really asleep now, holding Sally. Helen and Edward were asleep in the next room. It was time for me leave for The Starfish. I always looked in on Eva just before I left and again after I came home, though she would not see me until I woke up in the late afternoon.

It was a relief but also a deep sorrow when Eva stopped calling for her daddy and asking where Robert had gone. The smell of him faded from the house; I donated all of his clothes, shoes, pomades, combs, razors and shaving soaps to the Salvation Army.

One night while we were all eating our potatoes and cabbage, *Twilight Melodies* came on the radio. Robert was singing *My Blue Heaven* and I was playing the piano. Helen and I froze and Edward jumped up to change the station.

"Leave it alone, Edward," I said. "It's all right."

If Eva still recognized her father's voice, she gave no sign of it. His pictures were hidden in my drawers with pictures of David. I kept our records, but I never played them. The royalty checks from *Twilight Melodies* still came to me each month, only half as much as those for *Starfish Blues*. At least Robert had never tried to claim his half of the profits from the music we made together. Maybe deep down he knew that he only got the album and the tour because of me and he must have wanted some of his music to support his daughter.

I wrote letters addressed to the Bainworth mansion, most of which were returned to sender. I heard rumors that Robert and Audrey had moved out to California, but she also spent several months of the year in France and Italy. When I sent pictures of Eva, those were removed from the envelopes before they were sent back. I suspected that Robert kept her picture in his wallet, unbeknownst to Audrey or anyone else.

Mr. and Mrs. Schumann considered Robert dead to the family. He had abandoned me and Eva and also his parents when he eloped with Audrey. Elaine's divorce had been embarrassing but forgivable. She had been abandoned by Wayne, who her parents never liked, and they may have been secretly relieved that she had a chance to remarry, even though she and Oliver could never take communion again. Oliver Untermeyer was always respectful to Mr. and Mrs. Schumann and they liked the fact that his parents were German immigrants too. Mr. and Mrs. Schumann treated Eva and me as lovingly as ever, but would not speak of Robert.

The week after Robert had left, I asked Mrs. Schumann "Have you heard anything from Robert?"

She said to me "Marlene, we have no son."

Mr. Schumann sat in his carved wooden chair, imperious and unforgiving as a Norse god.

"Do not speak his name to us again," said Mr. Schumann.

Eva never asked her grandparents about Robert. I had waited until she was out in their backyard to ask them about him. I wished that we could comfort each other, as my family did in any time of trouble, but the only Schumann who would honestly speak from her heart was Elaine. Mrs. Schumann must have been twice as hurt and disappointed as I was, but I respected her wishes and kept silent.

Everyone at The Starfish was sympathetic after my divorce. The band was patient with me when I made mistakes and pretended not to notice if I shed a few tears during sad songs. Zach and Dennis gave me many free gin and tonics.

The night after Robert and Audrey's wedding announcement appeared in the paper, Iris whispered to me "I know what Robert did and I think he will regret it for the rest of his life."

Iris surprised us all by accepting a marriage proposal from her boyfriend Wendell Jackson. I did my best to be happy for her.

At the Starfish, women told me stories of their own no-good men and men (mostly intoxicated) assured me that I could find someone better. (I hoped they were not referring to themselves.) Even Chauncey, who never thought much of me, made the most sympathetic remark he could muster.

"I knew that Robert Schumann was no damn good!"

One night, about a week after the divorce, Al asked me to stay late at work. Dennis was leaving early and he needed someone else to help him count the money. He had never asked me to count money before so I asked:

"Is there anything else you need?"

"There's something I want to talk to you about," he said. " I'll give you a ride home."

I thought he must be disappointed that I looked so sad and even shed tears on stage. The Starfish was supposed to be an oasis from the desert of The Great Depression, a place where people came to escape their troubles. My music was supposed to bring others happiness and if I wallowed in my own misery, I could not be true to my music and my audience. Sad songs had their own kind of comfort and I had grown to love the blues, but my own sorrow was beginning to taint everything I played. I could hear in my head all the things Al would say to me.

Everyone left The Starfish one by one. Dennis washed the glasses. Chauncey stacked the chairs on the tables and blew out all the candles. Emmett swept and mopped the floor. Al switched off the yellow and green starfish lights on the walls and left on a few red lanterns by the bar to give us light to count by.

"Will you be needing anything more, boss?" asked Emmett.

"No, thank you, Emmett," said Al. "I'll close up."

Al and I neatly stacked the coins and bills on the bar: pennies, nickels, dimes, quarters, ones, fives, tens and so on. Al wrote down the amount in a ledger, then swept all the money into his brown leather satchel.

"Thank you, Marlene," he said.

"You're welcome, Al."

My hands felt grimy from handling all that money, so I washed up at the sink, turning my back to Al.

"You had something you wanted to tell me."

"Yes. I think I'll wash up too."

I sat on the bar, bracing myself for bad news. Al looked serious but not angry. What he had to say burdened him, like a lump in his throat. Maybe my recent sadness embarrassed him. He held my right hand and fixed his shining black eyes on mine. My heart quivered like a frightened rabbit.

"When Blue Maria left me, she cut my heart in half. I couldn't tell anyone how much it hurt. I've always had plenty of girls and some of them have dropped me. I never thought anything of it and just felt lucky to have so many women fall for me. Never in my life did I feel lonely until Blue Maria jilted me."

His voice was soft and sad, a tone I'd never heard from Al. I squeezed his hand.

"She did know how much you loved her, Al."

"She was my true love. There will be others, but no one will keep up with me or understand me like Blue Maria. I'm telling you this now for two reasons. First, because I trust that you'll never tell anyone else that I still love her."

"I won't."

"You're the most loyal person I know," he said. "The second reason I tell you this is because I know how much it hurt you that Robert Schumann left you."

Tears welled up in my eyes and I let go of his hand.

"You can't understand that, how it feels to be divorced with a child."

"Yes I can, Marlene. I may not have a two-year-old daughter and a bill of divorcement, but I know what you feel in here."

He touched his heart.

"You feel like Robert cut out a part of your heart and you are empty inside. Every person in the world feels that sometime. The real heroism isn't to die for love, but to keep on living and giving it."

"I will go on. I'd never end my life for a man who hates me."

"I know you'll never give up, Marlene. I never doubted that for a minute. You've been the backbone of your family and the best damn musician who ever played on my stage."

"Thank you. That means a lot to me, Al. I never would have made a record or been on the radio if not for you and The Starfish."

"I want to give you something," he said.

Al held my hand and took a red silk scarf out of his pants pocket. It came from China and had a pattern of peonies and nightingales woven into its smooth surface. As quick as a magician, Al wrapped the scarf around my neck and loosely tied it. The silk was still warm from his pocket.

"It's lovely," I said. "Thank you, Al."

"I got it at Wong's Imports in Central Market. I want you to know that there's beauty in this world no matter how bad it hurts you. And I want you to know that you are beautiful no matter what shit your husband said to you."

"You don't have to say that," I said, embarrassed.

"Don't be coy. It's the truth. Robert leaving is the best thing that happened to you."

"How can you say that? I love him. Eva needs her father."

"She needs a father, not a selfish coward. You and Eva deserve better than Robert and one day you will have it."

"How do you know?"

I was angry and near tears. To my great surprise, Al leaned forward and kissed me. I let myself kiss him back. Our lips parted and he looked down, his strong arms still wrapped around me.

"Do you think you can save me?" I asked rudely.

Al looked completely sincere and said "No, Marlene. I know you'll save yourself and Eva too. Come on, I'll drive you home."

We didn't speak on the ride home. I ran the scarf through my fingers like a rosary. I would tell everyone that I bought it on a whim. It was a singular event and I kept it a secret from everyone. The pain of losing Robert still pressed down on me, but I knew that the weight would lift one day.

When I got home that evening, I dug Robert's old portrait out of my drawer. I still had taken the picture of him in high school, when he first prepared to leave Laurel for New York. How young and handsome he looked in his tilted hat and three-piece suit! Now I saw the vanity in his pose, the self-satisfied smirk, the faraway look in his eyes that passed for deep intelligence. He hated Laurel and dreamed of an escape. He did not share his hopes and dreams with anyone, not with his family, with me or any friend. At age eighteen and at twenty-six, Robert Schumann lived only for himself.

I would keep some of his pictures for Eva because some day she would ask about him and want to see his face. I had saved her silver locket with the wedding pictures of us in my jewelry box, for the day she would be old enough to wear it. But this portrait in its black paper holder was my lost love, which I had unfolded on lonely nights in high school and at my uncle's farm. I had clung to it like an icon whenever I felt lonely, even when I married David I had kept this picture. Robert John Schumann, the actor, the singer, my soul mate, my white knight and my demon lover. Now I awakened from my dreams of him.

I carried the picture downstairs to the coal furnace and opened the metal trap door. I flung Robert's portrait on the orange coals and watched the edges curl up. There was vile black smoke from the film chemicals; the photograph burned slower than its black paper covering. The fire pierced Robert's right eye and a black hole spread out in place of his young and handsome face.

CHAPTER THIRTY-TWO

West Lemon Street was close enough to the railroad track that hoboes would come by begging for food. They moved along like shadows and most people pretended not to see them. The newspapers called them "the forgotten men" because their former employers, relatives and friends had dropped them like brown leaves, to drift or rot where they fell. Neighbors locked their gates to discourage hoboes and bought big dogs or guns. Only two people on our block would ever feed hoboes – Old Mrs. Taft and my sister Helen.

Helen would bake an extra loaf of cornbread or batch of biscuits and even set aside sausages, bacon and frozen orange juice, to be thawed out for "company". "Company" almost always meant hoboes. Helen never served orange juice to her friends and she scolded me once for drinking it.

"I bought the orange juice for the hoboes. They need some food with Vitamin C to avoid scurvy."

"So do we!" I said. "You feed those strangers better than you feed your own family."

"You know where your next meal is coming from. They don't," said Helen.

A dozen trains came through Laurel every day and at any hour between dawn and dusk we might get a knock on the back door. Hoboes knocked on the back door, too humble to climb the front steps. Also, the back door led directly into the kitchen, where they could look in through the bright windows and see Helen and me cooking or washing dishes. I felt embarrassed, though not fearful, and asked Helen to answer the door,

There would be one or two ragged men, smelling of cigarettes and old shoes and sometimes alcohol. Their clothes would be faded to brown and gray, whatever their original colors, and they would have beards or whiskers. They would hold their hats in their hands and humbly offer to rake the leaves or shovel the walk. Sometimes Edward had already removed the leaves or snow and Helen would ask the hoboes to carry wood from the woodpile; we burned wood in the fireplace sometimes to save coal.

No one ever got food without doing something for us; that was common courtesy. Almost all hoboes would offer their services at once, saying "Good afternoon, ladies. Is there any work you need done around the place?" They would mention that they were passing through Laurel and ask if anyone was hiring, which no one ever was.

If a hobo put out his hand and launched into a sob story about how his factory shut down and his wife ran off with the iceman, I would interrupt and say "Can you do something for us?"

"You have no patience, Marlene," Helen would whisper to me.

"No, I don't," I said. "Our father's dead. Your husband got laid off; mine abandoned me. Our lives are just as sad as most of theirs. The only difference is that we still have a house."

"We're lucky," said Helen. "It's only the grace of God that separates you and me from these men. We're not better people than them. What if you'd never found your job at The Starfish? You only found it because of Peggy Hobbes."

"I would have had to leave Laurel," I said.

I tried to imagine myself as one of these hoboes. I had met two transient women in The Starfish. They called themselves "road sisters" and traveled together for safety. They told stories of hopping trains and hitching rides and cried when they talked about the children they had left with relatives. Both of them planned to get work picking apples and send the money home. Their clothes were old, but clean, and their hair and nails neatly trimmed, unlike the dusty male hoboes. Women, no matter how destitute, had to dress and behave as if they had homes. They would ask for help from a church or wait in a bread line, rather than risk knocking on the door of a stranger who might take advantage of them.

"I think it's good that you want to help people," I said to Helen. "But we already do that with the money we put in the collection plate at Sunday mass. That goes to the St. Vincent de Paul Society and the soup kitchen downtown. That money helps people pay their rent and get a hot meal. I don't want you giving away our last biscuit to some old drunk who most likely ran out on his poor family."

"Marlene, you're jaded," said Helen. "I always give food, never money. I never give more than we can spare. There's no harm in it."

Edward worried about Helen's safety. We had never been robbed or threatened, but he feared the worst from strange men approaching the house. He still went out looking for odd jobs almost every day.

"Helen, you should never let anyone in the house when you're here alone, no matter how cold it is. What if some guy grabbed a knife and robbed you – or worse? Most hoboes carry knives anyway, if not guns."

"You always carry a jackknife yourself. So what!" said Helen. "I have a hatchet behind the stove if I ever have to defend myself."

"Don't be foolish, darling. Don't put yourself in danger because you want to be St. Elizabeth of Hungary. Tell them your husband insists they stay on the porch. Trust me, they've heard that before. And Mrs. Taft has that old outhouse if anybody needs it. You have to take it easy, Helen, if not for your sake, then for the baby's."

He didn't mean Grace; Helen and Edward were expecting another child. Pregnancy did not slow Helen down. My little sister had grown into a stout-hearted woman; she never complained of her swollen feet, aching back and touchy bladder.

"I think about how I love Grace and the new baby," Helen said, laying a hand on her belly. "And that doesn't make me afraid of hoboes and strangers. That makes me remember that every one of those men was once a baby in his mother's arms. A lot of people forget them, but I never will."

Helen agreed not to let anyone in if she was alone. When I was with her she would let hoboes wash and shave at the kitchen sink and use our bathroom. I hated to think of some strangers' grime sticking to my bathtub and sink, but I did sympathize with anyone who had no hot water and soap. I never squealed on Helen to Edward and scrubbed the tub and sink so he wouldn't see anyone else's whiskers or hair.

Mother also warned Helen to watch out for her safety, but admired her generosity.

"We all have to do what we can for the less fortunate," said Mother. "Amelia nurses people for free and Marlene gives people happiness with her music. Helen wants to do something about the Depression, not just for her own family, but for everyone she can possibly help. That is Christian and I am proud of it."

It was simple and uplifting to feed a stranger one meal and send them away smiling, imagining that they really might get that job in the factory in Pittsburgh or the cornfield in Iowa. I prayed that the two road sisters would find a way to get their children back.

Helen went into labor on a lilac-scented May night. Amelia and Katrina looked after her while I took a night off from The Starfish and watched Eva and Grace until noon the next day. When an old black hobo knocked on the door I gave him a bowl of potato kale soup and felt – for the first time in years – completely unselfish. While he pulled weeds for us I told Grace and Eva to pick tulips for Helen. They picked the best ones: red, yellow, white and pink, but I would not let them see her in labor, no matter how they whined and fussed.

"Thanks for feeding him," Helen said, catching her breath between labor pangs. "And tell the girls thanks for the flowers."

At about two in the afternoon, Helen's second daughter Julie was born. Grace and Eva were overjoyed to meet her. Grace clung to her mother and Eva asked if she could have a baby sister too. The Pipers and the Malones were very happy for Helen. Amelia and Arthur, Julie's godparents, gave a big garden party after her baptism, with pulled pork sandwiches and homemade strawberry ice cream.

That same week, Uncle Luke had a heart attack. He died in bed in Aunt Josie's arms. He had been sixty, but in good health until that time, like an old plow, working every day for decades, then cracking with no warning.

Sven went to Dutzer's junkyard that night to find Boyd, but his shack was abandoned. The next day Elias Dutzer told Sven he had fired Boyd two weeks prior for drinking canned heat and hadn't seen him since. Aunt Josie asked every friend and acquaintance of Boyd's if they had seen him, but most of them had not spoken to him in months. Boyd's church attendance was limited to Christmas and Easter, but the parish was shocked when he did not appear at his Luke Hayden's funeral or the rosary for him. Boyd was not present when a lawyer read Uncle Luke's will to his family, leaving the house and farm to Aunt Josie and his remaining money to Maud and Sven. Boyd got nothing except a watch and a Civil War medal from his Hayden grandfather, both of which he already had in his possession. Maud and Sven went to the police station to list Boyd as a missing person, and there was no news of him there either.

Boyd didn't show himself until June, when he met the family outside of St. Anne's as we left mass. I hadn't seen him in church, but later Maud told me he had been there. He had come in late, just before communion and sat in a back pew far from his family's usual place.

Boyd wore an ill-fitting navy suit coat, a green paisley bow tie and no hat. His blond hair was greasy and thinning in the back and his eyes were bloodshot. He wore too much cologne but still reeked of whiskey and sweat. He grabbed Sven by the sleeve, holding him back as Maud tried to pull him forward.

"Boyd, come with us to Aunt Aileen's," said Maud.

Mother, Aunt Josie and Joseph and Helen's families were already halfway up the block. None of them had seen Boyd. I stopped a short distance from Boyd, holding Eva's hand. She was restless, but I shushed her. I had to see what happened next, though I knew it wouldn't be good.

"Good morning, Boyd. How are you?" said Sven, twisting his strong arm out of Boyd's clutches.

"Miserable," said Boyd. "Old Man Dutzer claims he can't afford to pay me any more. I thought now would be a good time to move back to the old homestead. Besides, you'll need another hand on the farm with the harvest coming on."

"I have three hands now," said Sven. "And I just told Edward Malone that he could come out when we need another person for planting and picking."

Maud kept her arm linked with Sven's as if to protect him, even though she was half his size. Eugene clung to his mother's skirts and turned up his nose at his uncle.

Boyd kneeled down and stretched out his hand to Eugene.

"You'd love to have me around, wouldn't you, Eugene?"

"No!" Eugene yelled, slapping Boyd's hand.

"Maud, you got to discipline this boy," Boyd growled. "He's a real mollycoddle."

Maud's eyes narrowed.

"My Eugene is an angel! It's not his fault if he can't remember your face. It's bad enough you don't come to church or Sunday dinner anymore, but where were you when we buried Father?"

Boyd scowled and said nothing. Sven turned red and looked over to me, then at Maud.

"You girls should take Eva and Eugene and go on up to Aunt Aileen's."

Maud and I walked away with deliberate slowness, still listening to Sven and Boyd.

"You have to take me in! You have to!" Boyd shouted. "My mother won't stand for this!"

"Mama already told me she wouldn't have you under her roof until you quit drinking and got a job. She told Maud and me. Don't lie to me, Boyd. I could always tell when you lied."

"Don't you call *my* mother 'Mama'! Your mama's dead and rotten and she's better off not seeing what a bastard you turned out to be! You think you own Hayden farm? I'm the damn first born son!"

Onlookers peeked out of the windows of nearby houses and hesitated on the steps of St. Anne's. They tried to look disinterested, but the whispers sounded like the buzzing of a hornets' nest. Most of these people knew Boyd and Sven from church, Central Market and the neighborhood and had watched "that spoiled Hayden boy" pick on "the orphan from Norway" throughout their childhood years. I was probably not the only one who hoped Sven would knock Boyd out with one punch.

Sven did not raise his voice, but didn't show any fear either.

"I've been working Hayden farm since I was seven and you left it years ago. You didn't even show up for harvest last fall when your father needed you. You hate farm work, Boyd. You always have."

Boyd's face went red as he screamed.

"Dad would always take me back no matter what happened. I'm his flesh and blood and you're just a damn field hand!"

"It's my field," Sven said. "You're embarrassing yourself and me. Come to Aunt Aileen's with me and we'll talk this out like grown men."

Sven tried to put his hand on Boyd's shoulder, but Boyd shoved him.

"I'm not talking anything out, you fat bastard! You're not good enough to live in my house, work my land, or sleep with my sister!"

Maud and I had reached the corner. Eugene and Eva were looking backward at the commotion, which Maud pretended to ignore. I turned around to see Sven punch Boyd and knock him on his back on the sidewalk. Boyd didn't get up but he kept screaming and swearing incoherently as Sven walked away without a backward glance, pushing his way through the noisy crowd.

"Hurry up, Marlene, for God's sake," said Maud, pulling my elbow.

We did not see Boyd again or hear from him for a very long time. Cal heard that he hopped a train for Ohio, but no one had seen him leave. After that day, every time a hobo knocked on our door I feared it might be Boyd and prayed that he was safe and (with God all things are possible) sober.

In 1931, the Works Progress Administration began construction of new concrete sidewalks, four new parks and two concrete water towers in Laurel. Joseph and Edward Malone got jobs there.

Edward Malone became a foreman on the water tower project and after that, got work at Paulsens' Construction company. He and Helen began to save money again, although he still refused to use banks and kept it all in a fire-proof safe.

Helen felt crowded with Julie's crib at the foot of her bed and Grace and Eva still sharing their little bedroom. She and Edward still longed for their own house, but I asked them to stay with me for another year.

"I don't want Eva to have to lose anyone else. It was hard enough when she lost her father."

"Marlene, we won't move far away. We'll get a house in the neighborhood and I can still baby-sit Eva during the day. Edward can't feel independent until we have our own house. You must understand that, after all the struggles you went through with David to keep this house."

"I depend on you as much as you do on me," I said. "Please at least wait one more year."

Helen and I convinced Edward to wait one more year, save his money and look for a house within walking distance of mine. He agreed that Eva and Grace should not be separated just yet, but it was obvious that they would always be close friends as well as cousins.

Brendan still scraped by drawing portraits and finally getting some more contracts for illustrations. He and Isaac still lived in an old house somewhere in New York with an endless cast of roommates. Isaac worked at the greenhouse, tending the flowers and the accounts. Every winter, they worked at the ski lodge to put some money away.

On December 1, 1931 my mother turned sixty. Before the evening surprise party at Amelia's house, Mother had a real surprise. She heard a knock on her kitchen door and saw Brendan standing there.

"I was so happy to see Brendan," she told us that evening. "He just came in for an hour and then got back on the train. I couldn't make him stay, but it was so good just to see my son after all these years. He came all the way from Vermont. I told him to come back again, at least to visit, but I feel sure he won't. It's all right, though. I told him I always love him, wherever he is."

Joseph and Amelia were silent, perhaps thinking that Mother was too easy on Brendan in her old age. Helen and I were jealous that he hadn't come to see us. I had been writing to him for years asking him to visit mother, so I felt some satisfaction now. Mother had forgiven

Brendan for being different from all of us and he had forgiven her for trying to cut him into the shape of "a normal man". My Piper family had its flaws but I thanked God that none of us were normal, not my daydreaming father, my cobbler mother, one-legged Joseph, night nurse Amelia, "Saint Helen of the Hoboes", queer Brendan or me, the gin mill piano player.

CHAPTER THIRTY-THREE

I told myself that my life was fine. I was a good mother, a good daughter, a good sister, a good friend, and – without a doubt - a good musician. In spite of the Depression I still enjoyed birthdays and holidays with my loved ones and poured my heart out onstage at The Starfish. Blue Maria invited me to New York to play at The Queen of Clubs and we began to practice new songs for another album and talk about touring again. For two years after Robert left, I danced with traveling salesmen in Laurel and kissed sailors in New York City, but took none of them seriously.

One autumn day, Al slipped an invitation in my tip bowl. It was shortly before Christmas and the card only read:

Black Orchid
6 o' clock
Saturday
My treat
Love, Al

I hadn't been to the Black Orchid Café in five years, not since Robert took me there for my birthday before we were married. That was ages ago in the 1920's when all the shops were busy and we believed in the banks like churches. Now in 1933, it boggled my mind that some people were still rich and always would be. The wealthy rarely visited The Starfish and if any did "go slumming" they wore plain clothes to fit in. No wealthy matron would want to be spotted by her maid while quaffing old-fashioneds and no mill foreman would want to run into the men he had just laid off. Dennis and Zachary told me that the very wealthy had liquor delivered to their homes.

"Not by anyone we know, of course," Dennis said with a wink.

The Black Orchid looked just the same with its scarlet walls and ghostly pale orchids. The waiters swept past me in their starched collars pretending not to see my shabby coat and knitted hat. I glanced around, half-afraid I might see Elizabeth Campbell Sloane or Barbara Thompson, but none of the ladies in satins and furs were familiar. Audrey Bainworth was long gone from Laurel. Elaine had told me that Audrey and Robert had moved to Los Angeles. I would always think of her as Audrey Bainworth, never Audrey Schumann.

Since my divorce I had gone back to signing my name Marlene Piper and it seemed strange that it had ever been Marlene Schumann and Marlene Dunn. My memories of Robert at home and in The Starfish had been watered down and finally drowned by other memories of The Starfish Seven, of Al, of my family. Those places were mine before they were Robert's, but The Black Orchid was a place I had only visited with him. I missed Robert here as I had not missed him in months.

A white orchid stared at me like a hypnotic eye. If Al did not meet me here I would have to leave. I could not afford any item on the menu even if one of the waiters would stoop to bring it to me. They swooped past my table like magpies, not even bringing me a glass of water.

At last Al appeared, just five minutes after six. I had been hysterically early at five forty five. I didn't notice him until he pulled out the chair across from me and sat down. He was spotless and clean-shaven in a pinstripe suit and gray fedora. Al smiled at me and summoned the waiter with a simple tilt of his chin.

"I don't believe you wanted to meet me here," I whispered.

"You don't need to whisper, Marlene," Al said, patting my hand.

"How are you doing, Jimmy?" he asked the waiter.

"Just fine, sir," said the young man, embarrassed at being recognized from a drinking binge at The Starfish.

He brought us two water goblets with floating lemons and two menus, offered the special duck a la orange and Swedish meatballs.

"Get whatever you like, Marlene," said Al.

"Crab imperial and spinach salad with bacon dressing," I said, without hesitation.

Al had Beef Wellington with new potatoes and green beans. We sampled little bites of each other's dinners. I was glad that he wasn't fussy about table manners.

"Do you come here often?" I asked.

"Why? Would you like to?"

"No," I said. "I like the food but not the audience."

We glanced at the violinist, a blonde woman who looked like a wilted Easter lily in white satin and made her instrument whimper like a drowning kitten.

"The music isn't as hot as our place," said Al. "But she's so pretty I should give her my card."

"Yes you should," I said. "She might need to buy some resin or something."

Al grinned.

"I guess you're wondering why I brought you here. Aside from the atmosphere, I wanted to speak to you privately, without the band or your family interrupting or interfering. I want to make you a proposition and give you time to consider it. If you say 'Yes' I'll be delighted, but if you say 'No' I'll understand that too. You may want to consider the offer for a few days before you decide."

"I usually make decisions quickly," I said. "I can tell right away whether I want something or not. What's your offer?'

"Marlene, like ninety nine out of a hundred Americans, I have hoped and prayed for the repeal of Prohibition, but now that it's finally upon us, I know that it will be the end of The Starfish."

"What? Why should that be? Can't you get a liquor license and open the bar above ground? You could get more musicians now than ever and I'd be glad to play for you."

Al shook his head.

"I have political contacts," he said softly. "Which isn't all that shocking because politicians drink even more than journalists. When I looked into the possibility of a liquor license, I was not even allowed to apply. There will only be three bars in Laurel next year: one for the blacks, one for the poor whites and one for these snobs, owned and operated by the mayor's nephew."

He waved his hand dismissively.

"Are you sure, Al?"

"I've asked everyone I could think of to pull strings for me, but all I heard was 'Vintner, you made a ton of dough off Prohibition and the cops all looked the other way. You never got busted. You never went to jail. Just thank God you got away with it and move out of the way now that the honest businessmen of Laurel want to take over the bars, like they have everything else.' People don't like seeing a Portuguese Catholic with that much money. 'You sell hardware, Vintner, and that's all you're ever going to sell in Pennsylvania.' "

"What will you do now?"

"I'll put my money into my hardware business," he said. "I'll take good care of Mama in her old age and put my nephews and nieces through college. I like selling hardware, always did, and there's a lot of construction going on."

Al set his jaw with stubborn optimism, but couldn't quite smile.

"How long will The Starfish stay open?"

"Prohibition will end in December," he said. "The Starfish is history, Marlene."

"I'll still have the band," I said, but I doubted the words even as I spoke them.

Al's eyes were sad. In a few months there would be no more leather satchels stuffed with cash, no more Laurel Lager flowing from the faucet – and despite his prosperity – no more flappers turning their painted faces toward him like flowers following the sun.

"I'll really miss it," I said. "I love The Starfish. I know it's your baby."

I held his hand.

"You helped make it great," he said. "I'm going to say this to The Starfish Seven when you're all together. I already talked to the bartenders. Emmett and Chauncey have jobs lined up as delivery men, taking orders to Stolzfus and the other factories."

"That's good. What was the offer you wanted to make me?"

"I wanted to offer you a job too, Marlene. I know I've said this before but I wasn't joking. I want you to be my secretary."

I fumbled for an answer that was neither dishonest nor ungrateful.

"You know I can't type, Al."

"You'll learn. I learned, I just have other business to attend to and your letters read better than mine. Typing will be a lot easier to learn than piano."

"It's nothing like piano. I don't want you to give me a job just because you feel sorry for me."

"Easy, doll! I'm not the W.P.A. here. I've thought long and hard about this. You're one of few people I trust completely. You're honest, intelligent and you manage money well. You keep the dressing room spotless even when the rest of the band runs home early. You never come to work soused. You split up the tip money evenly, never taking a penny more than your share. I'd hire you for any job, Marlene, because you're sharp enough to train. Will you at least consider it?"

"Of course I will," I said.

I stretched my hand out to him, but he tucked his hand in his lap under the table.

"I don't want to disappoint you," Al said. "I don't want to make promises and break them. I want us to be good friends and I want you to find yourself a good man, not wait around for a two-bit skirt-chaser like me. You know I will never marry."

"Neither will I," I said. "I've had enough of that."

"Of love?" he looked amused.

"No, just marriage. I'll take all the love I can get."

"You should," he said. "Even if some man does sweep you off your feet and out of Laurel."

"I'd come back to Laurel," I said.

"Just consider my offer, that's all," said Al. "The job will always be there. And so will I, in one way or another."

He leaned forward and kissed me full on the lips. I closed my eyes and drank the kiss in like champagne. Customers whispered in shocked disgust and Jimmy the waiter clapped a hand over his chuckling mouth.

Al laid a generous tip on the table, linked arms with me and led me out.

"Come on, Marlene," he said. "Let's go home."

I knew he meant The Starfish. We lived there as much as in our houses (if not more) but were soon to be permanently evicted. Al and I had never been to The Starfish in the day time, but had no worries about being seen as we crept up the alley. Prohibition was almost over and no cop was going to bust us now.

The room was cold and silent as Al lit the red lanterns. He mixed us both gin and tonics and I held one up to toast.

"To our future."

"Our future."

We drank silently. In the red light he looked so handsome with his glossy black hair and classic profile. I thought of Dionysus the wine god finding Ariadne on the island of Naxos after Theseus abandoned her. Al was divinely beautiful and in spite of all his crimes and cruelties, his generosity was divine. As I watched him, he looked around the room at the stage with its purple curtain, the fish on the tile dance floor, the doors to the store rooms and dressing rooms where so many lovers had hidden.

"I named this place The Starfish because that's an animal that recreates itself," Al said. "Your Starfish Blues said it better than I ever could. I knew that even if I got busted by the cops, even if I lost all my money and went to jail, my life would have been worth it because I made some people happy. You do that, Marlene."

To Al's great surprise, I leaned across the bar and kissed him. He put his arms around me and I pulled myself up onto the bar, sitting on it as he stood. He pulled away from me and looked into my eyes, without his disarming smile or any charming words, but sincerely wanting me.

I told him "When Robert left me, you kissed me and told me my life wasn't over. Now I'm telling you that your life will go on."

I embraced him and breathed in his delicious scent of lime. His lips tasted like oranges. We kissed and bit each other's necks and tangled our fingers in each other's hair. I peeled off his green jacket and unbuttoned his clean white shirt. His skin was tawny and fine black hair covered his chest. He unbuttoned my dress and quickly unhooked my bra and garter belt. Al kissed my breasts and belly and parted my legs. I gasped, damp with sweat and longing. All my pain and loneliness melted under his tongue. He stood on a crate, so his hips were level with mine and I could unbutton his pants and caress him.

There on the bar that had given comfort to so many, Al Vintner joined himself to me. We moved slowly and deliciously, kissing and stroking each other. Al delighted me again and again before withdrawing at the crucial moment. He washed briefly at the sink, then held me until our heartbeats slowed down again. He handed me my clothes and found his on the floor.

"Don't fall in love with me, now," he said. "Live and love and make music, and don't let anything, especially not sentiment for me, hold you back."

"You've warmed my heart, but you won't break it," I said.

We kissed each other one more time before climbing up the ladder.

Within a week the other six musicians and I spoke freely about the closure of The Starfish and our future plans. We played better than ever and the house was still full and applauding loudly. It was hard to believe that it would ever end. The Christmas party (before Christmas Eve) and New Year's Eve parties were full, with many guests bringing us little gifts: jars of jam, smoked ham, knitted scarves and homemade lace. I danced with everyone who asked me and spent most of New Year's Eve in the dressing room with Al.

Nothing worried me until the night wound up and I saw Iris drinking champagne alone at the bar. She took off her shoes and rubbed her feet. She has told me in December that she was pregnant with her second child and would have to lay off the eggnog and rum punch. Iris stared at the glass of champagne and raised it to me, saying "This is my last drink."

"Just for seven months, Iris."

I sat down beside her.

"I can't keep doing this," Iris told me. "I need to be home with Benjamin. He's four already; I can't believe it. I'm tired of making the money. Wendell has his W.P.A. job now and Stolzfus is finally hiring again. He applied for his old job as night watchman and if he gets it, we'll be set. I won't have to work anymore."

"But you love drumming," I said. "You told me that you've drummed since you were two years old banging on your mother's pots and pans with a wooden spoon."

"I'll still drum at home and at church on holidays," she said, smiling to herself. "Howard and Jeremy want to play at Parker's when it opens and I'll back them up, but I'm through playing for white people."

"Are you through playing with white people?" I asked.

"Marlene, you know what I mean. I like you fine, but would we have ever even spoken to each other if we hadn't met down in this place?"

"I'm glad we did meet."

"Me too, but I'm not going to miss it. I'm sick of white men staring down my dress and mumbling 'I can't believe a woman can play the drums.' I'm sick of ignorant drunks who expect me and my brother to play minstrel songs. There are so many of my friends and relatives who won't come in here and mix with whites, but they'll see me at church and at Parker's."

Parker's would be the bar for Laurel's black citizens, with a full-service restaurant and three stories of dance halls. Its owners were James and Edward Parker, two butchers who had prospered even during the Depression. Parker's was a brick house three blocks from Buchanan Station. Every railroad porter and waiter would flock to it and it was close enough to its clients' neighborhood that most of them could walk home.

Neville's would be the bar for wealthy whites (named after Mayor Tate's idiot nephew) and midway between the Varsity Theater and the Franklin Opera House downtown. The watering hole for my class and would be Charlie's at the trolley stop after Stolzfus Silk Mill.

"Will you and I see each other again?" I asked Iris.

"I'll see you around," she said, as gently as she could.

Aaron Bauer overheard us and snapped "Don't be so damned sentimental, Marlene! How many bands do you know that have whites, blacks, Jews and girls playing together? Wake up, sister! This Little Rascals movie is over!"

I could no longer delude myself that The Starfish Seven would go on playing together or that any new members could replace or equal the originals. My band - white and black, male and female, Jew and Catholic and Baptist, jazz and rag and improvised genius – was broken and would not play anymore. We had worked out our differences miraculously and never let anyone's ego drown out our music. Every one of us had fans, people who came to The Starfish just to hear us, but that wasn't enough. No legal respectable bar would open itself to all seven of us. Recording would be impossible; none of us ever expected it. Now it hurt me to know that I would not hear The Starfish Seven play again. In January, the new bars would open and it would all be over.

Aaron Bauer was engaged and looking for accounting or bookkeeping work in New York City.

He said "I'll never perform again unless it's a band that can record some albums." This sounded like a boast, but I suspected he was really giving up. Maybe he played music to rebel against his modest doctor father and now he thought he was too old to show off anymore.

Frank Caprello would go back to the deli. Oliver Untermeyer would be a full-time plumber. Jeremy was head porter at the Ottoman Hotel and got Howard a job there driving patrons to and from Buchanan Station at all hours. They would play for their families and at parties but that was all.

"We've got families now, Marlene," said Frank. "We have responsibilities."

As if I had never had a family to worry about! As if I never paid bills or worried whether my labor could really feed five hungry mouths!

All I said was "I understand."

CHAPTER THIRTY-FOUR

All winter I prepared for the February day when I would leave for New York to start another tour with Blue Maria. We had recorded our third album, *Rocky Road Blues*, in May and would play and sell it in Cleveland, then Chicago, Minneapolis, Seattle, Portland, San Francisco, Los Angeles, Phoenix, Dallas, Houston, New Orleans, Atlanta, Charleston, Richmond and Philadelphia. We would be on tour for two months. Eva would stay with my mother from February until May when I returned.

Eva had cried a little in November when Helen, Edward, Grace and Julie had moved into their new house, even though it was only three doors down. Edward built gates in both of our fences so the girls could go through the alley from one yard to another. Grace and Julie each had their own rooms now, and a cherry tree to climb. Helen did not want Eva to live with them for three whole months; she and Edward were enjoying their space and freedom in their new home.

"I love Eva," Helen said. "But it's too much for me to look after her and Grace and Julie. Eva won't mind me as well as my girls do. She needs her hard-headed mom."

"You've spent as much time with my daughter as I have," I said. "And I'm very grateful but I don't want to be a burden to you."

Mother had suggested keeping Eva at her house.

"I'd like her company, Marlene. I raised all five of you kids and I know how to keep Eva from being bored and lonely and not spoil her too much."

Mother was not suffering for company; Mr. Dutzer came to court her and play pinochle with her three night a week. He asked her to marry him, and when she refused, he bought a house on our block to be close to her. One afternoon I walked in on them kissing and Dutzer put on his hat, tipped it to me, and rushed out the back door.

"Mother, you've still got it," I said, giggling.

"I've never loved anyone as I loved your father, but Elias is very dear to me," Mother said seriously. "I don't want a husband to cook and clean for, but at my age there's no harm in having an admirer."

Mother set the roses Mr. Dutzer had given her next to a Christmas card from Brendan, a pen and ink sketch of the Blessed Mother setting Jesus in the manger. He and Isaac were working at the ski lodge and my brother had gotten a great contract illustrating an encyclopedia.

Brendan had bought a house and invited us to visit him in the spring. Of all our family, only I went to see him.

It was a narrow, two-story red brick row house with window boxes full of parsley and mint. Brendan was now a "working artist" not a "starving artist" for the first time in years and could spend the rest of his life in New York.

When I visited, Isaac was at work at the greenhouse, but Brendan showed me the orchids and ferns he planted. On the wall were posters Brendan designed for theaters and bands: flappers in yards of pearls and smiling piano keys. Above the couch was his masterpiece: a painting of two boys fishing on a stone bridge. I recognized the boys as Brendan and Isaac at ten years old in straw hats and rolled-up pants. Whenever I missed my brother, I imagined him and Isaac sitting in that sunny room in New York beneath the painting of their boyhood, happy and safe together.

We sat on the leather couch petting Juno, their gray cat, and I told Brendan "You've really made it. I'm so proud of you."

"I'm proud of you too," he said. "I had an idea for your *Rocky Road Blues* album cover."

He showed me an all blue pen and ink sketch of a hobo jungle with trains and skyscrapers and tall water towers in the background and Blue Maria and me laughing, walking arm in arm down a gravel road.

"It's perfect," I said, already knowing that Blue Maria and the producer would agree.

Al had asked Emmett to photograph The Starfish Seven on stage on our last night together. The men all wore black suits and Iris and I wore our best dresses, hers silvery-white satin and mine pale blue with gauze ruffles. Al gave everyone in the band a gardenia corsage and a gold pocket watch with our names engraved on the back. Al was seated at the bar and Emmett and Chauncey were beside the ladder. Zach and Dennis stood the bar, mixing drinks and pouring Laurel Lager from the mysterious pipe that pumped in beer for the final time. At sunrise, we left one by one. Al had to shove me up the ladder so I wouldn't see the tears in his eyes. I hung the picture in my bedroom in a black frame. One day I would tell Eva all about it.

When I told Eva about my plans to go away, she took the news quietly and asked specific questions like "What day do you go?" and "What day do you come back?"

We marked the dates on the calendar. I would leave in February, under the picture of children exchanging Valentines and return in May, under a picture of a Maypole. I showed Eva my train route on a map, west from New York through Chicago to Seattle, down through San Francisco and Los Angeles and though Texas, New Orleans, Georgia, Charleston, Richmond and Philadelphia.

"Will you be here for my birthday?"

"Of course! Your birthday isn't until October twelfth."

Eva had stayed with Grandma Aileen many times when I went for a weekend in New York. Grandma Aileen showed her the room she would stay in, with a patchwork quilt on the bed and an old dollhouse that Amelia, Helen and I had played with. She would have all afternoon to play with her cousins. There were swings and slides on the playground at St. Anne's and Mill Creek close by.

"I'll send you postcards from every place I go," I said.

"Can I write you letters?" Eva asked.

I admired her ambition. She had just learned to write her name.

"No, honey. I'll always be going from one town to another, but I'll call you on the telephone every Sunday and we'll talk then."

Eva climbed up on my lap and hugged me around the neck.

"I'll miss you, Mama," she said.

Eva only said she'd miss me once, and then seemed to forget that I was leaving. We built snowmen with Grace and Julie and decorated our Christmas tree. Eva did not yet have to worry about or plan for the future.

Everything went agreeably until the February morning of my departure. I had been up all night packing the few remaining items for both of us. In the golden light of dawn, I had crept into her room and packed her Grimm's fairy tales and her slippers. Careful not to wake Eva, I watched her sleeping silently with her dark brown hair spreading over the pillow, her mouth like a pink primrose. The sunlight made her look like a holy card cherub. Too bad she had to wake up.

Eva hated getting up in the morning as much as I always had, but I had hoped she might go quietly through her routine, washing her face and hands, brushing her hair, eating her scrambled eggs and bacon. I had cooked her favorite breakfast, not our usual oatmeal, but Eva hadn't said a thing to me except "Good morning" when she first woke up.

After breakfast, I went upstairs to check the bathroom and our bedrooms for any little items we might have left behind. Eva followed me, dragging her red suitcase and holding Bob Bear in her arms. I tried to carry them for her, but she wouldn't let me. I hauled my big suitcases downstairs and stood before the piano for a minute, silently saying goodbye to it with my fingers on its closed lid.

"Mama, I don't want to go to Grandma Aileen's!"

Eva flung her red suitcase down, popping it open like a surprised mouth and spilling all her neatly folded clothes down the stairs. I could have slapped her. She had waited until I was at the bottom of the stairs, dumped the suitcase, then dashed back into her room. I rushed upstairs after her and flung her door open. Eva was sitting on her bed with fury in her dark eyes. Everyone else I knew feared my wrath, but my daughter never did. Either she knew I loved her too much to ever harm her, or – more likely - she knew her temper could match mine.

"Why did you do that? Why?" I screamed.

"Because I don't want to go!" Eva screamed back.

Taking a deep breath, I sat down on the bed beside her.

"Eva, you can't go on the train with me. I'm going to go to different towns every day and play piano late every night. I wouldn't have time to be with you. I need to go and make money for us and you need to stay here with Grandma Aileen."

Eva held my hand and looked sadly up at me.

"I can go too, Mama. I can sing great. You said so."

"Eva, you have to be a grown-up to sing in nightclubs. Little girls aren't allowed in there. You need to be here, honey, with the family."

"You're my family, Mama. If you love me, why don't you take me with you?"

"I love you more than anyone in the world," I said. "Even when I have to go far, far away from you, you are in my heart and I am in yours."

I put my hand over my heart and then over Eva's. Her little heart beat frantically like a sparrow that doesn't know which way to fly. One of her hot tears landed on my hand and she clung to me and cried.

"Mama, please don't go away. Daddy went away and he never came back."

"What? Do you remember that?"

"Yes. I remember Daddy. I remember he sang *My Blue Heaven* to me and rocked me in the rocking chair. I remember in winter when we walked in the snow and waited for Daddy to come off the train."

"You were only two then," I said, amazed. "Can you remember that far back?"

"Yes. I remember Christmas morning when I got my fairy book. Daddy said he told Santa I would like it. He held me on his lap and read me *Sleeping Beauty*. The prince in the picture looked like Daddy and I thought it really was Daddy. When he went away, I thought maybe the witch took him, but he would come back. But he never came back, Mommy."

"No, Eva, he never came back but nobody took him away. Your daddy didn't love me anymore. He loved another lady who was very rich. He thought she could make him a movie star, but she didn't. I loved him and I miss him too, but I know he'll never come back."

"Did he love me, Mommy?"

"Yes, he did Eva. He made a terrible mistake when he left you."

I hugged Eva and then looked into her eyes.

"You know I'm coming back, don't you, Eva? I'd never abandon you."

"Why do you have to go away all spring? Why does it take so long?"

"Blue Maria and I made a record and we have to go all over the country to sell it. We need the money. We need money to keep this house, for food, for clothes, for everything. But in the summer you and I will both be back here together. I need you to be brave while I'm gone, Eva."

She shook her head.

"I know it's hard. I'll miss you too. I love you Eva."

"I love you, Mama."

"Please help me pick up your clothes."

She picked up her clothes from the steps and I quickly packed them back in her suitcase.

"Are you ready to go to Grandma's now?" I asked.

Eva nodded.

"That's my good girl. I'm very proud of you, Eva."

We hurried to the streetcar. Eva sat on my lap quietly, almost asleep. Arguing with me had tired her out. She wanted me to carry her up to my mother's house, but I made her walk. She hugged and kissed her grandma quietly. Mother hugged and kissed her as they stood on the porch waving goodbye to me as I walked to the train station.

I looked back and waved to them three times before I turned the corner, but never set my suitcases down. I had to be resolute, for Eva. I told myself that she would get over missing me for one spring, but as much as I loved touring, I hated to leave her.

So many times I had worried that I would fail as a mother, that I would not love my child as much as I loved my music. I feared that I would fail her as Robert had, not by running away but by blaming others for my failures and closing my heart to Eva and cursing my roots in Laurel. Now I knew that was wrong, that the love in me was a living, growing tree, shading and supporting my mother, my child, my siblings, my friends and everyone I loved. My music and travels and the real joy of independence watered this tree. It didn't matter if I ever played Carnegie Hall as long as I never quit playing. I had not failed my music by having a child or failed my child by remaining a musician. No matter where I went or how I had to struggle, I would always go on playing and my daughter would never lose me, as long as I lived.

CHAPTER THIRTY-FIVE

Blue Maria and I planned to meet at Chumley's before we set off on the evening train. I sat in a dark wooden booth sipping a gin and tonic, inhaling the lime and juniper fragrance, savoring the bubbles and the pure clear happiness of drinking a cocktail in public. This was my first drink since the end of Prohibition, and with The Starfish closed and The Starfish Seven dissolved it seemed appropriate that I now drank alone.

In an odd way, the repeal had provided me with respectable work. This was the first tour where I did not have to worry about raids or find secret hideouts. When it was done I would return to my family and the office above Vintner's Hardware store. My life would finally go back to "normal", which I secretly dreaded.

For the rest of my life, I would miss The Starfish, the Starfish Seven and the way Al welcomed strangers and neighbors of every race, sex and creed into the sweet red light of his bar. I told myself that many more bars could open now, that thousands of broke people would find jobs as bartenders, barmaids, waitresses, bouncers, dishwashers and cooks. There would be more and better stages for musicians to play on.

Blue Maria and I had planned two or three stops in every town. Our agent, Henry Newell, would travel with us and sell copies of *Rocky Road Blues* to radio stations, record stores and to the audiences wherever we played. Like me, Blue Maria had to leave her daughter behind, with Kate and Big Jake. We would miss our daughters every day, call home often and send postcards from everywhere, but neither one of us would suffer from homesickness. It would be great to stay up late performing, drinking and dancing with all the men we wanted. When we came back, Big Jake invited us to play at The Queen of Clubs "any night until the joint closes or burns down".

I closed my eyes, folded my hands on the table and thanked God for my good life. I hoped that God would excuse me for praying in a bar, but my dear aunt, Sister Patricia, always said that God is everywhere and hears every prayer, so no one should hesitate to address Him. I thanked God for my daughter, my loving family, my many friends. I asked forgiveness for kicking David to the barn floor, for marrying Robert in secret haste. I asked God to take care of Eva, my mother and all my loved ones. I gave thanks for the chance to earn my living making music, to work in Al's office and play in Blue Maria's club. I wondered if the way I felt about Al was wrong, but at the same time I was grateful to have love without giving up my freedom. Finally I asked God to bless the album we had recorded and the tour we were about to begin.

Soon Blue Maria would meet me here, introduce me to Henry Newell and we'd be off to the train station. She would be kissing Violet goodbye now and Henry would be carrying her traveling trunk.

When I opened my eyes, I saw Robert Schumann sitting across the table from me. I gasped and slapped the table so hard that my gin and tonic bounced. Robert chuckled and grinned. He dressed as well as ever with pomade in his hair and a camel-colored jacket and pine green silk tie. His face was pale, his brown eyes not so bright as they once were. He was glad to see me but sadness clouded his voice.

"Hello, Marlene," he said. "It's wonderful to see you."

He took my hand and kissed it. I pulled it away as if it had been stung by a bee.

"I thought you and Audrey moved to Los Angeles," I said.

He tried to suppress a frown.

"Audrey's in Nice now and I'm here. I've been in New York for six months."

"Why did you leave Los Angeles?"

I sipped the gin and tonic, sensing that I would need liquid courage to hear what Robert was about to say.

"The studios own that town," he said bitterly. "If you so much as look at a director's daughter the wrong way, the studio loses your contract, cuts all your scenes from the picture and removes your name from the credits."

Did Robert say "you" instead of "I" to try and wring some empathy from me? Did he have any idea how many tears I had wasted on him?

"Is that what happened to you?" I asked.

"More or less," he said.

"I'm sorry," I said sincerely.

I held his hand.

"I took Eva to see *The Grand Hotel* because I heard you were in it."

He squeezed my hand and looked genuinely disappointed, but I didn't let him get a word in yet.

"I didn't tell her that she might see her daddy, but I looked for you in every single scene. I wanted to show you to her and tell her that her daddy is a movie star. Eva could be proud of that."

"I never got into that picture," said Robert. "I met the director at a party, but... how is Eva, Marlene?"

"She's wonderful," I said. "You left the best little girl in the world. She's more patient than me and more honest than you. I taught Eva a few songs on the piano and she has a great singing voice, which must come from you. She knows all her letters and can write her name and count to one hundred. She knows all the fairy tales in that book you gave her. Today she told me she remembered you reading her *Sleeping Beauty*."

I reached into my purse and drew out a photograph of Eva in a brown leather case. Eva's shoulder-length hair looked almost black and her brown eyes were bright. She wore a white lace dress and real rosebuds behind each ear. Tears welled up in Robert's eyes as he held his daughter's picture.

"I still have her baby pictures, but it's been so long. She's beautiful. My God, I've been so stupid."

He held one hand over his forehead and let the picture drop on the table.

"Why did you never write?" I asked. "If you've been in New York for six months, why did you never come to see us?"

"Would you see me, Marlene? I thought you'd tell Eva I was dead to make it easier for her."

"Why does everyone expect that?!" I almost shouted. "Nothing I could say would make it easy for Eva. I told her the truth. I told her that her daddy left us for a rich lady he loved better. I said her daddy made a terrible mistake."

Robert turned white with rage, like a pot about to boil over.

"How could you be so cruel? She'll hate me now. She'll never want to see me."

"If you want to come back into Eva's life, I won't stop you. Get on the train today and go to my mother's house. Tell Eva you love her and miss her. It would be the first unselfish act of your life. Eva will be angry at you, but you deserve that. If you love her, you'll show her that by not giving up. You can't just walk into a child's life and demand all her love for nothing. Eva isn't as stupid as I was."

"You were wonderful," said Robert, clasping both my hands. "You were the best wife any man ever had. You saved my life, Marlene. I never would have had a music or acting career if not for you. You did me more good than Audrey, even with no money. I can't believe how much you loved me."

I noticed that he wore no wedding ring.

"Did Audrey divorce you?" I asked.

"Yes," he said. "She left me because of the director's daughter and because of a sixteen-year-old blond boy. She tells everyone he's her nephew."

My eyes widened.

"Disgusting, isn't it? A woman of fifty-three! He could be her grandson! She went to Paris to get a divorce. My lawyer tried for a year to get some of the money but the judge insists that the Bainworth fortune is all Audrey's. Women are so cruel."

I pulled my hand away from his and held it over my smile.

"Well, you're not the first spouse to be jilted without a dime for a sixteen-year-old blonde," I said casually. "Tell me, Robert, what are you doing for a living now?"

"I'm in a W.P.A. program for out-of-work actors. I'm an assistant stage manager, but I'm sure I'll get a lead role soon."

"You were always about to get a lead role," I said.

He glanced down at my luggage.

"Are you in New York on a gig or on vacation?"

"I'm on tour, actually. Blue Maria will be here any minute to take me to the train station. We recorded a new album, *Rocky Road Blues.* It's all songs we wrote together. We leave tonight for Cleveland, then Chicago, Minneapolis, Seattle, Portland, San Francisco, Los Angeles, and back through Phoenix, Dallas, Houston, New Orleans, Atlanta, Charleston, Richmond and Philadelphia. We'll be gone three months. That's why Eva is staying with Mother."

Robert leaned toward me, wide-eyed and almost quivering with excitement. He grabbed my shoulder.

"Marlene, take me with you. Take me with you, honey. I love you. I need you. I know we can be happy together again. Let me open for you and Blue Maria; I've got some marvelous new songs. In three months we can mend all our old wounds. We can go back to Laurel and remarry and be a real family again. Think how happy Eva will be when you bring her father home. I know that you're angry, Marlene, but that's only because - deep down in your heart - you still love me and you can forgive me. I'll make it up to you, darling."

He leaned across the table and kissed my lips, but I shoved him away with all my strength and stood up.

"You are one piss-poor actor!"

Everyone in Chumley's heard me yelling, even the bartender, who dropped his white rag. Maybe the barflies had heard the whole damn conversation, but I was too irate to be embarrassed and I'd meant every word I said. Grabbing my suitcase, I tried to push past Robert. He jumped up and blocked my way.

"Marlene, I love you!" Robert screamed.

"BULLSHIT!" I screamed in his face. "If you loved me, you would have come home to see me and Eva long before this and begged for forgiveness. If I weren't on tour now you wouldn't even speak to me!"

"How can you be so bitter? How can you be such a bitch? You promised to love me forever!"

"I stopped loving you the day you walked out on me. It hurt like hell for a long time, but it doesn't hurt anymore. I'd like you to see our daughter, for her sake, but you will never live in my house or sleep in my bed or sing on a stage with me again."

"I'll go see Eva," he said. "I'll make it up to her. I'll take care of her while you're away. Just take me to the train station with you and buy me a ticket. Give me a chance, Marlene. Please!"

"Robert, I gave you everything I had to give and it wasn't enough. You're on your own now. Good luck to you."

I walked up to the bar to pay for my drink.

"Marlene, don't leave me!" said Robert. "I need you! I love you! Don't go!"

The bartender said "Mister, you have ten seconds to get out of here and leave this lady alone or you'll be 86'ed for life."

Robert turned on me, handsome and demonic as a hissing white swan.

"Your album will fail," he said. "You're not beautiful enough to be a star."

"I never needed to be a beautiful star," I said calmly. "I just needed to play the piano and I always will."

I smiled stoically as Robert stormed out the door.

"Eighty six!" yelled the bartender. "Here, honey, have yourself another gin and tonic, on the house. I think you've earned it."

Blue Maria came in a few minutes later. She looked like my own Statue of Liberty, in a blue-green coat, holding *Down the Rocky Road* sheet music instead of a torch. Over her shoulder, I glimpsed Henry Newell, a handsome blond man in a Packard waiting for us. I wanted to tell her about Robert, but not until we were on the train, for fear it might jinx our journey. It would be easier to tell her as we sat in our sleeping car gazing out at the starry horizon.

"I'm sorry I'm so late," she said. "It was hard to say goodbye to Violet. Henry is in the car outside. Are you ready for our whirlwind tour?"

"Yes," I said.

I took her hand and together we walked out into the sunshine. As the car wove through the streets of Greenwich Village, my heart felt light and my mind filled with the tinkling piano notes of all the songs I would play. My fingers moved already in my lap, full of the music, hot and cool jazz, moody blues and wild rag, the rhythm of my life that would never leave me.

THE END

Jill Charles' Biography

I grew up in Spokane, Washington and have three younger sisters: Molly, Clare and Megan. I majored in Creative Writing at Seattle University and wrote articles for Seattle's *Tablet: Magazine of Arts and Culture* and poems and stories for *Poetry Motel, Heliotrope* and *The Inlander,* an independent Spokane newspaper. I have lived in Spokane and Seattle, Washington and Florence, Italy and now live in Chicago. I perform poetry at open mics in the Chicago area, including Kafein and The Heartland Café. I have a blog at http://jill099.vox.com.

CPSIA information can be obtained at www.ICGtesting.com
Printed in the USA
LVOW010314151211

259361LV00006B/248/P